"It's impossible to think of the Louisiana bayou . . . without conjuring up scenes from James Lee Burke's Dave Robicheaux books" (*Chicago Tribune*)—savor his latest bestsellers featuring "one of the coolest, earthiest heroes in thrillerdom" (*Entertainment Weekly*)

THE GLASS RAINBOW

"James Lee Burke offers everything his readers expect—brilliant prose, prosaic situations that suddenly become mystic experiences, and a complex plot that repeatedly plumbs the depths of human depravity and the heights of nobility—in his superlative 18th novel."

—*Publishers Weekly* (starred review)

"Superb suspense. . . . A masterpiece of texture and mood."

—*Booklist* (starred review)

"Burke, whose sonorous cadences and obsession with the past have often recalled Faulkner, has never resembled the sage of Yoknapatawpha more closely than in this magnificent attempt to get it all down between one cap and one period."

—*Kirkus Reviews* (starred review)

"The suspense level is about as high as it gets in popular fiction."

—*Los Angeles Times*

**This title is also available from
Simon & Schuster Audio and as an eBook**

More praise for *The Glass Rainbow*

"Unlike his forebears, Sam Spade and Philip Marlowe, Robicheaux . . . is an evolving, dynamic character whose story is as crucial to the turns of the novel as is the gathering of clues and elimination of suspects . . . if the Robicheaux series might be considered as a whole, then *The Glass Rainbow* is its zenith—the point at which Robicheaux reaches his highest points of wisdom and humility. Gripping and tautly written throughout, Burke shows himself at his own zenith in the novel's magnetic and captivating conclusion: a startling tableaux where James Lee Burke, the hardboiled crime fiction writer, and James Lee Burke, the poet and sage, meet for a memorable conclusion, one that haunts the reader for days afterward."

—*Missoula Independent*

SWAN PEAK

"Sprawling, exuberant. . . . The violence is gruesome . . . the energy is bright-hearted."

—*The Oregonian*

"[A] meaty, thoughtful exploration of why men do the evil that they do. . . . A hell of a ride."

—*Miami Herald*

"If you love crime fiction . . . or if you just plain love good writing, *Swan Peak* will more than satisfy."

—*The Philadelphia Inquirer*

By the same author

JAMES LEE BURKE

THE GLASS RAINBOW

POCKET STAR BOOKS

New York London Toronto Sydney

Pocket Star Books
A Division of Simon & Schuster, Inc.
1230 Avenue of the Americas
New York, NY 10020

This book is a work of fiction. Names, characters, places, and incidents either are products of the author's imagination or are used fictitiously. Any resemblance to actual events or locales or persons, living or dead, is entirely coincidental.

Copyright © 2010 by James Lee Burke

Published by arrangement with Hyperion Books

First Pocket Star Books paperback edition August 2011

POCKET STAR BOOKS and colophon are registered trademarks of Simon & Schuster, Inc.

For information about special discounts for bulk purchases, please contact Simon & Schuster Special Sales at 1-866-506-1949 or business@simonandschuster.com.

The Simon & Schuster Speakers Bureau can bring authors to your live event. For more information or to book an event, contact the Simon & Schuster Speakers Bureau at 1-866-248-3049 or visit our website at www.simonspeakers.com.

Cover design by John Vairo Jr.
Spanish moss on bald cypress in mist © Atrendo Nature / Getty Images, Rowboat © Ulf Sjostedt / Getty Images

Manufactured in the United States of America

10 9 8 7 6 5 4 3 2 1

ISBN 978-1-4391-2831-2
ISBN 978-1-4391-3737-6 (ebook)

To my cousins, Alafair Kane,
Charlotte Elrod,
Karen McRae, and Mary Murdy

CHAPTER 1

THE ROOM I had rented in an old part of Natchez seemed more reflective of New Orleans than a river town in Mississippi. The ventilated storm shutters were slatted with a pink glow, as soft and filtered and cool in color as the spring sunrise can be in the Garden District, the courtyard outside touched with mist off the river, the pastel walls deep in shadow and stained with lichen above the flower beds, the brick walkways smelling of damp stone and the wild spearmint that grew in green clusters between the bricks. I could see the shadows of banana trees moving on the window screens, the humidity condensing and threading along the fronds like veins in living tissue. I could hear a ship's horn blowing somewhere out on the river, a long hooting sound that was absorbed and muted inside the mist, thwarting its own purpose. A wood-bladed fan revolved slowly above my bed, the incandescence of the lightbulbs attached to it reduced to a dim yellow smudge inside frosted-glass shades that were fluted to resemble flowers. The wood floor and the garish wallpaper and the rain spots on the ceiling belonged to another era, one that was outside of time and unheedful of the demands of commerce. Perhaps as a reminder of that fact, the only clock in the room was a round windup mechanism that possessed neither a glass cover nor hands on its face.

There are moments in the Deep South when one wonders if he has not wakened to a sunrise in the spring of 1862. And in that moment, maybe one re-alizes with a guilty pang that he would not find such an event entirely unwelcome.

At midmorning, inside a pine-wooded depression not far from the Mississippi, I found the man I was looking for. His name was Jimmy Darl Thigpin, and the diminutive or boylike image his name suggested, as with many southern names, was egregiously mis-leading. He was a gunbull of the old school, the kind of man who was neither good nor bad, in the way that a firearm is neither good nor bad. He was the kind of man whom you treat with discretion and whose private frame of reference you do not probe. In some ways, Jimmy Darl Thigpin was the lawman all of us fear we might one day become.

He sat atop a quarter horse that was at least six-teen hands high, his back erect, a cut-down double-barrel twelve-gauge propped on his thigh, the saddle creaking under his weight. He wore a long-sleeved cotton shirt to protect his arms from mosquitoes, and a beat-up, tall-crown cowboy hat in the appar-ent belief that he could prevent a return of the skin cancer that had shriveled one side of his face. To my knowledge, in various stages of his forty-year career, he had killed five men, some inside the prison system, some outside, one in an argument over a woman in a bar.

His charges were all black men, each wearing big-stripe green-and-white convict jumpers and baggy pants, some wearing leather-cuffed ankle restraints. They were felling trees, chopping off the limbs for burning, stacking the trunks on a flatbed truck, the heat from the fire so intense it gave off no smoke.

When he saw me park on the road, he dis-mounted and broke open the breech of his shotgun, cradling it over his left forearm, exposing the two shells in the chambers, effectively disarming his weapon. But in spite of his show of deference for my safety, there was no pleasure in his expression when he shook hands, and his eyes never left his charges.

"We appreciate your calling us, Cap," I said. "It looks like you're still running a tight ship."

Then I thought about what I had just said. There are instances when the exigencies of your life or profession require that you ingratiate yourself with people who make you uncomfortable, not because of what they are but because you fear their approval and the possibility you are more like them than you are willing to accept. I kept believing that age would one day free me of that burden. But it never has.

My introspection was of no relevance. He seemed uncertain about the purpose of my visit to Mississippi, even though it was he who had contacted me about one of his charges. "This is about those hookers that was killed over in your area?" he asked.

"I wouldn't necessarily call them that."

"You're right, I shouldn't be speaking unkindly of the dead. The boy I was telling you about is over yonder. The one with the gold teeth."

"Thanks for your help, Cap."

Maybe my friend the gunbull wasn't all bad, I told myself. But sometimes when you think you're almost home free, that indeed redemption is working incrementally in all of us, you find you have set yourself up for another disappointment.

"His nickname is Git-It-and-Go," Thigpin said.

"Sir?"

"Don't be feeling sorry for him. He could steal the stink off shit and not get the smell on his hands. If he don't give you what you want, let me know and I'll slap a knot on his head."

Jimmy Darl Thigpin opened a pouch of string tobacco and filled his jaw with it. He chewed slowly, his eyes hazy with a private thought or perhaps the pleasure the tobacco gave him. Then he realized I was watching him, and he grinned at the corner of his mouth to indicate he and I were members of the same club.

The convict's name was Elmore Latiolais. He came from a rural slum sixty miles northeast of New Iberia, where I was employed as a detective with the Iberia Parish Sheriff's Department. His facial features were Negroid, but his skin was the color of paste, covered with large moles as thick and irregular in shape as drops of mud, his wiry hair peroxided a bright gold. He was one of those recidivists whose lives are a testimony to institutional failure and the fact that for some people and situations there are no solutions.

We sat on a log in the shade, thirty yards from where his crew was working. The air was breathless and superheated inside the clearing, the trash fire red-hot at the center, the freshly cut pine limbs snapping instantly alight when they hit the flames. Elmore Latiolais was sweating heavily, his body wrapped in an odor that was like mildew and soapy water that had dried in his clothes.

"Why we got to talk here, man?" he said.

"I'm sorry I didn't bring an air-conditioned office with me," I replied.

"They gonna make me for a snitch."

"I drove a long way to talk with you, podna. Would you rather I leave?"

His eyes searched in space, his alternatives, his agenda, the pitiful issues of his life probably swimming like dots in the heat waves warping off the fire.

"My sister was Bernadette, one of them seven

girls that's been killed, that don't nobody care about," he said.

"Captain Thigpin explained that."

"My grandmother sent me the news article. It was from November of last year. My grandmother says ain't nothing been written about them since. The article says my sister and all them others was prostitutes."

"Not exactly. But yeah, the article suggests that. What are you trying to tell me?"

"It ain't fair."

"Not fair?"

"That's right. Calling my sister a prostitute. Nobody interested in the troot. All them girls just t'rown away like they was sacks of garbage." He wiped his nose with the heel of his hand.

"You know who's behind their deaths?"

"Herman Stanga."

"What do you base that on?"

"Herman Stanga tried to have me jooged when I was in Angola."

"Herman Stanga is a pimp."

"That's right."

"You're telling me a pimp is mixed up with your sister's death but your sister was not a prostitute? Does that seem like a reasonable conclusion to you?"

He turned his face to mine. "Where you been, man?"

I propped my hands on my knees, stiffening my arms, my expression blank, waiting for the balloon of anger in my chest to pass. "You asked Captain Thigpin to call me. Why me and not somebody else?"

"My cousin tole me you was axing around about the girls. But I t'ink you got your head stuffed up your hole."

"Forgive me if I'm losing patience with this conversation."

"There's no money in selling cooze no more. Herman Stanga is into meth. You got to come to Mis'sippi and interview somebody on a road gang to find that out?"

I stood up, my gaze focused on neutral space. "I have several photographs here I'd like you to look at. Tell me if you know any of these women."

There were seven photos in my shirt pocket. I removed only six of them. He remained seated on the log and went through them one by one. None of the photos was a mug shot. They had been taken by friends or family members using cheap cameras and one-hour development services. The backdrops were in poor neighborhoods where the residents parked their cars in the yards and the litter in the rain ditches disappeared inside the weeds during the summer and was exposed again during the winter. Two of the victims were white, four were black. Some of them were pretty. All of them were young. None of them looked unhappy. None of them probably had any idea of the fate that awaited them.

"They all lived sout' of the tracks, didn't they?" he said.

"That's right. Do you recognize them?"

"No, I ain't seen none of them. You ain't shown me my sister's picture."

I removed the seventh photo from my pocket and handed it to him. The girl in it had been seventeen when she died. She was last seen leaving a dollar store at four o'clock in the afternoon. She had a sweet, round face and was smiling in the photograph.

Elmore Latiolais cupped the photo in his palm. He stared at it for a long time, then shielded his eyes as though avoiding the sun's glare. "Can I keep it?" he said.

"Sorry," I replied.

He nodded and returned the photo to me, his eyes moist, his gold Brillo pad of a haircut popping with sweat.

"You said you hadn't seen any of the other victims. How did you know they lived south of the tracks?" I said.

"That's what I mean when I say you got your head up your ass. If they lived nort' of the railroad track, y'all would be tearing the state of Lou'sana apart to get the man who killed them."

Elmore Latiolais was not a likable man. In all probability, he had committed crimes that were worse in nature than those for which he had been punished. But the fact he considered Herman Stanga a cancer indicated, at least to me, that Elmore was still held together by the same glue as the rest of us. Herman Stanga was another matter. Herman Stanga was a man I hated, maybe less for what he was personally than what he represented, but I hated him just the same, to the degree that I did not want to be armed and alone with him.

I said good-bye to Elmore Latiolais.

"You ain't gonna he'p out?" he said.

"You haven't told me anything that could be considered of investigative value."

"'Investigative value'? Yeah, I like them kind of words. Herman killed a cousin of mine ten years back. He give her a hotshot and blew her heart out. When he knowed I was onto him, he paid a guy to joog me. Y'all wasn't interested then, y'all ain't interested now."

"I'm sorry for your loss," I replied.

"Yeah," he said.

• • •

HERMAN WAS ONE of those singular individuals for whom there is no adequate categorical description. He deliberately created addiction among his own people by giving what he called "entrepreneurial start-up flake" to teenage dealers. He encouraged his rock queens to eat fried food so their extra weight would signal to their customers that they were AIDS-free. He pimped off his white girls to black johns and his black girls to white johns. If a perv who liked it rough got into the mix, that was just the way it flushed sometimes. "Harry Truman integrated the United States Army. I'm taking multiculturalism and equal opportunity to a much higher level," he liked to say.

By his own definition of himself, he was always rocking to his own rhythms, high on his own rebop and snap-crackle-and-pop, and didn't "need to slam no gram to be what I am." He had the face of a pixie, his mustache trimmed into tiny black wings on his upper lip, his eyes bright with innocent mischief, the harmless satyr peeking out of the bushes. His physique was hard and lean, his skin stretched tight on his bones and tendons like a meth addict's, though he used drugs rarely, and only for recreational purposes. He liked to kick off his clothes by the poolside, down to his white silk boxer shorts, and sunbathe on a floating air mattress in the middle of his swimming pool, wraparound Ray-Bans on his face, a frozen daiquiri balanced on his stomach, his sunblock trailing off the ends of his fingers, his phallus as pronounced as the wood figure on a sailing ship's prow. The neighbors complained because of the exposure to their children, but Herman literally gave them the finger, hiking it in the air whenever he saw them gazing at him from their windows.

Herman Stanga was above convention. Herman Stanga was the iconoclast whose irreverence had made him rich while the assets of his neighbors drained through a sinkhole called the recession of 2009.

He had acquired his home on Bayou Teche, a faux antebellum two-story brick structure with twin chimneys, from a black physician who signed over the property for a minimal sum and left town with his wife and children and was never heard from again. Maintenance of the house and grounds ended the day Herman moved in. The hollow wood pillars were eaten by termites. The ventilated green storm shutters hung askew on their hinges; the rain gutters were clogged with pine needles and bled rust down the window frames. The manicured St. Augustine lawn was destroyed by mold and weed infestation and chains of red-ant mounds. Herman's Dobermans dug holes in the flower beds and downloaded piles of dog shit on every square inch of dirt they could squat on.

Herman, like a Leonardo da Vinci in reverse, had turned his own home into an emblematic masterpiece of suburban decay.

I rang the chimes, but no one answered. When I walked around back, I saw him cleaning leaves and pine needles out of the pool with a long pole, wearing Speedos that exposed his crack and his pubic hair. He had the most peculiar coloration I had ever seen in a human being. It was like black ivory that someone had poured liquefied gold inside. The afternoon sun had already dipped behind the oak trees on the bayou, and his wet hair and the oily glaze on his skin seemed touched with fire. A chicken was turning on a rotisserie over a bed of charcoals, next to a glass-topped table that was inset with an umbrella. In the shade of the umbrella was a cooler packed with crushed ice and bottles of Mexican and German beer.

"It's my man RoboCop," he said. "Sit yourself down, my brother, and open yourself a beer."

A striped robe like a Bedouin would wear hung over the back of a canvas chair. I picked it up and threw it at him. "Put it on."

"What for?"

"Your neighbor's kids are looking through the gate."

"You're right, it's starting to cool off," he said. He wrapped the robe around his midriff and tied it like a sarong, his chin tilted up into the breeze. The late sun's yellow glare on the bayou was like a match flame flaring just under the current. "Want to take a swim? I got a suit might fit you."

"I need you to look at some photos, Herman."

"Them girls over in Jeff Davis Parish that got themselves killed?"

"Why would you think that?"

" 'Cause you always looking for a way to jam me up. 'Cause y'all ain't got nobody else to put it on."

"Nobody else has talked to you?"

"There ain't been no ink on those girls in four months. What's that tell you?"

"You have to explain it to me. I'm not that smart."

"Give me them pictures," he said, ignoring my statement, his hand upturned.

This time it was I who ignored Herman. I laid the photos one by one on the glass tabletop. He waited patiently, an amused light playing in his face.

"Do I know them? *No.* Have I ever seen them? *No.* Would they be of interest to me? *No.* Why's that, you ax? 'Cause they're country girls with a serious case of ugly. Don't look at me like that."

"Who do you think might have murdered them?"

"It ain't a pimp. A pimp don't murder his stable. Check out their families. They probably been killing each other." He glanced at his watch. It was gold and had a black face inset with tiny red stones. "I got people coming over. We t'rew wit' this?"

The underwater lights in his swimming pool had just clicked on, creating a sky-blue clarity in the water that was so pristine I could see the silvery glint of a dime at the bottom of the deep end. Banana trees and a magnificent magnolia tree hung over the spiked fence that surrounded the pool. Potted plants bursting with flowers shaded his deck chairs and filled the air with a fragrance that was heavier than perfume.

"Your home is a study in contradictions. Your yard is carpeted with dog shit, and your house is being eaten to the foundation by termites. But your pool area is snipped right out of *Southern Living*. I don't get it."

"The uptown nigger who built this place wanted to be a character in *Gone Wit' the Wind*. Except Whitey on the bayou don't got no need for niggers pretending they're white people. So I give them a real nigger to weep and moan about. I own t'ree rentals, a condo in Lake Charles, and a beach house in Panama City, but I use this house to wipe my ass on. Every day I'm here, the value of my neighbors' property goes down. Guess who they gonna end up selling their houses to? That is, if I'm in the market for more houses.

"Know why there ain't been no media coverage on them girls for four months? Nobody cares. This is still Lou'sana, Robo Man. Black or white, it don't matter—if you got money, people will take your ten-inch on their knees. If you ain't got money, they'll cut it off."

"I think I'll let myself out."

"Yeah, fuck you, too, man."

"Say again?"

"Everyt'ing I tole you is true. But you cain't deal wit' it. And that's *your* problem, motherfucker. It ain't mine."

I LIVED WITH my wife, Molly, who was a former Catholic nun, in a modest frame house with a peaked tin roof among live oaks and pecan trees and slash pines and windmill palms on East Main, a half block from the famous plantation home known as The Shadows. There was rust on the roof and in the rain gutters, and it turned orange and purple in the late-afternoon sunset. Our lot was one acre in size and part of a historical alluvial floodplain that sloped down to Bayou Teche. The topographical contour of the land along the bayou had never been altered, and as a consequence, even though we were located close to the water, the houses in our neighborhood never flooded, even during the worst of hurricanes. Equally important for one who lives in the tropics, our house stayed in deep shade most of the day, and by the front walk, where we got full sun, our camellias and hibiscus stayed in bloom almost year-round, and in the spring our azaleas powdered the lawn with petals that looked like pink confetti.

It was a fine house in which to live, cool in the summer and warm in the winter, the ceiling-high windows outfitted with ventilated storm shutters, our new veranda a grand place to sit in wood rockers among our potted plants and house pets.

Alafair, our adopted daughter, had graduated

from Reed College with a degree in psychology, and now had taken off one semester from Stanford Law School to rewrite a novel she had been working on for three years. She had graduated Phi Beta Kappa from Reed and was carrying a 3.9 GPA at Stanford. She was a good writer, too. I had no doubts about the level of professional success that awaited her, regardless of the field she entered. My concern for Alafair's well-being was much more immediate and without any solution that I could see. In this case, the specific name of the concern was Kermit Abelard, the first man I believed Alafair was actually serious about.

"He's coming over here? *Now?*" I said.

I had just come home from work and had parked my pickup under the porte cochere. She was sitting in the rocker on the veranda, wearing a flowery sundress and white shoes, her skin dark with tan, her Indian-black hair burned brown on the tips. "What do you have against him, Dave?"

"He's too old for you."

"He's thirty-three. He calls it his crucifixion year."

"I forgot. He's also grandiose."

"Give it a rest, big guy."

"Is the convict coming with him?"

She made a face that feigned exasperation. Kermit Abelard, whose family at one time had owned almost half of St. Mary Parish, could not be accused of decadence or living on his family name. He had gone to acting school in New York and had published three novels, one of which had been adapted as a film. He had worked in the oil field when he could have been playing tennis and fishing for marlin in the Keys. Unfortunately, his egalitarian attitudes sometimes required others to pay a price, as was the case when he encouraged the entire crew on his drilling rig to join the union and got them and himself fired. Two years past, he had managed to work a parole from the Texas State Penitentiary at Huntsville for a celebrity convict author, a man who had been in and out of reformatories and jails since he was sixteen.

"Have you read *The Green Cage*?" Alafair asked.

"I have. I got it from the library. I didn't buy it."

"You don't think it's a brilliant piece of writing?"

"Yeah, it is, for reasons the author and his admirers don't seem to understand."

She wasn't taking the bait, so I slogged on. "It's a great look inside the mind of a sociopath and narcissist and manipulator. Count the number of times the pronouns 'I,' 'me,' 'mine,' and 'myself' appear in each paragraph."

"Somebody must have liked it. Robbie was a finalist in the National Book Awards."

"*Robbie?*"

"Argue with someone else, Dave."

I looked out at the evening traffic, at the birds gathering in the trees against a mauve-colored sunset. "Want to go for a run?" I said.

"I'm going to the park with Kermit. He's reading the revision I did on the last chapter in my novel."

I went inside the house. Molly had left a note on the kitchen table to the effect she was in Lafayette and would bring supper home. I changed into my gym shorts and a T-shirt and my running shoes, and in the backyard, under the supervision of our warrior cat, Snuggs, and our elderly raccoon, Tripod, I did fifty push-ups with my feet propped on a picnic bench, five reps of sixty-pound curls, three reps of military presses, and one hundred stomach crunches. It was cool and warm at the same time inside the shade of the trees, and the wind was blowing through the bamboo that separated our property from the next-door neighbor's, and wisteria was blooming in big blue and lavender clumps on the side of her garage. I had almost forgotten my worries regarding Alafair and her willingness to trust people she shouldn't; then I heard Kermit Abelard's black Saab convertible pull into the driveway and a car door open and close. I did not hear it open and close and then open and close again. Which meant Kermit Abelard did not get out of his vehicle and approach the gallery and walk Alafair back to the car and open the car door for her. In my view, no one could accuse Kermit Abelard of going out of his way to be a gentleman.

I walked to the edge of the backyard so I could see through the porte cochere into the front. Kermit was backing into the street, the top down on his convertible, the dappled shade sliding off the hand-waxed surfaces, as though the cooling of the day and the attenuation of the light had been arranged especially for him. Alafair sat next to him on the rolled-leather seat. In back was a man whose face I had seen only on the flap of a book jacket.

I jogged down East Main, under the canopy of live oaks that spanned the entirety of the street, past The Shadows and the bed-and-breakfast that had been the residence of the plantation's overseer, past the massive old brick post office and the Evangeline Theater, across the drawbridge at Burke Street and into City Park, where people were barbecuing under the shelters along the bayou and high school kids were playing a work-up softball game on the ball diamond.

I jogged for four miles, circling twice through the park. At the end of the second lap I hit it hard toward home, my blood oxygenated now, my breath coming regular, my heart strong, the sweaty glaze on my skin a reminder that once in a while you're allowed to reclaim a libidinal moment or two from your youth. Then I saw Kermit Abelard's Saab parked by the tin pavilion, checkered cloth and newspapers spread on a table, a mound of boiled crawfish and artichokes and corn on the cob piled in the center.

I didn't want to stop, but Alafair and her friends Kermit Abelard and the convict-author whose name was Robert Weingart had seen me, and now Alafair was waving, her face full of joy and pride. I tried to shine her on, to pretend I was committed to my run and couldn't stop. But under what circumstances do you embarrass your daughter in front of her companions, or indulge your enmity toward them at her expense? Or pass her by when perhaps she needs your presence for reasons she may not be able to acknowledge, even to herself?

I slowed to a walk, wiping my face with the towel I carried.

Kermit was a stocky man of medium height, with vascular, short arms and a cleft in his chin. He was built more like a dockhand than a descendant of local aristocracy. The top of his shirt was unbuttoned, his tanned, smooth skin exposed for others to look at. He had wide, square hands and fingers that were blunt on the tips. They were the hands of a workingman, but incongruously, the red stone of a Kappa Sigma ring twinkled on his finger.

"Come meet Robert, Mr. Robicheaux," he said.

"I'm pretty overheated. I'd better not get too close to you guys," I said.

Robert Weingart was sitting on top of the wood table, smiling good-naturedly, his alpine-booted feet planted solidly on the bench. He had fine cheekbones, a small mouth, and dark hair that was clipped neatly and wet-combed with a part that created a straight gray line through his scalp. His eyes were hazel and elongated, his cheeks slightly sunken. His hands were relaxed on his knees, his fingers tapered, like a pianist's. He conveyed the sense that he was a man with no hidden agenda, with no repressed tensions or problems of conscience. He seemed to be a man at peace with the world.

But it was the lack of balance or uniformity in his physiognomy that bothered me. He didn't blink, the way screen actors never blink. His mouth was too small, too quick to smile, his jaw too thin for the size of his cranium. His eyes stayed fastened brightly on mine. I kept waiting for him to blink. But he didn't.

"Looks like you've been pouring it on," he said.

"Not really."

"I thought your speed was pretty impressive."

"Have I seen you in the movies?"

"I don't think so."

"You remind me of an actor. I can't call his name to mind."

"No, I'm just a scribbler." He got up from the table, extending his hand. "Rob Weingart. It's a pleasure to meet you."

"It's not Robbie?"

"Just call me Rob if you like."

His handshake was boneless, unthreatening, cool and dry to the touch. There was a white shine on his teeth. He picked up a peeled crawfish and put it in his mouth, his cheekbones working slowly, his gaze never leaving my face. He touched at his lips with a paper napkin, his expression as benign as the weather was temperate, a bit like a man thinking of a private joke. "Is there something on your mind I can help you with?" he asked.

"I got it. It wasn't an actor. You remind me of Chet Baker," I said.

"The musician?"

"That's right. A tragic one, at that. His addictions ate him alive. You like jazz, Mr. Weingart? Have you done any professional performing? I'm sure I've seen you in a professional capacity."

"Let me fix you a plate, Mr. Robicheaux," Kermit said.

"No, I never was a performer," Robert Weingart said. "Why would you think that?"

"I just admire people who can teach themselves not to blink. When a person doesn't blink, you can't read his thoughts. All you see is one undecipherable expression. It's like staring into electrified silk."

"That's quite an image," he said to Kermit. "One of us ought to borrow that and give Mr. Robicheaux a footnote."

"You can just take it and use it in any fashion you choose. It's free," I said.

Kermit Abelard touched my forearm with a loaded paper plate.

"No, thanks," I said. "I'd better get back on my run."

"You're a police officer," Robert Weingart said.

"Alafair told you?"

"Usually I can spot a police officer. It used to be part of my curriculum vitae. But in this case I think your daughter told me. I'm almost sure of it."

"You think? But you don't know?"

Alafair's face was burning.

"Is my plate ready? I could eat a whale," Robert Weingart said, looking around, suppressing his amusement at the situation that swirled about him.

• • •

"I CAN'T BELIEVE you. Why didn't you punch him in the face while you were at it?" Alafair said to me after she returned home.

"That's a possibility," I replied.

"What did he do? The man was just sitting there."

"He's a mainline recidivist, Alf. Don't be taken in."

"Don't call me that stupid name. How can you know somebody five seconds and make judgments like that?"

"Anybody who's con-wise can spot a dude like that five blocks away."

"The real problem is you always want to control other people. Instead of being honest about your own self-centered agenda, you go after Kermit's friend."

"You're right, I don't know him."

"Why do you blame Kermit for what his family may have done? It's not fair to him, Dave, and it's not fair to me."

"There's no 'may have done' about it. The Abelards are dictators. If they had their way, we'd all be doing their grunt work for minimum wage, if that."

"So what? That doesn't mean Kermit is like the rest of his family. John and Robert Kennedy weren't like their father."

"What's with you two? I could hear you all the way out in the driveway," Molly said, coming through the back door, both arms loaded with groceries.

"Ask Dave, if you can get him to pull his head out of his ass," Alafair said.

"That's the second time someone has said that to me today. The other person was a meltdown on a road gang in Mississippi."

Molly tried to make it to the counter with the grocery bags. But it was too late. One of them caved, and most of our delicatessen supper splattered on the linoleum.

That's when Clete Purcel tapped on the back screen. "Am I interrupting anything?" he said.

CHAPTER 2

IT WAS THROUGH Clete Purcel that I had been over in Jeff Davis Parish asking about the seven girls and young women whose bodies had been found in ditches and swamp areas since 2005. Two weeks ago the remains of one of his bail skips were found in the bottom of a recently drained canal, her decomposed features webbed with dried algae, as though she had been wrapped in a sheet of dirty plastic. The pathologist said she had died of massive physical trauma. Perhaps she had been struck by a hit-and-run driver. Perhaps not.

Clete operated a private investigative service out of two offices, one on St. Ann in the French Quarter and the other on Main Street, here in New Iberia. His daily routine was one of ennui coupled with an almost visceral disdain for the people he routinely hooked up and delivered to two bondsmen in New Orleans by the names of Nig Rosewater and Wee Willie Bimstine, both of whom had been bankrupted after Katrina when FEMA transported their bonded-out clientele to faraway cities all over the United States. At one time Clete had been the best cop I ever knew, both as a patrolman and as a detective-grade investigator with the NOPD. But booze and pills and his predilection for damaged women had been his undoing, and he'd been forced to blow the country on a murder beef and hide out in El Salvador and Guatemala, where, as a mercenary, he got to see the murder of civilians on a scale that was greater than he had seen in Vietnam.

Insatiability seemed to have been wired into his metabolism. He fought his hangovers with uppers and vodka and tomato juice and a celery stick in a tumbler of crushed ice, convinced himself that four fingers of Scotch sheathed in a glass of milk would not harm his liver, and clanked iron daily to compensate for the deep-fried soft-shell crabs and oyster po'boy sandwiches and gallons of gumbo he consumed on a weekly basis. His courage and his patriotism and his sense of personal honor and his loyalty to his friends had no peer. I never knew a better and braver man. But threaded through all of his virtues was his abiding conviction that he was not worthy of a good woman's love and that somehow his father, the milkman who had made his son kneel on grains of rice, always stood somewhere close by, his face knotted with disapproval.

Clete was the libidinous trickster of folklore, the elephantine buffoon, the bane of the Mob and all misogynists and child molesters, the brain-scorched jarhead who talked with a dead mamasan on his fire escape, the nemesis of authority figures and anyone who sought power over others, a one-man demolition derby who had driven an earth-grader through the walls of a mobster's palatial home on Lake Pontchartrain and systematically ground the entire building into rubble. Or at least that was the persona he created for the world to see. But in reality Clete Purcel was a tragedy. His enemies were many: gangsters, vindictive cops, and insurance companies who wanted him off the board. Klansmen and neo-Nazis had tried to kill him. A stripper he had befriended dosed him with the clap. He had been shanked, shot, garroted, and tortured. A United States congressman tried to have him sent to Angola. But all of the aforementioned were amateurs when it came to hurting Clete Purcel. Clete's most dangerous adversary lived in his own breast.

I walked outside with him, into the coolness of the evening and the wind blowing through the bamboo that grew along the driveway. His skin was inflamed with fresh sunburn, and he was wearing a tropical shirt and mirrored shades that reflected the trees and clouds and his restored maroon Caddy with the starch-white top. He put his arm inside the driver's window and lifted an open can of beer off the dashboard, then stuck a filter-tip cigarette into the corner of his mouth and prepared to light it with his Zippo. I removed the cigarette and stuck it in his shirt pocket.

"Can't you stop doing that?" he said.

"No."

"What was going on in your kitchen?"

"I had some words with a convict writer who hangs out with Alafair's new boyfriend."

"This guy Weingart?"

"You know him?"

"Not personally. He knocked up a black girl who waits tables at Ruby Tuesday."

"How do you know?"

"She told me. He's a famous guy. She was impressed. I think he hunts on the game reserve. When they're nineteen and haven't been farther away than Lake Charles, it doesn't take a lot to get them to kick off their panties." He drank from his beer. The top of the can was covered with condensation from the coldness inside, and his mouth left a bright smear on it. "I've got a Dr Pepper in the cooler," he said.

"I just had one. Why'd you come by?"

I couldn't see his eyes behind his shades, but when he turned his head toward me, I knew he had caught the sharpness in my voice. "The feds are working those homicides in Jeff Davis Parish. Or at least they say they are. They're talking about a serial killer. But I don't buy it."

"Let it go, Clete."

"My bail skip was twenty-one years old. She'd had tracks on her arms since she was thirteen. She deserved something more out of life than being left in a rain ditch with all her bones broken."

When I didn't reply, he took off his shades and stared at me. The skin around his eyes looked unnaturally white. "Say it."

"I've got nothing to say," I replied.

"Rumdum PI's don't get involved in official investigations?"

"I went over to Mississippi and interviewed a brother of one of the victims. I also talked to Herman Stanga."

"And?"

"I came up with nothing that could be called helpful."

"So you're dropping it?"

"It's out of my jurisdiction."

"Meaning it's automatically out of mine?"

"I didn't say that."

"But you thought it."

"Only three of the seven dead girls and women are certifiable homicides, Clete. There's no telling how the others died. Drug overdoses, hit-and-run accidents, suicide, God only knows."

"Only three, huh?"

"You know what I meant."

"Right," he said. He put his shades back on and got in his Caddy, twisting the key hard in the ignition.

"Don't leave like this."

"Go back inside and fight with your family,

Streak. Sometimes you really put me in the dumps."

He backed into the street, lighting a cigarette with his Zippo simultaneously, an oncoming vehicle swerving around him, blowing its horn.

CLETE STARTED HIS search for Herman Stanga in New Iberia's old red-light district, down Railroad Avenue, where the white girls used to go for five dollars and the black girls on Hopkins went for three. He cruised past the corner hangouts and the old cribs, their windows nailed over with plywood, a drive-by daiquiri store, and rows of unoccupied houses in front of which bagged garbage and junked furniture and split mattresses were stacked three feet high. He passed a stucco bungalow that had been blackened by fire and was now used as a shooting gallery. He saw the peculiar mix of addiction and prostitution and normal blue-collar life that had become characteristic of inner-city America. Then he drove down Ann Street, where black teenage drug vendors stood one kid to each dirt yard, their faces vacant, their bodies motionless, like clothespins arranged on a wash line, their customers flicking on a turn signal to indicate they were ready for curb service.

The sky had the color and texture of green gas, the trees throbbing with birds. In the west, the sun was a tiny red spark inside rain clouds. Clete parked on a corner in front of a paint-peeling shotgun house and waited. His top was down, his porkpie hat tilted on his brow, his fingers knitted on his chest, his eyes closed in repose. Three minutes went by before he felt a presence inches from his face. He opened one eye and looked into the face of a boy who was not more than twelve, a baseball cap riding on his ears.

"What you want, man?" the boy asked.

"Affirmative action is forcing Herman Stanga to hire midgets?"

"I ain't no midget. You parked in front of my friend's house, so I axed you what you want. If you're looking for Weight Watchers, you're in the wrong neighborhood," the boy said.

"You're about to get yourself wadded up and stuffed in my tailpipe."

"Won't change nothing. You'll still be a big fat man calling other people names."

"I'm looking for Herman Stanga. I owe him some money."

The boy's expression showed no recognition of the lie. He stepped back from the Cadillac, nodding in approval, touching the chrome back of the outside mirror with his fingertips. His head was too small for his body, and his body too small for his baggy pants and bright orange and white polyester T-shirt.

"You just cruising around, handing out money? Leave it wit' me. I'll get it to the right person."

"What's your name?"

"Buford."

"Tell your parents to use a better form of birth control, Buford."

Then Clete saw a strange transformation take place in the boy's face, a flicker of injury, the kind that went deep and couldn't be feigned, like the pain of a stone bruise traveling upward from the foot into the viscera. Clete dropped his transmission into drive, then stuck it back in park. "What's your last name?" he said.

"I ain't got one. No, I take that back. My last name is Kiss-My-Ass-Fat-Man."

"Get in the car, Kiss-My-Ass."

The boy started to walk off. Four or five teenage boys were watching him from a side yard.

"Or go to jail," Clete said, opening his PI badge holder. "They have a new pygmy unit there. You can test-drive it and see if you'd like to stay around for a while. Forget your partners over there. After you're busted, they won't take time to piss in your mouth."

The boy hesitated, then got in the car, the big leather seat almost swallowing him up. He touched the polished wood of the dashboard and looked at the green glow of the dials. "Where we going?"

"Burger King. I eat five times a day. Right now my tank is empty. Can you handle a hamburger?"

"I ain't against it."

"If I catch you slinging dope again, I'll personally put you in juvie."

"If you was a cop, you'd know where Cousin Herman is at."

"Herman Stanga is your cousin?"

"I've seen you in front of your office downtown. You're a private detective."

"You're pretty smart for a midget. Where's your cousin, Kiss-My-Ass?"

"Where he is every night, at the club in St. Martinville. You a child molester?"

"What if I stop the car and use you for a tent peg and hammer you down into one of these dirt yards?"

"I was just axing. You look kind of weird. You need an elephant trunk on your face to make it complete." The boy put a mint in his jaw and sucked on it loudly. He glanced backward at the assembly of teenage boys disappearing into the dusk.

"What's the name of your cousin's club?" Clete said.

"Your stomach and your butt must weigh t'ree

hundred pounds by themselves. How you chase after people wit' all that weight? You must put cracks in the sidewalk. You be *T. rex. Jurassic Park* comes to New Iberia."

"The name of the club?"

"The Gate Mout'."

"Those guys back there were holding your stash?"

"Ax them."

"They'll chew you up and spit you out, Kiss-My-Ass. So will your cousin. You talk like an intelligent kid. Why not act like it?"

They were stopped at a traffic light now, the sky as purple as a cloak, cars streaming up and down a street lined with strip malls and discount outlets and fast-food restaurants. The boy whose first name was Buford opened the car door and stepped out and closed the door behind him. "T'anks for the ride, Mr. Fat Man," he said.

Then he was gone.

THE CLUB WAS located on a long two-lane state road that followed Bayou Teche into St. Martinville's black district, all the way to a town square that opened onto lovely vistas of oak trees and flowers and elephant ears planted along the bayou's edge, a historic Acadian church, and nineteenth-century frame buildings with balconies and wood colonnades whose soft decay only added to the aesthetic ambience of the square. But the black district was another world and not one that lent itself to postcard representation. The gutters were banked with beer cans and wine bottles and paper litter, the noise from the juke joints throbbing and incessant, each bar on the strip somehow connected to a larger culture of welfare and bail bond offices, a pawnshop that sold pistols that could have been made out of melted scrap metal, and a prison system that cycled miscreants in and out with the curative effectiveness of a broken turnstile.

The ceiling inside the Gate Mouth club seemed to crush down on the patrons' heads. The walls were lacquered with red paint that gave off the soiled brightness of a burning coal. The booths were vinyl, the cushions split, the tables scorched with cigarette burns that in the gloom could have been mistaken for the bodies of calcified slugs. The atmosphere was not unlike a box, one whose doors and windows were perhaps painted on the walls and were never intended to be functional. When Clete entered the room, he felt a sense of enclosure that was like a vacuum sucking the air out of his lungs.

He stood at the bar, his hat on, his powder-blue sport coat covering the handcuffs that were drawn through the back of his belt and the blue-black .38 he carried in a nylon shoulder holster. He was the only white person at the bar, but no one looked directly at him. Finally the bartender approached him, a damp rag knotted in one hand, his eyes averted, lights gleaming on his bald head. He did not speak.

"Two fingers of Jack and a beer back," Clete said.

A woman on the next stool got up and went into the restroom. The bartender shifted a toothpick in his mouth with his tongue and poured the whiskey in a glass and drew a mug of draft beer. He set both of them on napkins in front of Clete. Clete removed a twenty-dollar bill from his wallet and set it on the bar.

"Anything else?" the bartender said.

"I like the happy, neighborhood-type mood in here. I bet it's Mardi Gras here every day."

The bartender propped his arms on the bar, his eye sockets cavernous, his impatience barely constrained. "Somebody did you something?" he said.

"Is this place named for Gatemouth Brown, the musician?" Clete asked.

"What are you doing in here, man?"

"Waiting on my change."

"It's on the house."

"I'm not a cop."

"Then you got no bidness in here."

"The twenty is for you. I need to talk to Herman Stanga."

The muscles on the backs of the bartender's arms were knotted and tubular, one-color tats scrolled on his forearms.

"I'm out of New Orleans and New Iberia," Clete said. "I chase bail skips and other kinds of deadbeats. But that's not why I'm here. How about losing the ofay routine?"

The bartender removed the toothpick from his mouth and looked toward the back door. "Some nights we cook up some links and chops. They ain't half bad," he said. "But don't give me no shit out there."

"Wouldn't dream of it," Clete said.

Clete poured his Jack Daniel's into his beer mug and drank it. He walked through a back hallway stacked with boxes, and out the back door into a rural scene that seemed totally disconnected from the barroom. The back lot was spacious and dotted with live oaks and pecan trees, the limbs and trunks wound with strings of white lights. A barbecue pit fashioned from a split oil drum leaked smoke into the canopy and drifted out over Bayou Teche. People were drinking out of red plastic cups at picnic tables, some of the tables lit by candles set inside blue or red vessels that looked like they had been taken from a church.

Clete had never seen Herman Stanga but had heard him described and had no difficulty singling him out. Stanga was sitting with a woman in the shadows, at a table under a live oak that was not wrapped with lights. Both ends of the tabletop were covered with burning candles, guttering deep inside their votive containers. The woman was over thirty, heavy in the shoulders and arms, her blouse and dress those of a countrywoman rather than a regular at a juke.

Stanga tapped a small amount of white powder from a vial on the web of skin between his thumb and forefinger, then held it up to the woman's nose. She bent forward, closing one nostril, and sniffed it up as quickly as an anteater, her face lighting with the rush.

Clete walked closer, the tree trunk between him and Stanga and Stanga's female friend. A puff of wind off the bayou swelled the tree's canopy, rustling the Spanish moss, spinning leaves down on the tabletop and the shoulders of the two figures sitting there. Clete could hear Stanga talking with the kind of hypnotic staccato one would associate with a 1940s scat singer:

"See, baby, you ain't no cleaning girl I brung up from the quarters in Loreauville. You're a mature woman done been around and know how the world work. Ain't nobody, ain't no *man*, gonna make you do anyt'ing you don't want to. That's what I need. A strong woman that's a people person, somebody who know how to keep the cash flow going wit'out no hitches, midlevel management out there on the ground, keep these young girls in line. You be Superwoman. You ain't gonna be driving that shitbox of yours no more, either. Gonna put you in nice threads, gonna give you your own expense account, gonna dress you up, baby. I'll tell you something else. You a temptation, but bidness is bidness. Ax any nigger in this town. I respect a woman's boundaries. I'm here as your friend and your bidness partner, but the operational word in our relationship is 'respect.' You want some more blow, baby?"

The woman's eyes, which had seemed sleepy and amused by Stanga's monologue, wandered off his face to a presence that was now standing behind him. Stanga twisted his head around, the light from the candles flickering on his face, his tiny black mustache flattening under his nostrils. He laughed. "The American Legion hall is down the road," he said.

"A couple of your girls stiffed Nig Rosewater and Wee Willie Bimstine for their bail," Clete said. "I thought you might want to do a righteous deed and direct me to their whereabouts."

"Number one, I ain't got no 'girls.' Number two, I ain't no human Google service. Number t'ree—"

"Yeah, I got it." Clete removed his cell phone from his trouser pocket and opened it with his thumb. He looked at the screen as though waiting for it to come into focus. "A state narc friend of mine is sitting out front in my Caddy. He's off the clock right now, but for you he might make an exception. You want to take a walk down to the bayou with me or run your mouth some more?"

"Look, I ain't give you no trouble. I was talking to my lady friend here and—"

Clete pushed the send button on his phone.

"All right, man, I ain't in this world to argue. I'll be right back, baby. Order up something nice for us both," Stanga said.

Clete walked down the slope, ahead of Stanga,

seemingly unconcerned with the matter at hand, glancing up at the stars and across the bayou at the lighted houses on the opposite slope. The drawbridge was open upstream, and a tugboat, its deck and cabin lights blazing, was pushing a huge barge past the bridge's pilings. Clete stared at the shallows and at the bream night-feeding among the lily pads. He watched the gyrations of a needle-nosed garfish that was maneuvering itself on the perimeter of the bream that had schooled up underneath the lilies. He did all these things with the detachment of a resigned, world-weary man who offered little threat to anyone.

"So what this is, man, them two Jews in New Orleans cain't run their bidness wit'out siccing you on me?" Stanga said to Clete's back.

But Clete didn't reply. He adjusted his porkpie hat on his brow and stared at the dark green dorsal fins of the bream rolling in the water, the carpet of lily pads undulating from their movements.

"Hey, you just turn deaf and dumb or something? I been nice, but I got a short fuse with crackers who t'ink they can wipe their ass on other people's furniture. I ain't intimidated by your size, either, man. Have your say or call your narc friend, but you quit fucking wit' me."

"I identified one of the dead girls in Jeff Davis Parish," Clete said. "The guy who did her broke bones all over her body. Was she one of yours, Herman? How many girls do you have on the stroll over in Jeff Davis?"

Stanga snapped his fingers. "RoboCop sent you, didn't he? You got an office up on Main in New Iberia. You're RoboCop's windup for the jobs he cain't do hisself or he's already fucked up. Let me line it out for you, man. I ain't involved no more in certain kinds of enterprises. I don't know what you t'ink you heard me say to that lady back there, but I'm totally into new kinds of endeavors . . . Are you listening to me? I don't like talking to somebody's back."

Clete turned around slowly. "I'm all ears."

"What you heard me talking about is the St. Jude Project. It's an outreach program to he'p people nobody else cares about. That's what I'm doing these days, not pimping off people, not committing no homicides or whatever it is you t'ink I'm doing. Are you hearing me loud and clear on this?"

"St. Jude, the patron of the hopeless?"

"Hey, big breakt'rew. Let your brain keep doing those push-ups, you getting there, man. We done here?"

"No. You signed the paperwork on two of my bail skips. So under the the law, you're my collateral. Turn around and place your hands on the tree trunk."

Stanga shook his head in exasperation, the pixielike quality gone from his face, his expression almost genuine, devoid of guile or theatrics. "You making a big fool out of yourself, man. Busting me ain't gonna he'p no dead girls, ain't gonna get no money back for them Jews, ain't gonna make you look better in front of all these people. Grow up. I don't sell nothing to nobody they don't want. How you t'ink I stayed in bidness all these years? 'Cause I was selling stuff people didn't have no use for?"

"Turn around."

"Yeah, yeah, yeah, anyt'ing you want, man. Big pile of white whale shit go in a black man's club and blow his nose on people, bust some cat with recreational flake, make the world safe, and maybe get your fat ass on *COPS*! All of y'all are a joke, man."

"You better shut your mouth."

"Gets to you, don't it? Well, that's the way it ought to be. If you didn't have people like me around, you'd be on welfare. Look around you, man. Are all these people worried about me, or are they worried about you? Who brings the grief into their lives? Go ax them. There wasn't no problem here till you come out that back door."

Clete turned Stanga around and pushed him against the tree, trying to suppress the dangerous urge that had bloomed in his chest. When Stanga turned to face him again, Clete stiff-armed him between the shoulders. Then he kicked Stanga's feet apart and started patting him down, his face expressionless, trying to ignore the attention he was drawing from up the slope.

"What we're talking about here is hypocrisy, man," Stanga said over his shoulder. "I can smell weed on your clothes and cooze on your skin. Tell me you ain't had your dick in a black woman. Tell me you ain't been on a pad for them New Orleans dagos. You cain't see past your stomach to tie your shoes, but you t'ink a mail-order badge give you the right to knock around people ain't got no choice except to take it. I wouldn't let you clean my toilet, man, I wouldn't let you pick up the dog shit on my lawn."

Clete's right hand trembled as he pulled his handcuffs free from behind his back.

"Take out your cell-phone cameras," Stanga called to the crowd that was gathering up the slope. "Check out what this guy is doing. Y'all seen it. I ain't done nothing."

"Shut up," Clete said.

"Fuck you, man. I was in an adult prison when I was fifteen years old. Anyt'ing you can do to me has already been done, magnified by ten."

Then Herman Stanga, his wrists still uncuffed, turned and spat full in Clete's face.

Later, Clete would not be exactly sure what he did next. He would remember a string of spittle clinging to his face and hair. He would remember Herman Stanga's fingers reaching for his eyes; he would remember the sour surge of whiskey and beer into his mouth and nose. He would remember grabbing Stanga from the back, lifting him high in the air, and smashing him into the tree trunk. He knew he fitted his hand around the back of Stanga's neck and he knew he drove Stanga's face into the bark of the tree. Those things were predictable and not unseemly or uncalled for. But the events that followed were different, even for Clete.

He felt a whoosh of heat on his skin as though someone had opened a furnace door next to his head. His heart was as hard and big as a muskmelon in his chest, hammering against his ribs, bursting with adrenaline, his strength almost superhuman. One hand was hooked through the back of Stanga's belt, the other wrapped deep into the man's neck. He drove Stanga's head and face again and again into the tree trunk while people in the background screamed. Stanga's body felt as light as a scarecrow's in Clete's hands, the arms flopping like rags with each blow.

When Clete dropped him to the ground, Stanga was still conscious, his face trembling with shock, his nose streaming blood, the split on his forehead ridged up like an orange starfish.

The images and sounds Clete saw and heard as he stumbled up the slope toward the street would remain with him for the rest of his life. The witnesses who had gathered on the slope had been transformed into a group of villagers in an Asian country that no one talked about anymore. Their throats were filled with lamentation and pleas for mercy, their eyes wide with terror, their fingers knitted desperately in front of them.

Clete could smell a stench like stagnant water and duck shit and inflammable liquid bursting alight and straw and animal hair burning. He wiped Stanga's spittle off his face with his sleeve and pushed through the crowd, stumbling off balance, a man out of place and time, with no moat or castle to which he could return.

CHAPTER 3

I GOT THE PHONE call from the St. Martin Parish Sheriff's Department at 11:46 P.M. Clete had been barreling down the two-lane toward the Iberia Parish line when he hit the roadblock. Rather than think it through and let the situation decompress and play out of its own accord, he swung the Caddy onto a dirt road and tried to escape through a sugarcane field. The upshot was a blown tire, forty feet of barbed-wire fence tangled under his car frame, and a half-dozen Brahmas headed for Texas. The deputy who had called me was a fellow member of A.A. whom I saw occasionally at different meetings in the area. Her name was Emma Poche, and, like me, she had once been with the NOPD and had left the department under the same circumstances, ninety proof and trailing clouds of odium. Even today I had trepidation about Emma and believed she was perhaps one of those driven creatures who, regardless of 12-step membership, lived one drink and one click away from the Big Exit.

She lowered her voice and told me she was subbing as a night screw and that her call was unauthorized.

"I can't understand you. Clete's drunk?" I said.

"Who knows?" she replied.

"Say again?"

"He doesn't act drunk."

"What's all that noise in the background?"

"Four deputies trying to move him from the tank into an isolation cell."

The kitchen was dark, the moon high over the park on the far side of the bayou, the trees in the backyard full of light and shadows. I was tired and didn't want to be pulled into another one of Clete's escapades. "Tell those guys to leave him alone. He'll settle down. He has cycles, kind of like an elephant in must."

"That pimp from New Iberia, what's his name?"

"Herman Stanga?"

"Purcel tore him up at a bar in the black district. And I mean tore him up proper. The pimp's lawyer is down here now. He wants your friend charged with felony assault."

"Stanga must have done something. Clete wouldn't attack someone without provocation, particularly a lowlife like Stanga."

"He just poleaxed a deputy. You'd better get your ass up here, Dave."

I dressed and drove up the bayou ten miles to the lockup in the St. Martin Parish Sheriff's Annex, next to the white-columned courthouse that had been built on the town square in the 1850s. Emma Poche met me at the door and walked me down to the holding cell where Clete had been forcibly transferred. Emma was around thirty-five and had gold hair and was slightly overweight, her cheeks always pooled with color, like a North European's rather than a Cajun's. A softcover book was stuffed in her back pocket. Before we got to the cell, she glanced behind her and touched my wrist with her fingers. "Does Purcel have flashbacks?" she said.

"Sometimes."

"Get him moved to a hospital."

"You think he's psychotic?"

"Your friend isn't the problem. A couple of my colleagues have a real hard-on for him. You don't want him in their custody."

"Thanks, Emma."

"You can dial my phone anytime you want, hon." She winked, her face deadpan. Then waited. "That was a joke."

I wouldn't have sworn to that. She stuck me in the ribs with her finger and walked back down the corridor, her holstered pistol canting on her hip. But I didn't have time to worry about Emma Poche's lack of discretion. Clete looked terrible. He was alone in the cell, sitting on a wood bench, his big arms propped on his kneecaps, staring straight ahead at the wall. He didn't speak or acknowledge my presence.

Clete was a handsome man, his hair still sandy and cut like a little boy's, his eyes a bright green, his skin free of tattoos and blemishes except for a pink scar through one eyebrow, where another kid had bashed him with a pipe during a rumble in the Irish Channel. He was overweight but could not be called fat, perhaps because of the barbells he lifted daily and the way he carried himself. When Clete's boiler system kicked into high register, the kind that should have put his adversaries on red alert, his brow remained as smooth as ice cream, his eyes showing no trace of intent or anger, his physical movements like those of a man caught inside a photograph.

What usually followed was a level of mayhem and chaos that had made him the ogre of the legal system throughout southern Louisiana.

He turned his head sideways, his eyes meeting mine through the bars. The knuckles on his left hand were barked. "Just passing by?"

"Why'd you bust up Herman Stanga?"

"He spat on me."

"So you had provocation. Why'd you run from the St. Martin guys?"

"I didn't feel like putting up with their doodah."

He paused a moment. "I'd been smoking some weed earlier. I didn't want them tearing my Caddy apart. They ripped out my paneling once before."

So you wrecked your convertible for them, I thought.

"What?" Clete said.

"Did you knock down a screw?"

"I'm not sure. Maybe he slipped. I told those guys to keep their hands off me."

"Clete—"

"Stanga was playing to an audience. I blew it. I stepped into his trap. He claims to be a member of a street-people outreach program called the St. Jude Project. You ever hear of it?"

"That's not the issue now. I'll have a lawyer down here in the morning to get you out. In the meantime—"

"Don't shine me on, Dave. What do you know about this St. Jude stuff?"

"Either I stay here tonight to protect you from yourself, or you give me your word you're finished pissing off everybody on the planet."

"You don't get it, Streak. Just like always, you've got your head wrapped in concrete."

"What are you talking about?"

"We're yesterday's bubble gum. We're the freaks, not Herman Stanga. That guy has wrecked hundreds, maybe thousands, of people's lives. Guys like us follow around behind him with a push broom and a dustpan."

"What happened at the Gate Mouth?"

"I saw villagers in the Central Highlands. We'd lit up the ville. I heard AK rounds popping under the hooches. All the old people and children and women were crying. The VC had already blown Dodge, but we torched the place with the Zippo track anyway.

It was a resupply depot. Their wells were full of rice. We had to do it, right?"

I leaned my forehead lightly against one of the bars. When I looked up, Clete was staring at the back of the cell as though the answer to a mystery lay inside the shadows cast by the lights in the corridor.

On the way out of the annex, I saw Emma Poche in a small side office, reading her book. "Your friend quiet down?" she said.

"I'm not sure. Call me again if there's any more trouble."

"Will do."

"What are you reading?"

She held up the cover so I could see it. "*The Green Cage* by Robert Weingart," she said. "He's an ex-con who supposedly works with some kind of self-help group around here. What do they call it? He's hooked up with a rich guy in St. Mary Parish."

"The local rich guy is Kermit Abelard."

"Good book," Emma said.

"Yeah, if you like to get into lockstep with the herd, it'll do the trick," I replied.

"You're a joy, Streak," she said, and resumed reading.

BY NOON THE next day Clete had been charged with destroying private property, resisting arrest, and felony assault. I went his bond for twenty-five thousand dollars and drove him back to the motor court on East Main in New Iberia, where he lived in a tan stucco cottage, under spreading oaks, no more than thirty yards from Bayou Teche. He showered and shaved and put on fresh slacks and a crisp shirt, and I drove him to Victor's cafeteria and bought him a huge lunch and a pitcher of iced tea. He ate with a fork in one hand and a piece of bread in the other, his hat tilted forward, his skin lustrous with the energies that burned inside him.

"How you feel?" I asked.

"Fine. Why shouldn't I?" he replied. "I need to rent a car and get back to my office and talk to my insurance man."

"Why is it I think you're not going to do that at all? Why is it I think you've got Herman Stanga in your bombsights?"

The cafeteria was crowded and noisy, the sound rising up to the high nineteenth-century stamped-tin ceiling. Clete finished chewing a mouthful of fried pork chop and mashed potatoes and swallowed. He spoke without looking at me, his eyes intense with thought. "Stanga set me up and I took the bait. He'll be filing civil suit by the end of the day," he said. "I'm going to take Stanga down with or without you, Dave."

I paused before I spoke again. I could leave Clete to his own devices and let him try to resolve his troubles on his own. But you don't let your friends down when they're in need, and you don't abandon a man who once carried you down a fire escape with two bullets in his back.

"Robert Weingart may be hooked up with this St. Jude Project," I said. "At least that's the impression I got from Emma Poche."

"Weingart works with Stanga?"

"I'm not sure of that," I said.

Clete wiped his mouth with his napkin and drank from his iced tea, pushing his half-eaten lunch away. "Does the St. Jude Project have an office hereabouts?"

"Not exactly. Want to take a little trip back into 'the good old days'?" I said.

St. Mary Parish had a long history as a fiefdom run by a small oligarchy that had possessed power and enormous fortunes, actually hundreds of millions of dollars, at a time when the great majority of people in the parish had possessed virtually nothing. The availability of the ancient cypress trees, the alluvial soil that was among the most fertile in the world, the untapped oil and natural-gas domes that had waited aeons for the penetration of the diamond-crusted Hughes drill bit, and, most important, the low cost of black and poor-white labor seemed like the ultimate fulfillment of a corporate dream that only a divine hand could have fashioned. Even the curds of white smoke rising from the mills into the hard blue Louisiana sky could easily be interpreted as a votive offering to a benevolent capitalist deity.

To my knowledge, no members of the Abelard family had held rank of consequence in the Confederate army, nor had they participated in great battles, nor had their home been burned or vandalized by Yankee marauders. Nor did they choose to participate in the grand illusion that came to be known as the Lost Cause. In fact, rumors had persisted to the present time that the Abelards, originally from Pennsylvania, had gotten along very well with their Union occupiers and their cotton and molasses had been allowed to pass unobstructed up the Mississippi to markets in the North.

The patriarch was Peter Abelard. He had been a successful haberdasher in Philadelphia and New York City during the 1840s and had brought his wife and children to the South with one objective—to buy as much land and as many slaves as possible. By the outbreak of the war, he had owned 185 slaves and was renting fifty more, the latter in a category known as "wage slaves." After Emancipation, while others watched in quiet desperation as their fortunes went down the sinkhole or joined terrorist groups like the White League and the Knights of the White Camellia, Peter Abelard formed a partnership with the man who had converted Angola Plantation into Angola Prison and turned it into a giant surrogate for the slave-labor system that Lincoln had signed out of existence with one stroke of his pen. The two men created the convict-lease system that became a prototype throughout the South, resulting, in Louisiana alone, in the deaths of thousands of inmates, mostly black, who died of malnutrition, disease, and physical abuse.

The Abelard estate was down at the bottom of St. Mary Parish, where the land bleeds gradually into sawgrass and ill-defined marshy terrain that is being eaten away by saltwater intrusion as far as the eye can see. The Abelard house, with its Greco columns and second-story veranda, had once been a magnificent structure inside an Edenic ambience that John James Audubon had painted because of the beautiful birds that lived among the trees and flowers. But now, as Clete and I drove south on the two-lane asphalt road, the vista was quite different.

A ten-thousand-mile network of canals that had been cut for the installation of pipelines and the use of industrial workboats had poisoned the root systems of living marsh along the entirety of the coast. The consequences were not arguable, as any collage of aerial photography would demonstrate. Over the years, the rectangular grid of the canals had turned into serpentine lines that had taken on the bulbous characteristics of untreated skin tumors. In the case of the Abelard plantation, the effects were even more dramatic, due in part to the fact that the grandfather had allowed drilling in the black lagoons and hummocks of water oaks and gum and cypress trees that had surrounded his house. Now the house sat in solitary fashion on a knoll, accessible only by a plank bridge, the white paint stained by smoke from stubble fires, its backdrop one of yellowed sawgrass, dead trees protruding from the brackish water, and abandoned 1940s oil platforms whose thick wood timbers were as weightless in the hand as desiccated cork.

For whatever reason, for whatever higher cause, the collective industrial agencies of the modern era had transformed a green-gold paradisiacal wonderland into an environmental eyesore that would probably make the most optimistic humanist reconsider his point of view.

I had called ahead and had been told by Kermit Abelard that he would be genuinely happy if I would come to his home. I did not ask about his friend Robert Weingart, the convict-author, nor did I mention the reason for my visit or that I would be bringing Clete Purcel with me, although I doubted if any of these things would have been of concern to him. I did not like Kermit dating my daughter, but I could not say he was a fearful or deceptive man. My objections to him were his difference in age from Alafair's and that he was an experienced man in the ways of the world, and a great part of that experience came from the exploitive enterprises with which the Abelards had long been associated.

We rumbled over the bridge and knocked on the front door. A storm was kicking up in the Gulf, and the wind was cool on the porch. In the south I could see a bank of black thunderheads low on the horizon and electricity forking inside the clouds the way sparks fork and leap off an emery wheel.

"What a dump," Clete said.

"Will you be quiet?" I said.

He screwed a filter-tip cigarette into his mouth

and got out his Zippo. I started to pull the cigarette out of his mouth, but what was the use? Clete was Clete.

"Who's Abelard's cooze?" he said.

"*What?*"

"You heard me."

"Alafair is going out with him."

His face looked as though it had just undergone a five-second sunburn. "Why didn't you tell me that?"

"I thought maybe you'd figured it out."

"Is there another agenda working here, Dave?"

"Not a chance," I replied.

He lit his cigarette and puffed on it. When Kermit Abelard opened the door, Clete took one more drag and flipped the cigarette in the flower bed.

"How do you do?" Kermit said, extending his hand.

"What's the haps?" Clete replied.

"You're Clete Purcel, aren't you? I've heard a lot about you. Come in, come in," Kermit said, holding the great oaken door wide.

The interior of the house was dark, the furnishings out of the Gilded Age, the light fixtures glowing dimly inside their dust. The carpet was old and too thin for the hardwood floor, and I could feel the rough grain of the timber through my shoes. Clete touched his nose with the back of his wrist and cleared his throat.

"Something wrong, Mr. Purcel?" Kermit asked.

"I have allergies," Clete replied.

"I've fixed some drinks for us and a cold Dr Pepper or two and a snack if you'd like to come out on the sunporch," Kermit said.

I couldn't hold it back. "You're keen on Dr Pepper?" I said.

"No, I thought you might want—" he began.

"You thought I would like a Dr Pepper instead of something else?" I said.

"No, not necessarily."

"You have water?" I said.

"Of course."

"I'll take a glass of water."

"Sure, Dave, or Mr. Robicheaux."

"Call me whatever you like."

I saw Clete gazing out the side door onto the sunporch, trying to hide a smile.

"What is it I can help y'all with?" Kermit said.

"Is your friend Robert Weingart here?" I said.

"He's just getting out of the shower. We were splitting wood on the lawn. Robert is marvelous at carving ducks out of wood. Both of us write through the morning, then have a light lunch and do a little physical exercise together. I'm glad you came out, Mr. Robicheaux. I think so highly of Alafair. She's a great person. I know you're proud of her."

He was patronizing and presumptuous, but nevertheless I wondered if I hadn't been too hard on him; if indeed, as Clete had suggested, I'd had my own agenda when I'd brought Clete to the Abelard home.

When Kermit was only a teenager, his parents had disappeared in a storm off Bimini. Their sail yacht had been found a week later on a sunny day, floating upright in calm water, the canvas furled, the hull and deck clean and gleaming. I suspected that regardless of his family's wealth, life had not been easy for Kermit Abelard as a young man.

Earlier I mentioned that his ancestors had not invested themselves in the comforting legends of the Lost Cause. But as I glanced at a glassed-in mahogany bookcase, I realized that southern Shintoism does not necessarily have to clothe itself in Confederate gray and butternut brown. A Norman-Celtic coat of arms hung above the bookcase, and behind the glass doors were clusters of large keys attached to silver rings and chains, the kind a plantation mistress would wear on her waist, and a faded journal of daily life on a southern plantation written in faded blue ink by Peter Abelard's wife. More significantly, the case contained framed photographs of Kermit's grandfather, Timothy Abelard, standing alongside members of the Somoza family in Nicaragua, supervising a cockfight in Batista-era Cuba, receiving a civilian medal for the productivity of munitions that his defense plant had manufactured during the Vietnam War, and finally, Timothy Abelard overseeing a group of black farmworkers in a field of wind-swirling sugarcane.

In the last photograph, the cane cutters were bent to their work, their shins sheathed in aluminum guards. Only Timothy Abelard was looking at the camera, his pressed clothes powdered with lint from the cane. His expression was that of a gentleman who had made his peace with the world and did not consign his destiny or the care of either his family or his property to others.

Then I realized that I was being stared at, in a fashion that is not only invasive but fills you with a sense of moral culpability, as though somehow, through a lapse of manners, you have invited the disdain of another.

Timothy Abelard was sitting in a wheelchair no more than ten feet away, a black female nurse stationed behind him. Eight or nine years ago he had become a recluse without ever offering a public explanation of his infirmity. Some people said he'd developed an inoperable tumor in the brain; others said he had been dragged by his horse during an electric storm. His skin was luminescent from the absence of sunlight.

"Hi, Pa'pere. Did you want to join us?" Kermit said.

But Timothy Abelard's eyes did not leave my face. They had the intensity of a hawk's, and like a hawk's, they did not occupy themselves with thoughts about good or evil or the distinction between the two. He was well groomed, his hair thin and combed like strands of bronze wire across his pate. His smile could be called kindly and deferential, even likable, in the way we want old people to be wise and likable. But the intrusive nature of his gaze was unrelenting.

"How are you, sir?" I said.

"I know you. Or I think I do. What's your name?" he said.

"Dave Robicheaux, from the Iberia Sheriff's Department," I said.

"You investigating a crime, suh?" he said, his eyes crinkling at the corners.

"I had some questions about the St. Jude Project."

"That's a new one on me. What is it?" he said.

"I guess that makes two of us," I said. "Do you remember my father? His name was Aldous Robicheaux, but everyone called him Big Aldous."

"He was in the oil business?"

"He was a derrick man. He died in an offshore blowout."

"I'm forgetful sometimes. Yes, I do remember him. He was an extraordinary man in a fistfight. He took on the whole bar at Provost's one night."

"That was my father," I replied.

"You say he was killed on a rig?"

"Yes, sir."

"I'm sorry," he said, as though the event were yesterday.

I waited for Kermit to introduce Clete, but he

didn't. "Miss Jewel, would you get Pa'pere ready to go to Lafayette? He's having dinner with friends this evening. I'll have the car brought around."

"Yes, suh," the nurse said.

"Come on, Dave, let's go out here on the porch," Kermit said, jiggling his fingers at me, using my first name now, showing some of the imperious manner that I associated with his background. I was beginning to wonder if my earlier sympathies with him had been misplaced.

Entering the sunporch was like stepping into another environment, one that was as different from the interior of the house as a sick ward is from a brightly lit fairground on a summer evening. The windows on the porch were paneled with stained-glass designs of bluebirds and parrots, kneeling saints, chains of camellias and roses and orchids, unicorns and satyrs at play, a knight in red armor impaling a dragon with a spear. The western sunlight shining through the panels created a stunning effect, like shards of brilliant color splintering apart and re-forming themselves inside a kaleidoscope.

"Sorry to be late for our little repast," Robert Weingart said behind me.

He was wearing sandals and a terry-cloth robe that was cinched tightly around his waist, his hair wet and freshly combed, his small mouth pursed in an expression that I suspected was meant to indicate sophistication and long experience with upscale social situations. Kermit introduced Clete to him, but Clete did not shake hands. Nor did I.

A confession is needed here. Most cops do not like ex-felons. They don't trust them, and they think they got what they deserved, no matter how bad a joint they did their time in. In the best of cases, cops may wish an ex-felon well, even help him out with a job or a bad PO, but they do not break bread with him or ever pretend that his criminal inclinations evaporated at the completion of his sentence.

By no stretch of the imagination could Robert Weingart be put in a best-case category.

The glass-topped table was set with place mats and tiny forks and spoons and demitasse cups and bowls of crawfish salad, hot sauce, veined shrimp, dirty rice, and soft-crusted fried eggplant. Two dark green bottles of wine were shoved deep in a silver ice bucket, alongside two cans of Dr Pepper. Neither Clete nor I sat down.

"Well, time waits on no man," Robert Weingart said, sitting down by himself. He dipped a shrimp in red sauce and bit into it, then began reading a folded newspaper that had been in the pocket of his robe as though the rest of us were not there.

"You know Herman Stanga?" I asked Weingart.

"Can't say I've heard of him," he replied, not looking up from his paper.

"That's funny. Herman says he's working for the St. Jude Project," I said. "That's your group, isn't it?"

Weingart looked up. "No, not my group. It's a group I support."

"I'm familiar with Herman Stanga, Dave," Kermit said. "He doesn't work for St. Jude, but I've had conversations with him and tried to earn his trust and show him there's a better way to do things. We've gotten two or three of his girls out of the life and into treatment programs. You see a problem in that?"

"Down on Ann Street, I met this sawed-off black kid named Buford. He was slinging dope on the corner. He was probably twelve years old at the outside. He's Herman Stanga's cousin," Clete said.

"I guess Herman's outreach efforts don't extend to children or his relatives."

"Does Herman know this boy is dealing drugs?" Kermit asked.

"It's hard to say. I broke Herman's sticks at the Gate Mouth club in St. Martinville. He's in the hospital right now. You could drop by Iberia General and chat him up."

"Your sarcasm isn't well taken, Mr. Purcel," Kermit said. "You attacked Herman?"

"Your man spat in my face."

"He's not my man, sir."

"Is he your man?" Clete said to Robert Weingart.

"I don't know what you're talking about, my friend," Weingart replied.

"There's something wrong with the words I use? You can't quite translate them? How about taking the corn bread out of your mouth before you say anything else?"

Weingart put away his paper and unfolded a thick linen napkin and spread it on his lap. His robe had fallen open, exposing the thong he was wearing. "Have you ever tried writing detective stories, Clete? I bet you'd be good at it. I could introduce you to a couple of guys in the Screenwriters Guild. Your dialogue is tinged with little bits of glass that would make Raymond Chandler envious. Really."

Clete looked at me, his face opaque, his hands as big as hams by his sides, his facial skin suddenly clear of wrinkles. Don't do it, Cletus, don't do it, don't do it, I could hear myself thinking.

Clete sniffed again, as though he were coming down with a cold. He looked back at the doorway into the interior of the house. "You have rats?"

"No, not to my knowledge," Kermit said. "Mr. Purcel, no one meant to offend you. But what we're hearing is a bit of a shock. The St. Jude Project isn't connected with Herman Stanga, no matter what he's told you."

"We're glad to hear that, Kermit," I said. "But why would you be talking with a man like Stanga to begin with? You think he's going to help you take his prostitutes off the street?"

"I've spoken with Alafair regarding some of these things. I thought maybe she had talked with you. She's expressed a willingness to help out."

"You're trying to involve my daughter with pimps and hookers? You're telling me this to my face?"

Kermit shook his head, nonplussed, swallowing. "I'm at a loss. I respect you, Mr. Robicheaux. I respect your family. I'm very fond of Alafair."

I could feel my moorings starting to pull loose from the dock. "You're almost ten years older than she is. Older men don't have 'fond' in mind when they home in on younger women."

"Why don't I walk outside with Mr. Weingart and let y'all talk?" Clete said. "How about it, *Bob*? Can you hitch up your robe and tear yourself loose from that fried eggplant? What do you say, *Bob*?"

Inside my head I saw an image of hurricane warning flags flapping in a high wind.

Weingart rested his fingertips on the tabletop, his lips pursed, his cheeks slightly sunken, every hair on his head neatly in place. He seemed to be thinking of a private joke, his eyes lighting, a smile flickering at the corner of his mouth. "What would you like to do on our little stroll?"

"Robbie, don't do this," Kermit said.

"I just wondered what the big fellow had in mind. He looks like a gelatinous handful."

I saw the crinkles around Clete's eyes flatten, the

blood draining from the skin around his mouth. But he surprised me. "Time to dee-dee, Streak," he said.

Weingart repositioned his newspaper and began reading again, detached, wrapped in his narcissism and contempt for the world, indifferent to the embarrassment flaming in Kermit's face.

"Thank your grandfather for his hospitality," I said to Kermit.

"Mr. Robicheaux, I want to apologize for anything inappropriate that may have occurred here."

"Forget the apology. Don't take Alafair anywhere near Herman Stanga or his crowd. If you do, I'd better not hear about it."

Kermit blanched. "Absolutely. I wouldn't—"

"Mr. Weingart?" Clete interrupted.

"Yes?" Weingart said, reading his paper.

"Don't ever call me by my first name again."

"How about 'Mr.' Clete? Do come back, Mr. Clete. It's been such a pleasure," Weingart said. "Absolutely it has." He lifted his gaze to Clete, his eyes iniquitous.

I fitted my hand on Clete's upper arm. It was as tight as a fire hydrant. We walked back through the living room, past the photos of Timothy Abelard with members of the Somoza family, past a copy of a Gauguin painting, out the door and across the porch and onto the lawn. I could taste the salt in the wind and feel the first drops of rain on my face. Clete cleared his throat and turned to one side and spat. "Did you smell it in there?"

"Smell what?"

"That odor, like something dead. I think it's on the old man. You didn't smell it?"

"No, I think you're imagining things."

"He sends chills through me. He makes me think of a turkey buzzard perched on a tombstone."

"He's just an old man. He's neurologically impaired."

"I've been wrong about you for many years, Dave. You know the truth? I think you want to believe people like the Abelards are part of a Greek tragedy. Here's the flash: They're not. They should have been naped off the planet a long time ago."

"Get in the truck."

"Did you know Kermit Abelard was gay?"

"No. And I don't know that now."

"Weingart is a cell-house bitch. Those two guys are getting it on. Don't pretend they're not."

"Stay away from Weingart, Clete. A guy like that is looking for a bullet. Anything short of it will have no effect."

"You want Weingart around Alafair? You want his fop of a boyfriend around her? What's wrong with you?"

"Just shut up."

"The hell I will."

I ate two aspirin from a box I kept on the dashboard of my truck, started the engine, and hoped that a great hard gray rain would sweep across the wetlands. I hoped that window-breaking hail would pound down on my truck, clattering like tack hammers on the roof, filling the cab with such a din that I could not hear Clete talking all the way back to New Iberia. I wished somehow the sulfurous smell of the storm and the swirling clouds of rain and the bolts of lightning spiking into the horizon would cleanse me of the angst I felt about my daughter and her exposure to a tangle of vipers thriving on the watery southern rim of St. Mary Parish.

CHAPTER 4

THE STORM KNOCKED out the power on Main Street, so Alafair and Molly and I ate supper in the light of candles at our kitchen table while the rain beat down on the tin roof of our home and flooded the yard and danced on the surface of Bayou Teche. We had brought Snuggs and Tripod inside, and the two of them were eating out of their bowls on the floor. Tripod was old and sick and losing his eyesight, and I did not like to contemplate the choices we might have to make in the near future. As though she had read my mind, Molly got up from the table and wrapped him in a towel and placed him inside the cutaway cardboard box, lined with a soft blanket, where he slept whenever the weather turned bad.

She patted him on top of the head. "You still cold, little Pod?" she said. He lifted up his pointy face and stared at her, his nose twitching. She squatted down and continued to stroke his head. "You poor little guy."

When I first met Molly, she had been a nun, although she had not taken vows. She had been working with a relief organization that constructed homes for the poor and helped empower fisherpeople and victims of natural calamities. But she and her fellow nuns were of a different stripe than their antecedents, and they didn't confine themselves to the type of charitable activities that are usually considered laudatory but of no threat or consequence to corporate-scale enterprises. Molly and her friends began to organize the sugarcane workers. The workers who joined the union discovered they had twenty-four hours to get out of their company-owned houses. And that was just for openers.

Where did this happen?

You got it. In the medieval fiefdom of the Abelard family, St. Mary Parish.

Molly sat back down at the table and resumed eating, her thoughts hidden, the candlelight carving her features, flickering on her red hair and the strange brown luminosity of her eyes.

"I'm going to take him to the vet tomorrow," I said. "I think he might have distemper."

"I'll take him," she said. "I shouldn't have let him get wet this afternoon. I was late getting home, and his chain was wrapped around the tree. Where were you?"

We had gotten to the subject I didn't want to broach. "Clete and I took a ride to the Abelard home, down in St. Mary."

I heard Alafair stop eating. "Why would you want to go to the Abelard house, Dave?" she asked.

"A pimp by the name of Herman Stanga claims to be working for the St. Jude Project. Kermit Abelard says that's not so. His friend Robert Weingart claims he never heard of Herman Stanga. I think Weingart is a liar and a full-time mainline wiseass. Clete is hanging by a thread over the fire. He may go to prison because of Stanga, Alafair."

"Go to prison for what?"

"Stanga spat on him, and Clete did something he shouldn't have."

"So it's Kermit's fault?"

"I think Kermit is deliberately naive. He chooses not to see evil in men who are genuinely wicked. He told me he had talked to you about his contacts with Stanga."

"Kermit has a good heart. Maybe you'd find that out if you gave him a chance," she said.

The rain had slackened, and the light on the bayou was a dense green, the wake from a passing tugboat swelling over the banks into the roots of the cypress and oak trees. Our windows were open, and the air was cool and fresh, and I could smell the heavy, fecund odor of the bayou and the wet trees and the soaked ground, and I didn't want to talk about Herman Stanga and the Abelard family. No, that's not true. I did not want to hear my daughter speak as an advocate for the Abelards.

"I warned Kermit not to drag you into his association with Herman Stanga," I said.

"You did what?"

"Don't start, you two," Molly said.

"I'm not supposed to say anything when Dave insults my friends and patronizes me?" Alafair said. "You actually threatened Kermit? I can't believe you."

"I didn't threaten him."

"Then what did you say to him?"

"Weingart came to the table in a robe and a thong. He called Clete a gelatinous handful. This man is a walking regurgitant. Clete and I are not the problem."

"I am? That's the inference?"

I got up from the table and set my plate on the drainboard, half of my food uneaten. I took a carton of ice cream from the freezer and removed three bowls from the cupboard, unsure what I was doing. I opened the solid door to the back porch, letting in the wind. I could hear frogs croaking and rain leaking out of the oaks and pecan trees into the yard.

"Do y'all want strawberries with your ice cream?" I said.

"Why do you try to control other people, Dave? Why do you ruin everything?" Alafair said.

Molly reached across the table and grasped Alafair's hand. "Don't," she said.

"I'm not supposed to defend my friends or myself?"

"Don't," Molly repeated, shaking Alafair's palm in hers.

I put on my rain hat and walked downtown in the twilight. Customers were having drinks under the colonnade in front of Clementine's restaurant, and across the street, at the Gouguenheim bed-and-breakfast, guests were enjoying the evening on the balcony, and farther down the block a crowd was waiting under the colonnade to go inside Bojangles. I walked to the drawbridge over the Teche at Burke Street and leaned on the rail and looked down the long corridor of trees that was barely visible in the gloaming of the day. What is the proper way for a father to talk to his daughter when she has reached adulthood but is determined to trust men who will only bring her injury? Do you lecture her? Do you indicate that she has no judgment and is not capable of conducting her own life? It's not unlike telling a drunkard that he is weak and morally deficient because he drinks, then expecting him to stop. How do you tell your daughter that all your years of protecting and caring for her can be stolen in a blink by a man like Robert Weingart? The answer is you cannot.

I could not tell Alafair that I remembered moments out of her childhood that she considered of little consequence today or didn't remember at all: the burning day I pulled her from the submerged wreck of an airplane piloted by a priest who was flying war refugees out of El Salvador and Guatemala; her pride in the Donald Duck cap with the quacking bill we bought at Disney World; her first pair of tennis shoes, which she wore to bed at night, embossed on the appropriate tips in big rubber letters with the words "left" and "right"; her ongoing war with Batist, the black man who ran our bait shop and boat rental, because Tripod would not stay out of Batist's fried pies and candy bars; her horse, Tex, who threw her end over end into our tomato plants; Alafair, at age six, mallet-smashing boiled crabs at a screened-in restaurant by Vermilion Bay, splattering everyone at the table; Alafair, at age nine, fishing with me in the Gulf, casting two-handed with a heavy rod and saltwater reel like it was a samurai sword, almost knocking me unconscious with the lead weights and smelt-baited treble hook.

Do you approach your daughter and tell her that no man has the right to track his feet through a father's memories of his daughter's young life?

I walked home in the dark. The streetlamps were back on and the wind was up, and the frenetic shadows of the live oaks and the moss in their limbs made me think of soldiers running from tree trunk to tree trunk in a nocturnal woods, but I had no explanation why.

THE PHONE RANG at shortly after two in the morning. The caller sounded drunk and black and belligerent. I told him he must have misdialed, and started to hang up on him.

"No, I got the right number. Elmore said to call you. He's got to talk to you again," the caller said.

"You're talking about Elmore Latiolais who's in prison in Mississippi?"

"Yeah, I was in there wit' him. I got out yesterday."

"So you stopped by a bar and got loaded, then decided to call me up in the middle of the night?"

"I don't mean no kind of disrespect, but I'm going out of my way to make this call. Elmore seen a picture of a white guy in the newspaper. He said he was sure this white guy had been around his sister's house."

"What's the significance of the white guy?" I said.

"Again, I ain't meaning to disrespect you, but Elmore's sister was Bernadette. She was killed. This guy tole Bernadette he was gonna make her and her grandmother rich. She come to visit Elmore in jail, and she showed Elmore a picture of her and this white guy together. He's a famous guy, maybe a great humanitarian or somet'ing like that. Maybe he's been in the movies. I ain't sure."

"Elmore thinks Herman Stanga killed his sister. What's the white guy got to do with anything?"

"Elmore says the white guy knows Herman. I got to take a leak, man. You got what you need?"

"Give me your name. I'll meet you tomorrow in a place of your choosing."

"Lookie here, Elmore said send you a kite. That's what I done. Elmore showed the picture to Captain Thigpin and axed him to call you again. You ain't had no call from Captain Thigpin, have you?"

"No."

"'Cause Captain Thigpin ain't gonna be he'ping a black man on his road gang to bring down a rich white man. In the meantime, Elmore is going crazy in there. He keeps saying nobody cares about his sister. He says he's got to get out and find the people that cut her t'roat. 'She was just seventeen.' That's what he keeps saying over and over, 'She was just seventeen.'"

At this point I expected the caller to hang up. He had probably told me all he knew and was obviously tired, in need of a restroom, and wanting another drink.

"Lookie, the reason Elmore axed me to call you and not somebody else is simple," the caller said. "You said you was sorry for his loss. Ain't none of the hacks tole him that, but you did. I tole Elmore he better quit doing what he's doing or they gonna cool his ass out. But Elmore ain't a listener."

I WENT TO work early the next morning determined not to be drawn into problems outside my jurisdiction. Three years ago parish and city law enforcement had merged for budgetary reasons, and my office was now located in City Hall, on Bayou Teche, with a grand view of a religious grotto and wonderful oak trees next to the city library and, across the water, the urban forest that we call City Park. The sky was blue, the azaleas still blooming, wisteria hanging in clumps on the side of the grotto. I picked up my mail, poured a cup of coffee, and started in on the paperwork that waited daily for me in my in-basket.

But I could not get my two A.M. caller off my mind. In my wallet I found the cell-phone number of Captain Jimmy Darl Thigpin and punched it into my desk phone. My call went instantly to voice mail. I left a message. By eleven A.M. I had not received a reply. I tried again. At three in the afternoon I tried again. This time he picked up, but he offered no explanation for not having returned my earlier calls. "Is this about Latiolais?" he said.

"Yes, sir. I had a call last night from a man who

says Latiolais has some new information regarding his sister's homicide."

"How does a convict on a brush gang come up with 'new information'? Isn't it about time to give this a rest, Mr. Robicheaux?"

"The caller said Elmore Latiolais had seen a newspaper photo of a white man who knew his sister and is connected with a pimp and drug dealer here by the name of Herman Stanga."

"I don't know anything about this."

"Latiolais didn't tell you about the photo?"

"No."

"He made no mention of it to you?"

There was a pause. "I usually say things once. I do that because I tell the truth and I'm not used to having my word questioned."

"Can I talk with Latiolais?"

"You want me to put a nigra inmate on my cell phone?"

"Or you can have him call me collect on a landline."

"He's in lockup."

"There's no phone in your facility?"

"He doesn't have phone privileges there. That's why we call it lockup."

"Why is he in lockup?"

"He was acting like he had some jackrabbit in him."

"I need to speak to him, Cap."

"If you want to believe that boy's lies, that's your right. But I got a half-dozen inmates on my gang who would cut your throat for a dollar and lick the cut clean for an extra fifty cents, and I don't have time to be worrying about that little halfwit. I hope this is the last conversation we have on the subject."

"We can't promise that, Cap. We were hoping to get your cooperation."

"Who is 'we'?" he said. Then the line went dead.

Through my open door I saw the sheriff, Helen Soileau, pass in the corridor. She came back and propped one arm on the jamb. She was a trim, firm-bodied woman, attractive in an androgynous way, her expressions often enigmatic, as though she were vacillating between two lives even while she was looking into your face. "I was at a function in Lafayette last night," she said. "Timothy Abelard was there. He said you and Clete had been out to his house yesterday."

"That's true."

"What was Clete doing with you?"

"He came along for the ride."

She stepped inside the office and closed the door behind her, then sat down on the corner of my desk. She was wearing tan slacks and a pink shirt and her gun belt and half-top brown suede boots. "Clete is in a lot of trouble, Dave. But this time he's not going to drag his problems into our workday. Got me?" she said.

"My trip to the Abelards was off the clock."

"That's not the point."

"You know anything about this guy Robert Weingart?" I asked.

"He's a writer. What about him?"

"He and Kermit Abelard are involved with the St. Jude Project. Herman Stanga claims he is, too."

"That's not a crime."

"The fact that Weingart breathes our air is a crime."

"I like the way you leave your personal feelings at the front door when you come to work in the morning."

"I interviewed a convict in Mississippi who said Stanga is mixed up with the homicides in Jeff Davis Parish."

"When did you go to Mississippi?"

"When I took those two days' vacation time."

She lifted a strand of hair out of her eyes. "What are we going to do with you, bwana?"

"Weingart is a piece of shit. I think he has Kermit Abelard under his control. I think we're going to hear a lot more from him."

She was shaking her head, holding back something she didn't want to say.

"Go ahead," I said.

"Go ahead, what?"

"Say what's on your mind."

"Isn't Alafair seeing Kermit Abelard?"

"I don't know what the word 'seeing' means. It's like a lot of words people use today. I can't relate to their meaning. Does 'see' mean look at someone? Or sleep with someone? Alafair thinks both Abelard and Weingart are great writers. I heard Weingart's female lawyer rewrote most of his manuscript and got it published for him and that Weingart couldn't write his way out of a wet paper bag. I think Kermit is probably bisexual and in this guy's thrall."

"When you figure out how that translates into the commission of a crime, let me know."

"Why be everybody's punch?" I said.

"Want to rephrase that?"

"Bloodsuckers of every stripe come here and wipe their feet on us. We've turned victimhood into an art form. Weingart is a parasite if not a predator."

"Go back to that part about Abelard's bisexuality. I'd like to know how that figures into all this."

"I wasn't making a judgment about it."

Her eyes roamed over my face. "Tell Clete he's on a short tether. I always love chatting with you, Dave," she said. She winked at me and went out the door, closing it carefully behind her, like someone who does not want to be in the emotional debt of another.

TWO DAYS PASSED and I began to think less and less about the deaths of the women in Jefferson Davis Parish. The absence of news coverage about their deaths and the general lack of fear or outrage that their deaths should have provoked may seem bizarre or symptomatic of inhumanity among our citizenry. But serial killers abound in this country, and they often kill scores of people for a span of several decades before they are caught, if they ever are. Most of their victims come from the great uprooted, faceless population that drifts via Greyhound or gas-guzzler or motorcycle or thumb through trailer slums, battered women's shelters, Salvation Army missions, migrant worker camps, and inner-city areas that have the impersonality of war zones. The vagueness of the term "homeless" is unintentionally appropriate for many of the people inside this group. We have no idea who they are, how many of them are mentally ill or just poor, or how many of them are fugitives. In the 1980s, hundreds of thousands of them were dumped on the streets or refused admission by federal hospitals. The mendicant culture they established is still with us, although our problem of conscience regarding their welfare seems to have faded.

A local bluesman by the name of Lazy Lester once said, "Don't ever write your name on the jailhouse wall." Today it might not be a bad idea.

On Wednesday, just before quitting time, Helen came into my office with a back section of the Baton Rouge *Advocate* folded in her hand. "What was the name of the convict you interviewed in Mississippi?"

"Elmore Latiolais."

"I shouldn't do this."

"Do what?"

"Help you drag somebody else's problem into our workload." She dropped the newspaper on my desk pad.

I picked up the paper and read the story. It was four paragraphs in length. It was the kind of news story that any journalist or educated cop instantly recognizes as one that replicated a press handout or a statement made by a public information officer rather than an account based on an eyewitness interview. It was written in the passive voice and avoided specifics other than the fact that Elmore Latiolais, a man with a long criminal history, had been shot to death when he stole a pistol from a prison vehicle and threatened to kill a prison guard.

"Latiolais was a check writer and a bigamist and a thief. I don't see this guy threatening prison personnel with a stolen firearm."

"Pops, let the state of Mississippi deal with it."

"So why bring me the news story?"

"Because you have a right to see it. That doesn't mean you have a right to act on it."

"You brought it to me because you know this story sucks."

"Oh, boy."

"Listen, Helen—"

She walked out the door, shaking her head, probably more at herself than at me.

I called Jimmy Darl Thigpin on his cell phone,

expecting my call to go immediately to voice mail. But it didn't.

"Thigpin," a voice said.

"It's Dave Robicheaux."

"I figured."

"I just read the story on Latiolais's death. What happened?"

"I killed him. Somebody should have done it to that sonofabitch a long time ago."

"He had a gun?"

"That's right. He was getting it out of my cab."

The image his words conjured up didn't fit. "But he didn't actually have the gun in hand?"

"What did the newspaper say?"

"It stated he threatened you."

"'Cause that's what he did."

"How did Latiolais get access to the cab of your truck? What was an unsecured weapon doing in it?"

"A new man screwed up."

"Tell me straight-out, Cap, this man verbally threatened you while holding a loaded weapon in his hand. That's what happened? You were at mortal risk?"

"You're over the line, Mr. Robicheaux."

"The question stands. Will you answer it?"

"It *what*?"

"You put him in lockup because you said he had some jackrabbit in him. Then you took him out of lockup and left him unattended around a firearm. A man of your experience did that?"

"This conversation is over."

"Latiolais wasn't a violent offender."

"Did you hear me?"

"No, I didn't, not at all. Why didn't you call and tell me Latiolais had more information for me? I think you just killed a man who could have helped solve several homicides in our area."

"I've had about all this I can take. You stay the hell away from me."

He broke the connection. And I was glad he did. There were times in my job when I wanted to dig a hole in the earth and bury my shield and scrub my skin with peroxide.

IT'S THE CONTENTION of Alcoholics Anonymous that drinking is but the symptom of the illness. Those afflicted souls who quit drinking but do nothing else to change their way of life become what are called "dry drunks." Often they channel their bitterness and anger into the lives of others. They also seek to control everyone around them, and they accomplish this end by the most insidious means possible: the inculcation of guilt and fear and low self-esteem in those who are unfortunate enough to be in their sway.

A person who practices the steps and principles of A.A. has little latitude in certain situations. When we are wrong about something, we have to admit it promptly. Then we have to make amends and restitution. In moments like these, a person may yearn for an easier way—say, a tall glass packed with shaved ice, stained with four jiggers of Black Jack Daniel's, wrapped with a napkin to keep the coldness inside the glass, a sprig of mint inserted in the ice.

After supper, I watched Alafair feed Tripod and Snuggs in the backyard. She walked past me into the kitchen without speaking. I followed her inside and asked her to take a walk with me.

"I'm going out," she said.

"It won't take long."

"I have to dress."

"You going out with Kermit?"

"What about it? Should I arrange for him to pick me up somewhere else?"

"No."

"What did you want to talk about?"

Molly was watching CNN in the living room. I heard her turn off the television and walk into the hallway that gave onto the kitchen.

"Nothing. It's a nice evening. I just thought you might want to take a walk," I said.

I left the house and went down the street to Clementine's, where I knew I would find Clete Purcel at the bar. He was wearing cream-colored pleated slacks and oxblood loafers and a starched short-sleeved shirt printed with big gray and white flowers, his porkpie hat tilted forward on his head. He was sipping from a frosted mug of draft beer while the bartender poured his shot glass to the brim with Johnnie Walker. Clete looked at my reflection in the yellowed mahogany-framed mirror behind the bar. His eyes were lit with an alcoholic shine.

"You see the story about Elmore Latiolais?" he asked.

"Helen showed it to me."

"That gunbull friend of yours capped him?"

"Jimmy Darl Thigpin is not my friend."

"But he's the guy who capped Latiolais, right?"

"He's the one."

"How do you read it?"

"I'm not sure. Why are you drinking boiler-makers?"

"I only do it when I'm alone or with people. It's not a problem."

"It's not funny, either."

"Give Dave a soda and lime, will you?" Clete said to the bartender.

"Where have you been?" I asked.

"Chasing dead ends in Jeff Davis Parish." He squeezed his temples. "My lawyer talked to the DA in St. Martinville today. A half-dozen witnesses from the Gate Mouth club are prepared to testify against me. They photographed me with their cell phones while I was smashing Herman Stanga's face into a tree trunk. My lawyer says if I plea out, I'll have to do at least a year."

"We're not going to let that happen, Cletus."

"You know what the DA said? 'We're tired of this guy wiping his ass on us.'"

The bartender set a glass of ice and carbonated water, with a lime slice floating in it, on a paper napkin by my hand. "I'm sorry, I didn't order that," I said.

"You want coffee?" he asked.

"No, thanks."

"Let me know when you need something," the bartender said. He threw the carbonated drink into the sink and walked away. I had a hard time taking my eyes away from the back of his neck.

"Trouble on the home front?" Clete said.

"No, none."

Clete looked at me for a long time. "You dream about it very much?"

"About what?"

"You know what I'm talking about."

Don't enter into it, I heard a voice say. But I seldom take my best advice. "From time to time."

"What's in the dream?"

"Why be morbid? Nobody gets a pass on it. We have today. That's all any of us gets."

"Tell me what's in the dream."

"A square hole in the ground, deep in the forest. The wind is blowing, shredding leaves off the trees, but there's no sound or color in the woods. It's like the sun went over the edge of the horizon and died, and this time you know with absolute certainty it's never coming up again. When I wake up, I can't go back to sleep. I feel like weevil worms are eating their way through my heart."

Clete let out his breath, then drank the shot glass of Johnnie Walker all the way to the bottom, never blinking. He chased it with beer from his mug, his cheeks turning as red as apples. "Fuck it," he said.

A man on the next stool who had been talking with a woman turned and stared at Clete.

"Help you with something?" Clete said.

"No, sir," the man said. "I was just looking at the clock."

"Glad to hear it," Clete said. "Ralph, give this man and his lady a drink."

I got up from the bar stool and placed my hand on Clete's shoulder. I could feel the heat in his muscles through his shirt. "I'll see you tomorrow," I said.

"Don't let them get behind you," he replied. "The Bobbsey Twins from Homicide are forever. We were the only two beat cops the Panthers allowed into the Desire. Let somebody top that."

Clete's words would make no sense to anyone else. But what he said was true. In 1970 the Black Panthers took control of the Desire Project and reduced crime to almost zero. But the Panthers also had a violent relationship with the NOPD. Ironically, that era, in retrospect, seems innocent contrasted with the times we now live in.

Unfortunately, none of those thoughts were of comfort to me when I walked home under the glow of the streetlamps. I still had not resolved my situation with Alafair and was not sure that I could. At ten o'clock Molly went to bed and I sat in the living room and watched the local news. Then I turned out the light and sat in the darkness, the windows open, the wind sifting pine needles across our tin roof. At eleven-thirty I saw Kermit Abelard's car pull to the curb, and I saw Kermit and Alafair kiss on the mouth. Then he drove away without walking her to the door. I could hear myself breathing in the dark.

"You scared me," Alafair said, realizing I was in the living room.

"I was watching the news and fell asleep."

She looked at the darkened screen of the television set. "What did you want to tell me earlier?"

"I'm not sure."

"You're a case."

She went into her bedroom and put on her pajamas. I heard her pull back the covers on her bed and lie down. I took a blanket and a spare pillow out of the hall closet and went into her room and spread the blanket on the floor. I lay down on top of it, my arm resting on my forehead.

"Dave, no one is this crazy," she said.

"I know."

"I'm not ten years old anymore."

"You don't have to tell me."

"Stop acting like this," she said.

"To try to control the lives of other people is a form of arrogance. The only form of behavior that is more arrogant is to claim that we know the will of God. I owe you an apology. I've tried to impose my will on you all your life."

"I appreciate what you say. But that doesn't change the real problem, does it?"

"What's the real problem?"

"You don't approve of Kermit."

"I think at heart he's probably a decent man. But that's not my judgment to make."

"What about Robert Weingart?"

"I have nothing to say about him." The only sound in the room was the sweep of wind in the trees and the ping of an acorn on the roof. I propped myself up on my elbow. "You want to tell me something?" I asked.

"Robert met us at Bojangles," she said. "A Vietnamese girl works in there. She brought us our drinks, and he told her he'd ordered iced tea without sweetener rather than white wine. He said he was going to write tonight and he never drank before he wrote. But I heard him. He ordered wine. When she took it back, he watched her all the way to the bar with this ugly smile. Why would he do that?"

"Maybe he just forgot what he ordered."

"No, I could see it in his eyes. He enjoyed it."

"Where was Kermit when this happened?"

"In the men's room."

"Did you tell him about it?"

"No."

I didn't think it was the time to force her to think about the nature of Kermit's relationship with Weingart. "Maybe you should just forget about Weingart. Kermit will come to a resolution about him at some point in his life."

"What do you mean by 'resolution'?"

"They seem quite close."

"What are you implying?"

"Nothing. They're both artists. Kermit sees a different person in Weingart from the one you do, or at least the Robert Weingart you were sitting with tonight."

I heard her fix her pillow. Then she looked down at me. "Good night, Dave," she said.

"Good night, little guy."

"Little guy, yourself."

I rested my arm across my eyes and began to drift off to sleep. I felt her touch my shoulder. "I love you, Dave."

"I love you, too, Alf."

"Give Kermit a chance, will you?"

"I will. I promise," I replied.

CHAPTER 5

In the morning I used the Google search mechanism on the department computer to find the photograph that evidently Elmore Latiolais had seen in a newspaper. It took a while, since I had no cross-references except the mention by Elmore Latiolais's convict buddy that the man in the photo was white and a famous humanitarian. Or perhaps someone who had been in the movies.

I typed in Robert Weingart's name and got nothing but listings of book reviews and feature articles on the remarkable turnaround in the career of a lifetime felon whose autobiography had become the most celebrated literary work by a convict author since the publication of *Soul on Ice*.

Then I entered the name of Kermit Aloysius Abelard. The article and photograph I found had been published two weeks ago on the business page of a Mississippi newspaper. But the article was less about Kermit than his co-speaker at a civic gathering in Jackson, the state capital. The co-speaker was Layton Blanchet, one of those iconic, antithetically mixed personalities the American South has produced unrelentingly since Reconstruction. In the photograph, Kermit was seated at the speakers' table, his face turned up attentively toward Blanchet, who stood at the podium, his size and power and visceral energy as palpable in the photo as they were in real life. The cutline below the photo stated, "Self-made investment tycoon shares vision of a nation shifting its energy needs from oil to bio-fuels."

Layton had grown up in the little town of Washington, Louisiana, in St. Landry Parish, during an era when the sheriff and his political allies ran not only the gambling joints in the parish but one of the most notorious brothels in the South, known simply as Margaret's. His parents, like mine, were illiterate Cajuns and spoke almost no English and picked cotton and broke corn for a living. Layton attended trade school and business college in Lafayette, and sold burial insurance door-to-door in black neighborhoods and pots and pans in blue-collar Cajun neighborhoods. He also managed to get his customers' signatures on loan-company agreements that charged the highest interest rates possible under the law. Later, he worked at lower levels of law enforcement in both Lafayette and Iberia parishes, which was when I met him. Even then I felt Layton was less interested in a particular line of work than in determining where the sources of power and wealth lay inside a society, not unlike a blind man feeling his way through an unfamiliar room.

His singular gift was his ability to listen to every word people said to him, his blue eyes charged with energy and goodwill and curiosity, all in a way that was not feigned, his assimilation of other people's experience and knowledge an ongoing epistemological osmosis. He never showed anger or irritability. His square jaw and big teeth and radiant smile seemed inseparable.

I never doubted that Layton Blanchet was on his way up. But no one could have guessed how high.

When the oil economy collapsed in the 1980s, he bought every closed business, foreclosed mortgage, and piece of untilled farm acreage he could get his hands on, often at a third of its earlier valuation. Usually the sellers were only too happy to salvage what they could from their ruined finances, and Layton sometimes threw in an extra thousand or two if their situation was especially dire. Like a carrion bird drifting on a warm wind, he coasted above a stricken land, one that had not been kind to his family, and his ability to smell mortality down below was not a theological offense but simply recognition that his time had come around at last.

Layton owned a bank in Mississippi, a savings-and-loan company in Houston, a second home in Naples, Florida, and a condominium in Vail. But the center of his life, perhaps his visual testimony to the success his humble birth normally would have denied him, was the restored antebellum home where he lived on a bend in Bayou Teche, just outside Franklin.

It was a huge home stacked with a second-story veranda and dormers and chimneys that poked through the canopy of the two-hundred-year-old live oaks that shaded the roof. Every other year Layton had the entire house repainted so that it gleamed like a wedding cake inside a green arbor. He entertained constantly and imported film and television stars to his lawn parties. Stories abounded about Layton's generosity to his black servants and the Cajun families who farmed his sugarcane acreage. He was gregarious and expansive and wore his physicality in the way a powerful man wears a suit. I did not believe he was surreptitious or hypocritical, which is not to say he was the man he pretended to be. I think in truth Layton himself did not know the identity of the man who lived inside him.

Before quitting time, I called his house and asked if I could see him. "Drive on down. I'll put a steak on the grill," he said. "You still off the kickapoo juice? I always admired the way you handled your problem, Dave. I didn't catch the issue. What was that again?"

"I thought you might be able to help me with some questions I have about a couple of local guys."

"I'll tell Carolyn you're on your way."

"Layton, I can't eat. My wife is preparing a late dinner."

Forty-five minutes later he met me at his front door, wearing a muscle shirt and tennis shoes and beltless slacks that hung low on his hips. His swollen deltoids and his flat-plated chest and the slabs on his shoulders were like those of a man thirty years his junior. "Dave, you look great," he said.

Before I could reply, he called into the interior of the house, "Hey, Carolyn, Dave's here. Start those rib eyes I laid out."

"I have to head back home in a few minutes. I apologize for bothering you during suppertime."

"No, you got to eat something. Come in back while I finish my workout. You still pump iron? You look like you could tear the butt out of a rhinoceros. On that subject, how's Purcel? What a character. I tell people about him, but nobody believes me."

I followed him to the rear of the house, where he had turned a sunroom into a center for his Nautilus machines and dumbbells and weight benches. "Excuse me, all this fabric makes me feel like I'm inside mummy wrap," he said, working off his shirt, dropping it on the floor.

He lay back on a bench and lowered a two-hundred-pound bar from the rack onto his sternum. His straightened his arms, his tendons quivering, his shaved armpits stiff with tension, the outline of his phallus printed against his slacks, an easy smile on his mouth as he lifted the bar higher into the air. Then he lowered it to within an inch of his sternum and lifted the bar nine more times, his chest blooming with veins.

He notched the bar back on the rack, sat up, and put his shirt on, breathing through his nose, his eyes radiant. "Who are these guys you have questions about?"

"Kermit Abelard and Robert Weingart."

"I wouldn't say I know Kermit Abelard well, but I do know him. I never heard of the other guy."

"He's a celebrity ex-convict. He wrote a book called—"

"Yeah, I remember now. One of those books about how the world dumped on the author by making him rich."

"You and Kermit are doing presentations on biofuels?"

Layton was still seated on the bench, his knees spread. He pulled at an earlobe. "Not exactly. You're asking about the talk I gave in Jackson?"

"I saw something about it in a newspaper."

"Yeah, Kermit Abelard was there. But I'm not making the connections here. What are we talking about?" He sneaked a glance at his wristwatch.

"You ever hear of the St. Jude Project?"

"In New Orleans? I thought Katrina shut down all the welfare projects."

I didn't know whether he was being cynical or not. After Katrina made landfall and the levees burst and drowned over one thousand people, a state legislator stated that God in His wisdom had solved the problems in the welfare developments that man had not. The state legislator was not alone in his opinion. I knew too many people whose resentment of blacks reached down into a part of the soul you don't want to see. "The St. Jude Project is supposed to be a self-help program for people who have addiction problems. Junkies, hookers, homeless people, battered wives, whatever," I said.

"The big addiction those people have is usually their aversion to work. Not always but most of the time. I'm not knocking them, but you and I didn't have a charitable foundation to take care of us, did we?"

"Kermit Abelard never talked to you about the St. Jude Project?"

"Dave, I just said I've never heard of it. Hey, Carolyn, you got the meat on the fire?"

"You ever hear of Herman Stanga?"

"No, who is he?"

"A pimp and a dope dealer."

"I haven't had the pleasure. Before we go any farther with this, how about telling me what's really on your mind?"

"Seven dead girls in Jeff Davis Parish."

Layton's hands were resting in his lap. He gazed at the back lawn. It had already fallen into deep shade, and the wind was flattening the azalea petals on the bushes. The sun had started to set on the far side of the trees, and its reflection inside the room had taken on the wobbling blue-green quality of refracted light at the bottom of a swimming pool. Then I realized that the change of color in the room had been brought about by the sun's rays shining through a large dome-shaped panel of stained glass inset close to the ceiling.

"I'm not up on homicides in Jeff Davis Parish," Layton said. "Kermit Abelard is mixed up in something like that?"

"I was wondering why Kermit is doing biofuel presentations with you."

"He's interested in saving the environment and rebuilding the coastline. He's a bright kid. I get the sense he likes to be on the edge of new ideas. You drove all the way down here about Kermit Abelard? He's a pretty harmless young guy, isn't he? Jesus Christ, life must be pretty slow at the department."

"You know the Abelard family well?"

"Not really. I respect them, but we don't have a lot in common."

"Why do you respect them? Their history of philanthropy?"

"You go to a lot of meetings?" Layton asked.

"Sometimes. Why?"

"I've heard that when alcoholics quit drinking, they develop obsessions that work as a substitute for booze. That's why they go to meetings. No matter how crazy these ideas are, they stay high as a kite on them so they don't have to drink again."

"I was admiring your stained glass."

"It came from a Scottish temple or church or something."

"With unicorns and satyrs on it?"

"You got me. The architect stuck it in there. Dave, a conversation with you is like petting a porcupine. Ah, Carolyn with a cold beer. Thank you, thank you, thank you. You got some iced tea or a soft drink for Dave?"

His wife, Carolyn Blanchet, wore a halter and blue jeans and Roman sandals; she had platinum hair and the thick shoulders of a competitive tennis player. She had grown up in Lake Charles and had been a cheerleader and varsity tennis player at LSU. Now, twenty years down the road and a little soft around the edges, the flesh starting to sag under her chin, she still looked good, on the court and off, at mixed doubles or at a country-club dance.

Her laugh was husky, sometimes irreverent, perhaps even sybaritic, the kind you hear in educated southern women who seemed to signal their willingness to stray if the situation is right.

"I'm so happy you can have dinner with us, Dave. How's Molly?"

"She's fine. But I can't stay. I'm sorry if I gave that impression," I said.

"Your steak is on the grill," Layton said.

"Another time."

"She made a big salad, Dave," Layton said.

"Molly is waiting dinner for me."

"That's all right. We'll invite y'all out on another evening," Carolyn said. "I heard you talking about Kermit Abelard. Did you read his last novel?"

"No, I haven't had the chance."

"It's beautiful," she said. "It's about the Civil War and Reconstruction in this area. It's about this slave girl who was the illegitimate daughter of the man who founded Angola Penitentiary. A white Confederate soldier from New Iberia teaches her how to read and write. But more than anything, the black girl wants the recognition and love of her father. Do you know Kermit Abelard?"

"He's gone out with my daughter from time to time."

"I've never met him. But his father gave Layton the stained glass up there. At sunrise it fills the room with every color of the rainbow."

"I think the architect got that from Mr. Abelard, Carolyn. Mr. Abelard didn't give that directly to us," Layton said.

"Yes, that's what I meant."

"I'd better go now," I said.

Layton sipped from his beer, taking my measure. "Sorry you can't eat with us. You're missing out on a fine piece of beef."

He laid his arm across his wife's shoulders and squeezed her against him, his eyes as bright as a butane flame, the sweat stain in his armpit inches from his wife's cheek.

ON SATURDAY MORNING I drove to the rural community south of Jennings, where Bernadette Latiolais had lived with her grandmother. It had been raining hard for two hours. The ditches in the entire neighborhood were brimming with water and floating trash, the fields sodden, the sky gray from horizon to horizon. Few of the mailboxes had legible names or numbers, and I couldn't find the grandmother's house. At a crossroads, I went into a clapboard store that had a pool table in back and a drive-by daiquiri window cut in one wall. Through the rear window I could see rain swirling in great vortexes across a rice field that had been turned into a crawfish farm. I could see an abandoned Acadian cottage, its windows boarded, the gallery sagging, hay bales stacked inside the doorless entranceway. I could see a rusted tractor that seemed to shimmer to life when lightning splintered the sky. I could see thick stands of trees along a river that was blanketed with fog, the canopy green and thrashing inside the grayness of the day. I could see all these things like a transitional photograph of the Louisiana where I had been born and where now I often felt like a visitor.

One wall of the store was stacked from floor to ceiling with cartons of cigarettes. I bought a cup of coffee and started to ask directions to the grandmother's house from the woman behind the cash register. I had my badge holder in my hand, but I had not unfolded it. She interrupted me and waited on a car full of black men who had already ordered frozen daiquiris through the service window. She gave them their drinks and their change and shut the window hard, holding it firm for a second with the heel of her hand. Her arms and the front of her shirt were damp with mist, her physique bovine, her face stark, like that of someone caught unexpectedly in the flash of a camera. I identified myself and asked again for directions to the grandmother's house. She glanced at my badge and back at me. "All the daiquiris was sealed," she said.

"Pardon?"

"Ain't no law been broken long as I seal the cups. I know what they do when they leave here, but it ain't me that's broke the law."

"I understand. I just need directions to the home of Eunice Latiolais."

"The law says the driver ain't s'ppose to have an open container. That's all the law says."

"Will you give me the directions to the Latiolais house, please?"

"Go sout' a half mile and turn at the fo' corners, and you'll see it down by the river. People been dumping there. There's mattresses and washing machines all back in the trees. If you ax me, the people been doing this is the kind that just left here. I'm talking about the dumping." She paused. Her hands were pressed flat on the counter. She had run out of words. She looked out at the rain and at the backs of her hands. "This is about Bernadette?"

"Did you know her?"

"She use to come in for her Ho Hos every afternoon. The school bus goes close by her house, but she'd get off early for her Ho Hos and then walk the rest of the way."

"What kind of friends did she have?"

"Her kind ain't got friends."

"Ma'am?"

"There ain't no reg'lar kids anymore. One's drunk, one's smoking dope, one's trying to steal rubbers out of the machine in the bat'room. A girl like Bernadette is on her own. Come in here in the afternoon and see the bunch that gets off the bus. Listen to the kind of language they use."

"She was a good girl?"

"She was an honor student. She never got in no trouble. She was always polite and said 'yes, ma'am' and 'no, ma'am.' She wasn't like the others."

"Which others?"

"The other ones that's been killed. The others was always in trouble with men and dope. Her brother and sister wasn't no good, but Bernadette was sweet-sweet, all the way t'rew. She had the sweetest smile I ever seen on a young girl. The man who done that to her is going to hell. The man who killed her don't deserve no mercy. If he ever comes in here and I know it's him, he better look out."

"Do you know a man by the name of Herman Stanga?"

"No. Who's he?"

"A local character in New Iberia."

"Then keep him in New Iberia."

A palpable bitterness seemed to rise from her person, like a nimbus given off by a dead fire.

I followed her directions to the home of Bernadette Latiolais. The house was wood-frame, with fresh white paint and a peaked tin roof, set up on cinder blocks inside a grove of pecan trees and water oaks that had not yet gone into leaf. On the gallery were chalk animals of a kind given as prizes at carnivals, and coffee cans planted with begonias and petunias. One of the Jefferson Davis sheriff's detectives who had been assigned the case had given me as many details over the phone as he could. On a cold, sunlit Saturday afternoon, Bernadette Latiolais had entered the dollar store and bought two plastic teacups and saucers decorated with tiny lavender roses. After she paid, she walked out the door and crossed a parking lot and passed a bar with a sign in a window that said PAY CHECKS CASHED. She was five miles from her home with no apparent means of transportation. She was wearing a light pink sweater, jeans, a white blouse, and tennis shoes without socks. She was carrying the teacups and saucers in a paper bag. One week later, her body was found at the bottom of a pond, weighted with chunks of concrete. The knife wound to her throat was so deep she had almost been decapitated.

I picked up a paper bag off the seat that contained two books I had bought earlier that morning at Barnes & Noble in Lafayette. The grandmother invited me in, holding the screen with one arm as I entered. She was a big, overweight woman, obviously in poor health. She waddled as she returned to the couch where she had been sitting, as though she were on board a ship. When she sat down, she pressed the flat of her hand against her bosom, wheezing. "I'm s'ppose to be breathing my oxygen, but sometimes I try to get by wit'out it," she said.

"I'm very sorry about your granddaughter's death, Mrs. Latiolais. I'm also sorry about the death of your grandson Elmore," I said. "I interviewed him in Mississippi. Later he sent me a message about a photograph he'd seen in a newspaper. Elmore believed a man in the photograph was the same man who had told Bernadette he was going to make you and her rich. Did somebody tell you all that? That somebody was going to make you rich?"

"I didn't hear nothing about that, me," Mrs. Latiolais said. "It don't sound right."

I was sitting on a wood chair on the opposite side of a coffee table from her. I removed the two books I had bought and showed her the jacket photo on Kermit Abelard's novel about the Civil War and Reconstruction in Louisiana. "Do you know this man?" I asked.

She leaned over the book and brushed at the photo with her fingers, as though removing a glaze from it. "Who is he?"

"A writer who lives in St. Mary Parish."

"I don't know him."

"Look again. This is the man Elmore recognized in the newspaper photograph. He said Bernadette had had her picture taken with him. She showed it to Elmore when she visited him in jail."

"I ain't never seen him."

I pulled out the flap on my copy of *The Green Cage* and showed her the author photo. She looked at it for a long time. She tapped her finger on it. "That one I know," she said.

"You do? From where?"

"He was wit' a black man. The two of them was in the sto' buying some boudin. The white man wanted it warmed up, but the micro was broke and he was complaining about it. He wasn't from around here. He sounded like he was from up nort'. He said, 'I understand why y'all say t'ank God for Mis'sippi.' He said it like the people standing around him didn't have ears or feelings."

"Who was the black man?"

"I ain't seen him befo'. He had a li'l mustache,

like a li'l black bird under his nose. He was wearing a pink tie and a brown suit wit' stripes in it, what a downtown man would wear."

"Why would anyone tell your granddaughter he was going to make y'all rich, Mrs. Latiolais?"

"That's why I said it don't make sense. I own this house, but it ain't wort' a lot. Bernadette inherited seven arpents of land from her father. It's part of a rice field down sout' of us. Maybe somebody wanted to buy it a while back, but I don't remember. She wasn't gonna sell it, though. She said she was gonna save the bears."

"The bears?"

"That's the way Bernadette talked. She was always dreaming about saving t'ings, being a part of some kind of movement, being different from everybody else. I tole her them seven arpents was for her to go to colletch. She said she didn't need no money to go to colletch. She'd won a scholarship to UL in Lafayette. She was gonna be a nurse."

I talked to the grandmother for another fifteen minutes but got nowhere. The grandmother was not only afflicted with emphysema but was on kidney dialysis. Her life had been one of privation and hardship and loss, to the degree that she seemed to think of suffering as the natural state of humankind. The one bright prospect in her life had been taken from her. I have never agreed with the institution of capital punishment, primarily because its application is arbitrary and selective, but that morning I had to concede that the killer or killers of Bernadette Latiolais belonged in a special category, one that can cause a person to wonder if his humanity was misplaced.

THAT EVENING I hooked my boat trailer to my truck and picked up Clete Purcel at his motor court, and in the sunset drove the two of us up Bayou Teche to Henderson Swamp. The water in the swamp was high and flat, the islands of willow and cypress trees backlit by a molten sun, the carpets of floating hyacinths undisturbed by any fish that would normally be feeding at the end of day. No other boats were on the water. In the silence we could hear the rain ticking out of the trees and the whirring sound of automobile tires on the elevated highway that traversed the swamp. Up on the levee, which was covered with buttercups, the flood lamps of a bait shop and seafood restaurant went on, and I could see small waves from our wake sliding through the pilings into the shadows. When I cut the engine and let our boat drift between two willow islands that had turned dark against the sun, I felt that Clete and I were the only two people on the planet.

I doubted we would catch any fish that evening, but if possible, I wanted to get Clete out of his funk and his conviction that he was going to prison. The problem was, I thought that perhaps this time his perceptions were correct. I told him of my visit to the home of Bernadette Latiolais's grandmother. I also told him she had recognized the photo of Robert Weingart and that she had seen him with a black man who had a small mustache and wore a suit and a pink tie.

Clete flung a small spinner baited with a wriggler on the edge of the lily pads, his skin rosy in the waning light. "You think the black dude was Herman Stanga?"

"The grandmother said he looked like a 'downtown man.' She even said his mustache looked like a little black bird under his nose."

"What's this stuff about seven arpents of land?"

"It sounds like part of an undivided estate of some kind. Clete, maybe the Latiolais girl was just randomly abducted. Maybe her death doesn't have anything to do with Stanga or Robert Weingart. She was walking past a bar in broad daylight, and then she was gone. Maybe the wrong guy came out of the bar at the wrong time and offered her a ride. Maybe Bernadette Latiolais's death doesn't have anything to do with the deaths of the other victims."

"My money is still on Stanga," he said.

"Maybe he's involved, but I don't think he's the chief perpetrator."

"Because Stanga is kind to animals?"

"Because he has ice water in his veins. Stanga doesn't do anything unless it's of direct benefit to him. There is no known connection between him and the girl."

"On some level, Stanga is dirty. I just don't know how or why. Before this is over, I'm going to take him off the board." Clete retrieved his spinner and flipped it out again, his face empty.

I didn't want to hear what he had just said. "We'll get out of this one way or another, Clete. I promise. Your friends aren't going to let you down."

"I'm not going to do time. Before I go inside, I'll put a few guys in body bags or eat my gun."

"Not a good way to think."

"So I'll skip the country instead."

"How's your love life?" I said, changing the subject.

"I don't have one."

"You need to find a new girlfriend. This time get one your own age."

"Who wants a girlfriend my age?"

For the first time that evening we both laughed out loud, violating the stillness, as though three decades had not passed and we were both cops in uniform again, walking a beat with batons on Esplanade or Rampart. Then I saw the humor go out of Clete's face.

"What are you looking at?" I said.

"That boat out in the channel. Somebody is using binoculars on us. There. See the light glint on the lenses?"

I looked back toward the landing. In the gloom I could barely make out a male figure seated in the stern of a speedboat. Then I saw him lean over and dip his hand into the water and begin retrieving his anchor from the mud. Across the water, we could hear the dull thunk of the anchor clank in the bottom of the boat, then the buzzing sound of the electric starter turning over. The man in the speedboat pointed the bow directly toward us and opened the throttle, a frothy yellow wake fanning out behind him.

Clete reeled in his spinner and set down his rod on the gunwale. He took a po'boy sandwich from the ice chest, unwrapped the waxed paper, and bit into the French bread and fried shrimp and sauce piquant and sliced tomatoes and onions inside it, pushing the food back into his mouth with his wrist, his eyes never leaving the speedboat.

The driver made a wide circle and approached us so the sun was at his back and shining directly into our eyes. Clete shifted around in his seat, watching the speedboat, wiping mayonnaise off his mouth with his fingers. He pulled his right trouser leg up over his sock, exposing the hideaway .25 that was Velcro-strapped to his ankle.

The man in the speedboat cut his gas feed and drifted toward us, his boat rising on its own wake. "One of you guys named Dave Robicheaux?" he asked. His face was lit with an idiot's grin.

"What do you want?" I said.

"I want to know if I found the right man, the man I've been sent to find."

"You found me."

"My name is Vidor Perkins." His tan looked like it had been induced with chemicals or acquired in a salon. His shoulders were narrow and his dark hair oiled and conked on top and mowed into the scalp above his ears, exposing a strawberry birthmark that bled down the back of his neck. But it was his eyes that caught your attention. They were pale blue and did not go with the rest of his face. They seemed to have no pupils and contained the kind of lidless inner concentration that anybody who is con-wise immediately recognizes. In every stockade, prison, or work camp, there is at least one inmate no one deliberately goes near. When you see him on the yard, he might be squatting on his haunches, smoking a cigarette, staring into his own smoke with the concentration of a scientist, his hands draped over his knees like banana peels. At first glance, he appears to be an innocuous creature taking a break in his day, but then you notice that the other inmates divide around him the way water flows around a sharp rock. If you're wise, you do not make eye contact with this man or think you can be his friend. Nor, under any circumstances, do you ever challenge his pride.

The man who called himself Vidor Perkins fixed his mindless stare on Clete. "I bet you're Mr. Purcel," he said.

"We'd like to catch a fish before dark, provided this spot isn't already ruined. You want to spit it out?" Clete said.

"Man up at the bait shop sent me out here. Your daughter called, Mr. Robicheaux. She said there was an emergency at your house."

"Say that again," I replied.

"That's all I know. Sounded like a fire or something. I cain't be sure. He said something about an ambulance."

"Who said?" I asked.

"The man up at the bait shop. I just tole you." He killed a mosquito on his neck, lifted it from his palm with two fingers, and dropped it into the water.

"Why didn't you come straight out here? Why were you anchored?" Clete said.

" 'Cause I didn't know it was y'all."

I pulled out my cell phone and opened it. There was no service. "Were you in the bait shop when the call came in?"

"As a matter of fact, I was. This fellow took the call at the counter. He said something about paramedics. Or the voice over the phone said something about paramedics. I didn't get it all. If it was me, I'd haul freight on up there and see what the deal is."

"Let's see your ID," Clete said. "In the meantime, wipe that grin off your face."

The man in the speedboat gazed at the elevated highway and at the headlights streaming across it. He had a wide mouth that looked made of rubber, like the mouth of a frog or an inflatable doll, and his lips had taken on a purplish cast in the fading light. "I'd worry about my family and not about a fellow who's just trying to do a good deed," he said. "But I'm not you, am I?"

I got out my badge holder and opened it. "I want you to follow us in," I said.

He began picking at his nails. The wind came up and lifted the leaves on the willow trees and wrinkled the water's surface. Vidor Perkins pushed the button on his electric starter. "Bet I beat you there," he said. "I hope your family is all right."

Then he opened up his speedboat and rocketed across the bay, troweling a wide arc by the pilings under the highway, sliding across his own wake, his profile as pointed and cool as a hood ornament.

A minute later, he had disappeared down the channel, the darkness swallowing the yellow surge of mud rising in his wake.

The owner of the bait shop knew nothing of an emergency call; he also said the man in the speedboat had not been in his shop and had not used his concrete ramp to put his boat in the water.

I used the bait shop phone to call home. Alafair answered. "Is everything okay there?" I said.

"We're fine. Why wouldn't we be?"

"Clete and I are running a little late. I was just checking in."

"Something happen?" she said.

"You ever hear of a guy named Vidor Perkins?"

"No, who is he?"

"A meltdown I ran into. Don't let anybody in the house till I get home."

"What's going on, Dave?"

"I wish I knew."

EARLY SUNDAY MORNING I went to the office and put through a priority request with the National Crime Information Center for everything they had on Robert Weingart and the man who had given his name as Vidor Perkins. The electronic files and photographs that downloaded on my screen contained more information than I wanted or could possibly sort through. Perkins and Weingart had both been at the Texas State Penitentiary in Huntsville at the same time. Whether they knew each other was a matter of conjecture. Perkins had served time in

Alabama and Florida as well as Texas. Before Weingart went down for armed robbery in Texas, he had been arrested eleven times in Nevada, California, and Oregon, starting when he was sixteen years old. Unlike the majority of recidivists, neither man seemed to have a penchant for narcotics or alcohol. Most of their arrests involved fraud, robbery, or physical violence. As young men, both had been arrested on charges involving the jackrolling of elderly people and theft of the mails, which usually meant theft of Social Security checks. As a teenager, Weingart had been arrested for cruelty to animals and kept in a psychiatric facility for eight months. When he was nineteen, Vidor Perkins had been a suspect in an apartment-house arson that killed three people, one of them a child.

As with all sociopaths, the factual language used to describe their crimes said little if anything about their backgrounds or the influences that made them permanent members of an underclass that has one agenda—namely, to scratch their names on a wall in a way the rest of us will never forget. Maybe they grew up in shitholes. Maybe their fathers were violent drunks and their mothers wanted them aborted. Maybe they were crack babies, or they were born ugly or poor or stupid or were poorly educated and denied access to a better life. But when you have seen the handiwork of their kind up close and personal, none of the aforementioned seems to offer an adequate explanation for their behavior.

For some repeat offenders, jailing is an end in itself. They don't break out of jails; they break into them. But I doubted that was the case with either Weingart or Perkins. Actually, the only surprise in the electronic files I downloaded was Weingart's date of birth. He looked no older than thirty, but he was actually fifty-two. Either he shared much in common with Dorian Gray, or he had undergone a very good face-lift.

Monday morning I went into Helen Soileau's office with printouts of both men's rap sheets. I told her about my encounter with Vidor Perkins at Henderson Swamp and the lie he had told me about an emergency at my house. "Where's Perkins now?" she said.

"He has a rental house on Old Jeanerette Road."

"How'd you find him?" She was sitting behind her desk, her hands spread on top of the two rap sheets, her expression neutral.

"Called information and asked for new listings."

"You think he's delivering a warning on behalf of Robert Weingart?"

"Yeah, I do."

She stood up and looked at me, thinking thoughts whose nature I could only guess at, her eyes not really seeing me. "The thread on this is going to lead back to the Abelard house in St. Mary Parish, isn't it?" she said.

"If it does, it's because the Abelards are up to doing what they do best—screwing their fellow man."

She blew her breath up into her face. "Bring the cruiser around. Don't make me regret this, Pops."

We drove down Old Jeanerette Road through sugarcane acreage and meadowland, the wind riffling Bayou Teche in the sunlight, the rain ditches on either side of us littered with trash of every kind. We passed through a rural slum, then an experimental farm operated by the state, and rounded a bend where an old cemetery stood in a shady grove, the whitewashed crypts sunk at odd angles into the softness of the earth. Up ahead, just before the drawbridge, I could see Alice Plantation, built in 1796, and farther on a second antebellum home, one that is arguably among the most beautiful in the Deep South.

Across the drawbridge stood a trailer slum that looked like it was transported from Bangladesh and reconstructed on the banks of Bayou Teche. The house where Vidor Perkins had taken up residence was located back in a grove of slash pines and cedar trees, and offered a fine view of the economic juxtaposition that has always defined the culture in which I grew up. I doubted that Perkins was a student of history or sociology, or was even cognizant of what went on beyond the dermal wrap that probably constituted the outer layer of his universe. But the fact that he had moved into a comfortable bungalow in the midst of a breezy stand of trees situated between the two extremes of wealth and poverty in our state seemed more than coincidence. Or maybe that was just my fanciful way of looking upon an evil presence that had come into our midst, a phenomenon that was not without precedent.

His speedboat was parked on its trailer under a porte cochere, the trailer hitched to a pale blue paint-skinned pickup truck. In back, I could hear a radio playing and the sound of a rake being scraped across leaves and dirt. Helen and I walked into the backyard and saw a little black girl sitting in a swing that hung from a pecan tree. Vidor Perkins was hefting up great piles of leaves and pine needles and dumping them into an oil barrel that boiled with smoke. He was bare-chested and his skin was networked with rivulets of sweat, even though the morning was still cool. The little girl wore a pinafore and tiny patent-leather shoes powdered with dust. She was eating half of an orange Popsicle, watching us curiously.

Perkins squinted at Helen and me through the smoke, as though he couldn't recognize me or guess the nature of our visit. Then he pointed at me good-naturedly. "Mr. Robicheaux! Was everything okay at your house?"

"What was your purpose in trying to alarm me, Mr. Perkins?" I said.

"I didn't do no such thing. No, sir," he said, shaking his head. But it was obvious that he was less interested in me than he was in Helen. His gaze kept drifting to her, as though he were sneaking a look at a carnival attraction.

"I'm Sheriff Soileau. Filing a false police report is a felony in this state," she said.

A grin spread across his face. "A false police report? That's a good one. Y'all trying to play a prank on me?"

"You told a sheriff's detective about an emergency that didn't exist," she said. "Are you saying you didn't do that?"

"If the emergency didn't exist, that's not my fault. I was tole by the man up on the levee to carry a message to Mr. Robicheaux. Tell me the crime in that."

"Except the man up at the bait shop denies even seeing you," Helen said.

"Did I say which man give me the message? I most certainly did not. Maybe this fellow was some kind of jokester. Y'all want a cold drink or a Popsicle?"

"What are you doing in our parish?" Helen asked.

"Vacationing, looking for business opportunities and such." He was beaming as he stared at Helen, his gaze roving over her body in the way that ignorant and stupid people do when they're amused by a handicapped or minority person.

"You a friend of Robert Weingart?" she asked.

"The writer? I know who he is. Is he living here'bouts now?"

"He was in Huntsville the same time you were. You never buddied around with him?" she said.

"I spent most of my free time at Huntsville in the chapel or the library."

"Who's the little girl?" Helen asked.

"Her mother cleans for me. They're from right up the road, where all those trailers are at."

Helen went over to the swing. "Is your mommy home?" she said to the little girl.

"She's at work."

"Why'd she leave you here?"

"Mr. Vidor took me to buy clothes."

"Is somebody else at home right now?"

"My auntie."

"I want you to wait out front for us. We need to talk with Mr. Vidor. We'll drive you home in a few minutes. You're not to come back here again unless your mother is with you."

"Ma'am, you cain't tell that little girl what to do," Perkins said.

Helen lifted one finger toward Perkins, then looked back at the child. "You haven't done anything wrong. But you should be with your family and not in the home of a man you don't know well. You understand that?"

Perkins bit on a thumbnail, his grin gone. He stuffed a huge pile of blackened leaves and moldy pecan husks into the barrel, curls of smoke rising into his face. His conked hair was oily with sweat or grease or both, and the strawberry birthmark that bled like a tail out of his hairline seemed to have darkened in the shade.

Helen waited until the little girl had left the yard. "Here are the rules," she said. "You don't get near any children in this parish. If you try to harass a member of my department, if you look cross-eyed at somebody on the street, if you spit on a sidewalk, if you throw a gum wrapper out a car window, I'm going to turn your life into an exquisite agony."

He leaned on his rake, the sweat on his ridged stomach running into the waistband of his underwear. "No, you won't," he said. "Check my jacket. On my last jolt, I went out max time. I did twenty-seven months chopping cotton under the gun, just so I wouldn't have some twerp of a PO telling me what I could and couldn't do. You got no say in my life, Sheriff, 'cause I ain't broke no laws, and I don't plan to, either. Empty wagons always make the loudest rattle."

Helen brushed at her nose, the smoke starting to get to her. "You have anything you want to say to Mr. Perkins?" she asked me.

"You called Clete Purcel by name at Henderson Swamp. How'd you know who he was?" I said.

"He's got his big cheeks spread on a stool at Clementine's every time I go in there. He's usually drunk," Perkins said.

"When you see Robert Weingart—" I began.

"I don't see him," he said.

"Tell Weingart that for a mainline con, he's made a major mistake," I said.

Perkins laughed under his breath and bent to his work, dropping a rake-load of leaves and wet pine needles into the fire. Then he said something into the smoke.

"What'd you say?" Helen said, stepping toward him.

Perkins walked out of the smoke, blowing out his breath as though thinking of the right words to use. "I said maybe y'all ain't so damn smart. Maybe y'all are gonna wish you had me for a friend."

"Want to take the collard greens out of your mouth?" I said.

"I'm saying maybe I'm not the worst huckleberry in the patch. I'm saying there's some out yonder that is a lot worse than me," he replied. "They're home-grown, too, not brought from somewhere else." He peeled a stick of gum and rolled it in a ball and placed it behind his teeth, savoring the taste, his eyes filling with mirth as he stared Helen directly in the face. He began chewing, barely able to repress his amusement at Helen, his lips purple in the shade.

"You want to tell me why I interest you so?" she said.

"You put me in mind of a woman I knew in Longview. She could pick up a hog and throw it over a fence. She had a butch haircut that looked like the head of a toothbrush. It felt just like bristles when you ran your hand acrost it. I was sweet on her for a long time."

"Wait for me in the cruiser, Dave," she said.

"I'd better stay here."

"Dave?" she said. She waited. When I didn't move, she widened her eyes at me, her anger clearly growing. I walked close to Perkins, my face within inches of his, my back to Helen. I could see the tiny red vessels in the whites of his eyes, the dried mucus at the corner of his mouth, the strawberry birthmark that was slick with sweat.

"You get the fuck in your house," I said.

"Or what?"

Perkins's denim shirt was spread on the surface of a spool table. On top of his shirt he had placed his sunglasses, gold watch, cigarettes, and cell phone. I rolled them all in the shirt and tied it in a ball with the sleeves and dropped it into the flames. The denim burst alight and sank with its contents into the fire. "Welcome to Louisiana, Mr. Perkins. I love your place," I said.

CHAPTER 6

THAT AFTERNOON AN elderly cane farmer ten miles outside of New Iberia had been harrowing a field that was bordered by a coulee and a hedgerow of persimmon and gum trees. The lock on his gate had been broken by vandals driving ATVs, and the dirt road he used to get his machinery in and out of the field now gave access to dumpers who had thrown rubber tires and old furniture and raw garbage down the embankment of his coulee. He had called the sheriff's office to complain and had tried to bury or haul away the trash, then finally had given up.

The breeze was warm and drowsy, and he felt himself nodding off in the tractor seat. Up ahead, a flock of crows clattered into the air above the persimmon and gum trees. The farmer cut his engine, and in the shade of a canvas umbrella he had fastened above the tractor seat, he opened his thermos and poured himself a cup of Kool-Aid. From inside the trees, he could hear horseflies buzzing and see them clustering on the ground and rising suddenly in the air. The wind shifted out of the south, and an odor struck his nostrils that made his throat clench.

He walked into the trees, shielding his eyes from the sun's glare with one hand. At the lip of the coulee, someone had spaded the ground with a shovel and replaced the torn divots of grass with a rake, creating a broken pattern that made the farmer think of a root-bound plant in a cracked flowerpot. He found a long stick and began pushing the divots down the side of the levee, the clods of dirt rilling into the water.

Oh, *bon Dieu, bon Dieu*, he thought as the odor grew in strength and seemed to clutch at his face like a soiled hand. Then he touched something soft that made him drop the stick and step back, his eyes watering not from the odor but from what he thought he was about to see. He stumbled backward in the shade, away from the thing that was buried in the ground, unable to take his gaze from the hole his digging had created. But in the disturbed dirt, the only image he could make out was a plastic teacup that had a large piece broken out of it. The cup was painted with tiny lavender roses.

The coroner, the paramedics, a half-dozen uniformed deputies, two technicians from the Acadiana crime lab, and Helen and I all arrived at the scene within twenty minutes of one another. The body of the buried girl or woman was fully dressed and had been covered over by no more than a foot of soil. She was blond and about five and a half feet tall, and she wore the kind of tennis shoes a kid might, but because of the heat and the moisture in the ground and the piles of red ants that had been pushed into the depression with her, the decomposition was so dramatic that it was impossible to estimate her age.

Buried with her were two winter coats, an empty handbag, seven shoes, a polyester scarf, coils of costume jewelry, a tube of lipstick, two barrettes, a Bic lighter, and a saucer that matched the broken teacup the farmer had already unearthed.

The farmer had no idea when or how the body had gotten onto his land.

"Did you see any lights at night?" I asked.

"Kids running them ATVs all over my field. I called y'all fo' times, but ain't nobody done anything about it. You t'ink them kids done this?"

"I don't know," I said.

"I'm fixing to lose my farm. This land has been in the Delahoussaye family for a hundred and fifty years. I ain't never seen anything like this. Why ain't y'all done somet'ing?"

"You think someone has a grudge against you, sir?"

"You tell me. What it takes for a man to do his work and be let alone? Why ain't y'all kept them people off my land?"

"Sir, if you didn't want ATVs in your field, why didn't you buy a new lock for your gate?" Helen said.

"They broke t'ree of them. What was I s'ppose to do? Weld a chain on my gate 'cause y'all cain't do your job?" His face was wrinkled and brown and covered with sun moles, his eyes moist with tears. "She's just a young girl."

"How do you know that?" I asked.

"I just seen the coroner take off her shoe. Her toenails is painted, like young girls is always doing."

Helen and I looked at each other.

"I want you to think real hard about something, Mr. Delahoussaye," I said. "Did you ever throw any dishware out here? Did you ever see somebody else do it? Did you ever see any lying around on the ground?"

"No, suh, I ain't."

"And the last time you were in the grove was two weeks back?"

"Yes, suh."

"And the ground was undisturbed? There was no trash lying on top of it?"

This time he didn't answer but simply walked away, like a man who no longer cared what the world thought or did not think about him.

"What's the importance of the broken teacup?" Helen said.

"On the last day of Bernadette Latiolais's life, she went into a dollar store and bought two teacups and saucers. The cups were painted with lavender flowers."

"Where'd you get that?"

"I talked with a sheriff's detective in Jeff Davis Parish. A clerk in the store said she was carrying the cups and saucers in a paper bag. She walked past a bar with them and was never seen alive again."

Helen put on her sunglasses and looked at the yellow crime-scene tape vibrating in the wind. There were tiny beads of perspiration on her forehead and upper lip. The paramedics were zipping up the body bag on the remains of the female who had been buried among the trees. Red ants were crawling on the outside of the bag; the paramedics averted their faces when they picked up the bag and set it on the gurney, then one of them bent over and gagged in the weeds. Our coroner, Koko Hebert, a huge, sweaty, fat man, was blowing his nose into a dirty handkerchief. I could see Helen's chest rising and falling, her hands opening and closing at her sides. "The day it doesn't bother you is the day you should quit," I said.

"We're going to get whoever did this," she said.

THE NEXT MORNING Koko Hebert came into my office wheezing, a folder in his hand. When he sat down in a chair, his body seemed to deflate, like a giant air bladder collapsing upon itself. He smoked more cigarettes than anyone I had ever known, and he ate the most unhealthy food that was available in New Iberia's restaurants. He waged war against his own body and seemed to take pleasure in alienating himself from others. After his son was vaporized by a roadside bomb in Iraq, Koko attended the funeral service in Virginia by himself and told no one where he was going. He also refused to acknowledge the condolences of friends and colleagues. He lived alone in a house that was sheathed with broken asbestos shingles, and often occupied his time driving his lawn tractor up and down his two-acre lot on the bayou, mowing great swaths through the buttercups that tried to bloom on his property.

"Mind if I smoke?"

"There's no smoking anywhere in this building."

"Somebody just spat tobacco in the water fountain. Which habit do you think is worse?"

I gazed out my window at Bayou Teche and at the live oak trees in City Park. A young mother was sailing a Frisbee with her children by one of the picnic shelters. The children were leaping in the air and rolling in the grass and chasing one another in the shade. Their voices made no sound coming across the water, as though their lives were completely sealed off from the work we did in our building. I looked back at Koko. When I dealt with him, I had to remind myself that no matter what happened in my life, I would probably never be as unhappy a man as he was.

He leaned forward and pitched the folder on my desk. "She was mush inside," he said. "Approximate date of death is hard to say. My guess is she was in the ground at least two weeks. Age between nineteen and twenty-two. Evidence of rape? Not per se. Vaginal penetration? Almost any young girl these days has a train tunnel down there. A tattoo on the butt, one on the ankle, one on the shoulder. No traces of drugs. You got any coffee?"

I had to think before I could answer his question. "Downstairs." I waited for him to go on, but he didn't. I tried to hide my exasperation with both his callousness and his passive-aggressive behavior. I opened the folder on my desk blotter and glanced at autopsy forms he had filled out. His handwriting was indecipherable. "What's the cause of death?"

"What do you want?"

"What do *I* want?"

"Because it's take your choice. It wasn't blunt trauma. She wasn't shot or stabbed. Was she asphyxiated? Could be. But I doubt that's what did her in. It could have been an aneurysm or heart failure, maybe brought on by prolonged fear, asphyxiation, and general abuse. The big word in there is 'fear,' as in scared shitless." He was wearing an oversize Hawaiian shirt, and he began pulling at the fabric as though it was stuck to his body, shifting his shoulders around, putting on a performance. "Is your air-conditioning working?"

"What aren't you telling me?"

"It's written there on the first page, if you care to look at it. She had ligature marks on her wrist, deep ones. I think she was bound up for a long time. Her stomach was empty. Whoever grabbed her didn't feed her too good."

"Why do you say 'grabbed'?"

"She was obviously held against her will. That means she was probably abducted. Her tox screen was clear, which tells me she wasn't a prostitute. So I suspect she was grabbed off the street or lured into a captive situation. Maybe she met a guy on the Internet. You know how many bimbos are out there now flirting with guys who can't wait to tear them apart?"

"Koko, I just need the information. I don't need an interpretation of it. I don't need the drama, either."

"You trying to tell me something?"

"Yeah, everybody experiences loss."

He got up from the chair. His body had the sloping contours of a haystack. "Keep the file. I got the Xerox in my office," he said.

"You test people. That's all I was saying. It gets to be a drag."

"You want my opinion of how she went out? The Bible says Jesus sweated blood. At a certain level of fear and depression, it can happen. The capillaries pop, and blood issues from the pores with a person's sweat. You want to know if this girl suffered? You bet your ass."

When he closed the door behind him, his odor clung to the furniture like a gray fog.

A half hour later, Mack Bertrand, our chief forensic chemist, called from the Acadiana crime lab. He believed the saucer and teacup and shoes and lipstick tube and handbag and winter coats and the other items retrieved from the burial site on the Delahoussaye property had been placed inside the grave with the girl's remains and had not been dumped there earlier.

"How do you know?"

"Her body fluids are on every item we ran. Outside the immediate disturbed area, we found no buried garbage or debris of any kind."

"What do you have in the way of prints?"

"Either rainwater or mud ruined anything that

might have been there. If this is any help to you, the winter coats had levels of mold inside them that indicates they were stored a long time, probably in a damp place, before they went into the ground."

I called the sheriff's department in Jeff Davis Parish and then went into Helen's office and told her of the information I had gotten from Koko Hebert and the crime lab. "Has Jeff Davis Parish got a missing girl that fits the description of the vic?" she asked.

"Nope."

"Why did the perp bury her here?"

"Who knows? People dump dead animals out there. No one is going to pay attention to carrion birds circling around."

"Think we have a serial killer, a guy with a fetish?"

"Guys with a fetish don't give up their souvenirs. They move their hiding place around, but they don't give up their trophies."

She turned her swivel chair toward the window. Across the bayou, the children had gone and the park was empty. A birthday balloon, the air half gone, the painted face on the Mylar surface shriveled into a grimace, floated out of a tree onto the water.

"We need somebody in the box," Helen said. "This all started with that convict over in Mississippi, what's-his-name—"

"Elmore Latiolais."

"Right, the guy who was trying to dime Herman Stanga. Pick up Stanga."

"For what?"

"His front yard is covered with dog shit. He didn't brush his teeth this morning. His mother should have had herself sterilized. Any of those will do."

CLETE PURCEL'S OFFICE was located on Main, in a refurbished nineteenth-century brick building that had a steel colonnade attached to the front wall. He was proud of his office, and on the flagstone patio in back, he had placed a glass-topped table inset with an umbrella, and when life with his clientele was too much, he sat on the patio among the banana fronds and enjoyed a snack and read the newspaper or enjoyed the fine view of Bayou Teche and the drawbridge at Burke Street. When he went onto his patio, he entered his private domain, and his secretary was instructed not to bother him with any of the miscreants, addicts, and marginal hookers who visited and left and returned to his waiting room as though it were a social center.

If a client became disruptive or experienced a psychotic episode or began throwing furniture, the secretary called Clete on his cell phone. Otherwise, he ate his snack and gazed at the flowers and caladiums and oak trees and flooded elephant ears along the banks of the bayou and the passing tugs and workboats that were headed for the Gulf of Mexico. On this day in particular, Clete had resolved he would stop thinking about Herman Stanga and the jail time he might have to do for tearing the man up behind the Gate Mouth club. He had just set aside his copy of *The Daily Iberian* and nodded off in his chair when his secretary opened the French doors that gave onto the patio. "Mr. Layton Blanchet is outside," she said.

"What does he want?"

"He says he has an appointment. He said he called this morning."

Clete thought about it. "Yeah, he called, but he didn't have an appointment."

"What do you want me to tell him?"

Clete put a mint in his mouth and took his comb out of his pocket. He widened his eyes to wake himself up. "Send him on through," he said.

The nature of Clete's vocation did not allow him selectivity. Daily he came in contact with bail skips, pathological liars, bill collectors, loan-company operatives who ran sales scams in slums, wife batterers, runaway girls who had been raped by their fathers and brothers, attorneys who were kept on retainers by pimps and drug dealers, and insurance reps who convinced doped-up accident victims in hospital beds to sign claim waivers. The subculture that provided his livelihood was predatory and Darwinian and often without mercy, but to those who lived inside it, it was as natural a way of life as a zoning board licensing porn theaters and massage parlors in a residential neighborhood comprised primarily of elderly and poor people.

Clete dealt with problematic situations among his clientele in the way a field surgeon would treat a gangrenous wound, or perhaps in the way a nurse in a third-world typhus ward would treat her patients. He clicked off a switch in his head and did not think about what his eyes saw and what his thoughts told him and what his hands were required by necessity to do.

Dealing with people from the mainstream presented a different kind of challenge. Non-felons, people who attended church and ran businesses and belonged to civic clubs, upscale women whose faces wore the ceramic glaze of Botox, came to him in almost secretive fashion, explaining their problems in meticulous detail, keeping the wounds green and festering as they talked about seeking justice. Almost always they attributed the origins of their problems to the misdeeds of others. They considered themselves normal and without blinking lied both to him and to themselves. At the end of their relationship with Clete, no matter how positive the outcome, they had a way of not recognizing him on the street.

What bothered Clete most about Layton Blanchet was his manic level of energy and the power that seemed to flow through his arm when he shook hands, as though control of the other person was supposed to begin as soon as Layton's fingers crawled up someone's wrist. The freshness of Layton's expensive clothes and the intense clarity of his eyes made Clete think of a sailing ship bursting through waves, or in a darker mode, of an avaricious Greek warrior dropping from inside a wooden horse into the silent streets of Troy.

"This is where you work, huh?" Layton said, seating himself in the umbrella's shade without being asked. "Dave Robicheaux and I were talking about you not long ago. I'm glad you're making it in New Iberia. It can be a tough town for outsiders, you know, and all that antebellum family crap. Where'd you get that bunch in the waiting room? You bus them in from detox?"

"Jerry Springer does referrals for me."

But Layton didn't laugh. He looked at the backs of his hands, then at the bayou and at the old convent building on the other side of the drawbridge, deep in the shadow of the oaks. "I think I got a problem with my wife," he said. "One that's eating my lunch."

"You have security people who can handle that, Mr. Blanchet."

"It's Layton. 'Mister' is for the country club. My corporate employees don't need to know my family business. Carolyn is a good girl, but I think she's having an affair. Maybe it's middle age. Maybe she thinks she's losing her looks. Maybe she's tired of a man who talks about money all the time, although she has no trouble spending boxcar-loads of it. But she's getting it on with somebody, and I want to know who the guy is."

"How do you know she's unfaithful to you?"

"I can tell."

"How?"

"Do I have to go into detail?"

"It doesn't leave my office. It doesn't go into a written file."

"About nine o'clock she goes into the library and buries herself in a book. Or she's got a stomachache. Or she pulled a muscle on the tennis court. Look, I'm a realist. I'm fifteen years older than she is. But if some guy is in my wife's pants, he's not going to be out there laughing at me behind my back. Get me?"

"Not exactly."

"What is it I'm not clear about?" Layton asked.

"Are we talking about breaking somebody's wheels?"

"What difference does it make? You give me the information, then you're out of it."

"I don't like being party to a domestic homicide," Clete said. "Let me share a secret with you. Sometimes clients with problems like yours come in and tell me only half of the story. They're having affairs themselves, they're full of guilt, and they transfer it to the wife. So they spend a lot of money and accuse me of colluding with their old lady when I come up with nothing."

Layton stared out into the sunlight, his eyes as clear as blue glass. "You're good at what you do, Mr. Purcel, or I wouldn't be here. I don't assault or kill people, and I don't pay others to do it, either. As far as my own behavior is concerned, yeah, there have been instances when I haven't always done the right thing. But that's not the problem. I know my wife, and I know how she thinks, and I know she's pumping it with somebody. Can you help me or not?"

"It's a hundred and fifty dollars an hour and expenses."

"Done."

Clete rubbed at his mouth, wondering why Layton Blanchet had bothered him, wondering why a tuning fork was vibrating in his chest. The wind ruffled the canvas umbrella over his head. Layton continued to stare at Clete, either waiting for him to speak or taking his inventory or secretly savoring the moment after imposing his will on Clete. *The Daily Iberian* still lay on the tabletop. Its thickness was folded across the lead story. Clete flipped it open, exposing the headline. "That's too bad, isn't it?" he said to change the subject and end the conversation.

"What is?" Layton asked.

"Another young girl killed and dumped on a country road."

"It's going to continue till we get to the root of the problem."

"Pardon?" Clete said.

"Welfare, illegitimacy, people with their hand out. That's where it all starts. They've got their boy in the White House now. They'll be lining up for every dollar they can stuff in their pockets. Most of them would strangle on their own spit if you didn't swab out their throats for them."

Clete kept his face empty. "I'll give you a call when I have some information for you, Mr. Blanchet," he said.

"It's Layton."

HELEN SOILEAU HAD told me to bring in Herman Stanga and put him in the box. But Herman was an elusive quarry. He was not at his house, nor down on Hopkins or Railroad Avenue in New Iberia's old red-light district. I called the Gate Mouth club in St. Martinville, the place where Clete Purcel had broken open Herman Stanga's head against an oak tree. The man who answered the phone said, "You got the Gate Mout'. What you need?"

"Is Herman there?" I said.

"Who wants to know?"

I hung up without replying and called my fellow A.A. member Emma Poche at the St. Martinville Sheriff's Department and asked her to sit on the club till I got there.

"Maybe this is providential," she said. "I was thinking of calling you today."

"About what?"

"Some twelve-step stuff."

"You ought to take that up with your sponsor."

"I don't have one."

"Don't let Stanga go anywhere. I'll be there in fifteen minutes."

"You got a warrant?"

"He's not under arrest. We just need a little information from him."

"Sounds believable to me. Herman Stanga, friend of the court. Glad to hear about that," she replied.

I checked out an unmarked car and drove into

St. Martinville's black district and pulled in behind Emma's cruiser, which was parked two doors down from the Gate Mouth club. She was sitting behind the wheel, smoking a cigarette, the driver's window half down. She was wearing shades and looked thoughtful and pretty with her hat pushed back on her head. Her cheeks were pooled with color, the sunlight catching in her gold hair. I got in her vehicle and choked on the smoke. "Stanga is still inside?" I said.

"Unless he grew wings. You got a minute?" she said.

"Sheriff Soileau is waiting on me."

"I've got a situation on my conscience. I don't want to drink over it. It goes beyond even that. I'm desperate, Dave."

I wasn't sure what she meant. But I wasn't sure I wanted to find out, either. "You should be talking to a female sponsor. The two operative words there are 'female' and 'sponsor.'"

"My sponsor is in jail. Guess what for. Driving under the influence. Top that." She threw her cigarette into the street and rolled down the windows and turned on the air conditioner full blast. The sidewalk was empty, the front door of the club within easy view.

"I'll try to help if I can," I said.

"I've been seeing somebody. We had a relationship a long time ago, then we bumped into each other during Mardi Gras in New Orleans. We found out we were both going to the same party in the Quarter later, and we got pretty drunk and woke up at one in the afternoon the next day at the St. Charles Guest House. I've had bad hangovers, but never one that bad."

"Have you been to a meeting since?"

"Yeah, I went to a couple." She twisted her mouth into a button.

"Did you own up to a slip?"

"Not really."

"You haven't owned up to anyone?"

"That's what I'm doing now, right?"

I was beginning to feel I had been played. "I don't think you're going to get any peace on this until you come clean at a meeting, Emma."

"Last week my long-lost lover told me it was over. This was the same person who told me I smelled like the Caribbean and that my climaxes were like strings of wet firecrackers. I have to make some choices, Dave."

"I don't think we need all this clinical detail. Look, every guy who cheats on his wife tells his girlfriend his marriage is over, his girlfriend is the best human being he's ever met, that she has nothing to do with the breakup of his marriage, that she's beautiful and spiritual and loving and she has no reason to feel guilty about anything. He also indicates he's not sleeping with his wife. He usually says these things right up to the time he dumps his new pump of the week."

Emma removed her shades and stared into the glare on the street. A drunk black man had stumbled off the sidewalk and was trying to cross through the traffic while cars blew their horns at him. Emma brushed at her nose. "Get Stanga out of the club and I'll take care of the bowling pin out there."

"Don't be too hard on yourself. Sometimes we lose. It's nobody's fault, not yours, not the other person's. You just have to let it slide and say the short version of the Serenity Prayer. Sometimes you just have to say 'fuck it.'"

"You like being used, Dave? Did anyone ever screw you until your eyes crossed and you woke up in the morning aching for them to do it again? Then one day in a public place, the same person tells you that you deserve someone much better than them, and you know the person has told you this in public so you can't cry or break things or throw a drink in their face? When that happened to you, did you just say 'Fuck it, sports fans, I think I'll just go hit some tennis balls and go to a meeting'?"

I opened the door of the cruiser and got out on the sidewalk. The drunk black man had made it safely to the other side of the street. "I'm going to try to talk Stanga out of the club. If he gives me trouble, I want you there as a witness," I said. "If you can't do that for me, I need to call for backup. Tell me what you want to do, Emma."

She got out of the cruiser and slipped her baton through the ring on her belt. She removed her shades from her shirt pocket and put them back on. Her face looked hot and glazed. Her mouth was a tight line before she spoke. "I forgot you belong to that great fraternity of all-knowing A.A. swinging dicks. If I forget again, remind me," she said.

We found Herman Stanga at the back of the bar, where he was sipping from a demitasse of coffee, a tiny spoon and a single sugar cube on his saucer, his thin mustache winking with each sip. A big dressing was taped over the split Clete had put in his forehead, but otherwise he looked surprisingly well. "Hey, what is it, Robo?" he said. "Give my man a seltzer and ice and a lime slice, and wash out the glass good so it don't have no alcohol in it. You ain't got the Elephant Man out there, have you?"

"My boss wants to talk to you," I said.

"The champ of the Muff Diver '69 Olympics? How she been doing?"

"I wouldn't get on her wrong side."

"Man, I ain't getting on no side of that broad," he said. He looked at the bartender and laughed.

"Want to take a ride with me or sit in the cooler in St. Martinville while we work out legalities?"

Then he surprised me again. "Anyt'ing to he'p. You hear about my suit against that fat cracker? I'm gonna take both of his bidnesses, the apartment he owns in New Orleans, his car, his life insurance policy, his savings account, his guns, his furniture, and the waterfront lot in Biloxi he's making payments on in his ex-wife's name. When I get finished wit' him, he's gonna have a toot'brush and, if he's lucky, the tube of toot'paste that goes wit' it."

"You're the man, Herman," I said.

"You got that right, Jack. You kill me, Robo Man." He looked again at the bartender and laughed loudly, slapping the bar with the flat of his hand.

Emma Poche went back to the St. Martinville Sheriff's Department, and Herman Stanga rode with me back to New Iberia. I didn't like sitting next to him or talking to him or even acknowledging his presence. He smelled of hair cream and the decayed food in his teeth and the deodorant he used to overlay the sweat in his armpits. I cracked the window and kept my eyes on the road and wondered at the level of the enmity I felt toward him.

At the city limits, we entered a long corridor of oak trees. On the right-hand side of the road, set in deep shade, was a two-story antebellum home with a wide veranda, built out of wood in imitation of the columned brick Greek revival mansions down the Teche. The veranda sagged in the middle from either termite damage or settling in the foundation. The paint had turned gray in the smoke of stubble fires or dust blown out of the fields. A wash line was strung across the side yard, the clothes flapping in the wind.

"The man who built that house was a free man of color named Labiche," I said. "He owned a brick factory in town. He also owned slaves. He got rich selling out his own people. What do you think about that, Herman?"

"Say again? I was just starting to catch some Z's."

"The guy who built that home back there was a mulatto who bought and sold slaves and used them to make bricks that went into the construction of the biggest homes in this area before the Civil War. Some people would probably say he was just a creature of his times. My feeling is that he was probably an opportunist and a Judas. Since you're a man of considerable experience in racial matters, I wondered what your opinion is."

"What I t'ink is you couldn't find your own dick if you had a string tied to it. Wake me up when we're there," he replied.

It was almost five P.M. when I drove down East Main and turned in to the long driveway that led past the city library to the spacious brick building that served as both City Hall and the sheriff's department. Between the library and the wall of bamboo was a grotto dedicated to the mother of Jesus. The street and the buildings and the grotto were already deep in shadow under the oak trees. A crowd was gathered around the grotto, and at first I thought they were tourists or religious people; then I recognized Layton Blanchet in their midst and remembered he was a member of a live oak or historical preservation society, the kind of group that he would probably find useful in his machinations.

As I drove past him, he raised his hand in recognition, but I pretended not to see him. I put Herman Stanga in one of our interview rooms and went to Helen's office and told her I had delivered the freight. "Where you going?" she said.

"To my office, if you don't mind," I replied.

"I mind."

"Talking to Stanga is a waste of time."

"Humor me."

"The truth is, everyone would be a lot happier if Clete had taken him off at the neck. Stanga gets high on being rousted. He'll probably file a harassment charge against us and use it in his suit against Clete. The only thing Stanga understands is a club upside his head or a bullet in the mouth."

"Bwana no run the department. Bwana shut up. Bwana go into the interview room now."

Earlier in the day I had given Helen all my notes on the death of Bernadette Latiolais, my interview with her brother on the work gang outside Natchez, and my interview with the store clerk and Bernadette Latiolais's grandmother in Jeff Davis Parish. I also had given her my files on Robert Weingart and Vidor Perkins. When we entered the interview room, Stanga was sitting at the table, gazing out the window at a speedboat that was towing a girl on skis down the bayou. He put an Altoid in his mouth and sucked on it. "I got about fifteen minutes for this, then I need a ride back to my car. Y'all cool wit' that?"

"We appreciate your coming in," Helen said.

"You knew a convict in Mississippi by the name of Elmore Latiolais?"

"I been over that wit' Robo Man here. The answer is yeah, I knew that lying nigger for twenty years. He got hisself capped. Do I know why? Let me guess. He shot off his mout' to a peckerwood guard and ate a load of buckshot. Do I know anyt'ing about these girls that has gotten themselves killed? Let me guess again. They was working independent and messed wit' the wrong john and had the kind of date they wasn't expecting."

"Why were you over in Jeff Davis Parish with Robert Weingart?"

"The writer?"

"Yeah, the writer," Helen said.

"Who says I was?"

"A half-dozen people," she lied.

He opened his hands in disbelief. "What would I be doing wit' a writer? That's like axing me if I'm hanging out with the IRS."

"Maybe you were doing some work for the St. Jude Project."

"Yeah, I he'p out the St. Jude, but I don't know this writer. If you say I know him, then write that in my file. But I don't know him, and I don't know nothing about him except I seen him signing books at Books Along the Teche, and I'm tired of y'all getting in my face about this."

"Here's our problem, Herman," she said. "No matter what avenue we take into this investigation, your name comes up."

"What investigation? All them crimes, if there ever was any crimes, was in Jeff Davis Parish. But RoboCop and his friend Dumbo the flying beer barrel been trying to find a reason to drag their shit into my life."

"We had a body dumped in our parish, and we think the victim was connected to the homicides in Jeff Davis, Herman," Helen said, sitting on the corner of the table, her hands folded on one thigh. "If you're not involved in this, you have a good idea who is. Most people around here have one of two attitudes about you. A lot of them just laugh when your name is mentioned, like you're a funny hobgoblin that got loose from Railroad Avenue. Others say you're not at fault for what you are, that you never had a father and your mother had to turn tricks in a shack behind Broussard's bar and you grew up a raggedy-ass little boy who had to carry out the whores' pails from the back of the cathouses on Hopkins. But I always thought you were a smart man. I don't like what you do for a living, but there's no denying you're intelligent. That's right, isn't it? You're a smart man, aren't you, Herman? I knew your mother well. You were born premature, out in the hallway at Charity Hospital. I remember your mother's words: 'He wasn't no bigger than a squirrel.'"

Herman Stanga's face looked feverish, the skin moist, his eyelids stitched to his forehead. "Y'all t'ink you run t'ings. Y'all ain't nothing but a bunch of ants running around on a wet log, pretending y'all in charge, when the people that's running t'ings wouldn't let y'all squat on their commodes. But I got you, Robo Man. Your peckerwood friend is going to Angola. When he gets in there, he's gonna be the gift that keeps on giving. And Lady Hermaphrodite here is gonna keep using you to wipe her ass while I'm laughing at the bunch of y'all. I fucked you good, man, and you can t'ink about that all the way to your grave."

Helen got up from the table and stood at the

window, her back to us. She was silent a long time, the heel of her hand resting on the windowsill, her fingers tapping without sound on the wood. In the distance, I heard the whine of the speedboat fading, disappearing around a bend in the bayou. Without turning around, Helen said, "Make sure he gets back to his car all right."

CHAPTER 7

When Herman Stanga returned home from St. Martinville, the night sky was smoky with stars and moon glow, the underwater lights burning beneath the surface of his swimming pool, the wind ruffling the canopy of the trees along the bayou. While he undressed down to his white silk boxer shorts at his wet bar, kicking his trousers onto the rug, he called the home of his lawyer. The lawyer's message machine clicked on.

"Monroe, it's me. Pick up the phone," Herman said. "I got an update for you. I know you're there, man, so stop pretending you ain't. Dave Robicheaux ran me in this afternoon. He was talking in the car about niggers selling out niggers during the Civil War or some shit. He put me in a room wit' Amazon Woman. She was trying to make me admit I knew somet'ing about them girls that was killed in Jeff Davis Parish. She was calling my mother a whore. She didn't have a lot of nice t'ings to say about you, either. I'm telling you, Monroe, if I find out you're home and deliberately ain't picking up, your ass is grass. A couple of photos Doreen took of you wit' her sister are gonna be on the Internet. I'll be up late. Call me. I ain't just blowing gas here."

Herman slipped his feet into a pair of flip-flops and chopped up two white lines on a mirror, rolled a crisp one-hundred-dollar bill into a tube, and vacuumed up each line. He used the remote to turn on his giant flat-screen TV and flipped from channel to channel before he became bored and irritated and clicked off the set. He wiped the residue off the mirror with his finger and rubbed his gums with it and licked his finger clean.

The night was alive with sound. Leaves puffed out of the trees on the bayou. The neighbors' kids were playing tag in the dark. In the center of it all, his swimming pool glowed with an electrified blue clarity that seemed to answer all the mysteries about life and death, at least as far as Herman ever thought about them. He opened the sliding glass door and let in the night air and the smell of the flowers. Maybe he should relax and have Doreen over for a swim. Her sister, too. But Herman's spring was wound too tight to think very long about the recreational end of his profession.

He hit the speed dial on his cordless phone and got Monroe's message machine again. "Don't make me drive over there, Monroe," he said. "They messed wit' the wrong nigger. I'm gonna stick it to them, and you're gonna he'p me do it. You hearing me on this? You pull your dick out of wherever it is and pick up that phone! My tolerance for your lazy-ass behavior is wearing thin."

He opened his Sub-Zero freezer and took out a gallon container of French-vanilla ice cream and began digging chunks from it with a butcher knife, clunking each rock-hard piece into a bowl. His hand was wet and slick, his thumb hooked over the top of the knife handle, the coke singing in his blood, his ears thundering with the Herman Stanga national anthem, the latter a musical composition of angry self-righteousness that could blow windows out of buildings. Then he felt his hand slip and a sensation like an icicle slicing through his palm. The butcher knife clattered to the bottom of the sink in a rain of blood drops. He grabbed a dish towel and twisted it around his hand and cradled his arm against his chest. He picked up the phone and punched in 911 with his thumb, then thought about the consequences of his call and hung up. Coke on his wet bar, coke in his bedroom, coke in his bloodstream, paramedics and cops stomping around in his house with no need for a warrant because he had made the 911 call voluntarily. No way, ofay. He sat down in a chair and stared at the towel cinched around his hand. The bleeding had stopped. Give it a few minutes and he could drive himself to Iberia General, he told himself.

Time to coolerate his emotions, put things into perspective, and send another snow-white marching band up his nose. His hand was numb, the bloodstained towel a testimony to the dominion he could exert not only over pain but over the issuance of blood from a knife wound. Herman had taken control of the night. He was back in Chez Stanga, his Dobermans protecting him, his presence in the neighborhood a constant source of unhappiness to his neighbors, his power to upset and depress them always at the tips of his fingers.

He removed the cover from a silver cigarette box where he kept a small cake of virgin coke, the high-grade stuff the Colombians in Miami reserved for themselves. Herman's supplier said it lit the rain forests like summer heat lightning and cleansed the souls of unbaptized pagans. Right. That was why they all looked like overweight tomato pickers and thought the good life was hanging at the dog track and eating nachos and chili with their fingers. He lifted the spoon to one nostril and snarfed up the virgin flake and felt the hit all the way down to the soles of his feet, like an orgasm that had no erogenous boundaries.

But whether he was coked to the eyes or not, Herman's source of agitation would not go away. The problem was not his lawyer, nor the wetbrain detective who had run him in, or even that bucket of whale sperm Purcel. It was the hermaphrodite Amazon Woman and the things she had said about his mother and about him and the shack where he had grown up in New Iberia's old red-light district. How did she know Herman's mother had turned tricks behind Broussard's bar? How did she know his job had been to carry out the whores' pails to the rain ditch early Sunday mornings? Did his mother tell the dyke that, or was it common knowledge? Which was worse? Did his mother really say he looked like a squirrel when he was born in a hall-way at Charity Hospital in Lafayette? His own mother said that of him?

How had Amazon Woman described him? A raggedy colored boy? That was what he'd been, his knees and feet filmed with dust, lice nits in his hair, stink in his clothes, and skid marks in his underwear when a health official at the school made him pull down his pants to be checked for ringworm.

Herman tried to think of the words he should have said to the dyke, something that would have hurt her and made her feel ashamed and guilty about what she was. Words that would have made her feel like he felt, not only now but secretly every day of his life since he was a little boy.

The cut in his hand began to throb. Through the open sliding doors, he could hear the sounds of children playing tag in the dark and music from the lawn party down the bayou. But something was wrong. His Dobermans were easily agitated by music, sirens, or the noise of airplanes and usu-ally made howling sounds when they heard them.

In fact, when children were about, the Dobermans ran against their chains, sometimes almost snapping their necks.

Herman got up from the divan and opened the front door and looked outside. Except for the glistening piles of dog feces, the yard was empty. But the dogs had long chains and could have been around the side of the house. He started to walk outside and check, then hesitated and instead closed and dead-bolted the door. He went back through the kitchen and through the wet bar area and looked out at the pool and at the shadows the potted orchid and bottlebrush trees made on the flagstones. The wind gusted across the pool, wrinkling the water, smudging the brilliance of the underwater lamps, sending a peculiar chill through Herman's body. He realized he was still wearing only his silk shorts, that either the night had turned cooler or his air-conditioning was set too low and the ceiling duct was blowing directly on his head and shoulders.

He thought he saw a shadow move between one of the banana trees and the brick wall that separated him from the neighbors' property. Were the neighbors' kids in his yard again? They knew better than that. "Get out of there!" he shouted into the darkness.

Then the moon came out from behind a cloud, and the shadows by the wall disappeared and all he saw were flowers in his beds and the paleness of the moon glow on the banana fronds. He cradled his wounded hand against his stomach and went back to the wet bar. The pain in his hand had come back with a vengeance, and his heart was tripping as though it were tilted against a sharp object. He took a pitcher of orange juice from the refrigerator and drank directly from it, his breath coming short. His system felt poisoned. Was it the high-octane coke? Did one of the Colombians put a chemical surprise in his stash? Or was the odor rising from his armpits the old familiar stench of fear that his swagger and rebop and cynicism at the expense of others had tried to mask for a lifetime?

He sat down on one of the elevated stools at the wet bar and hit the speed dial on his cordless. Monroe's message machine kicked on, but this time, before the recording finished, Monroe picked up and started talking. "I was cutting the grass. I was just gonna call you," he said.

"So you listened to my message, then went back out and mowed the lawn 'cause you wanted to call me?"

"What?"

"Don't give me your trash, Monroe. I need you to drive me to the hospital."

"What's wrong?"

"I got a butcher-knife cut across my hand is what's wrong. Now get your sorry black ass over here."

"Who cut you?"

"That's what we're gonna talk about. You getting the implication? I been beat up, I been run in, I been threatened, I been racially humiliated, and now I been cut. Got the picture, Negro?"

"My recorder is still running. Hang on."

"Stop fucking with your machine and listen to me. We're gonna file a civil rights suit against the sheriff's department. They're gonna pay for what they done to me."

"I hear you, Herman, but who cut you?"

Herman's level of frustration and anger with Monroe was such that he could barely speak. Then he looked through the sliding doors and thought he saw a silhouette standing just to the side of an orchid tree. "I t'ink somebody is outside. I t'ink it's probably them kids from next door. Stay wit' me. If I tell you to call 911, that means get the Eighty-second Airborne out here, you got me, Monroe?"

Herman walked to the open glass doors, the cordless gripped in his left hand, a fist thudding inside his chest. "You in trouble?" he heard Monroe say.

"Hang on," Herman said.

He stepped outside and felt the wind blow on his face, drying the sheen of sweat on his forehead. The trees were rustling loudly, leaves drifting down on the brightness of the pool. He stared hard at a barrel-potted bottlebrush tree that in the shadows seemed fatter and denser than it should have been.

"I can't take this anxiety," Monroe said. "You all right, Herman? Tell me what's happening, man."

"Shut up, Monroe," Herman said, staring at a silhouette that disconnected itself from the bottlebrush tree and now stood framed against the moonlight that shimmered like a white flame on the bayou.

"Herman? You there?"

"Yeah, I'm here. There's somebody by the pool."

"Who?"

"If I knew, I'd tell you." Herman could hear a creaking sound in his ears, like water pressure at a great depth. "Monroe, stay wit' me and call the cops on your cell. Don't break the connection, you reading me on this?"

"I'm your cousin, man, I'm wit' you all the way. You got anything in your house you shouldn't have, get rid of it. Flush the bowl two or three times. Don't use the drains, either."

"Make the call and come over here, Monroe."

"I'm coordinating everything from right here.

It's under control. I got your back, man. This is the command center."

But Herman had removed the cordless from his ear and was no longer listening. "What are *you* doing here?" he said to the silhouette. He paused, but there was no reply. "I ain't big on this silent-treatment stuff. You got somet'ing to say that cain't wait till business hours, do it. But you're on my property, and I wasn't expecting no callers, except maybe a lady friend and her sister that's coming t'rew the door any minute now."

Again there was no response.

"How about saying what you got to say so I can go back inside and get dressed, 'cause I ain't comfortable walking around outdoors in my underwear talking to myself," Herman said.

"Herman, who you talking to?" Monroe's voice said.

But Herman was no longer thinking about Monroe or the cordless phone that hung uselessly from his hand. He wanted the children who had been playing tag in the dark to appear at his piked gate; he wanted someone from the lawn party to arrive by boat at the back of his property and invite him over; he wanted clothes on his body to take away the sense of nakedness and vulnerability that turned the backs of his legs to pudding.

He made a chugging sound when he cleared the clot in his throat. "Maybe it's my accent that ain't working here, 'cause you don't seem to understand what the focus is in our sit'ation. See, the focus is getting everyt'ing out on the table so we can look at it and resolve it and so it don't be a problem to nobody. But we cain't do that when we get inside this silent-treatment groove and try to scare the shit out of everybody. See, that's what John Wayne do in the movies, but in the real world, it gives everybody anxiety and the wrong idea about how t'ings are gonna work out.

" 'Cause look, this ain't funny no more. I ain't saying I necessarily got a weak heart, but I wasn't planning to get 'jacked in my own yard, I mean by my own pool, where I'm fixing to entertain these ladies that's coming over. 'Cause you're here to 'jack me, ain't you? Not nothing else? You can have my stash and my cash, it ain't a lot, but what more can I say, I ain't in this world to argue or give nobody trouble. I was just telling my attorney, he's on the line now if he ain't already on his way over, I'm a bidnessman and put deals together and ain't never been greedy about it and piece off the action and he'p as many people as I can if they want in on it, but I'm axing you not to point that t'ing at my face no more.

"Hey, I appreciate it. That's better. We just got to be a li'l more serene on some of this shit. I ain't no shrinking violet, but I t'ought my heart was gonna give out. No, wait a minute. No, no, hold on. There's another way to do this. What do you want? Just tell me and you got it. I'm here to please. We can always— Hey, fuck me, I'll get out of town, you want this place, it's yours. Don't do it. Please."

Later, the pathologist would say the first entry wound, under the left armpit, probably occurred when Herman spun away from the shooter, raising his arm defensively across his face. Even though the exit hole was the size of a quarter, the pathologist would report that the wound in itself was not a mortal one. In fact, the blood pattern on the flagstones indicated that Herman had tried to walk toward the far side of his pool, where his white ironwork chairs were positioned around a table centered with a beach umbrella. His movements were probably slow and precise, like those of a man trying to walk on a wire strung over an abyss, his gold-ebony skin glowing in the electric aura that rose from the pool. But his profile probably had the vulnerability of a cartoon cutout pasted on a target. The second round struck him in the mouth and took away most of his jaw. When he fell into the pool, he floated high above the columns of light that lit the deep end, his arms straight out, as though he were searching for something he had lost and could not find.

I CAME IN late that night. A bank of thunderheads had moved in from the Gulf, and the beginnings of a downpour had started to sprinkle on the trees in the yard and the tin roof of our house. To me, the rain in Louisiana has always worked as a kind of baptism. It seems to have the same kind of restorative properties, washing the dust from trees and sidewalks, rinsing the pollutants out of our streams, giving new life to the grass and flowers, thickening the stalks of sugarcane in the fields. When it rains at night in Louisiana, I remember the world in which I grew up, one that came to us each morning with a resilience and clarity that was like a divine hand offering a person a freshly picked orange.

I hung my raincoat in the hall closet. Molly was reading a book under a lamp in the living room. "Catch any fish?" she asked.

"One or two that I put back."

"Where's Clete?"

"I went by myself."

"Helen was trying to find you. You didn't have your cell phone on?"

"I left it in the truck. What did she want?"

"Someone murdered Herman Stanga."

I stared at her blankly. I could hear rain clicking against the window glass. "Stanga is dead?"

"At nine-thirty he was." Her eyes didn't leave my face. I could feel her trying to read my thoughts. "Helen asked where Clete was. I told her I thought he had gone fishing with you."

"I rousted Stanga this afternoon. Helen thought we could turn some dials on him."

"Why is she asking about Clete?"

"I'll talk to her in the morning."

"Does she think Clete—"

"No, that's ridiculous."

"How did you know what I was going to say?"

I didn't have an answer. "Did Helen want me to call her?"

"She didn't say. Dave, you never go off by yourself like that. Why tonight? Were you thinking about—"

"Drinking? Why would you think that?" I replied.

Her book was open on her lap, her reading glasses down on her nose. She took off her glasses and folded them and placed them in a case. Her face looked youthful and powdered with freckles under the lamp, her dark red hair touched with tiny lights. "I fixed some stuffed eggs and ham-and-onion sandwiches and a pitcher of sun tea," she said. "I haven't eaten yet. Did you eat at the landing?"

"No. You waited for me?"

"Alafair went out. I don't like to eat alone." Her eyes shifted off mine.

"She went out with Kermit Abelard?"

"They were going to a movie in Lafayette."

"Was Robert Weingart along?"

"I didn't look outside."

"It's all right. She has to work through it. Eventually she'll come out on the other side."

"Other side of what?"

"You want to know? You really want to know?"

"Dave, don't get angry with me."

"It's something dark. Clete sensed it when we were at the Abelard house. He said he could smell it on the old man. As sure as I'm standing in my own living room, we're dealing with something that's genuinely evil. Alafair is getting pulled into the middle of it, and I can't do anything about it."

Molly stared emptily into space.

THE NEXT MORNING the rain was still blowing in the streets when I went into Helen Soileau's office. The coroner's and the crime-scene investigator's reports were already on her desk. "I could have used you last night," she said.

"I'm sorry. I was at Henderson. I left my cell phone in the truck."

"It was after nine-thirty when I called you. You were still on the water?"

"I didn't check the time."

She was standing behind her desk, not quite looking at me, her thoughts hidden. A cassette player rested on her desk blotter. "The only witness we have wasn't at the crime scene," she said.

"Repeat that?"

"Monroe Fontenot, Stanga's cousin. Herman left two messages on Monroe's answering machine early last night, then made a third call that was recorded while the shooter was on the grounds. Here, listen." She pushed a button on the cassette player.

I had hated Herman Stanga, but I doubted that any civilized human being could take pleasure in the naked fear of a small, uneducated, pitiful man who had grown up carrying buckets filled with the washed-out product of other people's lust. While the tape played, I walked to the window and watched the rain dance on the surface of Bayou Teche. The last sounds on the tape were gunfire and the voice of Herman Stanga's cousin shouting into the phone. Helen pushed the eject button on the cassette player.

"We found only one slug," she said. "It hit the corner of the house. It's in pretty bad shape, but the lab says it's probably from a forty-five auto. There were no shell casings."

I nodded and didn't reply.

"What kind of shooters pick up their brass, Dave?" she said.

"Professional killers?"

"Who else?"

"All cops."

"Who else?"

"Ex-cops."

"Which leads us to a bad question. Maybe it's one you and I wouldn't ask, but somebody probably will."

"What's that?" I said.

"Who had the most motivation to blow Herman Stanga out of his socks?"

"Anyone who had the misfortune to know him."

"Wrong. Herman did business around here for a quarter century. He made money for lots of people. He greased cops and politicians and didn't make enemies of anyone who had the power to hurt him."

"I know that, Helen."

"Was Clete with you last night?"

"Ask him."

"I asked you."

"No, Clete was not with me."

"You said something to me yesterday that won't go out of my head."

"What's that?"

"You said the only thing Stanga understood was a bullet in the mouth."

"What about it?"

"Most of Stanga's jaw was blown off. Who saw you at Henderson Swamp last night, Pops? Don't break my heart."

"Nobody saw me. And I'm through with this conversation," I said.

AT NOON I found Clete sitting at the bar in Clementine's, a po'boy fried-oyster sandwich on a plate in front of him, a Bloody Mary in a big tumbler with a celery stalk stuck in it by his elbow. His loafers were shined and his slacks and Hawaiian shirt pressed, but the back of his neck looked oily and hot, and behind his shades, the skin at the corners of his eyes was white and threaded with lines. I rested my hand on his shoulder. It felt as hard as concrete.

"Helen Soileau wants you to come in," I said.

"For what?" he said, studying my reflection in the mirror behind the bar.

"She wants to know where you were last night."

"When I find out, I'll tell her."

"Rough night?"

"Probably. I don't remember. I woke up in the backseat of my rental, behind a filling station in Morgan City. My wallet was empty."

"You know about Herman Stanga?"

"I saw it in the paper."

"Helen just wants to exclude you."

"Good. Let me know when she does that," he said.

I tightened my hand around the back of his neck. "Come stay with us."

"I look homeless?"

"Just for a while, until we get through this stuff."

"I'm fine. I'm getting my Caddy out of the shop today. Everything is copacetic, Dave."

The waiter brought him a bowl of gumbo. Clete dipped the end of his po'boy sandwich into the bowl and began eating, drinking from his Bloody Mary, filling his mouth with French bread, oysters, lettuce and tomatoes, red sauce, and mayonnaise, stopping only long enough to wipe his chin with a white napkin. He took off his shades and turned toward me. His face looked poached and twenty years older than his age. "Stop staring at me like that," he said. "I'm not going to burn my own kite. You stop acting like I'm the walking wounded. Did you hear me, big mon? I can't take it."

Out of politeness, the bartender walked away from us. I went back outside, into the smell of wet trees and raindrops striking warm concrete, wondering at what point you have to honor the self-destructive request of the best friend you ever had.

At one P.M. Helen called me back into her office and told me that AFIS, the Automated Fingerprint Identification System, had found a match for the girl we exhumed at the Delahoussaye farm. "She was a Canadian runaway, from a place called Trout Lake, British Columbia. She'd been picked up in North Dakota and returned to a foster home in B.C." Helen opened a folder that was filled with printouts from both the National Crime Information Center and the Royal Canadian Mounted Police. "Her name was Fern Michot. I talked with an inspector with the RCMP. She seemed to have been a good kid, until her parents were killed in a car wreck and she got placed with a family that probably abused her. The social worker assigned to her case thinks the father in the family might have raped her. Anyway, here's a picture that was taken of her two years ago at age sixteen."

In police work, you see many kinds of photos, some taken in booking rooms, others at crime scenes, some in morgues. But the kind you're never prepared for is the picture of either the victim or the perpetrator when he or she was a child. The photo Helen handed me was of a beautiful blue-eyed, blond girl dressed in a Girl Scout uniform that had a maple leaf sewn on the sleeve. The girl was smiling and looked younger than her years, as though perhaps she hadn't outgrown her baby fat. She looked like a girl who had been loved and who believed the world was a good place where the joy of young womanhood waited for her with each sunrise.

"How did she end up down here?" I said.

"She had run away from British Columbia twice before. She must have run away again and crossed the border and this time kept going."

"But why here? How did she fall into the hands of the person who killed her?"

Helen put the photo back in the folder and placed the folder in my hand. "Find out," she said.

I turned to go.

"Streak?"

I hated what I knew was coming next.

"Did you talk to Clete?" she said.

"He was drunk last night. All he remembers is waking up in the backseat of his rental car in Morgan City."

"He has a blackout the same night Stanga is killed? What are the odds of that happening?"

"Clete is going through a bad time in his life. Why don't you cut him some slack?"

"All right, let's talk about you. You think I was too hard on you this morning, asking you where you were last night?"

"I didn't give it a lot of thought."

"Everyone knows you carry a forty-five auto, Dave. Everybody knows your feelings about Herman Stanga. Your best friend was about to be financially ruined and sent to Angola by a pimp you despised. You and Clete have been trashing legal procedure and stringing feces through courtrooms for decades. Both of you act like the world is a huge O.K. Corral. But I'm supposed to ignore all that to protect your sensibilities?"

"Why is it people remember Wyatt Earp's and Doc Holliday's names but not the names of the guys they shot?"

"That's exactly what I mean," she replied.

"My vote is still for Doc and the Earps."

"That's because you're unteachable," she said. "God!"

CHAPTER 8

HELEN HAD TOLD me to find out why the murdered Canadian girl, Fern Michot, had come all the way from British Columbia to southwestern Louisiana. But where was I to start? For openers, we sent out her photo to every newspaper and television channel in the state. I also called up a local printer and had circulars made that contained her picture and the words underneath: HAVE YOU SEEN THIS GIRL? CALL THE IBERIA PARISH SHERIFF'S DEPARTMENT. A twenty-four-hour number was printed at the bottom.

I spread all the material I had on Fern Michot and Bernadette Latiolais on top of my desk. I also opened up the file folders I had on the other women and girls who had died under suspicious circumstances in Jeff Davis Parish. But in actuality, what did I have? In general, the forensic connections were tenuous and perhaps even nonexistent. Some of the deaths may have been accidental, the kind of fate that often happens to marginalized girls and young women who find the wrong males and end up with an air bubble in a vein or who try to walk home dead drunk from a bar and never see the headlights they step in front of.

But there was one detail that was incontestable and would not go away. Bernadette Latiolais had bought two plastic teacups and saucers at the dollar store on the day of her disappearance. We had confirmed that the saucer and broken teacup buried with the body of the Canadian girl were of the same manufacture as the ones sold at the dollar store. There was little doubt that the two girls had been abducted and murdered or held in the same place by the same killer or killers.

But Bernadette did not fit the pattern of the other girls or women. She was not a runaway or a school dropout or a teenage addict or alcoholic. She had been an honor student who had won a scholarship to attend the University of Louisiana at Lafayette. She had been happy and confident about her future and was known for the sweetness of her personality. Perhaps more important from an investigative perspective, she was the only person among the eight women or girls who evidently had contact outside the small world in which they all lived. Her brother, the convict Elmore Latiolais, had recognized the newspaper photo of Kermit Abelard as the man who had promised to make her rich. Bernadette's grandmother had recognized the author's jacket photo of Robert Weingart as the man she had seen buying boudin in a store with someone whose description fit Herman Stanga's, which suggested at least the possibility that Bernadette had seen or known them.

But on what basis would Kermit Abelard or anyone else promise to make her rich? The grandmother had said Bernadette had inherited seven arpents of farmland that were part of an undivided estate. The arpent is the old French measure that is approximately one acre in size. Its value in that part of rural Louisiana was not great. In fact, Hurricane Rita, which struck the Louisiana coast three and a half weeks after Katrina, devastated the area.

Unfortunately, the story about Kermit Abelard's promise to Bernadette had its origins with Elmore Latiolais, a thief and a liar who probably bore a lifetime's enmity toward white people in general and cops in particular.

I twirled a ballpoint pen on my desk pad. Through my office window, I could see rain tumbling out of the sunlight onto the surface of Bayou Teche. In City Park, the old brick firehouse, now painted battleship gray, was deep inside the shadows of the oak trees. When I was a little boy, a French band used to play in the park on Saturday evenings, and the firemen, all friends of my father, boiled crabs behind the firehouse, and my mother and father would take me and my half brother, Jimmy, to eat with them. That was where I first listened to the song "La Jolie Blon," sung with the same French lyrics that had been sung in France in the eighteenth century. It remains today the saddest lament I have ever heard, one that you hear once and never forget for the rest of your life.

Where did it all go? I asked myself.

But I had to remind myself that neither our own passing nor the passing of an era is a tragedy, no matter how much we would like to think it is. If there is any human tragedy, there is only one, and it occurs when we forget who we are and remain silent while a stranger takes up residence inside our skin. Bernadette Latiolais had been robbed of her young life, and all her joys and choices stolen from her. Her mouth had been stopped with dust, and her advocates were few. Regardless of my promise to Alafair, it was time to make Kermit Abelard accountable.

CLETE PURCEL HAD gotten up early and showered, shaved, and brushed his teeth, then fixed a bowl of cereal and strawberries and taken it and a pot of coffee out on a table under the oak trees at the end of the driveway that divided the stucco cottages in the 1940s motor court where he lived. He had not taken a drink since lunch the previous day and had slept soundly through the night and awakened with his mind clear and his metabolism free of booze. It was a fine morning to be alive and to feel like a player again. A blue heron was standing in the shallows of Bayou Teche, pecking at its feathers, its legs as thin and delicate as strokes from a bamboo brush. An elderly black man sitting on an inverted bucket was bobber-fishing with a cane pole among the lily pads, raising his baited hook up and down as though the movement would make it more attractive to the fish hiding there. And sitting proudly in the shade, its maroon finish gleaming, its starched white top as immaculate as ever, was Clete's vintage Cadillac, just out of the repair shop.

He finished eating and washed his dishes, put on his porkpie hat, and went to the office with a song in his heart. Fifteen minutes after his arrival, he was reading a magazine article on Layton Blanchet and biofuels when his rosy-complected, top-heavy secretary, Hulga Volkmann, opened his door and leaned inside, her perfume drenching the room. "There's somebody out here who says his name is Kiss-My-Ass-Fat-Man," she said.

"What's he want?"

"He wouldn't say."

"Tell him the reparation issue for pygmies is off the table."

"Pardon?"

"Does he look like he might have a blowgun on him?"

"I'm confused, Mr. Purcel."

"Send him in, please."

The boy, who was not over twelve, came in and sat in a deep chair in the corner, his baseball cap sitting on his eyebrows. He gazed at the antique fire-arms mounted on the walls. "You cain't afford any kind of guns except junk?" he said.

"Your first name is Buford, right?"

"You can stick with Kiss-My-Ass. Or you can call me Mr. Kiss-My-Ass."

"You know I beat the shit out of your cousin Herman Stanga, don't you?"

"Yeah, at the Gate Mout'. I know all about it."

"Then why are you here?"

"My cousin wasn't no good. 'Cause I do what I do don't mean I liked Cousin Herman."

"I'm pretty busy, Kiss-My-Ass."

"Yeah, I can see that. Reading a t'rowaway maga-zine takes up a lot of time. There's a lady lives up the street from me on Cherokee. She's Vietnamese. She's a waitress at Bojangles. Know who I'm talking about?"

"No."

"She's a nice lady. She don't need no trouble from the wrong kind of guy."

"You got to be a little more specific."

"I was on my corner, and this white guy in a Mustang come by and wanted to buy some roofies. I tole him I don't handle that kind of stuff. So he axed me for some X. I tole him I don't have no X, either. I tole him that maybe I had some breat' mints 'cause that's what he needed."

"Why are you telling me this?"

"'Cause I seen this same car and this same guy dropping off the Vietnamese lady at her house. She don't need this guy slipping her roofies so he can do t'ings to her in his backseat."

"You remember what I told you I'd do if I caught you slinging dope again?"

"No disrespect, but you can go fuck yourself, too. You gonna he'p me or not?"

"Don't be surprised if you don't reach your next birthday. What's this cat's name?"

"I don't know, but I seen him before. He was at Cousin Herman's house. Herman said he was in the pen over in Texas. Herman said he wrote a book about it."

"Does the name Robert Weingart ring a bell?"

Buford shook his head.

"My fee is a hundred and fifty an hour. But we offer a pygmy discount," Clete said. He waited. "That was a joke, Kiss-My-Ass."

The boy gazed out the French doors at a tugboat passing on the bayou. "When the guy in the Mustang stopped by the corner, I wasn't slinging. I was waiting on some friends to go to the pool. If you want to make fun of me, go do it. But tell me if you gonna he'p or not, 'cause that man is fixing to do bad t'ings to a lady that been nice to every kid in the neighborhood."

"Why don't you tell her this yourself?"

The bill of the boy's cap was tilted downward, hiding his face. " 'Cause maybe I sold roofies before. 'Cause maybe I ain't proud about having to say that to somebody."

CLETE CALLED ME at the department after the boy left his office and told me of Robert Weingart's attempt to buy the date-rape drug known on the street as "roofies."

"What are you going to do?" I asked.

"Talk with the Vietnamese waitress and maybe chat up our celebrity ex-con scribbler."

"The latter isn't an option."

"The First Amendment has been suspended and nobody told me?"

I got up from my desk and closed my office door

and picked up the phone again. "Somebody did you a big favor when he helped Stanga into the next world. Don't blow it."

"Sounds a little cynical. You're not lighting candles for Herman?"

"We'll pick up Weingart and let him know his sexual behavior has come to our attention. In the meantime, you stay out of trouble. You're the human equivalent of a wrecking ball, Clete. Except you do most of the damage to yourself. You've never figured that out."

"My ex used to say the same thing. She used exactly the same words."

"Did you hear what I said?"

"Take an aspirin. Think cool thoughts. Nobody rattles the Bobbsey Twins from Homicide."

Did you ever conduct a conversation with a vacant lot?

I HAD MADE an appointment to interview Kermit Abelard at his house. I could have had him come in to the department, but I wanted access once again to the Abelard compound and the bizarre and insular world in which they lived, maybe for reasons I didn't want to admit to myself. Did I buy into the notion, as Clete had suggested, that the Abelards were players in an Elizabethan tragedy? No, I didn't. They certainly created the affectation of royalty in exile, but I doubted if even they were convinced by it. Someone once said that had Sir Walter Scott not written his romantic accounts of medieval chivalry, there would have been no War Between the States. I doubted if that was true, either. I believed the legend of the Lost Cause was created after the fact, when the graves of Shiloh and Antietam became vast stone gardens reminding us forever that we imposed this suffering on ourselves.

But if the Abelards and their peers were not created by the pen of an Scottish novelist, what were they? Clete Purcel had said either their house or the old man smelled of death. Was that just his imagination? Except Clete was nobody's fool and was not given to extravagant metaphors.

I signed out a cruiser and drove down to the watery rim of St. Mary Parish and thumped across the wood bridge onto the Abelard compound. The lagoon that surrounded the property was networked with algae, the moss in the dead cypress lifting in the wind off the Gulf, a solitary ventilated storm shutter slamming incessantly against an upstairs window. Out in the flooded cypress, I could see a man standing in a pirogue, his back to me, casting a lure in a long arc into the water. He was wearing a cap and a sleeveless denim shirt, and he had narrow shoulders and a suntan that had a strange yellow cast.

The black woman who let me in said Mr. Kermit was out in his boat but would be back momentarily; in the meantime, she said Mr. Timothy would like to see me out on the sunporch.

"You're Miss Jewel?" I said.

"Yes, suh. That's my name. I've taken care of Mr. Timothy for many years."

"And you know my daughter, Alafair?"

"Yes, suh. She's very nice."

I took unfair advantage of my situation and asked a question I should not have asked. "I was trying to remember when Alafair was out here last. Do you recall?"

"I take care of Mr. Timothy. I don't study on everyone who comes and goes, suh."

She escorted me to the sunporch. Timothy Abelard was reading in his wheelchair, canted sideways to catch the sunlight on the page, his entire person bathed in the rainbow of color that shone through the stained-glass windows. He looked up at me, smiling, with the expectation one might associate with a tiny bird in the bottom of a nest. "It's very nice of you to come out and talk with an elderly man," he said.

I wondered if he was simply being polite or if he was confused about the purpose of my visit. But perhaps a bigger problem for me was that I wanted to like Mr. Abelard. In all ways, he was genteel and seemingly thoughtful. Yes, his eyes were like those of a hawk. But for the elderly, a mistake in judgment about other people can have dire consequences, and it's hard to begrudge them their cautionary instincts in dealings with others. At least that was what I wanted to believe about this kindly old man.

"I'm here to see your grandson, sir," I said.

"He didn't run a traffic light, did he?"

"What are you reading?"

"I was just going to ask your opinion on it. Here, take a look. It's Kermit's new book."

I didn't want to see it, but he pressed it into my hand. The jacket was a wonderful collage of a plantation house burning against a plum-colored sky, a lovely woman holding the head of a wounded Confederate soldier in her lap, and a gallant officer with a plume in his hat rearing his horse in cannon smoke under the cross of St. Andrew. "Go ahead, read the first paragraph. Tell me what you think," Mr. Abelard said.

I had read none of Kermit's work, but I had to admit the opening scene in his new book was written by a very good writer. It described airbursts over Vicksburg in the summer of 1863, and a family of Negroes and one of poor whites trying to take cover in a cave they had dug in the bluffs with barrel staves. Kermit had even described the sound of hot shrapnel raining into the shallows of the Mississippi, a detail I would not expect a man with no war experience to know about.

"It's impressive, sir. I'll have to get a copy," I said, returning the book to him.

"Will you tell me the purpose of your visit?"

"I'm trying to exclude some possibilities in an investigation."

"Seems like you're an expert in vagueness, Mr. Robicheaux. Have you considered a career in politics?"

I had sat down in one of his rattan chairs. The bamboo creaked under me in the silence. It is difficult to describe the accent and diction of the class of people represented by Mr. Abelard. Their dialect is called plantation English and was influenced largely by British tutors hired to teach the children of plantation society. Unlike the speech of yeomen, it does not vary through the states of the Old Confederacy. If you have heard the recorded voice of William Faulkner or Robert Penn Warren, you have heard the same pronunciations and linguistic cadence characteristic of Mr. Abelard's generation in Louisiana. They could read from a phone book and you would swear you were listening to the cadences found inside a Shakespearean sonnet.

But well-spoken elderly gentleman or not, he had asked for it, I told myself. "In one way or another, my visit is related to your house guest, Robert Weingart. What kind of fellow would you say he is?"

"His prison background, that kind of thing?"

"For openers."

"The man's a mess. What else do you want to know?"

"Do you think it's good for Kermit to be hanging around with a fellow like that?"

"That's a bit personal, isn't it?"

"Have you checked out Weingart's criminal history?"

"You don't have to convince me of the evil that's in this world, Mr. Robicheaux. I've dealt with it in every form for a lifetime. Do you have a cigarette?"

"I don't smoke."

"Jewel!" he called.

Immediately, the black woman was at the door, waiting, her eyes not quite meeting his, her muscular body held straight and motionless, as though the virtue of patience had been ironed into the starch of her uniform.

"Get me a cigarette. Don't argue about it, either. Just bring me the cigarette and a match before Kermit comes back and starts fussing at me," Mr. Abelard said. He turned to me. "Don't get old, Mr. Robicheaux. Age is an insatiable thief. It steals the pleasures of your youth, then locks you inside your own body with your desires still glowing. Worse, it makes you dependent upon people who are a half century younger than you. Don't let anyone tell you that it brings you peace, either, because that's the biggest lie of all."

Jewel returned and placed a single cigarette in his hand, then lit it for him with a paper match. He puffed on it, wetting the filter, seemingly more pleased by the acquisition of the cigarette than his smoking of it. He continued talking about almost every subject imaginable except the presence of a career criminal like Robert Weingart in his house. I looked at my watch. "Where's your grandson, sir?"

"Out yonder, almost to the salt. They'll be back momentarily," Mr. Abelard said.

"They?" I said.

"Jewel, will you bring me an ashtray?" he called out.

"Sir, who is 'they'?"

But he turned his attention away from me to acquiring the ashtray, then began fumbling with it until he had positioned it in his lap. "You'd think by this time the woman could figure out that a man in a wheelchair can't smoke a cigarette without something to put the ashes in."

I had given up trying to find out who was in the boat with Kermit. Or maybe I didn't want to know. "Miss Jewel seems like a devoted caretaker," I said.

"I wish Jewel had a better life than the one she was given. But how many of us see the consequences when we step over forbidden lines?"

"Pardon?" I said.

"The racial situation of the South is one we inherited, and for good or bad we did the best we could with it. I just wish I had shown more personal restraint when I was in my middle years."

"I'm not following you, sir."

"The woman is my daughter. What did you think I was talking about?"

There was a long silence, then I felt my stare break and I looked away at the flooded trees that had been killed by saltwater intrusion, the petrochemical sheen that glistened on his lagoon, the flaking paint on the pillars that supported his second-story veranda, the decay and sickness that seemed to infect the entirety of the Abelards' property, and I wondered why we had concentrated so much of our lives on hating or envying or emulating people such as the Abelards and the oligarchy they represented. Then I saw a motorboat with two figures in it come across the bay and enter the cypress trees, riding on its wake, passing the man who was fishing in the pirogue. Kermit sat behind the wheel, wearing Ray-Bans and a sky-blue cap with a lacquered black brim tilted on the side of his head. Alafair was sitting next to him, her hair and face damp with salt spray.

I got up from the chair, keeping my face empty of expression. "I'll walk down to your dock, if you don't mind," I said. "I enjoyed talking with you."

"You seem offended."

I looked at the boat and at Alafair sitting close to Kermit, clenching his arm. "You withheld information from me, Mr. Abelard."

"What your daughter does or does not do isn't my business, sir. I resented your indicating that it is."

I looked at him a long time before I spoke. He was infirm and, I suspected, visited in his sleep by memories and deeds no one wishes to carry to his grave. Or perhaps I was endowing him with a level of humanity that he didn't possess. Regardless, I had concluded that Timothy Abelard was not someone I would ever come to like or admire.

"Robert Weingart is in your home with your consent, sir," I said. "You're an intelligent man. That means his agenda is your agenda. That's not a comforting thought."

"Get out," he replied.

I walked outside and down the slope of the yard toward a wood dock, where Kermit was mooring his boat. Alafair stepped off the bow onto the dock and came toward me. She was wearing white shorts and a black blouse and straw sandals; her skin was dark with tan in the sunlight, her hair blown in wet wisps across her cheek, her mouth lifted toward me.

"I'm here to see Kermit. It has nothing to do with you, Alafair," I said.

"You gave me your word," she said.

"I promised I wouldn't interfere in your relationship. There're some questions Kermit has to answer. He can talk to me or he can talk to Helen Soileau. Or he can wait until he's contacted by the FBI."

She walked past me without replying, glancing at me once, her eyes dead.

Kermit stood on his dock, his hands on his hips, gazing at the hammered bronze light on the bay and at the moss straightening on the cypress snags and at the man fishing in the pirogue. When he heard my footsteps behind him, he turned and extended his hand, but I didn't take it. The smile went out of his face.

"Did you know Bernadette Latiolais?" I asked.

He held his eyes on mine, more steadily than was natural, never blinking. "The name is familiar," he said.

"It should be. You were photographed with her."

"Oh, yes," he said. "One of the scholarship girls, I believe."

"She was a murder victim. She said you were going to make her rich. How were you planning to do that?"

"Wait a minute. There's some confusion here."

"Are you telling me you weren't photographed with her?" The truth was I had never seen the photo, and I knew of its possible existence only because Bernadette's brother, Elmore, said she had shown it to him when she visited him at the work camp in Mississippi.

"I'm saying I remember her name because my family belongs to the UL alumni association, and I was at the ceremony at Bernadette's high school when she was awarded a scholarship that we endow. At least if we're talking about the same person. Why don't you check it out?"

"I don't have to."

"Why is that?"

"Because you're lying. I think you have blood splatter all over you, podna, and I'm going to nail you to the wall."

"I don't care if you're Alafair's father or not, you have no right to talk to me like that."

"Who's the dude in the pirogue?" I asked.

"He looks like a fisherman."

"His name is Vidor Perkins. He did a stretch in Huntsville Pen with Robert Weingart, the guy who's made you his bunkie. He was also in the Flat Top in Raiford. That's where they keep the guys they couldn't legally lobotomize. In Alabama he cut up the face of a female convenience-store clerk with a string knife. He was also arrested for the rape of a five-year-old girl. If that man comes close to my daughter, your grandfather won't be able to protect you, Kermit."

"Say that stuff about a 'bunkie' again?"

"That's prison parlance for 'regular punch.'"

The veins in his forearms were pumped with blood, his hands opening and closing at his sides, his cheeks flaming. "You're old and you're a guest in our home. Otherwise, I'd knock your teeth down your throat."

"At my age, I don't have a lot to lose, kid. You're a good judge of character. Look at my face. Tell me I'm lying."

CLETE PURCEL HAD parked his Caddy a hundred yards down the two-lane from the motel in St. Martin Parish where Carolyn Blanchet, Layton

Blanchet's wife, had rented a room. It had not been a productive day for Clete. After Herman Stanga's little cousin Buford, also known as Kiss-My-Ass-Fat-Man, had visited Clete's office to tell him of his fears that Robert Weingart was planning to drug and seduce a Vietnamese waitress at Bojangles, Clete had gone to the girl's house and tried to warn her. He had tried to warn her in language that would not alarm or offend her. The mother, who spoke little English, thought he was a bill collector and told him to get out. The girl followed him outside, and Clete tried again.

"You know what Rohypnol is? It's a very powerful tranquilizer," he said. "It's called the date-rape drug. It takes only twenty or thirty minutes to turn a person into Play-Doh. The effects can last several hours."

"Robbie wants to do this to me?"

"'Robbie' is a douchebag and a bum. He has spent most of his life in prison for serious crimes. He made a black girl at Ruby Tuesday pregnant, then told her to get an abortion if she didn't want the kid. Here's my business card. If he bothers you, call me."

"You make me scared, Mr. Purcel."

"I'm not the one to be afraid of. Don't cry. You haven't done anything wrong. You're a good person, you hear me? That's why I'm here. Robert Weingart should have been ground into fish chum a long time ago. I'm sorry for upsetting you. Come on, don't do that. I apologize for the way I say things. My best friend tells me I have the sophistication of a junkyard falling down a staircase."

His attempt at humor did not work. "I think you're a nice man, but you must go back to your work now," she said.

"You're going out with this loser?"

"It isn't right to condemn people without giving them a chance to defend themselves."

She turned and went back into her house.

I tried, Kiss-My-Ass, Clete said to himself. But his words seemed self-mocking and were of poor consolation to him.

Now, in the twilight and the throbbing of birds in the trees, he was looking through his binoculars at a lounge with a blue-white neon champagne glass glowing over its entrance. He saw no one he recognized going in and out of the lounge. The motel was set behind the lounge and had a stucco arch over its driveway. At 7:13 P.M. Carolyn Blanchet emerged from her room in a swimsuit and dove into the pool, swimming cleanly through the water, taking long, powerful strokes, her platinum hair dark at the roots. She climbed up the steps in the shallow end, spread her feet slightly, and began cross-touching the tips of her toes, the backs of her thighs flexing, her bottom tightening against her swimsuit. Close by, two men playing cards at a table suddenly developed problems in their concentration.

Since being retained by Carolyn's husband, Clete had pieced off the job to a private investigator who operated out of Morgan City. The Morgan City PI had followed Carolyn in a rainstorm to a houseboat in the Atchafalaya Basin, where she had gotten into a shouting argument with someone who had been waiting for her. The other person had left in an outboard, wearing a raincoat that had a hood on it. The PI could not make out the person's face through his binoculars. The houseboat was owned by Carolyn's husband.

The next day the PI followed Carolyn to a hotel on the Vermilion River in Lafayette, except he didn't get into the lobby fast enough to see which floor her elevator had stopped on. On the odd chance he might get lucky, he prowled the hallways but saw no sign of her. The desk clerk said no one using her name was registered at the hotel. The Morgan City PI waited in his automobile for three hours. When Carolyn came out of the hotel, a beach bag swinging from her arm, she was by herself. His surveillance had been a waste. Plus, she had stared straight at him, boldly, through his windshield, giving him a triumphant look.

The next afternoon the PI tailed Carolyn to the motel outside St. Martinville. He called Clete and asked him what he wanted to do.

"You're doing a good job. Stay on it," Clete said.

"I think she's made me. If you ask me, she's had a lot of experience at this."

"I'll relieve you. Fax me your notes and hours, okay?"

"You got it. When you find out who the guy is, let me know."

"What for?" Clete asked.

"Maybe I can get on as his bodyguard. You ever hear the story about the football coach over in Texas that made a pass at her?"

"No."

"They took it outside and fought in the street. Blanchet blinded him. It cost him millions."

Clete looked through the binoculars again. Carolyn was reclining in a beach chair, a towel spread from her thighs to her breasts, her eyes closed. She seemed to doze off, then turned on her side, her hands pressed together and inserted under her cheek as though she were at prayer. Her mouth was soft-looking, her eyelashes long, the tops of her breasts white below her tan line.

But where was the lover? Clete resolved that

this would be the last time he would do scut work for jealous cuckolds or wives who wanted their husbands photographed in flagrante delicto. Why anyone romanticized the life of a PI was beyond him. Jobs like this one made him feel he was one cut above a voyeur. Second, the information he was paid to deliver ruined lives. Maybe the involved parties brought it on themselves, but there was no doubt in his mind that it was he who loaded the gun.

He also felt his work made him a hypocrite. His own marriage had been a nightmare of pills and booze and weed and infidelity. He tried to blame his problems on his wife, who had fallen under the influence of an alcoholic Buddhist guru in Colorado. Then he tried to blame his problems on the fact that he worked Vice and lived in an amoral netherworld that was not of his making. He blamed the basket of snakes he brought back from Vietnam and even blamed the mamasan he accidentally killed in a hooch in the Central Highlands and whose forgiveness he still sought in his sleep. He blamed the corrupt cops who pressured a young patrolman into going along with them when they planted a throwdown on an unarmed black man they had shot and killed. He blamed the bookies and Shylocks he owed, the tab he didn't have to pay at a couple of skin joints owned by the Giacanos, the script doctor who gave him unlimited amounts of downers, the watch supervisor who told him he either went on a pad for the greaseballs or he got assigned a beat at the Desire. And more than any of these, he blamed the easy female access that yawned open on Bourbon Street when his wife locked the bedroom door and said she could no longer live with a man who slept with a .357 Magnum and threatened to use it on himself because he believed the downdraft of helicopter gunships was shaking the plaster out of their apartment walls.

The light was tea-colored on the sugarcane fields and the oak trees along the Teche. A truck had parked next to the lounge, obscuring Clete's view of the swimming pool and the reclining figure of Carolyn Blanchet. He started up his Caddy and drove on the berm the hundred yards down the road to the lounge and parked by the side of the building so he could see both the entrance to the motel and the row of rooms that gave onto the pool.

He hadn't eaten since lunch, nor had he brought along his cooler that he usually kept stocked with po'boy sandwiches, Gatorade, a Ziploc bag of hard-boiled eggs, a jar of fresh orange juice, a pint of vodka, and a mixed dozen of longnecks and sixteen-ounce cans of Bud. This Layton Blanchet gig was a nuisance growing into a migraine that he didn't need. What was even worse, he told himself, he had taken the job out of pride rather than financial need because he didn't want to feel he couldn't handle a self-inflated manipulator like Blanchet. It was like mashing down the sole of your shoe on bubble gum to prove you weren't afraid of it.

What a fool he had been. Not only with Blanchet but with almost everything he touched. He'd lost it with Herman Stanga and had set himself up for a civil suit and criminal prosecution. Now he was running on dumb luck, a liver that he tried to revitalize with handfuls of vitamin B, and what he called the hypertension buzz, which produced a sound in his head like a fallen power line lying in a pool of water.

He was over the hill and lived alone and had no pension plan except a small SEP-IRA. The last woman he had loved and slept with had been an Amerasian FBI agent he had met in Montana. She had come to New Orleans with him, but as always happened with a younger woman, the discrepancy between youth and age finally had its way, and in this instance, the languid, subtropical heat and pagan excesses of southern Louisiana were no match for the techno-predictability of southern California, where she had grown up.

A woman in her mid-thirties came out the back door of the lounge and began walking toward the motel. She had gold hair that was cut short and wore jeans and suede half-topped boots and a canary-yellow cowboy shirt with purple roses sewn on it. She was looking straight ahead; then she saw the Caddy and Clete behind the wheel and smiled hesitantly, as though uncertain whether to approach the car or to continue on toward the motel. Finally, she walked to the driver's window and propped her hand on the roof. "Remember me?" she asked.

"It's Emma, right?" he said.

"Yeah, Emma Poche. I'm the deputy who called Dave Robicheaux the night you got brought in for that deal involving Herman Stanga at the Gate Mouth club. Looks like you got your car fixed."

"Yeah, look, Emma—"

"You on the job?"

"Something like that."

"My uncle is visiting from California. I'm supposed to meet him at the lounge, but he must have got lost. A guy has the phone tied up inside. I was gonna use the phone in the motel. Can I borrow your cell?"

He handed it to her. She went around the corner of the building and then came back to the Caddy, this time leaning down inside the passenger's window. She dropped his cell phone on the seat.

"Thanks. You get loose, come have a drink. My uncle is a no-show. What a drag, huh?"

Clete sat for another forty-five minutes in the Caddy. The sunset turned into long strips of maroon clouds, backdropped by a moment of robin's-egg blueness on the earth's rim, then the light drained from the sky and he could hear frogs croaking in a field down by the bayou and the first mosquitoes of the evening droning inside his vehicle.

He started the engine and rolled up all his windows and turned on his air conditioner full blast. Carolyn Blanchet got up from the recliner and went back inside her room. No one joined her. Twenty minutes later, she reemerged fully dressed, a fabric tote bag hanging from her shoulder. She opened a compact and studied her reflection in the mirror. She closed the compact and dropped it back in her bag. Then she got in her Lexus and drove away, the taillights disappearing in the gloom.

Clete picked up his cell phone off the seat and speed-dialed the private number Layton Blanchet had given him. He hoped he would get Blanchet's voice mail so he would not have to talk personally with the man again. No such luck.

"What do you want?" Blanchet said.

"Maybe I should call another time. Or just send you a fax. I can do that," Clete said.

"Sorry to sound short. I'm a little jammed up these days. You got something for me?"

"No, I've found nothing that could be considered significant. There's no charge for my time. I'll send you a bill for expenses and for the hours another guy put in. So this call in effect terminates my situation with you."

"Hold on there. What do you mean you're terminating the situation? What do you mean when you say you didn't find anything 'significant'?"

"Nothing we've uncovered puts your wife with another man. You know what I suggest sometimes in situations like this? I tell the husband to take his wife out to dinner. Buy her flowers. Put some music on the stereo and dance with her on the patio. Pay more attention to her and forget all this other bullshit. It's not worth it, Mr. Blanchet. Not financially, not emotionally. If our marriages are flushed, they're flushed. If they're salvageable, we salvage them."

"You said you were sending me a bill for another guy's hours. You shared this information with other people?"

"Yeah, I pieced off the job. That's how it works. I'm one guy, not the CIA."

"Then I want the names of everybody involved."

"We're done on this."

"Oh, no, we're not."

"My sympathies to your wife," Clete said, and clicked off his cell phone. He rubbed the ennui and fatigue out of his face and rested his forehead on the steering wheel. The air-conditioning was cold on his skin, the air freshener that the repair people had hung from his mirror smelling of lilacs, of spring, of youth itself. He remembered the excitement and romance of being twenty-three and returning home in Marine Corps tropicals, a recipient of the Navy Cross and two Purple Hearts, riding the Ferris wheel high above Pontchartrain Beach, the rifles in a shooting gallery popping far below him, the waves of the lake capping on the sand, a young woman clinging tightly to his arm.

But youth was a decaying memory, and no matter what a song lyricist might say, you couldn't put time in a bottle.

He went inside the lounge. Emma Poche was sitting by herself at a table in the corner, her canary-yellow western shirt lit by the glow of the jukebox. She had put on fresh lipstick, and her eyes were warm with an alcoholic sheen. "Sit down, handsome, and tell me about your life," she said.

He pulled out a chair and signaled the waitress. Emma was drinking out of a tall Collins glass, one packed with crushed ice and cherries and an orange slice. "I thought you knew Dave through the program," he said.

"Not really. Our ties go back to NOPD."

"You're not in the program?"

"I've tried it on and off. I got tired of listening to the same stories over and over. Were you ever in A.A.?"

"Not me."

"Yeah, stop drinking today and gone tomorrow. Why not party a little bit while you have the opportunity?"

"That's the way you feel about it?"

"I'm gonna die no matter how I feel about any of it, so I say 'bombs away.' If you ask me, sobriety sucks."

He tried to reason through what she had just said, but the jukebox was playing and the long day had landed on him like an anvil. The waitress came to the table and Emma ordered a vodka Collins and Clete a schooner of draft and a shot of Jack. He poured the whiskey into his beer and watched it rise in a mysterious cloud and flatten inside the foam. He tilted the schooner to his mouth and drank until it was almost half empty. He let out his breath, his eyes coming back into focus, like those of a man who had just gotten off a roller coaster. "Wow," he said.

"You don't fool around," she said.

"I spent most of the day firing in the well, then having a conversation with a world-class asshole. Plus I have complications with a dude by the name of Robert Weingart. Know anything about him?"

"I read his book. Weingart is the asshole?"

"Weingart is an asshole, all right, but I was talking about a client. Have you heard anything in St. Martin Parish about girls getting doped with roofies before they're raped?"

"I've heard about it in Lafayette but not around here. Weingart is doing that?"

"I'm not sure." Clete finished his boilermaker and ordered a refill. When it came, he sipped the whiskey from the shot glass and chased it with the beer.

"Your stomach lining must look like Swiss cheese," she said.

"My stomach is fine. My liver is the size of a football."

"Maybe you ought to ease up."

He could feel the alcohol taking hold in his system, restoring coherence to his thoughts, driving the gargoyles back to an unlighted place in his mind, releasing the cord of tension that often bound his chest and pressed the air out of his lungs. "I appreciated you calling Dave when I was in that holding cell. Some of those guys in St. Martin Parish carry resentments. That was a stand-up thing to do."

"You had the same kind of trouble at NOPD as me and Dave. The unholy trinity, huh?" she said, watching him lift the shot glass to his mouth again.

"I brought most of my trouble on myself."

"Save it for Oprah. I worked with those shitheads. What was the deal outside there?"

"What deal?"

"In your Cadillac. You were on a stakeout?"

"I wouldn't give it that kind of depth. Anyway, I pulled the plug on it."

"You like being a PI?"

"I don't think about it a lot."

"That's a good way to be. My job is okay, but I miss life in the Big Sleazy." She put her hand on his wrist when he started to lift his schooner again. "Better eat something."

"Yeah, maybe." His eyes moved sleepily over her face. She pretended to be looking at the bar, but he knew she was aware he was staring at her with more than curiosity. His gaze drifted to her ring finger. "You ever been married?"

"I woke up once with a rock-and-roll drummer who said we'd gotten hitched in Juárez, but I never saw a certificate. The guy got hit by a train, anyway. I was seventeen. I always call that part of my life the downside of that old-time rock and roll."

She looked back at the bar, straightening her shoulders slightly, her breasts stiffening against her shirt. Clete studied the clearness of her complexion and her pug nose and the pools of color in her cheeks and the redness of her mouth and the cuteness of her profile. She removed a strand of hair from her eyebrow and looked him in the face. "Something wrong?" she said.

"Did you have dinner yet?"

"No, I was supposed to eat with my uncle."

"Let's have another round and I'll buy you supper at Possum's."

"Dutch treat," she said.

"No, it's going on my expense tab, and I'm sending it to the world-class asshole."

"Who is he?"

He upended his shot glass and winked at her. When she sipped from her vodka Collins, her mouth looked cold and hard and lovely. She fished a cherry out of the ice and held it by the stem and placed it behind her teeth. When she bit into it, the juice ran over her lip. She caught it on one knuckle, smiling. She wiped her hand on a paper napkin. "I'm a mess," she said.

"You look good to me."

"Ready to rock, big guy?" she said. She bit down on the corner of her lip, her eyes fixed on his.

CHAPTER 9

I WOKE BEFORE SUNUP the following day and fed Tripod and Snuggs on the back steps, then fixed a bowl of Grape-Nuts and sliced bananas and sat down on the steps and ate breakfast with them. The dawn was a grayish-blue, the fog so thick on the bayou that I couldn't see the oaks on the far bank, the house and yard quiet except for the ticking of moisture out of the trees. It was one of those moments in the twenty-four-hour cycle of the day when you know that the past is still with you, if you'll only take the time to listen to the voices inside the mist or watch the shapes that are sometimes printed on a patch of green-black shade between the live oaks.

I sometimes subscribe to the belief that all historical events occur simultaneously, like a dream inside the mind of God. Perhaps it's only man who views time sequentially and tries to impose a solar calendar upon it. What if other people, both dead and unborn, are living out their lives in the same space we occupy, without our knowledge or consent? Buried in the mudflat down Bayou Teche from me were the remains of a Confederate gunboat. I knew this to be a fact because in the year 1942 my father pulled a huge rusted spike from one of its beams and gave it to me, along with sixteen balls of grapeshot he found inside the cavity of a rotted oak not thirty yards away. On the street in front of my present home, twenty thousand Yankee soldiers marched down the Old Spanish Trail in pursuit of General Alfred Mouton and his boys in butternut, their haversacks stuffed with loot, their wounds from a dozen firefights still green, their lust for revenge unsated. As I sat on the steps with Snuggs and Tripod, I wondered if those soldiers of long ago were still out there, beckoning to us, daring us to witness their mortality, daring us to acknowledge that it would soon be ours.

I have had visions of them that I do not try to explain to others. Sometimes I thought I heard cries and shouts and the sounds of musket fire in the mist, because the Union soldiers who marched through Acadiana were turned loose upon the civilian populace as a lesson in terror. The rape of Negro women became commonplace. Northerners have never understood the nature of the crimes that were committed in their names, no more than neocolonials can understand the enmity their government creates in theirs. The pastoral solemnity of a Civil War graveyard doesn't come close to suggesting the reality of war or the crucible of pain in which a soldier lives and dies.

But in spite of the bloody ground on which our town was built, and out of which oak trees and bamboo and banks of flowers along the bayou grew, it remained for me a magical place in the predawn hours, touched only cosmetically by the Industrial Age, the drawbridge clanking erect in the fog, its great cogged wheels bleeding rust, a two-story quarter boat that resembled a nineteenth-century paddle wheeler being pushed down to the Gulf, the fog billowing whitely around it, the air sprinkled with the smell of Confederate jasmine.

I heard the screen door open behind me. I turned and looked up into Alafair's face. She was still wearing her nightgown, but she had washed her face and combed her hair. I had not spoken to her since my confrontation the previous day with Kermit Abelard on the lawn of his house. "Got a minute?" she said.

I made room for her beside me. Both Tripod and Snuggs looked up from their bowls, then resumed eating. "Can I get you a cup of coffee?" I asked.

"I've made a couple of decisions. I don't know how you'll feel about them," she said.

The tenor of her voice was of a kind I never took lightly. Alafair made mistakes, particularly of the heart. She could be emotional and impetuous, but once she made up her mind about a matter of principle, she stayed the course, no matter how much she got hurt.

"I didn't go to the Abelard house because of your relationship with Kermit," I said.

"It doesn't matter. One way or another we're at a juncture, Dave. Until I work my way through a couple of things, I think it's better I move out."

"This is your home, Alafair. It's been your home since I pulled you out of a submerged plane."

There was no question I was using emotional blackmail against her, but I didn't care. I couldn't believe that either the Abelard family or my own ineptitude had brought us to this point. Also, there are times when loss is not acceptable under any circumstances.

"This has less to do with you and Molly than it does me," she said. "I know you want what's good for me, but no amount of reasoning has any influence on you. Yesterday Kermit and I went out in the boat to talk about my novel. His agent is flying in today. Kermit has already sent him a couple of chapters. The agent thinks he can sell my novel as a work in progress. Kermit's agent is with William Morris.

I should be delighted. But I have a serious problem. Know what it is? I think maybe I shouldn't let Kermit's agent represent me. Why? Because maybe you're right and I shouldn't be around the Abelards or Robert Weingart. Maybe I'm taking advantage of my relationship with Kermit to get an introduction to a publisher in New York. Or maybe the opposite is true. Maybe I'm about to throw it all away to satisfy my father's obsession about people who he thinks have too much money and power."

"Listen, forget Weingart and the Abelards. Yesterday there was a man fishing in a pirogue out in the cypress trees in front of the Abelard house. Do you know who that man was?"

"Somebody Robert is trying to help."

"His name is Vidor Perkins. He did time with Weingart in Huntsville Pen. He's the same guy who told me I had an emergency call at the bait shop on Henderson levee."

"Are you sure?"

"You think I'd forget the guy who said there was a fire at our house and that you were in trouble and that I'd better haul my ass up to the levee?"

She leaned forward on the step, clasping her ankles. She was barefoot and the tops of her feet were pale, and there was a solitary mosquito bite on her skin just above her left big toe. Her hair was raven-black with shades of brown, and I could smell the odor of shampoo in it. "Kermit isn't a bad person," she said.

"I have some photos at the office that maybe you should look at. One shows the body of a girl named Bernadette Latiolais. She was an honor student and about to enter the nurses' program at UL. The guy who killed her virtually sawed her head loose from her shoulders. I also have a picture of a

Canadian girl named Fern Michot. She was probably abducted, bound with ligatures, starved, and kept in a state of constant fear, at least according to the coroner. The same person or persons killed both girls. Kermit knew the Latiolais girl but did not indicate that to anyone until we got the information on our own. Robert Weingart was in the Latiolais girl's neighborhood, probably with Herman Stanga. Maybe these guys are innocent of any wrongdoing, but no matter which turn the investigation takes, their names keep coming up again and again."

She watched Snuggs and Tripod eating. I put my hand on her back. Her skin was still warm from sleep.

"He was the only one," she said.

"Pardon?"

"Kermit was the only one."

"You don't have to go into detail if you don't want to."

"He said he'd had other girlfriends, but none like me. He said I was the most talented writer he'd ever met. He said I was a lover and a sister to him. He said our souls knew each other in another time."

"Kermit was probably being honest with you. But maybe he has problems he can't overcome. Sometimes we have to let go of certain kinds of people and let them find their own destiny. But that doesn't mean we have to think less of them or less of ourselves for having known or liked or trusted them."

"I'm having dinner tonight with Kermit and his agent. Robert is going to be there, too."

"I see."

"Do you? Because I don't. I don't see anything. I feel stupid and gullible. I've never felt like this before."

"You didn't do anything wrong, Alf."

"When I was growing up, you weren't home half the time. You were always on a case. It seemed like everybody else's welfare came first. So I found somebody like Kermit. I never loved anybody as much. But he's like you."

"What?"

"Other people come first with him. I let myself see only half of Kermit. The other half belongs to Robert. He let Robert read my manuscript. He didn't see what Robert wrote at the bottom: 'This is wonderful. Package it with a free can of female hygiene spray and it should sell at least a hundred copies.'"

I couldn't think through what she was saying. "You believe I'm no different from Kermit Abelard? You're saying I put other people ahead of my family?"

She picked Tripod up and set him on her lap. She flipped him on his side, his thick tail slapping at the air. Her gaze seemed focused on him, but I'm not sure she saw anything at all. "You want me to move out?" she asked.

I got up from the steps and walked down to the bayou, wishing I could disappear into the fog and not hear the echoes of Alafair's words inside my head. I wished I could step onto the deck of a paddle wheeler and disappear inside the nineteenth century.

As soon as Clete Purcel woke in the refrigerated darkness of his cottage at the motor court, he sensed the absence on the other side of the bed even before he touched the empty depression in the mattress and the body warmth that was already dissipating in the sheets. Then he saw the note. When he pulled the pillow toward him and gathered the note in his palm, he could smell the odor of her hair and her perfume on the pillowcase. He felt the dry constriction of desire in his throat, a thickening in his loins, and the sick vapors of desertion and physical betrayal congealing around his heart. The note read:

Dear C.,
    Don't feel bad or worry about anything. I had fun. I put a couple of aspirins and vitamin B's and a glass of water on the drainboard. You know how to ring a girl's bell. Sweet dreams, big guy. Call me if you feel like it.
            E.

He got into the shower and turned on the water as hot as he could stand it and stayed inside the steam until his skin was red and his pores were running with sweat. Then he turned on the cold water and felt the shock go through him like an icicle. He dried off and put on clean skivvies and slacks and a freshly pressed shirt and tried to eat a half cantaloupe. But his hand trembled on the spoon when he attempted to gouge the meat out of the rind, and he drove the shank of the spoon into his palm with an impact like a nail striking bone and knocked his coffee off the table with his elbow.

He looked at his watch. It was 7:14 A.M. The day had hardly begun, and he felt as though he had already trudged halfway up the path to Golgotha and still had miles to go.

He drove to the office and parked in back. The fog was drifting off the drawbridge at Burke Street, and he could hear car tires crossing the steel-mesh grid and thudding onto the street that led past the old Carmelite convent. He unlocked the back door and sat down behind his desk and did not turn on the lights. He pulled his blue-black, white-handled .38 from his shoulder holster and set it in the middle of the desk blotter, although he could not explain why. He picked it up and felt its cold weight in his grasp and set it down again. He gazed at the round edges of the brass casings that were inserted in the cylinder, the sheen of oil on the steel surfaces of the frame, the knurled tip of the hammer, the fine white bead on the barrel sight. He opened the cylinder and rotated it slowly against the heel of his hand and pushed it solidly back into place, notching a loaded chamber under the firing pin.

He set down the .38 and pushed his swivel chair slightly backward, propping his hands against the desk as though positioning himself for an impending impact, perhaps like an air traveler realizing that something has just gone terribly wrong with the flight he is on. He breathed deeply, his blood oxygenating, his head seeming to swell to the size of a basketball, the veins in his scalp tightening against his skull. He picked up the .38 and curled his thumb over the hammer and pulled it back two clicks to full cock. He thought he heard the machinery on the drawbridge ratcheting disjointedly into place and a boat's horn blowing incessantly inside the fog, as though the elements in his environment had formed a single voice and were saying, *It's time, bub. Aren't you weary of the hassle? Everybody gets to the barn. It's only bad when the trip is prolonged and degrading.*

He laid the .38's frame flatly against his upper chest, the barrel aimed upward at a point midway between his throat and chin. He straightened in his chair, his left hand resting on his thigh, his gaze fixed on a 1910 photograph of the St. Charles streetcar headed down the neutral ground through a tunnel of trees, the wood seats loaded with Mardi Gras revelers.

His phone buzzed. He picked up the receiver slowly and placed it to his ear. He thought he could hear a sound like a metal top spinning on a wood floor.

"Mr. Purcel?" said Hulga, his secretary.

"Yes?"

"I got here a little early. I wasn't sure that was you in there."

"It's me."

"Are you all right?"

"Why wouldn't I be?"

"You sound strange."

The frame and grips of the pistol had grown warm inside his hand. He touched the barrel to the roll of flesh under his chin, as though reminding himself about an unfinished chore.

"Do you want me to get you coffee?" she asked.

"What day is it?"

"Friday."

"Funny how the week slips by. Everything is simpatico here, Hulga."

"Mr. Purcel, I don't want to say the wrong thing, but you don't sound like yourself at all."

"I broke the coffeemaker yesterday. Can you go down the street for some?"

"Maybe I shouldn't do that right now."

"Why not?"

"Oh, Mr. Purcel, what can I say? You're such a good man. You use profane language and have rough ways sometimes, but in your heart you're always a gentleman. I'm proud to work for you."

"I wouldn't say I'm a gentleman. But thank you."

"You were going to dictate a letter to the state

attorney's office yesterday. Can I come in there now and get that out of the way?"

"It can wait."

"Let me come in there or call someone for you. Can I call Mr. Robicheaux?"

"No, you can't."

"Mr. Purcel, I know the signs. My husband died by his own hand. I apologize, but I'm going to call Mr. Robicheaux. It's just something I have to do. Be mad at me all you want. Did you hear me, Mr. Purcel?"

He didn't remember what he said next or even if he said anything. He remembered replacing the receiver in the phone cradle and easing the hammer down on the .38 and removing his finger from inside the trigger guard. Then the .38 was back in its holster, hanging below his left nipple and the top of his rib cage. He opened the door to the main office and made sure Hulga could see him. He smiled at her and put on his sport coat and his porkpie hat. He put on his aviator shades and tucked his shirt into his belt with his thumbs, his grin still in place, like a man on his way to the track or to buy a lady a bouquet. Then he went outside and started his Caddy and drove it down a brick alleyway onto Main Street, with no clue as to his destination, with a dead space like an ice cube in the center of his mind, with no solutions in sight, no mojo, no booze, no weed, to deal with the centipedes, his body dead to the touch except for an enormous weight that seemed to crush down on his shoulders like a cross that could have been fashioned from railroad ties.

Main Street was still partially in shadow, the steel colonnades beaded with moisture, the air smelling of flowers and coffee and hot rolls and the odor of fish spawning in the Teche. He saw a white Mustang

convertible pull to the curb in front of the Gouguenheim bed-and-breakfast. The driver got out and
stepped up on the sidewalk and dropped his cigarette on the concrete, exhaling his last puff into the
breeze. He mashed the cigarette with his foot and
fixed the collar on his pleated white shirt, one that
was unbuttoned halfway down his chest. He wore
black trousers and a gold watch with a black face.
With his neatly clipped dark hair and clear skin,
he reminded Clete of a Spanish matador who had
started to go soft around the edges. Clete turned the
Caddy out of the traffic and parked a short distance
from the Mustang just as Robert Weingart, combing
his hair as he walked, went inside the Gouguenheim.

Clete lounged against the front fender of his
Caddy and watched the customers going in and
out of Victor's cafeteria, then a tug passing on the
bayou, his gaze shifting sideways through the front
door of the bed-and-breakfast, where Weingart was
speaking with a woman at the registration desk. It
was cool and breezy in the shadows, but Clete's skin
was hot, as though he had experienced a severe sunburn and the heat was radiating through his clothes.
He could also feel a pressure band threading itself
across the side of his head. When he adjusted his
hat, hoping that somehow the pressure would go
away, he felt the veins in his scalp tighten like pieces
of kite twine.

The Gouguenheim was a restored nineteenth-
century building with iron-scrolled balconies, tall
windows, ventilated storm shutters, high ceilings,
wood-bladed fans, glowing hardwood floors, and
plaster walls painted with pastel colors that, along
with the potted palms inside the entranceway,
gave the visitor the sensation that he was stepping inside a historical artwork. The view in the

morning from the balconies was not unlike looking out over the rooftops and canopy of trees in a Caribbean city at the end of the colonial era. Clete bit on a thumbnail and studied Robert Weingart's back. Why did the Robert Weingarts of the world always manage to find and appropriate the last good places? Sometimes it took a while, but sooner or later they emerged from the weeds and slithered their way up the trunk of a tree heavy with fruit or, at the least, more prosaically, left fecal prints on everything they touched. Clete folded his arms across his chest, opening and closing his hands, breathing through his mouth, a sodden crescent of perspiration forming inside his porkpie hat. He straightened his back and lowered his hands to his sides when Weingart walked out from the building. "How's your swizzle stick hanging, Bob?" he said.

"Patrolling the sidewalks today, are we?" Weingart said.

"That's why I'm called the mayor of Main Street. You checking in to the Gouguenheim?"

"Not me. The agent who'll probably be representing Mr. Robicheaux's daughter will be staying there. Of course, you're familiar with the William Morris Agency, aren't you?"

"They sell insurance?"

"Oh, that's very good. Would you like to join us for dinner? I understand you're a wonderful raconteur. I'm sure everyone would be fascinated with the tales you could relate. Industrial espionage, CIA intrigue, that sort of thing."

Clete folded his arms again and grinned and pushed his aviator shades up on the bridge of his nose with one finger. "I dig your wheels, Bob. You don't mind if I call you Bob, do you?"

"It's Robert. But call me whatever you wish."

"No, you're right. Bob is too commonplace. What about Roberto or Ro-bear, the way the French say it? No, that's too foreign. How about the Bobster? Kind of like a name a welterweight might have. You duck, you weave, you bob, you're slick as grease, you pop out their lights before they know what hit them. You're the Bobster."

"To be honest, Mr. Purcel, I don't think you have many arrows in your quiver."

"Remember that nineteen-year-old waitress at Ruby Tuesday you knocked up? The one you told to get an abortion? Did that Mustang fire up her hormones? I wish I could have a car like that and get my ashes hauled by teenage girls with ninth-grade educations. You couldn't bum the price of a box of rubbers off her?"

"Just stay on your Jenny Craig diet and keep saying your morning prayers, and you can drive a car like mine. But that might produce conflict for you. I suspect you're a nice soft hump for Mr. Robicheaux. I imagine in a time of AIDS, a few extra pounds can give comfort on a couple of levels."

Clete stuck a cigarette in his mouth but did not light it. He scratched at a mosquito bite high up on his arm, examining the flesh around the bite while he did it. "Good try, bub, but I checked you out. Over in Huntsville, you were lots of things, but straight wasn't one of them. The warden said you chugged pug for every swinging dick on the yard. That brings up a question I've always had. Is it true the Midnight Special originally meant a late-night freight train up the ass, maybe with a three-hundred-pound black guy driving the locomotive?"

"Funny man," Weingart said. "But answer me

this, Mr. Purcel. Alafair's breakthrough in New York will probably come about because of her friendship with me and Kermit. How does it feel to be stuck in a place like this? Why is it she's with us and not you?"

Clete watched silently as Weingart started his car and drove away. Then Clete got into his Caddy and followed him around the block and all the way down to the old brick post office and the plantation house known as The Shadows and finally back onto Main Street, where Weingart parked his vehicle and went into Lagniappe Too and sat down behind the picture-glass window and ordered breakfast.

I GOT THE call from Hulga Volkmann two minutes after I had picked up my mail and sat down behind my desk. "He told me not to call you, Mr. Robicheaux, but I'm doing it anyway, whether you or he like it or not," she said. "He's under great stress, and I think he's not entirely rational. He's also drinking too much. Now this Mr. Blanchet is calling. He's not a nice man and Mr. Purcel does not need to put up with that kind of abusive behavior at a time like this."

"Sorry, I'm not tracking the message here."

"I think Mr. Purcel is having a nervous breakdown. Mr. Layton Blanchet just called and accused Mr. Purcel of violating his confidence and hurting his family. He also said some very unpleasant things of a personal nature to me. He told me to write all this down and to read it back to him and then give it to Mr. Purcel, as though voice mail had not been invented."

"How does this relate to your concerns about Clete this morning?"

"I just told you, Mr. Robicheaux. Mr. Purcel left

the office in his automobile and then parked down the street from where this convict author had parked his little white convertible."

"No, you did not tell me about Robert Weingart. You were talking about Layton Blanchet."

"I already dealt with Mr. Blanchet. If I quote what I said to him, I would be taking license with you and acting disrespectfully. My concern is Mr. Purcel."

"What did you tell Blanchet, Miss Hulga?"

"I told him I would not be writing down any of his ugly remarks or allow them to be recorded on Mr. Purcel's phone. I also told him we do not welcome his kind of clientele in our office. I told him he was ill-mannered and ill-bred and unappreciative of Mr. Purcel, who works hard on behalf of his clients." She paused, as if energizing herself to cross the finish line. "I told him he was a self-important idiot and he could kiss my bottom."

"I see. And where is Clete now?"

"That's what I have been trying to tell you. He followed that criminal author down the street to Lagniappe Too and went inside. He doesn't like this man and considers him a degenerate who preys on uneducated young women. I don't think this is a matter of oil and water. It's more like one of gasoline and matches. Mr. Robicheaux, will you please stop this good-hearted man from doing more injury to himself?"

You could do worse than have a person like Hulga Volkmann on your side, I told myself.

CLETE SAT DOWN at one of the checker-cloth-covered tables in the corner of the restaurant, with a view of the intersection and the dark structural mass of The Shadows looming inside acres of live oaks bordered by a piked fence and walls of bamboo. Thirty feet away, Robert Weingart was buttering a roll and sip ping his coffee. When Weingart's phone rang, he examined the caller ID, then closed the phone without taking the call. He turned in his chair and glanced at Clete and seemed to laugh under his breath before sipping from his coffee again. He gazed lazily out the window at the flow of traffic on Main Street.

Clete gave his order to the waitress. "Coffee, orange juice, a breakfast steak, two fried eggs on top, grits, no butter, please, hash browns, and biscuits, with a bowl of milk gravy on the side."

"No butter," she said, making a special note.

"Yeah, I got hypertension and have to watch it."

"Anything else, Mr. Clete?"

He nodded toward Weingart's table. "Put Mr. Weingart's breakfast on my bill. He might get called away and not have time to go to the cash register. Same with me, Miss Linda. Let me pay you in advance. If I have to leave, just box up my food and put it in the refrigerator."

"If that's what you like," she said, clearly trying not to show any expression.

Clete handed her two twenty-dollar bills.

"That's too much," she said.

"Not really," he said. "Fine day, isn't it? I love coming here."

He sat erect in his chair and watched the back of Weingart's head and neck. Clete picked up his fork and flipped it over and over between his thumb and forefinger on his napkin. He drank his water glass empty and finished his coffee and orange juice and tapped the soles of his loafers up and down on the floor. He fitted his hands inside his coat sleeves and ran his palms up and down his forearms. He fished a piece of ice out of the bottom of his water glass with a spoon and put it in his mouth and sucked loudly on it. Weingart yawned and drew doodles on the cloth napkin with his ballpoint. Then he got up from his table and went down a narrow hallway to the men's room in back.

As Clete followed, he tried to convince himself that he had no plan in mind for the next few minutes. In reality, he probably did not, in the same way that an electric storm blowing out of the Gulf does not have a plan when it makes landfall. But as he walked down the old brick passageway toward the restroom, he was already reaching for the polyethylene gloves that he carried as a matter of course in his coat pocket.

Clete turned the handle on the men's room door, but the door was bolted. "Bob, got a minute?" he said.

He heard water running, then the faucet squeaking as someone turned it off. "Bob, is that you?" Clete said.

"What do you want?" Weingart said.

"Just a word or two."

Weingart slipped the bolt. When Clete opened the door, Weingart had gone back to examining his face in the mirror, tilting his nose up, pulling a hair from a nostril, touching the flesh along his jaw. "Say whatever it is and close the door when you leave, please."

"I talked with the Vietnamese girl who I think you're planning to seduce with roofies. I didn't make much headway, though. Know why that is? She thinks you're a decent person and you deserve a chance to defend yourself. That creates a quandary for us, Bobster. Both you and I know you're not a decent person, that you're mean to the bone and you get off on using people, particularly when it comes to unlimbering your big boy."

Weingart took out his pocket comb and began slicking back the hair on the sides of his head, his gaze never leaving his reflection. "Heard of Lexis-Nexis?" he said.

"What about it?" Clete asked.

"I did a little research on you." Weingart wet his comb and tapped the excess water off on the rim of the sink, his eyes shifting in the mirror to Clete's reflection. The skin at the corner of his mouth wrinkled with his smile. "When you were a cop in New Orleans, you were on a pad for the Giacano family. You popped a federal witness, a guy by the name of Starkweather. You were either taking juice from pimps or freebies from their whores. You had to hide out in Central America. You did scut work in Vegas and Reno for Sally Dio. You're lecturing me about morality?"

Weingart drew his comb through the top of his hair, stooping slightly to examine a thinning spot. Then he scraped a piece of mucus loose from inside one nostril, put away his comb, and wiped his hands clean on a paper towel. "Something you want to say, Mr. Purcel?"

"Not really, Bob."

"Because you don't look too well. A bit blotchy, in fact. Have a bad night? You smell like you might have stayed late at the grog shop. Funny how the booze gets in your system and poisons your blood and eats your organs and shrivels up your equipment and leaves you flaming in the morning, usually when your boy or your milk cow of the moment isn't handy—"

Clete wasn't sure anymore what Weingart was saying. He knew that Weingart was speaking because his mouth kept opening and closing; he knew that Weingart was fully engaged in a rehearsed analytical dissection of Clete's life, each noun and adjective wrapped with razor wire. He knew that

Weingart's face was filled with a self-satisfied confidence and an imperious glow, like a flesh-colored helium balloon floating above all the rules of mortality. Weingart's sense of invulnerability was characteristic of most psychopaths. Clete had helped convict a killer who had to be wakened from a sound sleep on the afternoon of his execution. Clete became convinced that the condemned man's lack of fear was not an indicator of courage but instead his belief that the universe could not continue without his being at the center of it. The only difference between Weingart and other sociopaths was his level of intelligence and his ability to wound with words and talk without pause, dipping into a dark well of invective that seemed inexhaustible.

Except, try as he might, Clete could not hear what the man was saying. If he heard any sound at all, it was that of the polyethylene gloves he was snapping tight on his hands and that Weingart did not seem to take notice of.

A bucket of cleaning materials sat under the lavatory. It contained scrub brushes, a container of Ajax, a spray can of Lysol, a roll of paper towels, grimed rags, a plumber's helper, and Brillo pads that were congealed with rust and a bluish detergent that had dried into glue. Clete leaned over and dipped his hand into the bucket, clanking various objects around inside until he found the things he was looking for. When he raised up, Weingart was still talking.

"You've got a serious case of logorrhea, Bobster. We need to do something about that," Clete said. "Easy now, hold still. No point in struggling. Come on, you were in Huntsville, Bob. I bet you pulled a train your first night down in the bridal suite. Hey, thatta boy."

Clete had fastened his left hand under Weingart's chin, sinking his fingers deep into the man's throat, pinning him against the wall. Weingart's jaw dropped, and his words gurgled and died on the back of his tongue. Then Clete shoved two Brillo pads into Weingart's mouth, packing them tight with the heel of his hand. "Okay, Bobster, time to freshen up," he said. "When you collect your thoughts, we'll talk a little more."

Clete plunged Weingart's head into the toilet bowl, pushing the flusher at the same time, plugging the hole at the bottom with the crown of his head. Weingart was on his knees, trying to find purchase on the bowl's rim with his hands, the water swelling up past his neck. The more he fought, the harder Clete pressed him down into the bowl, until the water was sloshing on the floor.

Then Clete pulled him up, the Brillo pads still packed in Weingart's mouth, his face and hair streaming. "You don't get near the Vietnamese girl again, right, Bob?" Clete said. "You lock a stainless-steel codpiece on your flopper, and you leave young girls in this parish alone. Nod if you understand. No? Okay, let's tidy up a little more."

Clete drove Weingart's head into the bowl again, this time pressing it down with both arms, the water heaving over the sides onto the floor, Weingart's legs thrashing. Ten seconds passed, then twenty, then thirty. The water kept curtaining over the toilet rim, an inch backing up against the walls, Clete's loafers squishing in it.

Clete ripped Weingart's head into the air just as I came through the door. "Hey, Streak, what's the haps?" Clete said. "I was just talking to Bob about the advantages of personal restraint. I think he was just coming around to our perspective on that. Can you hand me a couple of paper towels?"

CHAPTER 10

I PUT DOWN THE lid on the toilet and picked up Robert Weingart and set him on top of it. One of the Brillo pads had already fallen from his mouth; I lifted the second one gently from behind his teeth and dropped it in the wastebasket, then wiped his face with a handful of crumpled paper towels and placed a couple of dry towels in his hand. "Tilt your head back," I said.

He raised his eyes to mine, then cleared his throat and spat into one of the towels. "You saw what he did," he said.

"No, I'm not sure what happened here," I replied. "It looks like a personal dispute that got out of control, maybe."

Weingart propped his hands on his knees, his gaze still fastened on me, his pupils dilated. He resembled a man who had looked into a great darkness and could not readjust to light. "He almost drowned me."

"If you like, you can file charges, Mr. Weingart," I said. "I'll contact the police reporter at *The Daily Iberian* and give him the details about what happened here. I'll also pass on what appears to be the issue between you and Mr. Purcel. If I understand correctly, Mr. Purcel believes you've been preying on some teenage waitresses in New Iberia. I'll call *The Daily Advertiser* in Lafayette and the Associated Press in New Orleans to get maximum coverage for your situation. Normally, media would blow off a minor beef like this, but a story about a writer with your reputation would probably earn their immediate attention."

"What do you say, Bobster? Don't just sit there picking steel wool off your tongue. Show a little respect," Clete said, slapping him on the side of the head.

"Mr. Purcel, I want you to wait outside on the curb," I said.

Clete gave me a look.

"*Out,*" I said.

Clete pulled the polyethylene gloves off his hands and threw them in the waste can. He stuck a cigarette in his mouth, lit it, and blew the smoke in Weingart's face. "The Abelard family isn't going to be able to help you. In my opinion, every guy like you I take off the board is a star in my crown. Know that expression about the shit hitting the fan? Your journey through the fan just started. You mentioned Sally Dio. Use your LexisNexis to find out what happened to Sal and his fellow gumballs and the plane they were flying on in western Montana. You ever see pulled pork raked out of a ponderosa tree?"

I wanted to punch Clete in the side of the head.

Ten minutes later we were outside on the sidewalk, Clete with his boxed-up breakfast tucked under his arm, a fresh unlit cigarette hanging from his mouth. I pulled it out and threw it in the street. "How much trouble can you get into in one day?" I asked.

"Who told you I was here?"

"Who cares? It doesn't matter where you go. Five minutes after you arrive, plaster is falling out of the ceiling. You're like a train trying to drive down a dirt road."

"Weingart deserves a lot worse than he got."

"That's not for you to decide."

We were in the shadow of the building. People were passing us on the sidewalk, glancing away when they heard the tenor of our voices. "I got to go," he said.

"Where?"

"To check on a lady I was with."

"You mean last night?"

"Maybe."

"Who was she?"

"Her name escapes me."

"You were still drunk this morning. Weingart could have died of a coronary. How long was his head under water?"

"Her name is Emma Poche," he said. "I got it on with her."

"Are you out of your mind?"

"What's wrong with Emma?"

"Do I have to tell you? You're not interested in any woman who doesn't have biker tats or a history at the methadone clinic."

"She has a butterfly on her butt. That's the only one. I think it's cute."

"Cute?" I repeated.

"Lighten up, Streak. It's only rock and roll." His eyes were still lit with an alcoholic glaze, his throat nicked in two places by his razor, his cheeks bladed with color.

I gave it up, in the way you give up something with such an enormous sense of sadness rushing through you that it leaves no room for any other emotion. "What are we going to do, Cletus?"

"About what?"

"You."

"We all end up in the same place. Some sooner than others. What the hell. We're both standing on third base," he said.

I wanted to say something else, but I couldn't find the words. I left him there and walked down the street and got in my cruiser and returned to the office, an image in my mind I couldn't shake: that of a flag being lifted from a coffin and folded into a military tuck by a white-gloved, full-dress marine, his scalped head and hollow eyes as stark as bone. Would Clete Purcel's life focus into that one bright brassy point of light and then disappear with the firing of blank cartridges into the wind? Was this ultimately the choice we had made for both of us?

KERMIT ABELARD AND Robert Weingart and Kermit's agent, Oliver Fremont, picked up Alafair in a white stretch limo, and all of them headed up the St. Martinville highway toward Breaux Bridge and the Café des Amis. Alafair wore a simple black dress and black sandals and silver earrings, and sat on the rolled leather seat close to the door, while Kermit poured drinks out of a cocktail shaker. Oliver Fremont had a degree in publishing from Hofstra University yet spoke with an accent that was vaguely British. He was blond and tall and handsome, and he had perfect manners, but it was his accent, or rather his candor about it, that became for Alafair his most engaging quality.

"Did you live in England?" she asked.

"I've traveled there some, but no, I never lived there," he replied.

"I see," she said.

"You're wondering about my accent?"

"I thought you might have gone to school in the UK."

"It's an affectation, I'm afraid. When the upper echelons in publishing have a few drinks, they start sounding like George Plimpton or William and

James Buckley. My father sold shoes in Great Neck. He'd be a little amused by me, I think."

Alafair looked at his profile and the evening light marbling on his skin. He gazed out the tinted window at the oak trees and the sugarcane fields sweeping past. "This is a grand area, isn't it? I can see why you write with such fondness of it. I love the chapters Kermit sent me. I can't wait to read more," he said.

"Her father is a sheriff's detective," Robert Weingart said. "I think he gives her a lot of material. It's pretty feisty stuff, if you ask me."

"No, my father's experience doesn't have much to do with what I write," Alafair said.

Weingart was on his third mint julep. He wore gray slacks and tassel loafers and a blue-and-white-striped shirt with white French cuffs and a rolled white collar; his plum-colored tie had a gold pin in it. There were abrasions around his temples that disappeared like orange rust into his hairline. When he spoke, his mouth seemed to keep twisting into a bow, as though it were cut or bruised inside.

"I understand you're writing a sequel to *The Green Cage*," Oliver Fremont said to Weingart. "That must be a hard act to follow. I thought *The Green Cage* was a stupendous accomplishment, better than *Soul on Ice*, maybe better than *On the Yard* by Malcolm Braly. Did you ever read Malcolm? He was a great talent."

"Why do you compare my work to prison writing only?"

"Pardon?"

"You ever see *Straight Time*? Dustin Hoffman, Gary Busey, Harry Dean Stanton. Box-office bomb. Edward Bunker wrote the novel it was based on. I knew him inside. Good writer, good story, commercial bomb. Why? All prison stories are alike. They're about professional losers, and if there's any sin in this country, it's losing. *The Green Cage* deals with the entirety of the system, neoliberalism and the culture that creates criminality. It deals with the origins of the existential hero. It's not an account about jails. If it has any antecedent, it's *Shane,* not some crap dictated into a recording machine by an Oakland shine who doesn't know the difference between Karl and Groucho Marx."

"I think Oliver was saying your book goes way beyond categorical limits, Rob. That's why it's such a great accomplishment," Kermit said.

"Why don't we ask Alafair?" Weingart said. "I can't believe at some point you haven't been influenced by your father and his colleagues. Do they ever discuss their recreational activities? Do you know that most cops will admit, usually when they're sloshed, that they would have ended up stacking time if they hadn't gotten badges?"

"No, I didn't know that," Alafair said.

Weingart drank from his julep glass, his eyes never leaving hers. "Daddy doesn't talk about that at the dinner table?" he said.

"Rob, Alafair isn't responsible for any disagreements Mr. Robicheaux might have had with others," Kermit said.

"I probably am," Alafair said. "My father is a fine man and often comes home exhausted from dealing with people who belong in iron boxes that should be sunk in the ocean. Sometimes I lose sight of that fact and only add to his burden. I've done this on many occasions."

"Oh, wilderness enow," Weingart said. "I suspect the world of chick lit will wet its pants over sentiment like that. I often thought the best title for one of those books was *The Cave,* a title that suggests an infinitely receding vagina."

"I'd like to see the rest of your manuscript," Fremont said.

"That's very kind of you," Alafair said.

"Kermit, would you either give me a refill or pass me the bloody shaker so I can do it myself?" Weingart said.

"Sorry, Rob," Kermit said, tilting the cocktail shaker over Weingart's glass. "Rob took the speedboat out by himself today and ran through a tree limb. Luckily, he wasn't hurt more seriously."

"I don't think anyone is interested in my boating misadventure. Unless Alafair would like to use it in her novel-in-progress. Otherwise, I'd appreciate the conversation being shifted off of me," Weingart said.

Kermit folded his hands and gazed at the sunset and at the wind blowing on the sugarcane fields, obviously avoiding eye contact with Weingart. By the time the limo reached the restaurant in Breaux Bridge, Weingart's resentment seemed to have hardened into silent detachment. After they ordered, he stared out the window at the elevated sidewalks and old brick buildings and wood colonnades on the main street and the rusted iron bridge that spanned Bayou Teche. He broke a breadstick and bit down on it, then winced and touched his lip.

"Hurt yourself?" Oliver Fremont asked.

"I have an impacted tooth."

"Those are painful," Fremont said.

"Why are we here?" Weingart said, addressing himself to no one in particular.

"We're here because they serve fine food. Let's enjoy ourselves, Robert," Kermit said.

"Thanks for correcting me, Kermit. Alafair, did

you know that Kermit let me read your manuscript?" Weingart said.

"Yes, I became aware of that when I saw the note you wrote on the last page," Alafair replied.

"What note?" Kermit said.

"Evidently you didn't see it," Alafair said. "Why don't you ask Robert what he had to say?"

A waitress was pouring wine into their glasses. Outside the French doors, the sky was purple, the streets thick with shadow. The lights on the drawbridge had just come on. "Robert, what did you say about Alafair's manuscript?" Kermit asked.

Weingart lifted his eyes to the stamped ceiling of the restaurant, as though searching for a profound meaning inside the design. "No, it escapes me. Do you remember, Alafair? I hope you found it helpful."

"I believe you said it might sell a hundred copies if it was packaged with a hygiene promotion."

"No, I think I said 'female hygiene.'"

Kermit Abelard looked straight ahead, his gaze focused on the other diners, the white-aproned waiters and waitresses working their way between the tables. "I think Robert probably meant that as an indictment of the industry, not your book," he said. "Isn't that true, Rob?"

"I'm afraid I'm clueless. I can't even remember the story line at this point," he said. "Can you give me a nudge, Alafair? Something about first love, teenage girls being kissed on the mouth under the trees, Daddy hovering in the background. Sound familiar? It was tingly stuff through and through."

"That's not the story at all," Kermit said.

Weingart leaned forward on the tablecloth, his cheeks sunken, as though he had drawn all the spittle out of his mouth. "Did you tell Alafair what you and I were doing before you gave me the manuscript? In the boathouse? Because you couldn't wait to go inside?"

"I think you carry a great injury in your soul, Robert. And no matter what you do or say, I forgive you for it," Kermit said.

"Oh, good try. I think I now know where Alafair gets the unctuous goo she uses in her dialogue," Weingart said. "You *forgive* me? Oh, that's wonderful."

"You shouldn't have written that remark on her manuscript," Kermit said.

"I didn't just write the remark, I *said* it to you, Kermit. To your face, two feet from your ear. Tell me I didn't or that you didn't hear me. The kitty cat got your tongue?"

"Why are you acting like this?"

"Because you're just so *you*, Kermit." Weingart drank from his wineglass and smiled at the waitress as she placed his food in front of him. "My, red snapper and a stuffed potato. Do you mind if I start now? It's not very good if it's cold. Alafair looks a little conflicted. What does your father call you? It's Alf, isn't it? Talk with Alf, Kermit." Weingart inserted a forkful of potato and sour cream and parsley and bacon bits in his mouth.

Alafair's gaze was fixed on the French doors and the sunset on the bayou. She waited for Kermit to speak again, to say something in his own defense if not hers, to be more than the thing she feared he was. But he remained silent. When she glanced sideways at him, his hands were limp on the table, his eyes lowered, his expression a study in gray wax. The most incongruous aspect of his demeanor was the muscular configuration of his torso, his square, blunt-tipped workingman's hands, the cut of his jaw, the dimple in his chin, all of the physical elements she associated with his youthful masculine vigor, all of it now insignificant in contrast to the mantle of cowardice that Robert Weingart seemed to have draped on his shoulders.

"Mr. Fremont—" she began.

"It's Oliver," he said.

"I wouldn't have met you without an introduction from Kermit," she said. "Unlike many people who come to your agency, I made only a partial submission. I'm flattered by your comments about my work, but I think I'm getting special treatment. I think I'll feel more comfortable about my submission if you can look at the finished manuscript and then tell me if you think it's publishable."

Fremont leaned back in his chair, a bead of light in one eye. He massaged his temple with two fingers. "Not too many writers tell me that," he said.

"It seems like a reasonable point of view," she said.

"Not in my world."

Weingart had been snapping his fingers at the waitress for more tartar sauce. "Sorry, I didn't catch that. Telling the in-house secrets, are we?"

"You're a special kind of fellow, Robert," Oliver Fremont said.

"Care to elaborate on that?"

"Not really. Some writers become the stuff of legends for different reasons. Harold Robbins's agent used to lock him in a cottage at the Beverly Hills Hotel and not feed him until he shoved four pages of finished manuscript under the door. Supposedly Louis Mayer had Hemingway kicked off the MGM lot. Hart Crane threw his typewriter through a glass window into Dorothy Parker's yard. But I think you might become one of those guys for whom the rest of us are only a footnote."

"One of which guys?"

"Special guys. Legends. Guys people talk about at cocktail parties for many years. Their legends take on a life of their own and grow over the years. Eventually the legends become far more interesting than their work. Finally nobody remembers anything except the legend. The writer becomes something like a scarecrow in an empty field."

Weingart had stopped eating. "Let me explain what 'special' is and why I'm not 'special.' Special people need special handling. I'm not an aberration or a curiosity. I've read more books than most university Ph.D.'s. I'm more intelligent than they are, more knowledgeable of the real world, more erudite in front of their students than they are. In short, I'm a civilized man and not 'special,' my friend. See, 'special' is for the guys who stay in twenty-three-hour lockdown and get two showers a week if they're lucky. 'Special' is for the guys who have to brush their teeth with their finger because they melt the handles of their toothbrushes over a Bic lighter and mold them into shanks. I'm on a first-name basis with a few cell-house acquaintances that are in the 'special' category. If you like, I can introduce you to them. Then you'll be in possession of some hands-on knowledge about 'special' guys, and you can impress your friends with it. Want me to arrange a meeting or two before you leave for New York? These guys will love your accent."

Alafair got up from the table and used the telephone at the bar to call a cab. Then she went outside and waited by the curb without returning to the table. It was dark now, and the lights on the iron drawbridge over the Teche were iridescent with humidity. She looked back over her shoulder. She had thought Kermit Abelard might follow her out of the restaurant. Instead, he was arguing with Weingart at the table. No, "arguing" was the wrong term, she thought. When people argued, they spoke in heat, leaning forward with wrinkled brows, their throats corded, the flesh around their mouths bloodless. But Kermit kept pausing to allow Weingart to speak, lowering his long eyelashes, his face colored by embarrassment rather than passion. Oliver Fremont rose from his chair, his gaze fixed on Alafair, and walked between the tables and out the French doors, speaking to neither Kermit nor Weingart.

"Just a thought or two for you to keep in mind, Ms. Robicheaux," he said. "When I said I loved your work in progress, I meant it. I think your talent is enormous. Do whatever you wish about submission. Finish the manuscript or send it along in chunks. But send it to me, understand? No one else. I want to be your agent, and it's not because you're friends with Kermit. I think you're going to be hugely successful."

"Thank you."

"What I've told you is not a compliment, it's a fact. Second, that guy Weingart is a world-class jerk nobody in the industry takes seriously. He's an embarrassment to his publisher and a self-important moron who will probably crash and burn on a live TV show when he's drunk or insulting a woman or making racist remarks. But it's going to happen, and when it does, his phone calls won't be answered and his publishing contracts will disappear. Because he's a megalomaniac, he'll never figure out what brought about his downfall, and he'll spend the rest of his life blaming everyone else. You got all that?"

"I think so," she replied.

"You want me to escort you home?"

"No, I'm fine. You're a nice man."

"That looks like your cab," he said. After the cab pulled to the curb, he opened the back door for her and closed it after she was inside. The window was open. He leaned down toward it. "You're going to have a great career. Weingart couldn't shine your shoes, and frankly, neither could Kermit."

But it wasn't over. Kermit Abelard virtually plunged out onto the sidewalk, both hands held up to stop the cabdriver. He grabbed the back door, leaning inside. "Don't leave like this," he said.

"Like what?" she asked.

"Mad, hurt, upset, whatever you want to call it."

"I'm none of those things, Kermit. I made a mistake. It's on me, not you. It's not even on Robert in there. So now I'm going home."

"What mistake?"

"About who you are. You're somebody else. Or maybe you have two or three people living inside you."

"If I'm not the person you thought I was, then I'd appreciate your telling me who I am."

"I'm not sure. But I won't be there to find out, either. You were the only one, and I want you to remember that as long as you live."

"Only one what? I don't know what you mean. You mean sexually? What are you talking about?"

"You'll figure it out. But when you do, remember I just spoke of you in the past tense. That will never change. Good-bye, Kermit," she said.

As she sat back in the seat and the cab pulled away, she could see the wind riffling the leaves on the trees along the bayou. The reflection of the lights from the drawbridge on the leaves and the electric glitter they created made her think of thousands of green butterflies fluttering inside a dark bowl.

On Sunday morning I woke before dawn. I'd had a peculiar dream, one that was actually about a dream. Many years ago on a Christmas Eve, in a Southeast Asian country, I had been asleep on top of a poncho liner, under a parked six-by. Somewhere out there beyond the elephant grass and the rice paddies and the hills that had been chemically defoliated or burned by napalm, Bedcheck Charlie was prowling through the darkness in black pajamas and a conical straw hat and sandals fashioned from the rubber strips he had sawed out of a truck tire. In his hands was the blooker he had taken off the body of a dead United States soldier who had been in my platoon. The launch tube was painted with gold and black tiger stripes. Every hour or so during the night, Bedcheck Charlie lobbed a round in our direction. Often it exploded in the paddy, sending up a geyser of water and mud and metal fragments that rained back down harmlessly. Or if it landed in the elephant grass, it blew a mixed smell of burned explosive and torn sod and root systems into the breeze, a combination that wasn't altogether unpleasant. Once, Bedcheck Charlie got lucky and nailed the shit barrels in a latrine. But Bedcheck Charlie was a tactician, not a strategist. When he was on the job, you crosshatched your molars and slept with a frown, as though a fly were walking across your brow, waiting for the next plunking sound of a grenade leaving the launch tube. At dawn, you started the new day as though you had spent the night humping a sixty-pound pack.

Except on this particular Christmas Eve, for whatever reason, Bedcheck Charlie gave it a rest. I fell into a deep sleep and dreamed it was Christmas in New Iberia. I dreamed I was a child and in my bed, and through the window I could see the pecan and oak trees in the yard and the frost on our grass and, through the branches of the trees, the Star of Bethlehem burning brightly against an ink-black sky. It was a wonderful dream, and I wanted to hold on to it and wake to a Christmas morning that was shining with dew and filled with all the joy of the season.

Except when I awoke under the six-by, I was not looking at the Star of Bethlehem. On the far side of the rice paddy, a pistol or trip flare had popped high in the air and was floating down to the earth, trailing strings of smoke, its phosphorescent glow swinging back and forth, illuminating the landscape with the trembling white-and-black severity of a filmstrip that has gone off track inside the projector. Then three other flares popped in succession right after the first one. On the slope of a low hill that had traded hands a half-dozen times, a piece of worthless defoliated real estate the marines later named Luke the Gook's Slop Chute, thirteen grunts returning from an ambush had been caught in a burned-out area where the tree trunks looked like skeletal fingers protruding from the ash. The column froze, and each man in it tried to transform himself into a stick. But their disguise was to no avail. VC sappers were in the elephant grass, and their automatic-weapons fire turned the column into a bloody mist.

Now, on a Sunday morning in the spring of 2009, I woke from a dream about a dream in a small sugarcane town on Bayou Teche, the slope behind the house white with ground fog, the overhang of the trees dripping on the tin roof. Freud said our dreams are manifestations of our hopes and fears. Did my dream represent a desire to return to the childlike innocence of the Cajun world in which I was born? Or did it indicate a warning from the unconscious, a telegram from the id telling me to beware of someone whose behavior I had been too casual about?

I looked through the window and saw a large man coming around the side of the house, his suit streaked with moisture from our camellia bushes, his eyes as cavernous as inkwells, his jaw crooked with indignation.

Molly was still sound asleep, the sheet molded by her hip. I slipped on my khakis and loafers and unlocked the back door and went outside. The man in the suit stood deep in the shadow of the house, opening and closing his fists, oblivious to the moisture leaking from the rain gutter on his head and shoulders. "You want to tell me what you're doing in my yard at six on Sunday morning?" I said.

"I need some information, and I need it now. And I don't want any mouth off you about it, either," he said.

"How about putting your transmission into neutral, Layton?"

"Where's Clete Purcel?"

"How would I know?"

"You're his buddy. You're the one who recommended him to me."

"No, I didn't."

"Don't lie."

"You're not going to talk to me like that."

"I'm not, huh? You got some damn nerve. I'm an inch from flattening you on your butt."

I propped my hands on my hips and looked at Tripod's hutch and at the trees in the fog and at an empty rowboat floating down the bayou, its bow turning slowly in the current. "You're a more intelligent man than this. Regardless, it's time for you to go."

For just a second, he seemed to take heed of my words. "I can't find my wife. She didn't come home last night. But I found this in her dresser." He pulled a business card from his shirt pocket. "It's Clete Purcel's. There's a phone number on the back. The phone number belongs to the Hotel Monteleone in New Orleans. How did Purcel's business card get in my wife's dresser drawer?"

"I don't know."

He threw the card at my chest. "I'll tell you how. While I was paying him to follow her around, he was sleeping with her. That pile of offal was in the sack with my wife."

"You're dead wrong. Now get out of here."

"I've got the goods on your friend, Robicheaux, and maybe you, too. I've got sources inside your department. They say Purcel is being investigated for the killing of that black pimp. The word is maybe you're not above suspicion, either. Maybe the two of y'all capped the pimp together because he was about to send Purcel to Angola."

I heard the bedroom window slide open. "What's the trouble, Dave?" Molly said.

"It's Layton Blanchet. He's about to leave. Right, Layton?" I said.

"This doesn't concern you. Close the window," he said to Molly. He faced me, his feet spread slightly, his height and breadth and the corded tension in his body not to be taken lightly. "Where is Purcel? I'm not going to ask you again."

Out of the corner of my eye, I saw Molly's face leave the window, then I heard the window close and the shade go down on it.

"I'm going inside now. I'll call either a cab or a

cruiser for you. Tell me which you prefer," I said.

"You were a guest in my home. Carolyn fixed supper for you. What kind of people are you?"

"Who are you talking about?"

"You. All of you."

His face was dilated, his breath rank, an odor like testosterone or dried sweat wafting off his body. His fists looked like big rocks at his sides.

I said, "I think you need help, partner. Clete hasn't harmed you, and neither have I. I'll drive you home myself. Maybe your wife will be there when you get back. Everybody has marital problems, but they pass. How about we let go of all this backyard bebop?"

Molly opened the screen door and came out on the steps, her robe cinched around her hips, her red hair hanging in her eyes. Layton turned and stared at her as though he had forgotten who she was or why she had come outside. She stepped into the yard, pushing her hair back with her fingers. "Listen to my husband, Mr. Blanchet," she said. "He's a truthful man, and he has nothing but good intentions toward you. You can leave or you can stay and have coffee with us, but you're not going to come here and threaten people. *That* ends right now."

He looked at her a long time, a behemoth of a man in a stained three-thousand-dollar suit, the shame of the cuckold as visible on his face as antlers painted on canvas in medieval portraiture. "Thank you," he said.

"Do you want to come in?"

"No," he replied. "No, I'm sorry for coming here like this. I'm sorry for many things." He bent over and picked up Clete's business card from the apron of bare ground around Tripod's hutch. He stared at it blankly, then inserted it in his shirt pocket and walked down our driveway to his vehicle, brushing against the side of my pickup, oblivious to the muddy smear it left on his clothes. Molly continued to gaze down the driveway as Layton drove away. "You once quoted a convict about the relativity of doing time," she said.

"His name was Dock Railroad. He was an old-time Pete man who did scores for Didoni Giacano. Clete and I caught him burning a safe in the back of Nig Rosewater's bail bond agency. Dock was already a four-time loser. Clete offered him a cigarette and said, 'Sorry about this, Dock. You're probably going away on the bitch.' Dock said, 'Don't worry about it, Purcel. Everybody stacks time. Inside the fence or outside the fence, we all stack the same time.'"

"Do you believe that?" she asked.

"No," I replied.

"Let's fix some breakfast, troop. Then we can both use a little more sack time. Are you up for that?"

CHAPTER 11

WHEN I FOUND Clete that afternoon, he was polishing his Caddy at the motor court, dressed in a freshly ironed sport shirt printed with tropical birds and an outrageous pair of scarlet nylon Everlast boxing trunks that extended to his knees. He was humming a tune, passing a clean cotton rag back and forth across the dried wax on the finish, pausing to blow a bug off the starched top so he would not have to smack it and stain the immaculate starchlike whiteness of the canvas. Behind him, under the trees, a pork roast was cooking on his rotisserie barbecue pit. "How's it hanging, big mon?" he said.

Without all the deleterious influences of booze and weed and cigarettes in his system, Clete looked ten years younger, his eyes clear, his skin rosy. I hated to ruin his day. "Layton Blanchet was in my backyard this morning. He seemed a little unhinged."

"Tell me about it. He's left a half-dozen messages on my machine."

"Are you going to talk to him?"

"I tried that. If you ask me, the guy is a head case. He's got some other problems as well. I did a little checking on him. His bank in Mississippi is under SEC investigation. The fed I talked to said Blanchet has been running a Ponzi scheme since back in the nineties. He gets retirees to roll over their pension plans and SEP-IRAs into his bank and promises them a minimum of ten percent on their investment. Most of them are going to lose every penny they gave him."

"He says he found your business card in his wife's dresser."

Clete had been polishing a back fin on the Caddy. He hand slowed and then stopped. He popped the rag clean and seemed to study the smoke drifting off his barbecue pit into the trees and the way the sunlight glittered like yellow diamonds on the bayou. "What would she be doing with my business card?" he asked.

"Evidently he's convinced himself that you and Carolyn Blanchet were getting it on while you were working for him."

"Not that I wouldn't like to, but he's full of shit."

"The number of the Monteleone Hotel was on the back of the card," I said.

"Layton Blanchet thinks I hang out at the Monteleone on my income? What an idiot."

"Where do you think she got the card?"

"From any one of half the lowlifes in South Louisiana."

"He said a couple of other things, Clete. He says he has a source inside the department. He says you're still getting looked at for the Stanga homicide, and maybe I am, too."

"Because the shooter was using a forty-five?"

"That and a few remarks both you and I made about Stanga."

"Blanchet knows I'm being looked at but you don't? Does that make sense to you?"

"Helen Soileau doesn't always take me into her confidence."

"Well, that's not my problem. Check out the day. Who cares about this stuff? We're on the square, aren't we? You know how many people have messed with the Bobbsey Twins from Homicide and are now in the ground? Get me a Bud from the icebox and a Diet Doc for yourself. I don't want to hear any more about Layton Blanchet."

"Watch your back, Cletus."

"And take away your job? What kind of guy do you think I am?" he said. He went back to polishing his car, his leviathan shoulders rolling inside his shirt. I went into the cottage and opened a Dr Pepper and a Budweiser, and we drank them in the shade.

ON MONDAY MORNING, when both Molly and I were at work and Tripod was in his hutch, his hind leg had begun to tremble for no reason. Alafair had folded a soft blanket in the bottom of a cardboard box and taken him to the vet. In the rearview mirror, she noticed a pale blue pickup truck turn behind her, then reappear a block later and make a second turn with her. When she parked in front of the veterinary clinic, the truck drove on by and caught the state road leading to a drawbridge in the distance.

Tripod had a form of distemper, one that came and went and seemed to steal more of his life each time. The veterinarian gave him a shot and some medicine that was to be mixed with his food. Alafair put Tripod back in his box and placed the box on the passenger seat of her old Honda and headed home. It was a fine morning. A sun shower had left the streets damp and the trees dripping, and the new sugarcane was green in the fields and bending in the breeze. She rolled down the windows to let in the cool air, and Tripod popped his head out of the box, his nose pointed into the wind like a weathervane.

She passed a redbrick Catholic church with a spire and a cupola on the roof, and rumbled across the drawbridge and stopped at a fruit stand on the far side of the bayou. Next to the fruit stand, a man was selling shrimp and crawfish out of the back of a refrigerated truck. Alafair got out of her car and closed the door. "I'll be right back, Pod," she said.

But there were three people ahead of her who could not decide what they wanted, and she had to wait. The Amtrak passed on the railroad embankment behind her, and traffic stalled at the intersection. On the other side of the state road, known as Old Spanish Trail, was a dry canal that emptied into Bayou Teche. Along the banks of that same canal, unknown to most people driving by it, Confederate infantry had dug a skirmish line in the year 1863 to cover the evacuation of wounded from the Episcopalian church on the west end of the town. Kermit Abelard had been fascinated with the site and had climbed down into it with a spade and a metal detector in search of minié balls, in spite of Alafair's warnings, streaking his skin with poison ivy. But that was months ago, when the Kermit she knew and loved was more boy than man, in the best possible way, unmarked by avarice or false pride or dependence on others. In her mind, there had been a purity about Kermit—in his vision of the world, in the books and stories he wrote about the antebellum South, in his conviction that he could change the lives of others for the better. Had she been totally wrong about him? Had the innocent boy in him died simply because of his association with Robert Weingart? Or had the innocent boy never existed except in Alafair's imagination?

The sun had broken out from behind a rain cloud, and she had to shield her eyes against its brilliance. Across the road, the oak trees along the bayou were deep green from the rain and swelling with wind, the sound of car tires on the bridge steady and reassuring, like a testimony to a plan, perhaps a reminder that life was basically good and that she was surrounded by ordinary people who shared a common struggle. A vendor had broken open a sample watermelon that he said came from the Rio Grande Valley in Texas, and he cut a slice for Alafair and put it on a napkin and placed the napkin in her palm.

"I have a sick raccoon. He'll love this," she said. "Let me pay you."

"No, ma'am, I wouldn't take a dime for that," he replied.

Wasn't it time to forget about Kermit Abelard? she asked herself. To leave him in the past, as she had promised both him and herself? To enjoy the day, to work on her book, to take care of animals, to give up resentment of herself and the wrong choices she may have made, to forgive Kermit Abelard for being weak and not defending her, even forgive him for allowing himself to be demeaned and humiliated in public by a man as loathsome as Robert Weingart? If she could forgive Kermit for not being what she thought he was, and forgive herself for her excess of love and trust, then she could let go of both Kermit and the past. Wasn't that how it worked?

No, it didn't. The man she had loved may not have been real. But the man she had given herself to, imaginary or not, would always live on the edges of her consciousness. And for that reason alone, she would always feel self-deceived and robbed at the same time, as though she had cooperated with a thief in burglarizing her own home.

"You want some shrimp or crawfish?" the vendor with the refrigerator truck asked. He was a tiny man dressed in strap overalls, his white shirt buttoned at the wrists, his spine bowed in a hump.

"Yes, I'm sorry. Two pounds of veined shrimp, please," she said, opening her purse.

"You're Mr. Robicheaux's daughter, aren't you?"

"Yes, I am."

He raised his eyes to hers, then looked past her in the direction of her Honda. "I saw you drive up in your li'l car," he said.

"Yes?"

"You know that fella?"

"Which fellow?"

"That one there," the man said, nodding toward her car, his mouth down-hooked at the corners.

She turned around. The skinned-up pale blue truck she had seen earlier was parked behind her Honda. A man was leaning inside the passenger window, his shoulder and elbow making a pulling and pushing motion. She left both the shrimp and her money on the vendor's worktable and went to the car. "What do you think you're doing?" she said.

The man straightened up. His hair was gelled into the shape of a cupcake, the skin fish-belly white where it was shaved above the ears. A strawberry birthmark bled out of his hairline into his collar. His mouth was a wide slit not unlike a frog's, the upper lip duck-billed. There was a rolled newspaper in his hand. "I was playing with your pet," he said.

"Were you poking him with that paper?"

"I don't know if I'd call it that. No, I was just

letting him paw and mouth it a little bit. I wasn't poking him at all."

"He's sick and he's old and he doesn't need anyone messing with him. You step back from my car."

"You don't remember me?"

She gazed at him as one does at a pornographic image thrust unexpectedly before one's eyes, not wanting to engage him, not wanting to enter the moral vacuity of his eyes, not wanting to look at the flare of his mouth and the wetness on his teeth and the yellowish discoloration in his skin that affected a suntan. "You were fishing out at the Abelard place," she said.

"That's right. My name is Vidor Perkins. I'm pleased to formally meet you. I'm one of the many unfortunates that is being he'ped by Robert Weingart and the St. Jude Project. I know a lot about coons. This one don't look sick. If you ask me, he looks fat enough for roasting. Spoiled is what I'd call him. We're not doing animals a favor when we spoil them." He reached inside the window with the rolled newspaper and tapped it up and down between Tripod's ears. "Bet he's a twenty-pounder."

"You get away from my animal or I'm going to slap you cross-eyed."

"I'm just trying to be kindly. When critters are sick, and I mean real sick, like you're telling me about this one, you got to put them down. Cheapest and best way to do it is with a burlap bag and some rocks."

She reached in her purse for her cell phone.

"Calling your daddy? He burned up my gold watch, my cell phone, my sunglasses, and my cigarettes. Know why he did that? He was protecting that lesbian he works for. He thought she was gonna lose it and try to hit me upside the head. I admire a man like that."

Alafair's hand trembled as she punched in 911 on her phone.

"You're a excitable thing, aren't you?" he said. He wiped two fingers along her jaw and stuck them in his mouth, licking them from the knuckle to the nail as he removed them. "You doin' anything tonight?"

TEN MINUTES LATER she was at my office, carrying Tripod with her, his head sticking out the top of the box. She told me everything that had just happened by the fruit stand. "I want to get a concealed-weapons permit," she said.

"It's not a bad idea," I said.

"I stopped by the restroom and washed my face. My skin feels like a snail crawled across it. Are you going to have him picked up?"

She waited for my answer. I realized I was gazing at her without seeing her. "It's what he wants," I said. "It's obvious Robert Weingart sicced him on you, but I think Weingart's motive has less to do with you than me."

"How do you know this?"

"Because they're both con-wise. They have an agenda. It's about the St. Jude Project or the deaths of the girls in Jeff Davis Parish or the Canadian girl we found buried on the Delahoussaye property. It also involves the Abelards and, I think, Layton Blanchet. The connections are all there, but I can't get a net over them."

I saw Helen through the glass window in my door. She pointed at me and mouthed the words "My office," then walked away.

"How dangerous is this guy Perkins?" Alafair asked.

"He has no moral bottom. He's probably killed people. He and Weingart both jack-rolled Social Security recipients. He was a suspect in an apartment-house fire that killed a child."

Her eyes filmed. "You're telling me I've been a fool?"

"No, I'm saying you're like most good people, Alafair. Our greatest virtue, our trust of our fellow man, is our greatest weakness."

Tripod had started to climb out of his box. She picked him up and straightened his blanket and forced him to lie down again.

"I think he's feeling better," I said.

"How do I get the gun permit?"

I took an application form out of my desk drawer. Many years ago I had started keeping the forms there for one reason and for one reason only: I had finally stopped pretending to people who had been stalked, terrorized by mail and over the phone, sexually degraded, assaulted with a deadly weapon, tortured, and gang-raped. No, that's badly stated. I had stopped lying about how our system works. Perpetrators of horrific crimes are often released on bond without either the victims or the witnesses being notified. Witnesses and victims are told they need only to testify in a truthful manner and the person who has made their lives a misery will be put away forever. In law enforcement, bromides of that kind are distributed with the blandness of someone offering an aspirin as a curative for pancreatic cancer. Visit a battered women's shelter and come to your own conclusions about how successfully our system works. Or chat up a judge who releases child molesters to a counseling program and lectures a rape victim on her provocative way of dressing.

These aren't hyperbolic examples. They're as common as someone spitting out his bubble gum on a sidewalk.

"You're not going to bring Perkins in?" Alafair said.

"I'm not sure. While you fill this out, I need to talk to Helen."

"About bringing in Perkins?"

"So far we haven't found any handles on these guys, Alf."

When I entered Helen's office and saw her face, I knew we were not going to be talking about Alafair's encounter with Vidor Perkins. A gold pen, inside a small Ziploc bag, was sitting on top of Helen's desk blotter. "Recognize that?" she asked.

"Not offhand."

"Look at it closely."

I picked up the Ziploc bag and, with two fingers, held it up against the light from the window.

"Can you read the inscription?" she said.

"It says 'Love to Clete from Alicia.'"

"Who's Alicia?" she asked.

"Alicia Rosecrans, an FBI agent Clete was involved with in Montana."

"Involved with?"

"They were an item for a while. What's the big deal about the pen?"

"A pool cleaner found it at the bottom of Herman Stanga's swimming pool this morning."

"What's the pool cleaner doing at the house of a dead man?"

"Stanga had paid three months in advance for the service. Why is the first thing out of your mouth a question about the maintenance man rather than how the pen got in Stanga's swimming pool?"

"Maybe Clete went to see him."

"I talked with Clete two days after Stanga was murdered. He said he had been by Stanga's house but had never been on the property. You look a little uncomfortable."

"Clete wouldn't shoot somebody in cold blood."

"By his own admission, he was in a blackout the night Stanga died. He doesn't know what he did. How is it that you do? Tell me how you acquired this great omniscience, Dave."

"Don't buy into this crap, Helen."

"You get your damn head on straight. This pen puts Clete at the scene of a homicide. He denies ever having been there, but he admits he had a blackout the night of the crime. What if a perp said that to you?"

I tried to speak, but she interrupted me. "You've spent years attending meetings. Why do people usually have alcoholic blackouts?" she said.

"They're caused by a chemical assault on the brain."

"Try again."

"Sometimes drunks can't deal with what they've done."

"Good. We got that out of the way. Now get out of here and do some serious casework and stop fronting points for Clete. I'm really tired of it."

"Has the pen been to the lab?"

"Yeah, it has."

I waited for her to continue, but she didn't. "Whose prints are on it?" I said.

"Nobody's."

"That's funny, isn't it? Clete's pen doesn't have Clete's prints on it? Maybe he was wearing latex when he put it in his pocket." I could see her chest rising and falling, her irritation reaching critical mass, but I didn't care. I went on, "Vidor Perkins put his hand on my daughter's face this morning. At the fruit stand by the bayou."

"Tell Alafair to file battery charges."

"Maybe we should bust Perkins for littering as well."

She picked up the Ziploc bag with the gold pen inside it and dropped it again. It hit the blotter with a sound like a rock falling. "You want to make clever and cynical statements? That's fine. But this pen won't go away. How do you think I feel about investigating an old friend like Clete? You think you're the only person in the department with feelings?"

"What's the name of the pool cleaner?" I asked.

I found him three hours later in St. Martinville, dragging an underwater vacuum on a telescopic pole along the bottom of a swimming pool behind a house owned by a black city councilman. I had known him for years. His name was Felton Leger, and he used to coach Little League baseball in New Iberia. He had a deformed foot and had to wear a special boot for it, but he had always been a man of good cheer and goodwill who was known for his decency and his loyalty to his family and friends. Why do I mention these things? Because I wanted the pool man to be someone else, someone whose word was suspect and who would be willing, if the price was right, to set up Clete Purcel.

But no such luck. Felton Leger was an honest man. "There was a lot of slash-pine needles on the bottom, big globs of them," he said. "I almost didn't see the pen. Then the vacuum sucked up a bunch of needles and I seen the pen lying there like a big gold bug. So I fished it out wit' the seine and dumped it in a paper bag and called the sheriff's department, 'cause I figured y'all would be wanting to look at it. I didn't like the man who lived there. But it was the law's job to get rid of him, not some killer."

"Did you touch it or dry it off?"

"I knew better than to do that. I dropped it right in the bag."

"You did the right thing, Felton. When was the last time you cleaned the pool?"

"One month ago."

"Could the pen have been in there then?"

"No, sir. When I clean the pool, I clean the pool."

"How many people know your schedule?"

"Just me. Sometimes I might tell my wife where I'm gonna be on a particular day."

"How many people know you serviced Herman Stanga's pool?"

"Maybe I said something to my wife. Maybe not. I don't remember. The bank owns the house now. Stanga had borrowed a bunch of money on it and wasn't making his payments."

"Didn't he always pay you in advance?"

"'Cause I made him. I knew he was a deadbeat. If you ax me, I think he was fixing to leave town. That's why he let the lawn burn up and the dogs dump all over the place. He kept up the pool to entertain his chippies."

"I see. Where's your wife work?"

"At the sheriff's department. She's a night dispatcher."

I tried to place her but couldn't. "In New Iberia?"

"No, here in St. Martinville. This is where we live now," he said.

• • •

IT WAS AFTER three P.M. when I got back to town. I called Clete's office and was told by Hulga, his secretary, that he was at Baron's health club. I found him in a back room alone, dressed in sweatpants, his T-shirt splitting on his back while he squatted and hoisted a two-hundred-pound bar above his head, his neck bulging, his face almost purple.

"Have you lost your mind? You're going to slip a disk," I said.

He dropped the bar on the floor, his breath escaping like air from a collapsed balloon. "Dave," he gasped, unable to finish the statement.

"What?" I said.

"*What?* You ask *what?*" He sat on a bench and put his face in a towel. "Will you give me a break? I'd rather be married. You follow me everywhere I go. I get no peace. You're worse than my ex." He breathed slowly, in and out, sweat leaking out of his eyebrows. "What are you doing here?"

It was not a time to be completely honest. I told him what had happened to Alafair at the fruit stand and made no mention of the gold pen that had been found at the bottom of Herman Stanga's pool, one inscribed to him by the FBI agent Alicia Rosecrans. He listened quietly, wiping his throat and the back of his neck with the towel. "Say that last part again. He put his hand on her cheek and licked his fingers?"

"Something like that," I replied.

"Let me shower and get dressed and we'll pay him a visit."

"I'll handle it."

He looked at me from under his brow. "Like how?"

"I'm not sure yet. When Helen and I rousted him at his house, he seemed to suggest he could be a friend to the department, like he knew about the inner workings of an operation that was larger in importance than he and Robert Weingart were."

"You ever know a meltdown who was different? They bypassed toilet training and shoe tying, but they're experts on everything from brain surgery to running the White House. Why would Perkins want to help y'all? He's not on parole, and he doesn't have any charges hanging over his head. This guy wouldn't lift a toilet seat unless there was something in it for him."

"Money."

"From who?"

I let the thread die. I still had not broached the question about the gold pen, primarily because I was in the position of investigating a friend I wanted to protect against the consequences of the investigation I was conducting. I tried to convince myself I was "excluding" Clete as a suspect in the death of Herman Stanga. But Clete's history of violence, even though most of it was on the side of justice, indicated a level of rage that had little connection to the miscreants he visited it upon and everything to do with a young boy who was not allowed to eat supper and was forced to kneel for hours on rice grains and, with regularity, feel his father's razor strop whipped savagely across his buttocks. The thought of Clete Purcel in a blackout, in proximity to a sneering misogynistic pimp like Herman Stanga, made me shudder. The fact that Stanga had publicly gloated over the prospect of sending Clete to Angola made me wonder if indeed the most logical suspect on the planet for the Stanga homicide wasn't sitting three feet from me.

I went back to the entrance of the barbell room

and shut the door. I saw the expression change in Clete's face. "What's the deal?" he asked.

"Where's the gold pen Alicia Rosecrans gave you?"

His T-shirt was gray with sweat. He pulled it loose from his neck and shook the fabric to cool himself, his green eyes empty. "I don't know. Maybe at my office. Or in my dresser," he said. "I don't like to think about Alicia a lot. I thought maybe she and I would be together for a while. Like always, that didn't happen. What's so important about the pen?"

"When is the last time you saw it?"

"I don't remember. What is this crap?"

"It showed up in an unlikely place. Stop avoiding the question, Clete."

"I don't remember where I put it. I didn't want to see it again. I wish I had thrown it away. Every time I looked at it, it made me feel bad."

"Who had access to it?"

"How do I know when I don't remember where I put it?" Then, illogically, he said, "My secretary comes in my office. The skells come in my office. People visit my cottage. The cleaning woman. Look, I remember Wee Willie Bimstine borrowing it once. Maybe he didn't give it back. Or maybe it was Nig who borrowed it."

"It was found at the bottom of Herman Stanga's swimming pool."

He widened his eyes and squeezed his mouth with one hand and wiped his hand on his pants. "Who found it?"

"The pool cleaner. He's a straight-up guy."

We were both silent. Somebody opened the door and started to come in. "We're tied up in here right now," I said.

The door closed and the person went away.

"Helen says you told her you were never on Stanga's property," I said.

"That's right, I was never there."

"Who might have taken the pen out of your office or your cottage?"

"Layton Blanchet came to my office when he hired me to follow his wife around. I've had a couple of female guests at the cottage. I'm not necessarily talking about the boom-boom express, maybe just for drinks or something to eat before we went to the casino."

"Emma Poche was one of them?"

"Definitely."

"But what?"

"That *was* the boom-boom express—in the sack, on the furniture, in the shower, maybe on the ceiling. I crashed into the wall with her and cracked the plaster. She deserves her own zip code down there. It was like swimming in the Caribbean. I told her she was part mermaid."

"Will you stop that?"

"I'm trying to tell you we were occupied. She wasn't rifling my dresser or closet or whenever I lost that damn pen."

"You didn't sleep?"

"I think both of us kind of passed out."

"So you don't know what she did?"

"She's not that kind of person, Dave."

"Yeah, I know. You told me she's cute because she has a tattoo on her butt."

"You ought to see it."

"When are you going to grow up? Don't you realize how serious this is?"

"What am I supposed to do, go into mourning for myself? I don't care if I was blacked out or not. I didn't pop Stanga. If other people don't believe me, that's their problem. How about I treat you and Molly and Alafair to dinner at the casino tonight? You're giving me a headache here."

I LEFT THE health club and called Molly and said I was working late and that I was not sure when I would be home.

"Alafair told me about her encounter with that creep Perkins," she said. "Is this related?"

"I'm not sure where he is right now."

"Is Clete with you?"

"No, I just left him at the health club."

"Let Helen and the department handle this."

"Sure."

"Do you think I'm an idiot?"

"I'm not sure what you mean," I said.

"If you're going after this guy, I want to be with you."

"I'll call you back later. Everything is fine. I just got a little behind in my schedule today."

"Don't you hang up on me."

"I'm losing the signal," I said.

My statement to Molly had not been a total lie. In truth, I had no plan about Vidor Perkins. He was obviously a psychopath, inured to threats and pain and deprivation by a lifetime of institutionalization. Worse, he delighted in attention, particularly when he had an audience. Any con who turns down parole from a joint like Huntsville and of his own volition does twenty-seven months in a cotton field under the tender and loving supervision of mounted Texas gunbulls has demonstrated a degree of toughness that cannot be dismissed easily. Also, I still believed that Perkins had an agenda that may have involved betrayal of either the Abelards or Layton Blanchet or Robert Weingart. But I couldn't be sure.

In fact, I could not be sure about anything in this case, except that Perkins had to leave my daughter alone.

I drove down Old Jeanerette Road through fields of waving sugarcane and past the whitewashed crypts that stood in a shady copse, the ground green with lichen that looked as soft as felt, all of it five feet from a bend in the road, like an abiding visual reminder, at least for me, of the earth's gravitational claim upon the quick.

I pulled into Perkins's gravel driveway. His stucco bungalow was already deep in shadow inside the pecan trees and slash pines that surrounded it, his pickup truck parked under the porte cochere. His flower beds were mulched and blooming with azaleas and impatiens and rosebushes. A water bird jittered a rainbowlike haze across the front lawn. On the far side of the two-lane, the property extended all the way down to the Teche, a long grassy slope pooled with the shade of giant live oaks that were silhouetted against a red sun. It was an idyllic scene except for the little black girl who sat on the front steps, her knees pinched close together, her hands knotted in her lap.

I got out of my pickup and walked toward her. From the backyard, I could hear a thick, whapping sound, like a hard object striking a canvas or plastic cover. The little girl was the same one Helen and I had told not to visit Vidor Perkins's home by herself again.

"Remember me?" I said.

"Yes, suh. You and the lady drove me home," she replied.

"You promised us you wouldn't come back here without your mommy."

"She dropped me off. She takes care of a sick

lady. My auntie couldn't keep me." She spoke in a monotone, her face empty.

I sat down on the steps, one step lower than she was. I gazed at the bayou. "Your name is Clara?"

"Yes, suh."

"Did something bad happen at Mr. Vidor's house today, Clara?"

In the silence, I could hear the slash pines swaying in the wind, the pine needles tinkling on the rain gutters.

"Clara, nothing bad will happen to you for telling the truth. Did Mr. Vidor do something he shouldn't have?"

"I want to go back home now."

"I'll take you there, I promise. But you need to tell me what Mr. Vidor did."

"Took my picture."

"In what way?"

"Suh?"

"How were you dressed when he took your picture?" I heard the whapping sound from the backyard again. "Were you wearing your dress and your shirt just like you are now?"

"Mr. Vidor tole me to lie on the couch. He tole me to put my thumb in my mout'. Then he tole me to put my hands behind my head."

"How many pictures did he take of you, Clara?"

"Two or t'ree."

"Did Mr. Vidor touch you at all in a place he shouldn't have?"

"No, suh. He just took the pictures. I tole him I didn't want to do that no more, and he stopped."

"Okay, Clara. I want you to wait here while I straighten out a couple of things with Mr. Vidor. Then I'll take you home and a lady will come out from the sheriff's department and stay with you until your mommy gets off work. But you remember what I say: You're a good little girl. You've helped out a police officer, and that's what good guys do. You're one of the good guys, do you understand that?"

I walked around the side of the house just as Vidor Perkins pulled back an archer's bow and drove an arrow into a plastic bull's-eye draped across a stack of hay bales. He glanced over his shoulder at me, then pulled another arrow from the quiver on his back and fitted the shaft on the bow string. "I figured you'd be along directly," he said. He lifted the bow, pulling back the string, his shoulders taut with tension. A second after he released the shaft, it whapped dead center in the target, quivering with a sound like a twanged bobby pin.

"Help me out here, Mr. Perkins," I said. "I think Robert Weingart told you to give my daughter the worst time you could. But I think the motivation is more than simple jealousy. You guys want to become known as victims of police harassment because you know you're going to be suspects in a homicide investigation. Let me take my theory one step further. You have a personal agenda, and it involves selling out both the Abelards and your jailhouse podjo and maybe even Layton Blanchet."

"Cain't say as I know Mr. Blanchet, although I've heard his name. But I'll give your words some study and get back to you on that."

"My daughter has applied for a concealed-weapons permit. In the meantime, I'm giving her a Smith and Wesson Airweight thirty-eight. If you come near her again, she's going to blow your head off. If she doesn't, I will. We'll sort out the legalities later. But you won't be there to see it."

He took another arrow from his quiver but did not notch it on the bow string. He blew on the feathers, then stroked them into shape with his fingers. "She smells like peaches when you peel the skin off," he said. "Must be a treat to have something like that around the house."

"I want you to go inside now and get your camera and bring it back out here."

"Why would I do that?"

"Because the photos you took of that little girl probably don't meet the standard of prosecutable evidence. In a borderline case like this, you'll probably skate. But that doesn't mean you'll be allowed to keep the pictures or put them on the Internet. What that means, Mr. Perkins, is you're going to voluntarily destroy the memory card or the film or whatever is in your camera."

"Come back with a warrant and you can discuss it with my attorney."

"I see," I said.

"You look like you got shit on your nose, Mr. Robicheaux."

"We don't come up against your kind every day, so you'll have to excuse me. You're pretty slick."

He gazed at me a long time, his skin a chemical yellow in the sun's glow, the wind puffing his shirt, his arrow notched now, his fingers relaxed on the string. "Your daughter could have filed battery charges, but she didn't. Know why?" he said. "She don't want to admit in a courtroom she cain't handle a man's attentions. They all got the same weakness. The big V. Vanity. Like the Bible says."

I turned and walked out of the yard. "You cain't touch me, Mr. Robicheaux," he called at my back. "I'm floating outside your window like a hummingbird. I'll always know where you and your family

are at. But you won't know where and when I might
show up. Till one day I come peekaboo-ing by."

I opened the door to my pickup and felt under
the seat. The baton was an old one, the only sou-
venir I took with me when I was fired from the
New Orleans Police Department. It was made of
oak, knurled on the grip, lathe-troweled with three
rings below the tip, drilled through the center and
filled with a steel bolt, its black paint nicked, a
leather thong threaded through the handle. In the
old days, when Clete and I walked a beat on Canal
and in the Quarter, a cop in trouble or chasing a
perp would whang his baton on the pavement or
a curb as a distress signal to other cops. There was
no concrete in Vidor Perkins's yard and no other
cops in the vicinity. And no one else in his backyard
except him and me. He had just fired an arrow at his
target and didn't hear me coming. I bent low when
I swung the baton and caught him high up on the
calf, right behind the knee. His mouth fell open and
he dropped to the ground like a child genuflecting in
church.

He breathed loudly through his mouth, as though
his tongue had been scalded. Then he squeezed both
hands behind his knee, his face splitting with a grin,
his eyes closed in slits. "Oh, Lordy, that's a mean
stripe you lay on a man, Mr. Robicheaux," he said.
He let out a gleeful howl as though blowing a storm
out of his chest. "I understand she's your foster kid.
I hear that opens up the parameters. I bet when she
was eighteen, a man had to tie a board acrost his
rear end not to fall in."

I could feel my fingers finding new purchase on
the baton's handle, the leather thong looped loosely
on my wrist bones. I could feel a vein of black electricity crawling through my arm into my shoulder,

down my right side, and through my back and chest. He made me think of a medieval jester mocking his executioner as he knelt before the chopping block. I could feel my whole body becoming a torqued spring that would find release only when I whipped the baton across Perkins's temple and watched his eyes go senseless and dead. The procedural explanation was already available. I wouldn't even have to use a throwdown. He had committed a crime upon a child. I had tried to search him before hooking him up. He had whirled and gotten his hands on his archer's bow. The blows I'd delivered were in self-defense and not intended to be fatal. As I had these thoughts, I saw Vidor Perkins's time on earth coming to an end.

Then I heard the little black girl. She was standing at the back corner of the house, weeping and hiccuping, shaking uncontrollably, unable to deal with what she had witnessed. "It's okay, Clara," I said.

"You lose again, Mr. Robicheaux," Perkins said.

"I guess you could say that."

"I ain't hurt that little girl. Down deep inside you know it."

"'Better they fasten millstones about their necks and cast themselves into the sea.' Know where that comes from, Mr. Perkins?"

"Jesus was talking about the scribes and Pharisees that misled the innocent, not the likes of me. I ain't mussed a hair on that girl's head. No, sir."

"I'll be around."

"Come back any time."

I went inside his house and came back out with a camera I found on the kitchen table. I set it on the back step and smashed it into junk with my foot. Perkins had pulled himself up by holding on to the trunk of a pine tree. He continued to grip it, like a man on board a pitching ship. He gazed at a black cloud moving across the sun. "The devil is fixing to beat his wife," he said. "When you were looking at my jacket, did you check my IQ? My grammar may not be too hot, but my IQ is higher than Robert's. Down the road, you'll see who walks away with the most marbles. It ain't gonna be Robert Weingart or them Abelards, either."

I drove the little girl to her house and walked her inside just as a shower of hailstones clattered on her roof and danced on the dirt yard.

CHAPTER 12

EARLY THE NEXT morning, I went into Helen's office and told her of my visit to Vidor Perkins's house.

"Go over that last part again," she said.

"Which part?"

"About the baton."

I did, describing in detail how I pulled it from under the seat of my vehicle and went after him, whipping one leg out from under him. While she listened, she held my gaze, her face impassive. She took an Altoid out of a box on her desk blotter and put it in her mouth. "Why are you telling me this?" she asked.

"Because you need to know."

"No, it's because you think my office is a confessional."

"Maybe."

"There's no maybe about it, Dave."

I waited for her to go on, but she didn't. I suspected she had reached that point in dealing with others when we finally accept people for what they are and stop contending with their character defects.

She sucked on the mint and pushed the box toward me. "You want me to bring him in?" she asked.

"My vote is we ignore him for the time being. He's energized by attention. Leave him alone, and I think he'll offer us a deal of some kind on Robert Weingart. My guess is they were buds in Huntsville, and now Weingart is an international celebrity, while Perkins gets treated like toe jam. I suspect Perkins is driven by greed and envy and resentment. I think he wants to make the big score at Weingart's expense."

"What is it we're not talking about here, Dave?"

"Pardon?"

"For want of a better word, *duh*. The gold pen. The one that has Clete's name on it that ended up at a homicide scene."

"He doesn't remember where he put it, and he doesn't remember the last time he saw it. He says a number of people may have had access to it, including Layton Blanchet. Also, a number of women have been visitors at his cottage."

"Like which women?"

I had to wonder for a second if Helen's curiosity went beyond the professional. Years ago she and Clete had become involved romantically and had crossed lines in ways that surprised even them.

"The only one he mentioned was Emma Poche," I replied.

"From NOPD?"

"She's a deputy in St. Martin Parish now. What do you know about her?"

"Not much. As I recall, she had a history as a boozer." Her eyes slipped off mine, and I knew there was something she wasn't saying.

"What else do you know about her?" I asked.

"She sleeps around. Or she used to. Let's talk about the gold pen."

"Somebody planted it on Stanga's property. You know it, Helen, and so do I. Drunk or not, Clete Purcel wouldn't shoot down an unarmed man, even one he hated."

"That might be true, but Clete invites chaos and

self-destruction into his life at every turn. In this case, he's making us do his enemies' dirty work. I don't want to be part of the script any longer."

"I can't blame you."

She got up from her desk. Her windowsill was lined with potted flowers. A motorized houseboat was passing on the bayou, its deck dotted with people from a movie company who were looking for sites they could use in their film production. Helen leaned on the windowsill and gazed at the boat, her back as hard-looking as iron against her shirt. "That's what we should all be doing," she said. "Having fun, enjoying our lives, riding on a boat with people we like. How'd we let dope and pimps and degenerates get into our communities?"

"They've always been here," I said. "They come out of the woodwork when they have sanction."

"My ass," she said.

You're wrong, I thought. But I didn't say it.

"You want to add something?" she asked.

"Nope."

Then Helen made one of those remarks that always atomized my defenses and left me feeling that maybe I'd done something right: "You think you're tough-minded, bwana, but your heart gets in your way. I don't know what I'd do if something happened to you."

I WENT BACK to my office and stared at my file cabinet where the crime-scene and coroner's photographs of Fern Michot and Bernadette Latiolais were tucked inside case folders. My file cabinet did not function simply as a place where I put things. In this instance, the sightless eyes and decomposed features of two homicide victims had disappeared from my view and were pressed between departmental

forms and Xeroxes from the authorities in Jeff Davis
Parish and fax and Internet printouts from Baton
Rouge and time logs and sheets of lined paper torn
from my notebook and legal pad. And all of it was
encased in a rectangle of darkness bordered by the
metal drawer and the shell of the file cabinet, not
unlike the contents inside the sliding refrigerated
tray used in a mortuary storage area, all of it safely
sequestered, the degree of the victims' suffering
placed in abeyance, so I would not have to reflect
upon what the world had done to them.

But I could hear their voices, even though I
had never known either girl. Their killers (I was
convinced now that more than one individual was
involved) did not understand that the dead find a
conduit into the minds of the living, particularly
when they have been robbed of their lives and all
the promise and happiness that had awaited them.
When Bernadette's executioners wired her body to
chunks of concrete and sank her in a pond, and
shoveled dirt into the eyes and mouth and over the
brow and hair of Fern Michot, they had not appreciated the enormity of the theft they had just committed. I do not believe the rage the dead experience
can be contained by the grave. How many people
can understand what it means for an eighteen-year-
old girl to be in love, to wake every morning and
feel that something extraordinary and beautiful is
about to happen on that particular day? How many
understand the joy a young girl experiences when
she is kissed on the mouth and eyes by a man who
loves her, or the sensual pleasure of dancing barefoot on a lawn at an open-air concert, throwing
her rump around in an innocent celebration of her
sexuality, to see her own skin glow in the mirror, to
see her breasts swell, and to hear her heart's blood

race when she says the man's name in the silence of her bedroom?

How can all of that be ripped loose from a young woman's chest in moments, unexpectedly, through guile and treachery, without a psychic scream leaving the soul, a scream that is so loud it wraps itself around the world?

I closed the blinds on my windows and my office door and clicked off the overhead lighting and sat in the air-conditioned gloom, my arms motionless on top of my desk blotter. What were the two girls trying to tell me?

But I knew, in the way that all fathers who raise a teenage girl know. At a juncture in their lives, Bernadette Latiolais and Fern Michot had trusted a man they thought was special. He was probably handsome, older, better educated than they, and wise in the ways of the world. He was confident and reassuring and seemed to dismiss or solve problems in a magical fashion. At some point in their association with him, he had performed an act, seemingly unknown to himself, that was both kind and strong. After that moment, they made a compact with themselves and decided he was the one to whom they would give their entire heart and soul.

Who was the man who fit all the criteria? I saw his face float in front of me like a chimera painted on air. I saw the slyness in his eyes, the plastic surgery that had tugged his flesh back placidly on the bone, the lips that were slightly puckered to hide the smirk flickering on his cheek.

I had to blink to make sure I was not actually looking into Robert Weingart's face. Unconsciously, I brushed my right hand against the checkered grips of my holstered .45. I lifted my hand back onto the desk, like a child in puberty obsessed with concerns about impure thoughts and touches.

I jerked open the blinds and did not let myself dwell upon the choices that I was making already, my hand clenching and unclenching at my side.

OVER THE YEARS, I had come to believe that almost all homicides, to one degree or another, are premeditated. A man who enters a convenience store with a loaded pistol has already made a decision about its possible use. A person who commits an abduction, knowing nothing about the victim's heart condition or that of the victim's loved ones, has already decided on the side of self-interest and is not worried about the fate of others. Even a man in a barroom fight, when he continues to kick a downed opponent trapped on the floor, knows exactly what he is doing.

In my view, there is an explicit motivation in almost every homicide, even one committed in apparent blind rage. Was the motivation in the death of the two girls sexual? Possibly, but I doubted it. Robert Weingart was in the mix, and I believed the Abelards were, too, and possibly even Layton Blanchet. Sex was not a primary issue in their lives. Money was. When it comes to money, power and sex are secondary issues. Money buys both of them, always.

But what was to be gained financially by the deaths of two innocent girls? Perhaps the answer lay in what I considered a long tradition among people like the Abelards. Historically, they had acquired their wealth off the backs and sweat of others. Nor, when push came to shove, were they above the use of the lash and branding iron and selling off families to different parts of the country. In their journey from the role of newly arrived colonials escaping from Old World despots to a time when they themselves became slave owners, they managed to do considerable damage to the earth as well, burning out the soil by not rotating crops and turning old-growth forests into stump farms.

But how could two teenage girls with no apparent agenda, from poor families, be an obstruction in someone's monetary scheme to the extent that their lives would become forfeit? It made little sense. I suspected the answer lay in the obvious, perhaps a detail I had missed or already passed over. As an addendum to this reflection, the word "motivation" suggests complexity that is often not there. Ask any detective who has heard the confession of a murderer. When the killer finally explains his rationale for committing the worst act of which human beings are capable, the speciousness and absurdity of his thinking is of such a mind-numbing magnitude that the detective's response is usually one of silence and blank-faced disbelief. Fortunately, he often has a legal pad and felt pen close by, almost like stage props that he can slide across the table to the suspect while he says, simply and quietly, "Write it down."

At 11:23 A.M., Helen opened my office door without knocking. "Layton Blanchet and his wife just T-boned a black woman's car with their Lexus at Burke Street and the drawbridge," she said.

"So?"

"They're trying to leave the scene."

"Why are you telling me?"

"The Blanchets aren't going to smash up somebody's car in our parish and drive away like their shit doesn't stink. I'll meet you out front."

The drive to the accident scene was only three

blocks down East Main, past The Shadows and the old Evangeline Theater where a street named for a pioneer Irishwoman fed into the drawbridge. Coincidentally, the accident scene was a short distance from the back of the brick building where Clete Purcel kept his office.

Two cruisers had arrived ahead of us. A Mazda had been crushed against a telephone pole, its passenger-side doors driven into the seats. Glass and strips of chrome molding lay in the street. Amazingly, the woman driving it was unharmed; she was sitting in the backseat of a cruiser, talking to a paramedic who kept moving a finger back and forth in front of her face.

If anyone was injured or impaired by the accident, it was Layton Blanchet. While his wife argued with a sheriff's deputy, Layton sat behind the steering wheel of his Lexus with both the driver's and passenger's doors open to let in the breeze. He looked like a man afflicted with a fatal disease. Helen and I parked in front of the domino parlor on Burke Street and walked toward the accident. As soon as Carolyn Blanchet saw me, she disengaged from her argument with the deputy. "Dave, thank God you're here. Can you do anything for us?" she said.

"Like what?"

"Layton is having a nervous breakdown. I was taking him to Our Lady of Lourdes in Lafayette," she said.

"He's having a breakdown but you let him drive the car?" I said.

"It was the only way I could get him out of the house," she replied.

"So why were you downtown and not on the highway to Lafayette?" I asked. Inside the shade at the back of the brick building, I could see the umbrella on Clete's office patio ruffling in the breeze. Carolyn's eyes followed mine, and I knew that whatever information she was about to give me would come a teaspoon at a time and would reveal only enough to ensure that her account was credible.

"He wanted to talk to your friend Clete Purcel. About a business matter of some kind," she said.

Carolyn had shown no acknowledgment of Helen's presence.

"Have you met Sheriff Soileau?" I asked.

"Hi," Carolyn said, and returned her attention to me. "I've got to get him to this psychiatrist who's waiting for us at Lourdes. The black woman ran the stop sign. No one is injured. I don't want to see her ticketed or hurt financially. We'll fix our own car. Maybe Layton will even fix hers. But we didn't cause this, and we don't have time for a lot of paperwork and stupid questions. Now, are we done here?"

"No, madam, you're not," Helen said.

"Then tell me what I can do to make this right so I can take my husband to the hospital."

"Normally when people try to leave the scene of an accident, it's not for humanitarian reasons," Helen said. "Your husband is going to take a Breathalyzer test, and you're going to file a report at the Iberia Parish Sheriff's Department. You're going to do that now, not later. That means you get in the back of that cruiser by the bridge, of your own volition, and you do it without further discussion. If you say anything more, you're going to jail in handcuffs."

"This is ridiculous," Carolyn said.

"Not to us, it isn't. Would you like to say something else?" Helen said.

Carolyn Blanchet's platinum hair looked as bright as a helmet in the sunshine, her contacts as blue as the sky. Her skin made me think of brown tallow. She held her gaze on Helen, never blinking, her expression impossible to read. "I apologize if I seemed abrupt. May I call my attorney?" she said.

"Please do. The reception in the backseat of the cruiser is excellent," Helen said.

"This is such a lovely little city. The word 'quaint' comes to mind. It's like a place out of a fable. Is it the fable about a big fish in a small pond? Or is that about something else? I'm probably confused," Carolyn said.

But Helen was already walking away from her, her arms pumped, her attention focused on the black woman and the ruined Mazda and Layton Blanchet sitting slack-jawed behind the wheel of his Lexus. I followed her up onto the sidewalk at the edge of the drawbridge, out of earshot of Carolyn Blanchet.

"She's been married to Layton too long," I said.

"Forget about it. I think her problem isn't with us or the accident," Helen said. "I think she doesn't want us talking to her husband."

"I think you're right," I replied.

"What's going on between Clete and Layton Blanchet?"

"Layton thinks somebody is pumping his wife. He hired Clete to find out who."

"And?"

"Clete came up with zero."

"But that's not why she wants to keep us away from her husband. I want you to get Layton alone and find out what's going on."

"You've never met Carolyn?"

"Why?"

"You seem a little charged up."

"I was taking graduate courses at LSU when that snooty bitch was a cheerleader. She got a friend of mine kicked out of her sorority because my friend was a lesbian."

"I see," I said, my gaze shifting off Helen's face to the oaks on the lawn of the old convent across the bayou.

"You see what?"

"Nothing."

"Dave, do you think you're the only person in the world who resents rich people treating us like we're their personal servants?"

"I'll see what I can get out of Layton," I replied.

"Do that," she said. She put on her sunglasses and placed her hands on her hips, her gaze riveted on Carolyn Blanchet. "They're not going to wipe their feet on us. Not this time."

"When did they do it before?"

"Everybody does."

"You sound like me."

"I know. It's depressing," she replied. Then she hit me on the arm.

Layton took the Breathalyzer test and came up negative. Helen rode back to the department with a deputy, and I put Layton in our cruiser and drove across the drawbridge, past the former convent, and into City Park.

"What are we doing?" he asked.

"It's time for a sno'ball. You'd rather sit in an interview room down the hall from a holding cell or have a sno'ball with me in the shade?"

For the first time since we had arrived at the accident, he tried to smile. Then the humor faded from his eyes and he stared at some children turning somersaults on the grass in the park. "I was a good cop, wasn't I?" he said.

In my opinion, Layton had used police work solely as a threshold into more lucrative enterprises. "I didn't know you real well back then, Layton. I suspect, like most of us, you did the best you could."

"I mean, I never jammed anybody. I never knocked the blacks around."

"That's right."

"When I sold pots and pans and burial insurance in black neighborhoods, I tried to give them a break, at least as far as my boss would allow."

I parked on the grass under a spreading oak that shadowed a long concrete boat ramp that dipped down into the Teche. I bought two sno'balls from the concession truck and walked back to the cruiser with them, the spearmint-stained ice sliding over my fingers. "Try this, podna. It's like a cool breeze blowing through your chest," I said.

"What I'm saying is, I never set out to screw anybody," he said. "I tried to be a decent man. I worked hard for what I got."

"Who said otherwise?" I said, sitting down in the driver's seat, leaving the door open and putting down all the windows with the power buttons.

"These federal investigators, they're taking me apart. Look, I wasn't running a Ponzi scheme. It's like any kind of investment. The people who get in early make the big money. The ones who come along later don't always do as well. All investment is speculative in nature."

It was time to change the subject. "Why'd you want to see Purcel?"

"I think my wife is having an affair. I think Purcel knows who it is."

"If that's true, why wouldn't Clete tell you?"

"Maybe somebody got to him."

Layton kept staring straight ahead, the sno'ball melting in his hand. At one time or another, we have all met someone whose fate we secretly pray will never be our own. The person upon whom a premature death sentence has been imposed will use every medical procedure he can afford to re-purchase his life; he will be brave and humble and for a while will even pretend that willpower and prayer and holistic medicine will give him back the sunlit mornings that he once took for granted. But eventually a shadowy figure will step in front of his eyesight and his face will forever be darkened by the experience. I believed that Layton Blanchet had become that man, and it was very hard to feel anger or indignation toward him.

"Clete didn't stiff you. He's an honest man," I said. Then I shifted the direction of the inquiry again. "Did Clete lend you his gold pen?"

I could see Layton's mouth moving, as though re-peating my question. "Gold pen? Why would I want his pen? What are we talking about?"

I was convinced his confusion was not manufac-tured. "It's not important," I said. "I don't believe the possibility of your wife's infidelity is the issue, Layton. I think those dead girls are. Maybe it's time to come clean and get it behind you. Your parents were honest working people. What would they tell you to do?"

"Don't you try to use my family against me," he replied. But he spoke without passion, the sno'ball melting and running down his wrist. I took it from his hand and threw it out the window.

"You denied a personal relationship with the Abelards," I said. "But Kermit Abelard was with you when you gave a talk on biofuels in Jackson,

Mississippi. You also have stained glasswork in your house that either he or his father gave you."

"Maybe it's him."

"I'm not following you."

"Kermit Abelard. Maybe it's him my wife is sleeping with."

"I've got news for you. Kermit has a boyfriend."

Layton looked at me as though he were coming out of a trance. "This writer who was in Huntsville?"

You just stuck your foot in it, bud, I thought. "Yeah, *that* writer. So you know a lot more about the Abelards and their friends than you've been willing to admit. Right?"

"I don't care about them one way or another."

"I would. They're about to take you down. You have resources, Layton. You're an intelligent man. Don't take the weight for these bums."

Then he said something that convinced me I would never reach the engine that drove Layton Blanchet. "A year ago I took Carolyn to a state fair up in Montana," he said. "I always loved fairs and carnivals and festivals and circuses and rodeos when I was a kid. It was a summer evening, and the sky was pink and green above the mountains, and this ride called the Kamikaze was lit up against the sunset. I couldn't recall a more beautiful moment. We were eating candied apples on a bench and watching all these kids get on and off the Kamikaze, and we were surrounded by all these working-class families that were grinning up at the Kamikaze like it was a big piece of magic in the sky. But they looked like people of five hundred years ago. Their faces were just like the faces you see of peasants in paintings of fairs in the Middle Ages. And I said that to Carolyn."

"Said what?" I asked.

"That nothing has changed. That we're still the same people, doing the same things, not knowing any more than we knew back then. I told Carolyn, 'We're all dust. At a moment like this, you get to look through a glass rainbow and everything becomes magical, but when all is said and done, we're just dust. Like the people in those paintings. We don't even know where their graves are.'"

"Maybe life is ongoing. Maybe we all get to see one another again," I said. "But no matter how it plays out, why not get on the square? You've come through hard times before. Maybe things aren't as bad as you think."

"She laughed," he replied, as though he had heard nothing I'd said.

"Who?"

"Carolyn laughed and threw her candied apple in the trash. She said, 'Honey, you're telling this to the gal who's seen you take an old widow for her last cent. Lose the role of the poet, will you?'"

I started the cruiser and drove us out of the park, over the drawbridge, and back onto Main Street. One of Layton's eyes bulged from his head, like a prosthesis that didn't fit the socket.

CHAPTER 13

IT WAS STILL raining when Clete Purcel went to sleep that night. He slept peacefully in his cottage at the motor court on the bayou, his air conditioner turned up full blast, a pillow on the side of his head, a big meaty arm on top of the pillow. Inside his sleep, he could hear the rain on the roof and in the trees and hear it tinking on the air conditioner inset in the window. At a little after five A.M., he heard a key turn in the lock. Without removing the pillow from his head, he slipped his hand under the mattress and worked his fingers around the grips of his blue-black snub-nose .38.

In the glow from the night-light in the bathroom, he saw a figure enter the room and close the door softly and relock it. He removed his hand from the pistol and shut his eyes. He heard the sounds of someone undressing; then he felt a person's weight next to him and a hand tugging the pillow loose from his face.

Emma Poche bent down over him and put her mouth on his and touched him under the sheet and then slid her tongue over his teeth. "How you doin', honey-bunny?" she said.

He pulled back the covers and took her inside them and held her close against his body. He could feel the heat in her skin and the weight of her breasts against his chest. "I didn't think you got off till oh-six-hundred," he said.

"Somebody is covering in the log for me," she said.

"That's a good way to get in trouble."

"No, oh-four-hundred to oh-seven-hundred is all dead time. The drunks are either under arrest or home, and normal people haven't left for work yet."

"You got it figured out," he said.

"Always," she said, and bit him on the ear. She placed her knee across his thigh and touched him again and blew on his cheek and neck and chest and ran her tongue down his stomach. Then she mounted him and lifted his phallus and placed it inside her, her eyes closing and her mouth opening. "Did you miss me?"

"Oh, boy," he said, more to himself than to her.

"No, tell me. Did you miss me? Did you have dreams before I got here?"

"You bet," he said, his voice as thick as rust in his throat.

"You like me, Clete? You like being with me?"

"Don't talk."

"No, tell me."

"You're great," he said.

"You're my big guy. Oh, Clete, keep doing this to me. Just do it and do it and do it." Then she said "Oh" and "Oh" and "Oh" and "Oh," like the rhythm of waves hitting on a beach.

When it was over, his heart was pounding and his loins felt drained and weak and empty and his skin was hot to his own touch. She curled against his side and put her fingers in his hair and placed the flat of her hand on his chest. He could hear her breath rising and falling. Outside, the rain was ticking in the leaves, and through a crack in the curtains, he could see that the sky was still dark with thunder-clouds, a tree of lightning blooming without sound on the horizon.

"I have to ask you something," he said.

"You heard stories about my time at NOPD?"

"Who cares about NOPD? They almost sent me up on a homicide beef."

"Then what is it?"

"I had a gold pen. I'm pretty sure it was in my dresser. No, I'm not just pretty sure. I know it was in my dresser."

"Yeah?" she said.

He turned on his side so that his eyes were only a few inches from hers. Her face was heart-shaped, her pug nose tilted upward, her eyes crinkling. She lowered her hand and squeezed him inside the thigh. But he removed her hand and held it in his. "Dave is bugging me about this pen. I mean, in a good way. He wants to clear me in the Herman Stanga shooting."

"I don't get what you're saying."

"A maintenance guy found my pen in Stanga's swimming pool."

"So the Iberia Department is trying to put his death on you?"

"Not exactly. But they can't ignore the evidence, either. My name is inscribed on the pen."

"You're asking me about it?"

"Dave won't get off my back about it. I had to give him the names of everybody who'd had access to my cottage and office. I mentioned your name, among others. I felt rotten about it. I felt rotten not telling you."

"You think I stole from you?"

"No."

"Or that I tried to set you up?"

"No, I don't think that."

"Then why'd you give Dave Robicheaux my name? Why'd you tell him about us?"

"You care whether people know we're seeing each other?"

"It's not their business."

"I was just wondering if maybe you saw the pen. I'm always dropping things or lending or handing people stuff and forgetting it."

He could feel her draw away from him, her hands receding back into the bedcovers, her body somehow growing smaller. "You just said one of the shittiest things anyone has ever said to me."

"I didn't mean to. I was trying to tell you I felt guilty about mentioning your name to Dave. I felt I was disloyal not telling you about it."

She sat up on the side of the bed, the sheet and blanket humped over her shoulders. "You don't trust me, Clete. It's that simple. Don't make it worse by lying."

"I think you're swell. I'm crazy about you."

"But maybe I'm a Jezebel, right? I'll see you around. Look the other way while I dress."

"Come on, Emma. You're reading this all wrong."

"Boy, can I pick them. Yuck," she said.

After she went out to her car, he slipped on his trousers and followed her, barefoot and bareheaded and wearing a strap undershirt in the rain. "One last try: Come back inside," he said.

"I let people hurt me only once, then I get even. With you, I don't have to. You'll never know the opportunity you just threw away. Bye-bye, big boy."

She got in her car and started the engine, her face still pinched with anger through the beaded glass. He watched her taillights disappear in a vortex of rain on East Main Street. Then he went back inside and took off his wet clothes and sat naked on the side of his bed in the dark, staring at nothing, his hands like empty skillets at his sides.

• • •

THE CALL CAME in from the sheriff in St. Mary Parish at 10:17 the same morning. Helen was out of the office, and the call was rerouted to my extension. The sheriff's name was Tony Judice. He was a firm-bodied, rotund, and congenial man, less political than most public servants here, and was known for his integrity as a sugar farmer and manager of the local sugar co-op.

"Did y'all have Layton Blanchet in custody yesterday?" he asked.

"Not exactly. He and his wife were in an accident. We took them in for an interview, primarily because they were giving the responding officers a lot of trouble and trying to leave the scene. How'd you know about it?"

"One of my deputies was over there. This is out of your jurisdiction, Dave, so I don't know if y'all want to be bothered with it or not," he said. "A guy running a trotline in the Basin called on his cell and said he found a dead man in a rowboat. The description of the dead man sounds like Blanchet. The rowboat is close by the fish camp he owns. I'm about to head out there in a few minutes. I'll wait for you if you're interested in Blanchet for reasons other than traffic accidents, or I can call you when I get out there."

"Why would you think I'd have a special interest in Layton?"

"The guy's businesses are unraveling. I think every law enforcement agency in the government is taking a look at him."

It took me under a half hour to meet the sheriff at an airboat dock on the edge of the great watery expanse known as the Atchafalaya Basin, and it took even less time to cross a wide, flat bay dimpled with raindrops and enter a bayou that wound between flooded gum and willow trees from which flocks of egrets rose clattering into the sky. The Basin isn't one entity but instead an enormous geographical composite, bigger than the Florida Everglades, containing rivers, bayous, industrial canals, flooded woods, hummocks, and wetlands that bleed as far as the eye can see into the Gulf of Mexico. It is also a cultural redoubt, one where people still speak French and live off the computer. It's a place where, if need be, you can escape through a hole in the dimension and say *au revoir* to the complexities of modern times.

The airboat sailed sideways over sand spits that were as slick as a wet handkerchief and dented the trees with the backdraft and scattered leaves on the bayou's surface. Suddenly we were in open water, where a houseboat was moored between an island of hard-packed sand and a levee that was green from the spring rains and dotted with buttercups inside the gloom, all of it capped by a sky laden with clouds that still flickered with electricity from last night's storm.

A powerboat with a crime scene investigator and two uniformed deputies in it had already arrived at the levee, and the deputies were stringing yellow tape through the cypress trees that grew in the shallows around the houseboat. The wind was blowing out of the south, and it had pushed an aluminum rowboat into the cypress knees that protruded from the water's surface along the edge of the island. The pilot of the airboat cut the engine and let our momentum slide us up on the levee, twenty yards past the far side of the tape.

Sheriff Judice and I crossed a plank walkway onto the island and walked toward the rowboat that seemed locked inside a scrim of floating algae. "Did you talk much with Blanchet yesterday?" he asked.

"Yeah, at some length."

"How would you describe him?"

"Depressed, not quite rational."

"Suicidal?"

"It's possible. But I don't know if I'd go that far."

"Why not?" he asked.

"My experience has been that most suicide victims want to leave behind a legacy of guilt and sorrow. They're angry at their fate, and they have fantasies whereby they survive their death and watch other people clean up the mess they've made. They tend to favor shotguns, razors, and big handguns that leave lots of splatter."

"Blanchet wasn't angry?"

"I'm not much of an expert on these matters, Sheriff."

"Say what's on your mind, Dave."

"My experience has been that when Layton's kind lose it, they write their names on the wall with someone else's blood, not their own."

Out of the corner of my eye, I saw the sheriff look at me. "You were in Vietnam?" he said.

"What about it?"

"People can dwell on the dark side sometimes. Hell, I do."

I started to speak, then let his remark slide.

"Jesus Christ, look at this," he said.

The rowboat was rocking slightly in the wind, the aluminum hull knocking against the cypress knees and a chunk of concrete in the shallows. Inside it lay a huge athletic man dressed in golf slacks and a tropical-print sport shirt and wearing a Rolex watch. He was on his back, as though he had been trying to find a comfortable place to rest inside an impossible environment, a hole the size of a dime under his chin. His skullcap and most of his brains were hanging in the lower branches of a willow tree that extended over the water. His eyes were open, the brilliant butanelike glow replaced by a color that reminded me of soured milk. The index finger of his right hand was still twisted in the trigger guard of a 1911-model .45 auto. The crime scene investigator stood to one side, snapping pictures. A single brass shell casing rolled back and forth in a half inch of rainwater in the bottom of the boat.

It was spring, but the air was unseasonably cool, a cloud of fog rising from a wooded island on the far side of the bay. In a tropical country many years ago, a philosophical line sergeant once told me, "You're born alone, and you die alone. It's a giant clusterfuck out there, Loot." I had told my friend the sergeant he was wrong. But as I stared at the ruined and disbelieving face of Layton Blanchet, and at the expensive clothes he had died in and the way the sun-gold hairs on his wrist curled around the band on his Rolex watch, I doubted Layton would have disagreed with him.

A black Ford pickup was parked on the levee, the windows down. "We'll run the tag, but I'm pretty sure I've seen Blanchet or his wife driving that truck around Franklin," the sheriff said, squatting down, looking more closely at the body. He glanced at the top of the levee and at the truck again. "Why would he leave the windows down? It was raining all night and into the morning. Think he just didn't care?"

"Good question," I said.

The sheriff pulled a pair of polyethylene gloves over his hands and slipped the .45 from Layton's finger, pointing the muzzle at the water, away from me and his deputies. He depressed the release button on the magazine and dropped it from the frame into a Ziploc bag, then pulled back the slide and ejected the live round from the chamber. There were flecks of blood on the steel sight and around the .45's muzzle. There was no question about the distance of the gun from the wound it had inflicted. The hole under Layton's chin was seared around the edges from the muzzle flash, puffed on one side from the gases that had tunneled upward with the bullet through Layton's mouth and brain cavity.

The sheriff placed the .45 in a separate Ziploc bag and the spent casing and live round with it. "Let's take a look in the houseboat," he said.

The door was unlocked. The interior was immaculate, the bunks made, the galley squared away, the pots and pans gleaming and hung from hooks, the propane stove free of even water spots, the teakwood wheel in the pilot's compartment freshly polished, all the brass fittings rubbed as smooth and golden and soft-looking as browned butter.

By the propane stove was a paper shopping bag, and inside it were pieces of a broken drinking glass. A coffee cup and a bottle of vodka had been left on a yellow linoleum counter by the sink. In one corner I could see tiny splinters of glass that someone had not swept up.

"What do you make of it?" the sheriff asked his crime scene investigator.

The investigator shrugged. "He had a drink and then went outside and did it? Search me."

"What do you think, Dave?" the sheriff said.

"I don't understand why Layton would come out here to shoot himself," I replied.

"I think you just don't buy Blanchet as a suicide," the sheriff said.

"I don't. But I'm often wrong. You haven't talked with his wife?"

"I can't find her. From what I hear, that's not unusual."

"That's my point, Sheriff," I said. "Layton thought his wife was sleeping around. If Layton was going to punch somebody's ticket, I think it would have been hers or her lover's or both of them."

"What if he was drunk?" the crime scene investigator said.

"Layton didn't get drunk. Maybe he had a psychotic break. It happens. Maybe I don't want to admit I grilled him pretty hard yesterday and helped push him over the edge."

But I had lost the attention of both the sheriff and his crime scene investigator. "The coroner should be here in a few minutes," the sheriff said. "We'll get an estimated time of death and bag it up here. What's bothering you, Dave?"

"Everything," I said. "He drives out here in his truck, in the rain, with his windows down. He walks down the levee in the rain, unlocks the houseboat, and maybe has a drink by the sink. Except he doesn't track up the floor. Then he goes back outside, again in the rain, and sits in a rowboat and blows off the top of his head."

"Maybe he was never on the houseboat," the crime scene investigator said.

"Then who left it unlocked?" I said.

"People forget to lock their doors, Robicheaux," the crime scene investigator said. "There's nothing rational about suicidal behavior. That's why it's called suicidal behavior."

The wind had started gusting, cutting long V-shaped patterns on the surface of the bay. I was out of my bailiwick and did not want to seem contrary and grandiose. Police officers in Louisiana are underpaid and are often forced to give special consideration to people whom they despise, and I did not want to show disrespect to either the sheriff or his men. But I had known Layton Blanchet for decades, and they had not. So I simply said, "I appreciate y'all inviting me out here."

We went back up the plank walkway onto the levee. I didn't want to look at Layton again. I couldn't say I had ever admired him or had been sympathetic to his problems or was even sympathetic to the fact that he, like me and others, had been born poor to parents who picked cotton and broke corn for a living. Layton was not a victim or an aberration; his way of life and his fate were of his own creation. Ultimately Layton was us. He had learned his value system from the oligarchy, people who possessed one eye in the kingdom of the blind. Like Huey Long, Layton became the dictatorial and imperious creature he hated. His egalitarian ways and personal generosity were a fraud. The antebellum home that resembled a wedding cake couched in a green arbor was now someone else's, beckoning to the rest of us, telling us it could be ours, too. What a folly all of it was, I thought.

As we passed the rowboat, I lowered my eyes so I would not have to look upon Layton's face. Then I stopped.

"What is it?" the sheriff asked.

The wind had divided and separated the net of algae that had blown against the rowboat and the bank. In an inch of water sliding up and down on the silt, between the aluminum hull of the boat and a cluster of cypress knees, I saw a metallic glint. I squatted down and lifted up a .45 casing with the tip of my ballpoint pen. "He either fired once and missed, or blew his head off and then fired a second time for recreational purposes," I said.

"Or the blowback caused an involuntary trigger pull and discharged the second round," the scene investigator said.

"Could be, but that almost never happens on the 1911-model forty-five. The grip safety on the frame requires too much pressure from the heel of the hand," I said. "Plus, all the motors in his head were cut when the first round emptied his brainpan."

"What do you think happened?" the sheriff asked.

"I think somebody shot and killed Layton, then put the forty-five in his hand and fired a second round so a gunshot residue analysis would show burnt gunpowder on his skin. But whoever did it couldn't find the second casing."

"So why didn't he take the one in the bottom of the boat?" the sheriff said.

"Maybe he just didn't think it through," I replied.

"Yeah, and maybe the second casing has been lying there days or weeks," the scene investigator said.

"That's possible," I said.

"So we just don't know," the sheriff said.

"I guess not," I said.

I walked back to the airboat by myself and waited for the coroner and said no more on the subject. The sheriff and his investigator wanted to wrap it up. I couldn't blame them. I turned around and faced the bay and let the wind and rain blow in my face. I breathed in the damp cleanness of the air and the smell of fish spawn and humus and wet trees back in the swamp. None of it cost five cents, and that was a thought I hoped to keep in the forefront of my mind as long as I lived.

SOMETIMES IN POLICE work you get an undeserved break. Or the bad guys do something that's really dumb. Or the bad guys turn out to be more deranged than you thought they were. The day after Layton Blanchet's death, our dispatcher buzzed my extension. "There's a guy out here to see you," he said.

"Who?" I asked.

Wally, our three-hundred-pound hypertensive dispatcher, was known as the department's comedian and professional cynic. Essentially he was a good soul, but he invested most of his energy in trying to convince people otherwise. "He won't give his name. He says he'll only talk to you."

"What's he look like?"

He thought about it. "I'd say he looks like the bore brush you run through a gun barrel. He's also got a birthmark running out of his hair down the back of his neck, like maybe a bird with the red shits sat on his head."

"What's this fellow doing now?"

"Eating a Big Mac and drinking a soda and wiping his mout' on the paper towels he got out of our can."

"Get a deputy to escort him up here. Also tell Helen that Mr. Vidor Perkins is in the building."

Then Wally said something that was unusual even for him. "Dave, who is this guy?"

"The real deal, Wally."

When Vidor Perkins sat down in front of my desk, he was holding a clipboard in one hand and a ballpoint in the other, his idiot's grin firmly in place. "Thanks for seeing me, Mr. Robicheaux," he said. "Let me explain the purpose of my visit."

"I'd appreciate that."

"I'm writing my own book. Folks have always tole me I have a flair for it."

"That's interesting. How can I help you with that?"

Aside from their moral vacuity, Perkins's eyes had another abiding and singular characteristic: The pupils seemed to remain the size of pinheads, regardless of where he was. I remembered something Elmore Latiolais had said when I interviewed him on the prison work gang in Mississippi: "There's no money in selling cooze no more. Herman Stanga is into meth."

"Where were you educated, Mr. Robicheaux?" Perkins asked, crossing his legs at the knee, his expression anticipatory, respectful, his pen poised over his clipboard.

"I don't think my background will be of great interest to your readership."

"Don't underestimate either yourself or my book. This is gonna be a humdinger of a story. I'll let you in on a secret. Rob Weingart's book got wrote mostly by his female attorney. Mine is gonna be written by my own hand, without no he'p from people who have no idea how things really work."

I looked at his eyes and the manic way he smiled and the twitches under his facial skin, and I had little doubt that Vidor Perkins not only had an addiction but that it had moved into overdrive. "Something happen between you and Weingart?" I said.

"I wouldn't say exactly between me and him. More like between me and that nasty old man."

"Mr. Abelard?"

"He tole Rob he don't need the likes of me hanging around his island. I bet you think that's 'cause of my prior troubles with the law."

"I wouldn't know." Over his shoulder, I saw Helen look through the glass in my office door. Then her face went away.

"It don't have anything to do with my history. It's because of the class of people I come from. In Mr.

Abelard's mind, I'm po' white trash from a tenant farm in north Alabama. It's in my diction and my frame of reference. For a man like Mr. Abelard, those things are worse than the mark of Cain. It ain't much different here'bouts, is it?"

"I have no idea what goes on in Mr. Abelard's mind."

"Let me set y'all straight on a couple of things. I never intentionally harmed a person in my whole life."

"Your sheet seems to indicate otherwise."

He nodded as though agreeing with me. "When we lived in the projects, I took Social Security checks from some old people's mailboxes. But it was two other boys done the beating up on them, not me. And I got a lot of gone between me and them boys later on."

"You were also arrested in an arson that killed three people. One of them was a child."

"No, sir, I had nothing to do with that fire. I knew who did, but I kept my mouth shut. That wasn't easy for a boy who was fifteen years old and getting hit upside the head with the Birmingham telephone directory."

"Why are you here, Mr. Perkins?"

As he gazed around my office, his pale blue eyes shone with the self-satisfied pleasure of a man who knew that he was one of the very few who understood the complexity of the world. "You think I'm trying to fool you about my book. I called a literary agent. Man from the William Morris Agency. Same man your daughter had dinner with when he was visiting here. He said soon as I'm done to fire off my manuscript to him. What do you think about that? Your daughter and me might end up colleagues."

"That last part isn't going to happen."

"Maybe not. But I know a bunch of people that's going down. And I'm gonna put it all in my book. I'll give you a little tidbit here, Mr. Robicheaux. About twenty years back, Kermit Abelard's parents disappeared from their yacht out in the Bermuda Triangle, didn't they?"

"The story is they were lost in a storm off Bimini."

"'Story' is the word. That nasty old man who don't want me on his island was doing business with the Giacano family in New Orleans. Their business was running weed and coke into Florida, Louisiana, and Texas. Mr. Abelard didn't pay his tab with the dagos, and the dagos had both his son and his daughter-in-law wrapped with chains and sunk in about sixty feet of water."

"Was Weingart mixed up with this?"

"Ask him, or read my book when it comes out. Now, tell me a little bit about your education and service record and war experiences, if you've had any. Stuff I can kind of soup up the description with."

"Who killed the Canadian girl and Bernadette Latiolais, Mr. Perkins?"

He gazed earnestly into space. "I'm a blank on that one."

"I just noticed the time. I'm sorry, I have an appointment. Here's my business card. Give me a call whenever you want."

He pointed a finger at me playfully. "You know what, you're not a bad fella."

After he was gone, I opened the windows, then went down to Helen's office and told her what had happened. "You think he's just nuts?" she said.

"I think he's a psychopath and typical white trash who hates people like the Abelards. I think he wants to hang Robert Weingart out to dry as well."

She massaged her upper arm, a tinge of fatigue in her face. "You think Perkins killed the girls?"

"Maybe."

"For what motive?"

"A guy like that doesn't need one," I replied.

"You see the newspaper this morning?"

"No."

"Layton Blanchet's death is being called a suicide."

"Well, it's bullshit."

"Cut loose of it, bwana. We have only one homicide to concentrate on in our jurisdiction—the murder of the Canadian girl, Fern Michot."

"Everything we've talked about is part of one package. You know it, and so do I," I replied.

"Yeah, I do, but our limitations are our limitations. That's the way it is."

I started to speak, but she went back to her paperwork and didn't look up again until I was outside her door.

CHAPTER 14

THE PECULIARITY OF entering one's eighth decade is that questions regarding theology do not sharpen but instead become less significant. Better said, need for proof of the supernatural becomes less imperative. At a certain point, perhaps we realize that we have been surrounded by the connections between the material and the unseen world all our lives, but for various reasons, we chose not to see them.

Years ago dead members of my platoon used to call me up long-distance during electrical storms. So did my murdered wife, Annie. A psychiatrist told me I was experiencing a psychotic break. But cold sober and free of all the ghosts I had brought back from a land of rice paddies and elephant grass and hills that looked like the summer-browned breasts of Asian women, I had seen my father standing in the surf south of Point Au Fer, the rain tinking on the hard hat he was wearing when he died in an offshore blowout. In the oil field, he had always been called Big Aldous Robicheaux, as though the three words were one. In his barroom fistfights, he took on all comers two and three at a time, exploding his fists on his adversaries' faces with the dispassionate ease of a baseball player swatting balls in a batting cage. My mother's infidelities filled him with feelings of sorrow and anger and personal impotence, and in turn his drunkenness and irresponsibility robbed her of any happiness she'd ever had and finally any possibility of belief in herself. My parents ruined their marriage, then their home and their family. But in death, when the wellhead blew out far below the monkey board on the rig where he was racking pipe, Big Aldous clipped his safety belt onto the Geronimo wire and jumped into the blackness, brave to the end, swallowed under a derrick that collapsed like melting licorice on top of him. A survivor said Big Aldous was smiling when he bailed into the stars. And that's the way I have always remembered my old man, and I have come to learn that memory and presence are inextricably connected and should never be thought of as separate entities.

So I have never argued with people about the specters I have seen or the voices I've heard inside the static of a long-distance phone call. I know that the dead are out there, beckoning from the shadows, perhaps pointing the way for the rest of us. But I don't fear them, and I conceive of them as friends whom I don't think I'll mind joining. It's not a bad way to be.

Early in the A.M. the day after Vidor Perkins's visit to my office, I woke in the grayness of the dawn to the clanking sounds of the drawbridge at Burke Street. The fog had rolled up Bayou Teche from the Gulf and hung like wet strips of gray rag on the ground and in the oak trees. I fed Tripod and Snuggs, then fixed a fried-egg and bacon sandwich and took it and a cup of coffee and hot milk and a folding chair down the slope of my backyard. I sat down by the water's edge and ate breakfast and watched Tripod and Snuggs come down the slope and join me, sniffing at the breeze, their tails flipping back and forth. The green and red lights on the drawbridge were smudged inside the fog, the steel girders hardly visible. Evidently the great cogged wheels that raised and lowered the bridge had gotten stuck. Then I heard the machinery clank and bang loudly, and each side of the bridge rose at forty-five-degree angles into the air and what I thought was a huge two-deck quarterboat slid through the open space and came down the bayou toward me, a hissing sound rising from its stern.

But it was not an offshore quarterboat. It was a nineteenth-century paddle wheeler, with twin fluted stacks, a lamp burning inside the pilothouse. A massive bare-chested black man, wearing no shoes and dressed only in a pair of flared work trousers, was coiling and stacking a thick length of oiled rope on the bow. The side door to the pilothouse was open, and inside I could see a skipper at the wheel, smoking a cob pipe and wearing a billed mariner's cap and a dark blue coat with big buttons. He seemed to study me, then removed his pipe from his mouth and touched the bill of his cap. I waved back at him, unsure what I was seeing. I thought the boat was a replica, one with screws under it, perhaps part of a tourist promotion of some kind. But I saw a woman in a hooped dress standing in a breezeway, looking at me as though I were an oddity she didn't understand; then the stern passed not ten yards from me, the ground quaking with the roar of the steam engines, cascades of silt and yellow water sliding off the paddle wheel.

I put my food down and stood up from my chair and stared in disbelief as the bow and the lighted pilothouse and the rows of passenger compartments and the woman in the hooped crinoline dress and the stern of the boat were enveloped by the fog, the wake landing on the bank with a loud slap.

"Dave?" I heard someone say.

I turned around. Alafair was standing twenty feet behind me in her bathrobe and slippers.

"Did you see that?" I asked.

"See what?"

"That double-decker that just went by."

"No, I didn't see anything. What are you doing down here?"

"The drawbridge was stuck. It woke me up. A paddle wheeler just went down the bayou."

She walked down to the water's edge, leaning forward, peering southward into the fog. "Just now?"

"Thirty seconds ago."

She looked at me strangely. I took out my pocket-knife and cut my sandwich in half and handed her my plate with the half on it that I had not bitten into. But she ignored the gesture. "You're telling me you just saw a riverboat, the kind with the big paddle wheel in back?" she said.

I sat down next to her and glanced at the eastern sky. "How about that sunrise? Isn't that something?" I said.

If you're lucky, at a certain age you finally learn not to contend with the world or try to explain that the application of reason has little or nothing to do with the realities that exist just on the other side of one's fingertips.

THAT SAME MORNING, Clete Purcel drove to the cottage on Bayou Teche that Emma Poche rented just outside St. Martinville. It was a restored cypress structure, perhaps over a century old, unpainted, set back in deep shade under live oaks, its small gallery hung with baskets of impatiens. Emma's car was parked on the grass under a tree, a back window half down. On the seat he could see an oversize tennis racquet and a can of balls. The surface of the bayou was wrinkling in the breeze. In the distance he could see a graveyard filled with whitewashed crypts and the back of the nightclub where he had torn Herman Stanga apart.

It was Emma's day off. When she came to the screen door, she was wearing sweatpants and a T-shirt, her face unwashed and lined with sleep. She gazed at him a moment and said, "What do you want, Clete?"

"To take you to breakfast," he said.

"What's the point? It's over."

"If you say so. But it shouldn't end over a mis-understanding about that pen. Any one of a half-dozen skells could have creeped my place, somebody working for the guy who popped Stanga."

He could barely make out her features through the grayness of the screen. Her eyes were lowered, as though she were considering his words. "I need to get in the shower. Fix some coffee if you want," she said. She unsnapped the latch on the door and walked toward the back of the cottage. A few moments later, while he poured coffee grinds in the top of an old-time drip pot, he heard the sound of water hitting on the tin walls of the shower stall. A wood-bladed fan spun slowly on the ceiling of the living room. The furnishings in the room were sparse and looked thread-worn or purchased secondhand. A bookcase next to the television set contained mostly popular music CDs and a few paperback editions of novels that seemed to have no thematic connection and probably had been picked up at yard sales. But one book caught his eye. It was a blue hardcover and was stamped with the words THE BOOK OF AL-COHOLICS ANONYMOUS. Clete picked it up and sat down in a stuffed chair that puffed up dust when his buttocks sank into the seat cushion. He opened the book and heard the spine make a cracking sound. On the title page, someone had written:

To Emma,
> With hopes that you won't misplace this one.
> All the best from your easy-does-it friend,
> Tookie

Clete replaced the book on the shelf. Emma came out of the back dressed in a fresh pair of jeans and a cowboy shirt. She had put on makeup and perfume and earrings and looked lovely framed against the window and the view of the trees and the bayou outside.

"I fixed coffee," he said.

"Yeah, I smelled it."

"Where are the cups?" he said.

She rubbed her forearm, her expression a mixture of indecision and frustration. "Clete, I don't know how else to say this. You treated me with distrust and disdain. You hurt me deeply. And you did it after we made love. The word is 'after.' You made me feel dirty and cheap."

"It wasn't intentional. It just worked out that way." He stared hopelessly at the ceiling. "What should I have done? Not tell you that somebody planted a gold pen with my name on it at a homicide scene?"

But she made no reply.

"Who's Tookie?" he said.

She had to think a second to make the connection. "Where'd you hear about Tookie?"

"I just saw her name in your book."

"Which book?"

"Your A.A. book. She wrote a note in there."

Emma was frowning, obviously not understand-

ing. He reached up on the shelf and opened the blue
hardcover on his lap and turned to the title page.
"See, she wrote—"

"Tookie Goula was my sponsor for a short time.
She has jailhouse tats all over her arms. She used to
hook in truck stops in the Upper South. Truckers
call them 'pavement princesses.' Tookie looks more
like the Beast of Buchenwald now. Or a reverse
Beast of Buchenwald. A fat, lumpy lampshade with
tats."

Clete tried to assimilate what he had just heard.
In the silence, Emma seemed to grow even more irritable. "Does that answer your question?" she asked.

"I guess. You play tennis? I saw the racquet in
your car."

"I hit a few balls on the wall at the park sometimes."

"I'd like to take that up myself," he said.

She began taking down cups and saucers from
one of the kitchen cabinets. Then she stopped and
turned around. "I've already moved on, Clete. I
don't hold what you did against you. But you need
to find somebody else."

"You've got another guy?"

"That's my business."

"Your friend Tookie, the one who gave you the
book, you'd already read her inscription in there?"

"Yeah, she gave me the book. To tell you the
truth, I think you should see a counselor. Or go to
A.A. meetings or spend more time with Dave Robicheaux, because I think both of you have broken
glass in your head."

"I think you're right."

"What's that mean?"

"I've got some terrible character defects, the chief
of which is I'm a rotten judge of people."

"Say again?"

"Nope. I'm eighty-sixing myself from your house," he replied, blowing out his breath.

He went outside and let the screen slam behind him. He walked toward his Caddy, across the lawn, past her car, glancing inside again at the tennis racquet and the can of balls. Clete knew little about the cost of tennis racquets, but the logo on the cover of this one indicated that it was probably expensive and not of a kind that a casual player would purchase, particularly one who lived on a parish deputy's salary. He heard the screen door open behind him.

"Clete?" she said. She was standing on the gallery, her hands on her hips. "The coffee is ready. Come back in and have a cup. We're still friends. I didn't mean to talk so harshly."

A smile wrinkled at the corner of her mouth. The wind blew a strand of hair on her cheek. She squared her shoulders slightly, tightening her breasts against her cowboy shirt. Clete folded his big arms across his chest and seemed to think for a long time, as though trying to recover a detail from his memory that was of enormous importance. "I dug your butterfly tattoo. The truth is, I dug you, too, Emma," he said. "But when somebody lies to me, it's like somebody spitting in the punch bowl. I find another watering hole."

Then he got in his Caddy and drove away, clicking on a CD of Bob Seger's "Old Time Rock and Roll" full-blast.

HE CAME TO my house early Saturday morning and said he wanted to go fishing, but I didn't believe that was the reason for his visit. Clete's external scars and his indifference to them belied the level of injury that he often carried inside him. Regardless of how badly he was treated by women, or how treacherous they turned out to be, he always blamed himself for the failed relationship. Even more paradoxically, he refused to speak ill of them under any circumstances and would not allow others to do so, either. Like most Irish, the pagan in him was alive and well, but he kept a pew in a medieval cathedral where the knight-errant genuflected in a cone of stained light, blood-soaked cloak or not.

"You think I just blew it, or maybe—" he said.

We were sitting in his Caddy, the top down, under the overhang of the trees on East Main. The morning was still cool, the sunrise barely visible through the canopy. "Maybe what?" I said.

"She's dirty."

"Dirty on what?"

"Everything. I started running the tape backward in my head. When I'm surveilling Carolyn Blanchet at the motel, Emma comes walking out of the lounge and sees me and says she's waiting for her uncle. Except the uncle never shows up, and I end up getting loaded with her and in the sack with her later that night. Then my gold pen disappears and shows up in Stanga's swimming pool. Then I see this expensive tennis racquet in her car and I start thinking about who else plays tennis. Like Carolyn Blanchet. Then Emma lies to me about seeing the inscription in the A.A. book. That book had never been opened. Then she tries to get me to come back in the house, maybe for some more high-octane boom-boom. I got to admit it was a temptation." Clete rubbed the tops of his bare arms. "I feel like I've walked through cobwebs."

"You're trying to put yourself in the mind of a wet drunk."

"I *am* a wet drunk."

"No, you're not. You're still an amateur."

"Will you stop trying to make me feel better? Do you think I got taken over the hurdles or not?"

"Why would Emma Poche want to help somebody frame you for clipping Stanga?"

"I don't know. That's what I'm asking you."

"You think she was at the motel to meet Carolyn Blanchet?"

"It occurred to me," he replied. "But if she's a lesbian or a switch-hitter, she had me fooled. When you take a ride with Emma Poche, there's no eight-second buzzer."

"Will you grow up? This woman is trying to ruin your life, and you talk about her like you're seventeen years old."

"What's wrong with that?"

"Vidor Perkins came to my office."

"Are you serious?"

"He says he's writing a book. He says Timothy Abelard, Kermit's grandfather, was involved in the drug trade with the Giacano family. He claims Timothy Abelard stiffed the Giacanos, and they had his son and the daughter-in-law wrapped in chains and dropped in sixty feet of water."

"Abelard got his own kid killed?"

"That's what Perkins says."

"And he's putting this in a book and telling you about it?"

"That's about it."

"Is he trying to extort the Abelards or get himself killed?"

"I think he genuinely believes he's a great talent. He's already contacted a literary agency and says he and Alafair are going to be colleagues."

Clete rubbed his forehead. He'd had a haircut

the day before and a good night's sleep, and his face looked pink and youthful, his intelligent green eyes full of warmth and mirth, the way they were years ago when we walked a beat on Canal. "We've had a good run, haven't we?" he said.

"The best," I said.

He rested the palms of his big hands on the steering wheel. He watched a solitary leaf spin out of the canopy of live oaks above us and light on the waxed hood of the Cadillac. "You don't figure Layton Blanchet for a suicide?" he said.

"I'm not objective. Most people looking at the scene evidence would put his death down as self-inflicted. I think Layton was too greedy to kill himself. He was the kind of guy who clings to the silverware when the mortician drags him out of his home."

"Let's go out there," Clete said.

"What for?"

"Maybe the guy was a butthead, maybe not, but he was my client. Maybe if I had found out who his wife was pumping, he wouldn't be dead," he replied.

I told Molly where we were going, and we hitched the boat to the back of my pickup, put our rods and tackle boxes and an ice chest inside, and drove down through Jeanerette and Franklin to the Atchafalaya Basin. I didn't particularly want to revisit the scene of Layton's death. To me, he was not a sympathetic victim. He reminded me of too many people I had known, all of whom had become acolytes in a pantheon where the admission fee was the forfeiture of their souls or at least their self-respect. But unfortunately, like drunks driving at high speed through red lights, the Layton Blanchets of the world made choices for others before they self-destructed. Bernadette Latiolais and Fern Michot didn't get to vote when their lives were arbitrarily taken from them, and I believed I owed both of them a debt.

We drove down the same levee where Layton had parked his pickup truck on the last day of his life. The water was high from the rain, lapping across the cypress knees, the strings of early hyacinths rolling in the waves. The sky was overcast, the wind steady out of the south, and in the distance I could see a flat bronze-colored bay starting to cap and moss straightening on a line of dead cypress trees. I pulled the truck to a stop and cut the engine. Leaves were blowing on the water where Layton's houseboat was moored, and the yellow crime-scene tape strung through the gum and cypress trees had been broken by wild animals. The aluminum rowboat was lifting and falling with the waves, clanking against a cypress knee or a chunk of concrete. For some reason, maybe because of the grayness of the day, the entire scene made me think of a party's aftermath, when the revelers return to their homes and leave others to clean up.

Clete stared through the windshield, screwing a cigarette into his mouth. "What's she doing here?" he said.

"Good question," I replied.

But if Emma Poche, dressed in her deputy's uniform and rubber boots, took notice of us, she gave no sign of it. Her back was turned, a roll of fresh crime-scene tape hanging from her left hand. She slapped at an insect on her neck and wiped her palm on her clothes. Then she seemed to see us, smiling casually, not overly concerned by our presence. On the far end of the houseboat, I saw an outboard tied by its painter to the deck rail. Clete and I crossed the plank walkway and stepped onto the island. "Aren't you out of your jurisdiction?" he said to Emma.

"The St. Martin and St. Mary parish line runs right through this bay. In fact, no one is sure exactly where it is," she said.

"What are you doing?" he asked.

"None of your business," she said. But she was smiling with her eyes as she said it, looking at me as though the two of us shared a private joke. "We got a call that some kids were trying to get into the houseboat."

"I guess some people got no respect," Clete said.

"Why are you guys out here?" she asked.

"Entertaining the bass," I said.

"At this exact spot. My, my," she said.

"Yeah, what a coincidence," I said.

"Are you questioning my jurisdictional authority, two guys who have no business here at all?" she said.

"No, we're not, Emma," I said. "Did you know Layton?"

"I saw him around. Listen, Dave, if you have a question about my being here, call the dispatcher and have her check the log. Because I don't like y'all's insinuation."

"We just happened by," I said, walking to the rowboat. "How many shell casings did the St. Mary guys find?"

"I wouldn't know," she replied.

"If Layton used a semiauto, and there was a second shell casing, that would present quite a puzzle, wouldn't it?" I said.

"You'd have to ask somebody else that. Frankly, I don't care. That's why I'm in uniform and not a detective. I don't like carrying caseloads and taking the job home every day. Also, I'm not that smart."

I faced into the wind as though I had lost interest in the subject. "It's pretty out here," I said.

"Yeah, it is. Or it was," she said.

"Was?" I said.

"Fuck off, Dave," she said.

I smelled tobacco smoke. Clete had just lit his cigarette and was staring down at the rowboat, his gaze sweeping from the bow to the stern, lingering on the dried blood from Layton's massive head wound. "You don't mind if we just stand here for a little bit, do you?" he said to Emma.

"Do whatever you want. After I rewrap the scene, don't cross the tape again," she replied.

She walked into the shallows, among the flooded trees, and strung fresh tape through the trunks. Soon she was on the other side of the houseboat, out of earshot. Clete continued to puff on his cigarette, his attention still fixed reflectively on the rowboat. I pulled the cigarette gently from his fingers and flicked it into the wind and heard it hiss when it struck the water. His concentration was such that he didn't seem to notice. "So Blanchet was lying on his back, looking skyward, his head in the stern?"

"Right," I said.

"And the forty-five was in his right hand?"

"He had one finger in the trigger guard."

"Which way was the wind blowing when y'all found him?"

"Just like today, straight out of the south."

"Was the boat more or less in the same position, or did the paramedics move it?"

"It's exactly in the same position."

"How do you know?"

"The bow is right by that same piece of concrete," I said.

"Look at the willow tree."

"Yeah?"

"There's still exit matter on the lower branches. But the branches are three feet behind the stern. It's too far back."

"I'm not following you, Clete."

"Look, I'm speculating, but if he set the forty-five under his chin and pulled the trigger, the fluids and bone matter from the wound would have gone straight up into the tree's overhang. But what if somebody is in the boat with Blanchet and wants to distract him? Somebody with the forty-five hidden under a raincoat. He tells Blanchet to look up at a comet, a constellation, an owl or a hawk flying across the moon. Then the shooter plants one under his chin, and Blanchet's oatmeal flies into the tree."

"I think you're probably right, Clete, but I tried to sell that one to the sheriff, and it didn't slide down the pipe."

"Yeah, well, screw the sheriff. This is still St. Mary Parish, Louisiana's answer to the thirteenth century." Clete squatted down, steadying himself with one hand on the gunwale of the rowboat. "Think of it this way. If you're correct in your hypothesis about the shooter putting the forty-five in Layton's hand and letting off a second round, where would the shot have gone?"

I could see where he was taking his re-creation of the moments that had followed Layton Blanchet's death. Clete was still the best investigative detective I had ever known. He had the ability to see the world through the eyes of every kind of person imaginable; he knew their thoughts before they had them. The same applied to the physical world. Where others saw only an opaque surface, Clete saw layers and layers of meaning beneath it.

"Okay, so Blanchet's brains go flying into the

willow tree, and he falls backward into the stern of the boat, about two hundred and twenty pounds of hard beef," he said. "So what is our shooter going to do at this point? He's probably still in the boat with Blanchet. He can put the forty-five in Blanchet's hand and try to aim it away from him toward the levee. But he's going to blow gunpowder residue on Blanchet's clothes, plus deafen himself. Or he can climb out of the boat and stand in the shallows and point the forty-five toward the island, above the houseboat. The bullet should have carried across the bay and into the swamp. Hang on."

Clete climbed into the rowboat. His weight caused it to rock violently back and forth, then he sat down on one of the seats, stabilizing the hull, and eased himself into the position Layton's body had been in when we found it. Clete rested his head on the stern and let his right arm flop over the gunwale. He configured his thumb and index finger into the shape of a pistol and sighted as though aiming at a target. The tip of his finger pointed directly at the houseboat.

"Y'all didn't find anything in there that looked like a bullet hole, did you?" he asked.

"*I* didn't." Then I thought about it. "Good Lord."

"What?"

"In the galley there was a paper trash sack with pieces of a broken drinking glass inside it. But there were also some slivers of glass in one corner, under a window. I thought they were from the drinking glass and somebody had overlooked them when he was sweeping up."

Clete climbed back out of the boat, the water soaking his tennis shoes and the bottoms of his khakis. "Let's have a look," he said.

But Emma Poche was not in a cooperative mood. "You guys aren't going inside that boat," she said. "Number one, I don't have a key. Number two, you have to get permission from my boss or the St. Mary sheriff. Number three, I know how y'all think and operate, and I'm not gonna let either of you pick that lock."

"Do you mind if we look around outside?" I asked.

"Why, for God's sakes?" she said.

"I don't know. When we arrived here, I got the feeling you were looking along the bank for something," I said. "Maybe we'll find it for you."

"I just remembered why I don't go to A.A. anymore," she said.

"I'll bite. Why's that?"

"Because of the sexist male pricks I met there," she replied.

"We'll be out of your way in just a minute," I said.

"Be my guest. Take all the time you want. Like five minutes. And 'bite' is the word," she said. She stiffened an index finger and pointed it at me. Her cheeks were bright with color as she went back to work stringing tape in the trees, jerking it hard through the limbs.

"You'll never win their hearts and minds," Clete said to me.

"You wouldn't pick a lock at a crime scene, would you?"

"Emma might be a little nuts, but she's one cute, smart little package," he replied.

"I can't believe you."

"Give the devil her due. Look at the ass on her."

"I give up, Clete."

He slapped me between the shoulder blades, his

face full of play. Clete Purcel would never change. And if he did, I knew the world would be the less for it.

We stepped up on the houseboat and worked our way forward, examining the molding around the windows in the galley. A long chrome-plated bar that a person could use as a handhold was anchored along the roof of the cabin. At the approximate spot where I had seen glass slivers on the other side of the wall, I saw what looked like an empty screw hole in one of the metal fastenings on the bar. Except it was not a screw hole. I stuck my little finger inside and felt the rough edges of torn wood and a sharpness like splintered glass.

I removed my finger and put one hand on Clete's shoulder and stepped up on the deck rail so I could see across the top of the cabin roof. Eighteen inches from the chrome-plated bar was an exit hole in the roof. The .45 round had punched through the hand bar's fastening and clipped the top of the glass inset into the window, before surfacing obliquely from the treated plywood that constituted the ceiling to the galley.

"You were dead-on right," I said.

"You found it?"

"We've got the entry and exit holes, but no slug."

Clete pushed himself up on the deck rail so he could see. Emma Poche was watching us from out in the water. "You think this is going to make any difference with the sheriff in St. Mary?" he asked.

"Like you say, this is still a fiefdom," I replied.

"What are y'all doing up there?" Emma called.

We both stared at her without replying. The sun had come out, and her hair and face and uniform were netted with light and shadow.

"Did you hear me?" she said.

"Why'd you bring crime-scene tape on a 911 possible break-in?" I said.

"Because it was already in my goddamn boat," she replied.

I drummed my fingers on the cabin roof. "You ever carry a forty-five auto as a drop, Emma?" I asked.

She began to gather up the strips of crime-scene tape broken by deer or bear, and stuff them into her trouser pockets. "When I turn around again, you two cutie-pies had better be out of here," she said.

"My flopper just started flipping around," Clete said.

CHAPTER 15

MOLLY AND I attended four P.M. Mass in Loreauville that Saturday, with plans to go to dinner and a movie afterward in Lafayette. Alafair was at home by herself, working on her novel, when the phone rang. "Miss Alafair?" the voice said.

"Yes?" Alafair said.

"It's Jewel, Mr. Timothy's nurse."

In her mind's eye, Alafair saw the big, ubiquitous black woman in the starched white uniform who constantly attended Timothy Abelard in his home and took him everywhere he went. What was the rumor about her? That she was Abelard's illegitimate daughter?

"Mr. Timothy axed if you'd come out to see him," Jewel said.

"Then ask him to call me, Miss Jewel," Alafair replied.

"He's embarrassed."

"Excuse me?"

"By the way you were treated by Mr. Robert. He knows all about it."

"Miss Jewel, you've called me and done your job, so this isn't a reflection upon you. But if Mr. Abelard wants to talk with me, he needs to call me personally. You tell him I said that, please."

"Yes, ma'am. He said to tell you his son and Mr. Robert aren't there right now."

"I understand. Thanks for calling, Miss Jewel. Good-bye," Alafair said. She replaced the receiver and went back to her room and began work on her manuscript again. Through the back window she could see the shadows growing in the trees, the afternoon sun ablaze like a bronze shield on the bayou. The phone rang in the kitchen once more. This time she checked the caller ID. It was blocked. "Hello," she said, hoping it was not who she thought it was.

"Oh, hello, Miss Robicheaux. It's Timothy Abelard. I hope I'm not bothering you," the voice said.

"Miss Jewel gave me your message, Mr. Abelard. I appreciate your courtesy, but no apology is necessary regarding Kermit."

"That's very gracious of you. But I feel terrible about what's occurred. I don't know your father well, but I was quite an admirer of your grandfather, Big Aldous. He was an extraordinary individual, generous of spirit and always brave at heart. It saddens me that any member of my family or an associate of my family would offend his granddaughter in any fashion."

Timothy Abelard's voice and diction were as melodic and hypnotizing as branch water flowing over stone. The syllabic emphasis created an iambic cadence, like lines taken from an Elizabethan sonnet, and the *r*'s were so soft they almost disappeared from the vowels and consonants surrounding them. If an earlier development of technology had allowed the recording of Robert E. Lee's voice, Alafair suspected, it would sound like Timothy Abelard's.

"How can I help you?" she found herself saying.

"Jewel is only a couple of blocks from you. Let her drive you to my home. My son and his friend Robert are away right now. We'll have a cup of tea, and I promise Jewel will return you to New Iberia before dark."

"I don't know how that will serve any purpose, Mr. Abelard."

"I'm elderly and bound to a wheelchair, and I don't have many possessions I consider of value except the honorable name of my family. I feel, in this instance, it's been sullied. I ask you to visit me for no more than a few minutes. I will have no peace until you do so."

She thought about driving herself to the Abelard home, but her car was being serviced at the Texaco station down the street. "I'd be happy to come out," she said.

Moments later, the nurse pulled a Lincoln Town Car into the driveway, the oak leaves drifting out of the sunset onto the shiny black surface.

TIMOTHY ABELARD WAS on the lawn in his wheelchair when Alafair arrived on the island where his home seemed to rise out of its own elegant decay. He was dressed in a beige suit and an open-necked crimson shirt, one that had a metallic sheen to it, his black tie-shoes buffed to a dull luster. Since Alafair's last visit there, a landscape architect had hung baskets of flowers from the upstairs veranda and lined the walks and pathways with potted palms and orchid trees and flaming hibiscus, as though trying to import the season to a place where it would not take hold of its own accord. Against the backdrop of stricken trees in the lagoon and the termite infestation of the house, the transported floral ambience on the property made Alafair think of flowers scattered on a grave in an isolated woods.

"I'm so glad you could come," Mr. Abelard said, extending his hand.

Someone had already placed a beach umbrella in a metal stand on the lawn, and under it a chair for her to sit in. Timothy Abelard was sitting in the shade of the umbrella, a photo album open on his lap. When Alafair sat down, she found herself unconsciously pinching her knees together, her hands folded. Mr. Abelard smiled, his eyes examining her, one eye a bit smaller and brighter than the other. "I was just looking at some photos taken when I was a bit younger," he said. "In Banff and at Lake Louise, in Alberta. Here, take a look."

He turned the scrapbook around so she could see the photos in detail. In one, Abelard was standing on a great stone porch of some kind, perhaps on the back of a hotel. Behind him were banks of flowers that were so thick and variegated in color that they dazzled the eyes. In the distance were dark blue mountains razored against the sky, their snowcapped tops so high they disappeared into the clouds. In another photo, Abelard was eating on a terrace not far from a green lake surrounded by golden poppies. A glacier stood at the headwaters of the lake, and at the table where Abelard was dining sat a man with patent-leather-black hair. He was suntanned and wearing shades and a black shirt unbuttoned on his chest.

"That's Robert Weingart," she said.

Abelard turned the scrapbook back around on his lap. "No, you're mistaken. That fellow is someone else."

Before she could speak again, he said, "You have your father's features."

"Dave is my foster parent. He pulled me from a submerged airplane when I was very small," she said. "I think I was born in El Salvador, but I can't be sure. My mother died in the plane crash."

"I'm sorry to hear that. Are you a citizen today?"

"In my opinion, I am."

"Legality and morality are not always the same thing, is that it? That's an interesting perception. How is your novel progressing?"

"Fine. Thank you for asking. What is all this about, Mr. Abelard?"

When he grinned, his mouth exposed an incisor tooth, and the sunlight seemed to pool in the eye that was smaller and more liquid than the other. "In part, it's about what I just mentioned—morality as opposed to legality. This man named Vidor Perkins, a past associate of Robert Weingart, was hanging around the island. I had to run him off. Now Robert has informed me that Mr. Perkins is writing a book containing fabrications about my family. In the eyes of the law, this man has completed his prison sentence in the state of Texas, and legally, he has every right to be in our community. But in my view, he does not have the moral right, particularly when he slanders others. What are your feelings about that, Miss Robicheaux?"

"I don't have any feelings about it at all. I have nothing to say about this man except that I didn't bring him here."

"But I did?"

She looked at the sunlight on the dead cypress trees in the lagoon and didn't reply.

"Well, reticence is a statement in itself," Abelard said. "My grandson is weak. But I suspect you've learned that."

"Sir?"

"It's not his fault. His parents died when he was a teenager, and I protected and spoiled him. He's worked with his hands in the oil field and championed all kinds of leftist causes, but inside he's always been a scared little boy. So he attached himself to Robert and thought that would give him the masculine dimension he doesn't possess in his own right. Unfortunately for him, his dependency on Robert cost him his relationship with you, didn't it?"

"I don't dwell on it. I don't think you should, either."

"My hearing isn't all that it should be. Would you repeat that?"

"No."

"Beg your pardon?"

"No, I won't repeat it. And I won't talk about Kermit. You said your family's honor had been sullied and you would have no peace unless you set something straight. If you're telling me that somehow your family name has been tarred because of an offense committed against me, you're seriously overrating the importance of your family. I couldn't care less about what Kermit or Robert Weingart did or didn't do. I feel sorry for Kermit, but he made his choice. As far as Robert Weingart is concerned, if you wanted him out of this community, he'd be gone in twenty-four hours. Why don't you deal with your own culpability and stop demeaning your grandson?"

"You're speaking to me as though I'm benighted. Or perhaps condemned by God for my sins and unworthy of respect."

"I don't know what your sins are."

"Be assured they are many. But not of the kind you think—greed and misuse of power and all the kind of nonsense that liberals like to rave on and on about. If there is a great sin in my life for which I'll be held to account, it lies in not accepting the rules of mortality."

"Sir?"

"You're not deaf, are you?" he said, smiling, leaning forward in his wheelchair. "Paul Gauguin wrote, 'Life is merely a fraction of a second. An infinitely small amount of time to fulfill our desires, our dreams, our passions.' I've tried to buy back my youth, with various degrees of success. They say it can't be done, but they're wrong. Youth isn't a matter of physical appearance. It resides in one's deeds. It doesn't die until the heart and the brain and the glands die. Those who say different not only give up the joy of living but seek the grave."

"You've found the secret to eternal youth?"

"No, it's not eternal. But its pleasures can be magnified with age rather than surrendered."

"Why are you telling me this?"

"Because my grandson is a fool and didn't know what he had."

His mouth flexed slightly, and she saw the tip of his tongue wet his lip. An odor like menthol rub and dried perspiration seemed to rise from his clothes.

"I think I'll go now."

"I've offended you?"

"Not me. Perhaps God. But I'm not sure He would waste his time on you, Mr. Abelard."

"You're a mixture of Spaniard and Indian. Your heritage is the Inquisition and blood sacrifice on a stone altar. You think those are removed by a cleric splashing water on you? I read part of your novel, the one you gave to Kermit. You're a talented and intelligent young woman. Why do you talk the theological rot of a fishwife?"

She stood up from the chair and took a breath. "I'm going to walk across your bridge and down your road. You can send Miss Jewel to pick me up and take me home. Or you can decide not to, whichever you prefer."

"Stay," he said, one hand reaching out toward her like a claw.

Then she saw the speedboat out on the bay, Robert Weingart at the wheel, Kermit being towed on skis in the wake.

"You lied," she said.

"About what?"

"You told Miss Jewel to tell me they were away."

"They were. Out on the boat. That's what 'away' means. They weren't here."

"You had me fooled for a minute, Mr. Abelard," she said. "I thought you might be a genuinely wicked man. Instead, you're simply a cheap liar. Excuse me, sir, but you excite an emotion in me that I can only express as *yuck*."

She began walking across the bridge, her purse on her shoulder, her dress swaying on the backs of her thighs, her shoes loud on the planks. For a moment she thought she could feel the eyes of Timothy Abelard burrowing into her back; then she went around a bend in the road bordered on each side by undergrowth and thick stands of timber. A solitary blue heron glided above her, its wings stenciled against the sky. It turned in a wide arc and landed in the shallows of a green pond that resembled a giant teardrop. Through the trees she could see it pecking at its feathers, unconcerned about her presence or the sound of her footfalls on the road or the motorboat with Robert Weingart at the wheel streaking across the bay. Somehow the sight of the bird and its ability to find the place it needed to be seemed to contain a lesson that perhaps she had forgotten. In moments, the easy rhythm of walking and the wind bending the gum trees and the slash pines had erased the exchange with Timothy Abelard from her mind, and she concentrated on trying to get service on her cell phone.

ALAFAIR WAS STILL up when Molly and I got home from the movie theater in Lafayette. She told us what had happened on the Abelards' island.

"Abelard didn't send a car to take you home?" I said.

"No," she said.

"You had to walk all the way to the highway to get a cab?" I said.

"It wasn't that far." She was sitting at the breakfast table in the kitchen, her shoes off, a bowl of ice cream in front of her.

"Why didn't you call me?"

"Because I didn't want to take you away from your evening out. Because it's not a big deal."

I went to the telephone on the counter and picked up the receiver, then set it down again. "I suspect Abelard's number is unlisted. Do you have it?"

"He's just an old man. Leave him alone," she said.

"Don't underestimate him."

"He's pathetic. You didn't see him."

"You know the term 'the banality of evil'? When Adolf Eichmann was captured by Israeli commandos, he was working as a chrome polisher in an automobile plant, a guy who helped send six million people to their deaths."

"Mr. Abelard is a shriveled-up worm and should be treated as nothing less and nothing more," she replied. "Put it in neutral, big guy."

"Listen to Dave, Alafair," Molly said. "Timothy Abelard bought politicians and the law most of his life. No one is sure what kinds of crimes he may have committed. If he had you brought out to his island, it may have been for a purpose you don't want to think about."

Alafair set down her spoon on a napkin and looked at it. She rubbed her temple and picked up her bowl of ice cream and placed it inside the freezer. "He showed me some pictures that were taken years ago in the Canadian Rockies. In one of them, he was sitting at a table with a man who looked like Robert Weingart. Except Mr. Abelard looked twenty years younger in the photo, and Robert looked like he does today."

"Weingart has had plastic surgery. There's no telling how old he is," I said. "I've pulled his jacket in three states. He's been giving different birth years throughout his entire criminal career."

"You think Mr. Abelard showed me that photo by mistake, or he had an agenda?" she asked.

"I think he had one thing only on his mind, Alafair," I said.

"I want to take another shower," she said.

I went to the refrigerator and took Alafair's bowl of ice cream out of the freezer as well as an unopened half gallon of French vanilla, then got a jar of blackberries from down below and placed two more bowls on the counter. "A pox on the Abelards and a pox on Robert Weingart," I said. "Bring Tripod and Snuggs inside, and bring in their bowls, too."

"Dave, do you think Timothy Abelard killed those girls?" Alafair asked.

"Do I think he's capable of it?" I said. "I'm not sure. Mr. Abelard is a shadow, not a presence. I don't think he's like the rest of us. But I have no idea what or who he is."

ONCE IN A while, even the slowest of us has an epiphany, a brief glimpse through the shroud when we see the verities reduced to a simple equation. For someone whose profession requires him to place himself inside the mind of aberrant people, the challenge is often daunting. Then, as if you're tripping on a rock in the middle of a foot-worn, clay-smooth path, you suddenly become aware that the complexity you wish to unravel exists to a greater degree in your own mind than in the problem itself.

Early Sunday morning, while Molly and Alafair were still asleep, I walked down East Main in the fog, past The Shadows, hoping to find a breakfast spot open. On the far side of The Shadows, where a gravel drive leads down to the bayou between a long wall of green bamboo and the old brick Ford dealership that has been converted into law offices, I thought I heard footsteps behind me. When I turned around, I could see nothing but fog puffing through the piked fence on The Shadows' lawn, swallowing the streetlamps, rising into the live oaks overhead. I crossed the gravel drive and continued down the street toward the drawbridge, where I could hear a boat blowing its horn to gain the tender's attention. Then I heard footsteps behind me again. This time, when I turned around, I held my ground and waited, my gaze fastened on the figure walking out of the mist toward me.

A small pink digital camera, one that a woman might own, hung on a strap from one shoulder. A leather carrying case, one that could have held either binoculars or just odds and ends, hung from the other. Notebooks and several pens were stuffed in his shirt pockets. He wore a flat-brimmed straw hat that had a black band around the crown, the kind a nineteenth-century planter might have worn. But his shirt was tucked in and he wasn't wearing a coat and his hands were empty, and I thought it unlikely he had a weapon on his person.

What is the lesson that most cops and traditional mainline cons have learned since the 1960s regarding America's prisons? It's simple. With the exception of those caught up in the three-strikes-and-you're-out legislation of the 1990s, almost anyone who does time today either is incurably defective or wants to be inside. If you don't believe

me, check out who's on the yard. The swollen deltoids and shaved heads and outrageous one-color
tats are cosmetic. The first thing a frightened pagan
does is paint his face blue and disfigure his skin. The
simian brow and the wide-set eyes and the mouth
that is like a raw slit tell the story of the crowd on
the yard much more accurately. From the time most
of them threw a curbstone through a window or
set fire to their middle school or boosted a car and
drove it across spike strips at one hundred miles an
hour, they were looking for a way to punch a hole
in the dimension and return to a place where people
grunted in front of their caves and knocked down
their food with a rock. I can't say I blame them.
We're running out of space. But I think the crowd
by the weight sets on the yard would be the first to
say that societal injustice has little to do with the
factors that put them in prison.

"You wouldn't bird-dog a fellow on Sunday
morning, would you, Mr. Perkins?" I said.

"I was just taking a walk, not unlike yourself,
Detective Robicheaux," he said.

"You're ten miles from your house, Mr. Perkins."

"That's true. But I love New Iberia's downtown
area. As long as you're here, I'd like to ask you some
questions regarding my book. I watched Miss Alafair at Mr. Abelard's house through my field glasses
yesterday."

"You did what?"

"She was in no danger, sir. I had my eye on her
the whole time she was there. If anything had happened, I would have called you right away. Or I
might have taken action myself."

"You're spying on my daughter or the Abelards?"

"I'm not spying on nobody. I'm doing research
on my book. But I have to admit I've taken a liking

to you. Your daughter, too, yes, sir. You're dealing with a dangerous bunch. You're an educated and respectable man, so you see these people from the top down. I see them from the bottom up. I'm not sure what the bigger scheme is, but I know these people ain't what they pretend to be. Robert Weingart thinks he's got them outsmarted, but when they're done with him, he'd best look out, that's all I can say. What about you and me teaming up?"

"Say again?"

"We ain't so different. You got a keen eye about people, Detective Robicheaux. You know the Abelards for what they are. Their kind wouldn't spit in my mouth if I was dying of thirst in the Sahara. From what I hear, you grew up pretty much like I did. The Abelards and their ilk treat your folks pretty good?"

I gazed at the lunatical vacuity in his eyes and was convinced that whatever motives drove him, that whatever thoughts he actually had, that whatever his real life experience was, none of it would ever be known by anyone except God.

"Don't follow me anymore, Mr. Perkins. If you do, I'll have a cruiser pick you up," I said.

"That downright hurts my feelings."

"Call my business number if you need to. Or come by the office. Send me a postcard. But do not follow me or come near my house."

"I been watching your back. Your daughter's, too. Wake up and learn who your friends are. Maybe show a little humbleness and gratitude."

I crossed the street and headed toward Clementine's, hoping that an employee would be there and let me in and give me a cup of coffee and a beignet.

"Robert's got two hundred thousand dollars stashed away. That's the kind of money he's siphoned off the deal they got going," Perkins called after me.

I stopped and turned around again. I could see the drawbridge lifting in the fog, its girders beaded with moisture. "What deal?" I said.

"I don't know. That's why you and me got to team up. The weather is fixing to take a turn. The weatherman says a real frog stringer is about to blow in on us. I'd dress for it."

"Get away from me," I said.

I would find out later that my admonition had been neither wise nor fair.

WHEN I RETURNED home, Molly and Alafair were eating breakfast in the kitchen. Through the tree trunks and the gray-green shadows in our backyard, I could see the tidal flow of the bayou reversing itself, the surface undulating as though the current had been infused with a great cushion of air. I told Molly and Alafair that I was going to take a drive into Jeff Davis Parish and that I would be home after lunch.

"What for?" Molly said.

I didn't want to explain, so I said, "I have to check out a couple of things about the Latiolais girl."

"It's Sunday. Why not do it on the clock?" Molly said.

"Helen is not a big fan of my investigating a homicide outside our jurisdiction."

"I'll go with you," she said.

"If you want," I said, my gaze not meeting hers. "Look, I ran into Vidor Perkins on the street. I don't think he intends us any harm. Evidently he's convinced himself he's an author. But I had Wally put a cruiser in front of the house until I get back."

"What was he doing on East Main?" Alafair said.

"Following me."

"Early Sunday morning?" she said.

"He's a wack job. He says he was surveilling the Abelards' compound yesterday and saw you there. But his agenda is with them and not us."

"How do you know?" Molly asked.

"We don't have anything he wants. I'll be back in three hours."

"Dave?" Molly said.

But I didn't answer, in part because no matter how helpful Molly or Alafair wanted to be, I had to find an empty place in my head where I could see the detail I had missed, the image that had not recorded itself on my memory, the line of dialogue that had seemed inconsequential at the time, the finitely small symbol for the larger story that would explain the brutal murders of two innocent girls. Or maybe I would end up concluding that all my speculations were a vanity. Sometimes the clue is not there, or the case information is wrong, or somebody screwed up in the lab. But if Fern Michot and Bernadette Latiolais's killer or killers went not caught or taken off the board in a more primitive fashion, it wouldn't be because no one tried.

I took the old two-lane highway past Spanish Lake and turned onto I-10 in Lafayette and drove to Jennings, then down into the southern tip of the parish where the coastline dissolved into a marshy green haze and eventually became part of a saltwater bay. Just as I had placed Vidor Perkins into a much simpler category, one in which most miscreants have the wingspans of moths rather than pterodactyls, I tried to imagine the makeup of the person or persons who had murdered the two girls. I was sure that sex and misogyny were involved. But I was also sure that finance was as well. And when it came to the big score in Louisiana, from World War II to the present, what was the issue? Always? Without exception? I mean take-it-to-the-bank, lead-pipe cinch, what extractive opportunity in an instant created the sounds of little piggy feet stampeding for the trough?

How about oil? Its extraction and production in Louisiana had set us free from economic bondage to the agricultural oligarchy that had ruled the state from antebellum days well into the mid-twentieth century. But we discovered that our new corporate liege lord had a few warts on his face, too. Like the Great Whore of Babylon, Louisiana was always desirable for her beauty and not her virtue, and when her new corporate suitor plunged into things, he left his mark.

I didn't revisit Bernadette's grandmother; instead, I talked to people at a crossroads store, a bait shop, and a trailer settlement. Some of the damage done by Hurricane Rita was still visible: concrete foundations in empty fields, an automobile wedged upside down in a coulee, the wreckage of homes bulldozed in piles as high as small pyramids, and the tangled bones of livestock that had drowned by the tens of thousands, sometimes on rooftops or inside the second stories of farmhouses. But I was struck most by the riparian resilience of the land, the sawgrass that extended as far as the eye could see, the hummocks of gum and persimmon and hackberry and oak trees, the seagulls and brown pelicans that sailed over the mouth of a freshwater river flowing into the Gulf. In moments like these, I knew that Louisiana was still a magical place, not terribly different than it was when Jim Bowie and his business partner the pirate Jean Lafitte smuggled slaves illegally into the United States and kept them in a barracoon, somewhere close to the very spot I was standing on. If anyone doubts the history I've described, he can visit an island at the south end of this particular parish and perhaps find some of the skeletal remains for which it is known. The skulls and vertebrae and rib cages and femurs that have washed out of the sand belonged to a shipload of slaves abandoned by a blackbirder sea captain who left them to starve when he feared arrest. Louisiana is a poem, but as with the Homeric epic, it's not good to examine its heroes too closely.

I parked my pickup at the end of the road and got out on the asphalt and looked southward. In the alluvial sweep of the land, I thought I could see the past and the present and the future all at once, as though time were not sequential in nature but took place without a beginning or an end, like a flash of green light rippling outward from the center of creation, not unlike a dream inside the mind of God.

I could smell the salt out on the Gulf, the baitfish and shrimp in the waves, the warm and stagnant smell of wet sand and dead vegetation and ponded water in the marsh, and the distant hint of rain and electricity in the clouds. It was a grand place to be. Did the seven arpents of land that Bernadette had inherited from her father have anything to do with her death? Her grandmother had said Bernadette wanted to save the bears. The people I spoke to on the south end of the parish said they knew nothing of any attempt to save bears, nor were they sure where Bernadette's seven arpents might have been located, although they said that many years ago some of the Latiolais family had farmed some rice acreage that had been turned into commercial crawfish ponds. But the ponds had been abandoned because of the importation of Chinese crawfish, and the land was now little more than a soggy swamp.

Plus, Louisiana's land areas had been drilled and redrilled and offered little in the way of further exploration. The money was in offshore drilling, and to my knowledge, no new refineries were being built in Louisiana. What possible value could Bernadette's seven arpents have possessed?

At lunchtime I gave up my odyssey and went back to a crossroads service station where I had stopped earlier. I sat on a chair outside facing the Gulf and ate two microwaved lengths of white boudin and a pile of dirty rice and potato salad off a paper plate. Then I went back inside and bought a fried pie and a cup of Community coffee and ate the pie and drank the coffee while I looked out the window at a shrimp boat moving down a canal through the sawgrass, seagulls whirling and dipping over its wake.

"Find out any more about that property you were looking for, Mr. Robicheaux?" the clerk said. He was in his mid-twenties and wore a crew cut and striped strap overalls and a brown T-shirt.

"Not much," I said. "I'll probably go to the courthouse and check the records tomorrow."

"After you left, another man came in and asked me about that property. No, not exactly about the property, but about the girl, the one who was killed?"

"Bernadette Latiolais."

"Yeah, a man came in and said didn't that girl come from a family that had a rice or crawfish farm here'bouts."

"What did this fellow look like?" I asked.

"'Strange' is the word I'd use."

"Strange in what way?"

"His eyes, they didn't have any pupils."

"What color were they?"

"Blue. And he had black hair combed up on his head."

"What else do you remember about him?"

"He had a country accent, but not one from around here. He was grinning all the time, like there was some kind of joke going on between us. Except I couldn't figure out what the joke was. He had a binocular case hanging from his arm."

"What kind of car was he driving?"

"I didn't pay it much mind, sir."

"What did you tell this fellow?"

"Same thing I told you. I was in the army for the last six years and haven't kept up much with the news at home. You know this guy?"

"Yes, I do." I wrote my cell phone number on the back of my business card and gave it to the clerk. "If you see him again, call me. Don't try to detain him and don't provoke him."

"He's dangerous?"

"Maybe, maybe not. His name is Vidor Perkins. Personally, I wouldn't touch him with a soiled Q-tip. But that's just one man's opinion."

"A soiled Q-tip?" the ex-soldier said. He shook his head and stuck my card under the corner of his register.

I washed my hands in a sink outside the men's room and dried them on a paper towel. Through the window I saw a semi go through the intersection, hauling huge machinery of some kind that was snugged down on the flatbed with boomer chains. A low-slung white car, one with charcoal-tinted windows, was following close behind it. The hood was painted with primer so that it resembled a blackened tooth inset in the car body. The driver was obviously irritated by the slow momentum of the semi and kept gunning his engine, swinging out to pass, then ducking back behind the semi's rear bumper, so close he couldn't adequately see the road. His engine was loud and sounded too powerful for the vehicle. When he gained a clear spot on the road, he floored the accelerator, his vehicle sinking low and flat on the springs, blowing dust and newspaper in his wake, ripping a strip of gravel out of the road shoulder.

There was a Florida plate on the vehicle, the numbers obscured with dirt. There was also orange rust around the bottoms of the doors and fenders, the kinds of patterns you see in automobiles that have been exposed over a long period of time to a saltwater environment. Any Florida-licensed automobile, particularly one built for high speed, is suspect along the I-10 corridor that runs from Jacksonville all the way to Los Angeles. But for those who transport narcotics, and for the cops who try to put them out of business, the area of concern begins at I-95 in Miami. I-95 feeds into I-10 just north of Jacksonville, Florida, and a westward journey from that point on allows the transporter to make drop-offs in Tallahassee, Mobile, Biloxi, New Orleans, Baton Rouge, Lake Charles, Beaumont, and Houston. Like the modern equivalent of Typhoid Mary, one transporter can string systemic misery and death across 20 percent of the country.

Except the transporters have a problem they didn't anticipate. I-10 is heavily patrolled by narcs in the state of Louisiana, particularly in Iberville Parish. As a consequence, transporters often swing off the interstate and use Old Highway 90 or any number of parish roads that are not patrolled.

"Did you ever see that white car that just went south through the intersection?" I asked the clerk.

"It's funny you mention it. He drove by here a couple of times. Once right after the guy with the binoculars was in here."

"Did you get a look at the driver?"

"No, sir, I didn't. I only noticed him because of how loud his engine was."

"If he comes back and you get a look at his tag number, give me a call, will you?"

"Yes, sir, I can do that. What's the problem with this guy?"

"Probably nothing," I said.

I drove north on the road, retracing my route, my radio on, my windows down. The air was balmy, the cow pastures on either side of the road emerald-green and dotted with buttercups and pooled with shadows. But I couldn't shake a feeling that had occurred periodically in my life for decades, often without cause. It was like the tension in a banjo or guitar string that is wrapped too tightly on the peg. Or a tremolo that can travel through the fuselage of an airplane just before you glance out the window and see engine oil blow back across the wing. Or perhaps the cold vapor that wraps around your heart on a night trail, one sown with Bouncing Betties and Chinese toe poppers, or the peculiar distortion in your vision when you climb down into a spider hole and realize you have just touched a thin strand of trip wire attached to a booby-trapped 105 dud.

Years ago I could rid myself of my apprehensions with VA dope and Beam straight up and a Jax back. But I didn't have my old parachute anymore. So I said the Serenity Prayer that is recited in unison at the beginning of every A.A. meeting in the world. If that didn't work, I would use the short form of the same prayer, which is "Fuck it" and is not meant as an irreverent statement.

I pulled to the side of the road and took a deep breath. The wind was cool, and gulls were cawing overhead. Not far away, a black family was cane-fishing in a canal, swinging their bobbers onto the edge of the cattails. It was Sunday, I told myself. A day of rest. A respite from anxiety and fear and ambition and greed and all the other forces that seem to drive our lives. A truck pulling an empty cane wagon rattled past me, then a delivery van with a cargo door. A red airplane that looked like a crop sprayer came in low over a field and, just before it reached a power line, gained altitude again and disappeared beyond a windbreak that had been created by a hedgerow of gum trees.

Now the road was totally empty, both behind and ahead of me. I realized that although my radio was still on, I was unaware of what was being broadcast. It was a baseball game. I clicked off the switch and put my truck in gear. I had accomplished virtually nothing on my trip to Jefferson Parish. Maybe I should at least drop by the home of Bernadette Latiolais's grandmother, I thought. If nothing else, I could offer to drive her somewhere or do a chore for her that she could not do for herself. Something good could come out of my trip.

I parked in front of the grandmother's white frame house and tapped on the screen door, but no one answered. One of the coffee cans planted with petunias had been blown or knocked off the gallery into the yard. I opened the screen and knocked on the inside door. Then I twisted the handle. The door was locked. I walked around the side of the house and into the backyard. The rear door was locked as well, and all the curtains were closed. No vehicle was parked in the yard. I returned to the front yard and stared at the house. The pecan trees and water oaks on the sides of the house were in partial leaf, and the shadows they cast looked like rain running down the walls and tin roof. I picked up the spilled coffee can and repacked the dirt and uprooted petunias with my fingers, then replaced the can on the porch. Hard by the circular spot where the can had originally stood was a muddy smear, the kind the bottom of a shoe or a boot would make.

I was letting it get away from me. Maybe the grandmother had gone to the home of relatives for Sunday dinner. Maybe she was sick and in the hospital. Maybe she had died. I could not think of any reason she would be in danger.

Unless the seven arpents of land owned by Bernadette Latiolais had automatically reverted upon Bernadette's death to the grandmother.

I sat down on the steps and dialed 911 on my cell phone and told the dispatcher who and where I was. "Can you send out a cruiser? I'm a little worried about Mrs. Latiolais," I said.

"What's the nature of your emergency?"

"I'm not sure there is one. But I'm out of my jurisdiction, and I'd like somebody from your department to help me check things out."

"We'll send someone as soon as—" the dispatcher began.

I heard the door open behind me.

CHAPTER 16

"WHAT YOU DOIN'" on my gallery?" Bernadette Latiolais's grandmother said.

"I was looking for you," I replied, getting up from the step. I told the Jeff Davis dispatcher to cancel my request for a cruiser.

"I was taking a nap. I didn't know anybody was out here," the grandmother said. She was silhouetted behind the screen, her thick glasses filled with reflected images of the trees in her yard, her massive weight bent on her walking cane. "Where's that other one?"

"Other what?" I asked.

"I t'ought he was wit' you. He used your name. You're Mr. Robicheaux, aren't you?"

"That's correct. Who used my name, Mrs. Latiolais?"

"Mr. Big Foot did. Knocked my li'l flower can in the yard and didn't pick it up. Just drove on off. In his li'l blue truck."

"Did he give his name?"

"No, he just give yours. Said he was doing research and was a friend of yours, and wanted to know where my granddaughter's land was at."

"What did you tell him?"

"That it was part of a big estate that wasn't never divided. Maybe it's on top of the land, maybe it's underwater. Who cares? My family didn't even own the oil rights. They was sold for ten dollars an arpent back in the twenties. Why's he axing me questions?"

"What did this fellow look like?"

"He had a red birt'mark on the back of his neck."

"Mrs. Latiolais, this man is no friend of mine. He's an ex-convict by the name of Vidor Perkins. If he comes back, don't let him in your house for any reason. Call 911 and have a cruiser sent to your home."

She hobbled out on the porch. Her girth and stooped posture and the entreating manner in which she twisted her head up made me think of a female Quasimodo, stricken and cheated by the fates in ways that were too many to count. "You t'ink he had somet'ing to do wit' what they done to Bernadette?"

"Maybe, but I can't be sure." Then I thought about the words she had just used. "You said 'they.'"

"Suh?"

"When you mentioned your granddaughter's death, you indicated that more than one person was involved."

"'Cause that's what I t'ink. Bernadette didn't just go off wit' some man from a bar, no. She didn't have no interest in that kind of man. She was an honor student. She had a scholarship to colletch. It wasn't one man that tricked her or pulled her into a car or somet'ing like that. It took at least a couple of them cowards to do what they done."

I told her I was sorry for having disturbed her, and I got in my truck. I started the engine and called Clete's cell phone and ended up with his voice mail. "Clete, I'm just now leaving the home of Bernadette Latiolais's grandmother. A man who sounds like Vidor Perkins was here today. He was asking questions about the seven arpents of land Bernadette owned. Do those seven arpents coincide with anything you learned from the families of the other dead girls? Call me back ASAP. I might be here awhile."

As I drove away from the Latiolais home, I could see Mrs. Latiolais in my rearview mirror, still watching me from behind the screen, as though her conversation with me was her only conduit back to the girl who had been stolen from her.

I drove back to the parish road that led north to the interstate and back to New Iberia. But I couldn't give up my obsession with Bernadette Latiolais and the secrets she had probably taken to the grave. What did she mean when she said she was going to save the bears? What had been her relationship with Kermit Abelard? He claimed he had known her name only because she was a recipient of a scholarship his family had endowed. Was Kermit lying? Was he covering up for his grandfather or Robert Weingart or perhaps even Layton Blanchet?

I had never met Bernadette Latiolais, but I had come to admire her. In spite of the poverty in which she had been born, and the illiteracy and ignorance that surrounded her, she had graduated from high school with honors and had won a scholarship to a university. She had wanted to be a nurse and to help others and evidently had wanted to protect wild animals in a state where the hunting culture is almost a religion. Where were her friends and advocates now? I believed more and more that Bernadette had died for a cause and that her homicide was not a random one. And my experience has been that people who die for causes have few friends in death.

For reasons I couldn't quite explain, other than the fact that I believed somehow the geography of this area was linked to Bernadette's death, I drove down toward the river where I had seen an ancient

Acadian cottage that was being used to store hay. Most of the pioneer homes built by the original Acadian settlers have disappeared, destroyed by fire or plowed under by tractors or torn down for the two-hundred-year-old cypress planks in their walls. But each one of them, with its small roofed gallery and twin front doors and tall windows, is a reminder for me of the pastoral Louisiana of my childhood. Clouds had moved across the sun, and I could see rain falling on the south end of the parish. In minutes big raindrops and fine bits of hail were hitting my windshield. I parked by the abandoned Acadian cottage and turned off my engine. Down by the river, I could see the gum trees along the bank growing dimmer and dimmer, the clouds swollen and black as soot now and veined with electricity.

My cell phone rang. I thought it was Clete, but it was not. "Mr. Robicheaux?" a voice said.

"Yeah, who's this?" I could hear almost nothing except the booming of the thunder outside. "Who's calling? You'll have to talk louder. I'm in an electric storm."

"Marvin, at the store," the voice said. "You gave me your number."

The army veteran, I thought. "Right. What's happening?"

"The guy—"

"I can't hear you."

"The guy you said . . . he was . . . didn't know what kind of . . ."

"You're breaking up, partner," I said.

"My cousin saw . . . blue . . . the guy with . . . about three miles . . . help you."

"Move to a different spot. I'm not reading you."

"Three miles . . . the guy with the Florida . . . blue pickup truck . . . the guy . . . out and . . ."

"Hang up and call back. I'm going to move my truck."

"I'll . . . landline," he said.

"Hello?"

The transmission went dead. I started the engine and began to drive down to the trees by the river so I could get under some cover that would deaden the sound of the rain and hail on my cab. Before I had driven ten yards, the cell phone rang again.

"It's Marvin. I'm on the store phone now. Can you hear me, Mr. Robicheaux?"

"Yeah, but please repeat everything you said. Very little of it came through."

"My cousin came into the store and said some guys in a white car with a Florida tag got into it with a guy driving a beat-up blue pickup. Behind the old creamery about two miles south of me. My cousin said he thought they were just talking, but when he looked in his rearview mirror, he could see they were arguing. It was starting to rain, and he didn't see everything real good, but he thought a guy from the white car shoved the guy driving the pickup. My cousin thinks maybe the guy in the pickup was in deep shit. I don't know if this is any help to you or not."

"The guy in deep shit was driving a blue pickup truck?"

"That's what my cousin said. The guy had black hair that was combed up on his head in a square. That's how my cousin described it. He sounds like the guy you were looking for, doesn't he?"

"You bet he does. Does your cousin know where any of these guys went?"

"No, sir. He felt it wasn't his business, but then he got bothered about it. You know, two against one?"

"You did the right thing, and so did your cousin.

Call me back if y'all see any of these guys again."

"One other thing. My cousin said there was a van parked close by. He didn't know if anybody was in it."

"A cargo van?"

"He said a delivery van. Same thing, huh?"

"What color van?"

"He didn't say. Sir, can you tell us what's going on here?"

"When I figure it out, I'll get back to you," I replied.

"Where are you?"

"Why do you want to know?"

"Because to tell you the truth, I think you might be messing with some bad dudes. This place isn't like the place I grew up in, Mr. Robicheaux."

I closed my cell phone and drove in a wide arc behind the Acadian cottage, watching the rain swirl across the grass in the field and on the gum trees and on the surface of the river. I had lowered my windows a half inch and could smell the odor of the Gulf and feel the power the storm seemed to draw from both the sky and the land. The river was already running high and wide, the water way over its banks, a yellow froth scudding through the flooded tree trunks. Then out of nowhere, overhead, I saw the same red airplane I had seen earlier, except this time it was fighting hard against the wind, its wings buffeting, its landing lights sparking whitely. What was a crop duster—if that's what it was—doing up in weather like this? I asked myself.

When I turned back toward the paved road, trying to stay on the high ground as I passed the Acadian cottage, I stared through my windshield and realized I wasn't alone.

A dented, paint-skinned blue pickup truck had

come to a stop in the grassy field midway between the Acadian cottage and the road, its headlights on high beam and its windshield wipers flying. I pressed down on the brake and slipped my transmission into neutral and waited. But the blue pickup, the same one I had seen parked at Vidor Perkins's house, did not move. The sky was completely black now, the airplane gone, the entirety of the landscape so devoid of light that the pale grass in the fields seemed luminous by comparison. In the background the rain was blowing in gray sheets, smudging out the paved road and the farmhouses in the distance.

I took my pair of Russian field glasses from the glove box and focused them on the windshield of Perkins's truck. I could see a solitary figure inside, but I couldn't make out the features. I unsnapped the strap on my .45 and lifted it from its leather holster and set it beside me on the seat. The driver of the blue pickup remained motionless behind the steering wheel, the headlights smoking in the rain.

What's it going to be, Vidor? You just want to prove how crazy you are? Are you trying to impress someone? Is this your chance to take me off the board?

Or was the driver Vidor Perkins? The former soldier at the crossroads store had said a man who was probably Vidor Perkins had gotten into it with two men who had been driving a white car with a Florida tag. Had they commandeered his truck and perhaps weighted Vidor with a cinder block and dumped him in a pond?

But as though he had read my mind, the driver got out of the pickup and walked in front of his headlights and lifted his arms out from his sides. I refocused my field glasses on his face. There was no question whom I was looking at. There was also no doubt what he was trying to tell me: Vidor Perkins was unarmed and not a source of danger to me or anyone else. To emphasize that fact, he pulled off his shirt and dropped it in the weeds, the rain melting the grease in his hair, glazing his bare shoulders and arms against the beams of his headlights.

But there was a problem with Perkins's dramatic display of his innocuousness. Perkins had been jailing most of his life. He knew every ritual associated with every aspect of arrest at a crime scene. He knew what the cost could be for pulling a cell phone from his pocket or tucking the tail of his shirt into his trousers at the wrong moment. He knew how to keep both hands outside a car window if he was pulled to a stop on a road. He knew never to fumble in his glove box for his registration or reach into his coat for ID unless told to do so. He knew what to do on the yard if a warning shot was fired from a gun tower. He knew how to turn into a non-seeing, non-hearing piece of stone after somebody was shanked in a corner and the shank was passed hand to hand before it was thrown at someone's feet. Vidor was a walking encyclopedia of criminal knowledge. If he had wanted to demonstrate convincingly that he was unarmed, he would have turned his trouser pockets inside out and rotated in a full circle, his arms straight out at his sides, to show me that he did not have a pistol stuffed in his pockets or behind the back of his belt. Inexplicably, he was not doing what he knew I expected.

I turned my truck at an angle to him and rolled down my window. "On your face, Mr. Perkins," I said.

But he gave no reply.

"Guys like us are old school. Don't disappoint me," I said.

His gaze was riveted on me, the rain separating his hair on his scalp. I thought I could see his lips moving, but I wasn't sure. "Want to tell me something?" I said.

He started walking toward me, his hands out by his sides, his face twitching.

"That's far enough, Mr. Perkins."

He was close enough now for me to see him swallow. "I been trying to he'p," he said.

"I got that impression. You want to tell me what you're doing here?"

"Nothing. I saw your truck is all."

"Put your hands on your head."

"Sir?"

"Do it."

"Yes, sir."

"Now turn in a circle."

"I'm gonna get down on my face."

"No, you're not."

"I'm just trying to come into compliance here. I was doing my research. I went to the black lady's house—"

"You place your hands on the crown of your head and turn around, Mr. Perkins."

"Yes, sir, whatever you say." He knitted his fingers on top of his head and rotated in a circle. When he looked at me again, his chest was rising and falling, his mouth shaping and reshaping itself, like rubber, as though he wanted to speak words that he didn't know how to form. The skin around his eyes was bloodless, like that of a man who was seasick. There was a red knot on his collarbone, with two punctures in it, as though he had been bitten by a snake.

"Who was in that airplane, Mr. Perkins?"

"I didn't see no plane."

"Don't lie."

"I got nothing to do with no plane."

"Walk toward me."

"If you're gonna bust me, do it. I'm getting on my face. Hook me up. I ain't here to give you trouble. No, sir, that's not my way."

"No, you will walk toward me, then you will get on your knees. You will do that right now."

I picked up my .45 from the seat and opened the door and stepped outside. Then I realized I had missed something. Far behind Perkins's truck, on the opposite side of the paved road, a gray cargo van was parked under an oak tree, its sliding door open wide.

"Walk toward me," I said.

"No."

I cocked back the hammer on my .45. "Do it or I blow your fucking head off," I said.

"Mr. Robicheaux, I ain't a bad man. I didn't bargain for this. I didn't have no choice." He lowered one hand and touched the knot on his collarbone. "See."

"You have two seconds to move, Mr. Perkins. Look into my face and tell me I won't do it. No, don't look behind you. Look at me."

"Yes, sir, I believe you. I'm coming. I apologize for scaring your daughter. I apologize for messing in your life. Mr. Robicheaux, let me explain." But he couldn't control his fear. I could see tears welling in his eyes.

"Come toward me, Mr. Perkins," I said, pointing the .45 with both hands at the center of his face.

"Let me get on the ground, sir. Right now. I cain't walk no more. I went to the bathroom in my pants."

"No, you will do what I say."

I shifted my position so he was directly between

me and the parked van. He looked pleadingly into my eyes. "I didn't start that fire when I was a kid. It was them other boys. That's been on my sheet all these years, something I never did. I went from one state home to another. I learned how to draw trees for psychiatrists. If you cain't make the pencil line come back on itself, they say you're schizophrenic. That can get you a free pass out of a jail or the wrong foster home. That's how I grew up."

"Tell me about it later, bub. Who's in the van?"

I would never get a reply to my question. I heard a dull, wet pop inside the rain and simultaneously saw Vidor Perkins's jaw drop and an exit wound the size and shape of a watermelon plug fountain from just above his right eye. His motors were cut, and he went straight down on the ground, his eyes never closing, his head tilted upward like a man catching a glimpse of a bird streaking by overhead.

I was staring across the field at the rain-dimmed outline of the cargo van and the dark opening in its side, where I was sure the shooter was now sighting on me.

I piled inside the cab of my truck, my head below windshield level, just as two rounds blew out the glass in the driver's door. I had knocked my cell phone off the seat and could not find it on the floor. I tried to twist the ignition and start the engine, but the shooter changed his line of fire and went to work on the front of the truck, punching holes in the radiator, flattening the right front tire all the way to the rim, whanging at least two rounds off the engine block.

I found the two extra magazines I kept in the glove box. With my head still down, I opened the passenger door and rolled out on the ground, my .45 in my right hand, my cell phone still lost somewhere under a seat or a floor mat. The shooter let off three more rounds, one punching through the dashboard and ricocheting off the steering wheel. Ironically, the shooter, in flattening the tire, had improved my position. The right side of the truck had sunk almost to ground level, reducing my exposure, and from a kneeling position, I could steady my arm on the side of the headlight and aim on the van. Up until that point, I believed the shooter thought he might have nailed me. I could feel my heart pounding with adrenaline, my skin tingling with expectation. It's a strange moment, a euphoric high that probably goes back to the cave and later on makes you wonder if bloodlust isn't much more a part of your chemistry than you wish to concede. But everyone who has been there knows what I'm talking about. The dark corners of the mind are suddenly lit with a clarity that frees you from every fear you ever had.

I opened up in earnest, squeezing off one round after another, the heavy frame and checkered grips bucking solidly in my palm. The 1911-model army .45 is a lovely weapon to have on your side. Its reliability, power, accuracy, and the amount of damage it can create in a few seconds have no equal, at least in my view. No matter how well armed the person on the receiving end is, he knows he's not leaving the fight without a bloody nose. When the slide locked open, I pressed the release button on the empty magazine and let it drop from the frame. I shoved in another magazine and slammed it hard into place with the heel of my hand, then released the slide and let it chamber another round. But before I could fire again, I realized that I had more to deal with than the shooter in the van.

The low-slung white car with the charcoal windows and the hood spray-painted with primer had come up the road from the south and was now turning in to the field, the driver positioning his vehicle behind the rusted tractor that shimmered whenever lightning jumped between the clouds. I saw the front passenger window go down and an arm come out and the barrel of a weapon with a folding wire stock on it point in my direction. This time I wasn't going to be a stationary target. I got to my feet and started running through the field toward the river, sheets of rain swirling around me, the grass thick and sharp-edged and well over my knees, water and mud exploding from under my shoes.

I heard three shots from the automobile. I could also hear the driver gunning his engine, his tires whining as they slid over the muck in the field, and I suspected the shooter was firing wildly. I zigzagged as I ran, my lungs burning, the rain stinging my eyes. The Acadian cottage was behind me now, shielding me from the van, but I still had the shooter in the car to worry about. I turned in a circle, almost falling down, and let off one round at the car's windshield, but I heard no impact and suspected I had fired high. Then I ran full tilt down a coulee that was brown with runoff from the field, grabbing roots and morning glory vines on either side of it for support, until I splashed into a stand of willows and gum trees whose trunks were under at least two feet of water.

My chest was heaving, my clothes drenched and heavy. I waded downstream between the trees for thirty yards. The rain was striking the river so hard the air glowed with a misty yellow light six inches above the surface. I held on to a tree trunk and opened and closed my mouth, trying to clear my hearing of the kettledrums beating in my head. I stuck the .45 in my belt and swallowed hard and pushed my thumbs under my ears, but nothing worked. The world had become a cacophony of distorted sound that could have been a high-powered engine approaching the riverbank or the humming of the current through the flooded trees.

I waded back up on the bank, then got down on my knees and worked my way up a clay-slick slope, holding on to cypress roots, until I was in an eroded pocket where I could look out upon the field with minimum exposure. My .45 was smeared with a grayish-pink clay, and I wiped it clean with a wet handkerchief and pointed the barrel downward and hit it to free it of any obstructions inside. Then I raised my head above the embankment. I discovered I had dramatically underestimated my adversaries. These were not nickel-and-dime gumballs. They were cleaners.

The cargo van and white car were parked deep in the field now, and two men wearing dark raincoats with hoods were loading the body of Vidor Perkins into the van. One of them glanced back at the road, which was almost invisible inside the storm. They closed the van and joined three other men wearing the same type of raincoats, and the five of them began advancing through the grass, not unlike a line of hunters flushing quail from a field.

I had heard about their kind, and years ago I had even had an encounter with a paramilitary group that brought a black ops operation into New Orleans, but I had never seen them work up close. The urban legend was they sanitized crime scenes, vacuuming them and scrubbing them down with bleach and, if necessary, replacing walls and carpets and furniture and repainting walls and ceilings. The darker story was they carted off their victims and had them compacted inside junk cars

or ground into fish chum. These were stories I had
never wanted to believe, because the personnel who
did this kind of work were not products of the un-
derworld but had been taught their trade by their
government.

The five men in hooded raincoats were fanning
out, their weapons cradled across their chests. I
calculated I had perhaps twenty to thirty seconds
before they reached the edge of the embankment.
When that happened, I would be pinned down
and flanked on both sides. I looked behind me. I
could try to swim the river, but the opposite bank
was steep and clay-sided and devoid of any trees
along the mudflat. As soon as I was stranded there,
they could pot me as easily as shooting a coon in a
bare cornfield. I could try to swim to the next bend
downstream, but I would be visible and exposed for
at least a hundred yards, and my pursuers could run
along the bank and cut me to pieces.

What do you do under those circumstances? I
had eight hollow-point rounds in my .45 and a full
magazine in my back pocket. The storm had effectively isolated the environment I was in. Even if
someone passed on the paved road, it was unlikely
he would take notice of the events down by the
river. Over the years I had read of historical situations that were similar, and I had always wondered
what I would do. The French Legionnaires at Dien
Bien Phu, most of whom were Germans, had kept
repeating over and over "Cameroon," in memory
of the famous last stand their antecedents had made
in defense of Maximilian during Benito Juárez's war
for Mexico's independence. Crockett and Bowie
and Travis and 185 others went down to the last
man at the Alamo, Crockett run through against
the barracks wall, Bowie firing his pistols into his

executioners in the infirmary just before he was tossed on top of their bayonets. Custer and his men died bravely on the hilltop overlooking the Little Big Horn River, although as many as thirty troopers may have committed suicide rather than allow themselves to be taken half alive and subjected to a fiendish death.

The real question was not what I expected of myself but what my enemy expected of me. The man in the center of the line was probably the leader. I heard him give a muffled command, then the two men on either side of him began moving out farther and farther from him. My guess was they had already concluded I would either run or try to swim upstream or downstream, and they had come to this conclusion because that was what they would have done.

What was it they did not expect me to do? When we say someone will run like a rabbit, we are usually speaking derogatorily and not examining the content of our rhetoric. A cottontail rabbit does not run without a destination; he runs in a circle that leads him back to his starting place. Then he hides, leaving his pursuers to chase a scent that serves only to confound them.

I doubted if the cleaners expected me to go back to the coulee, the place where I had dropped out of sight and entered the river basin. But that was exactly what I did, running through the shallows, splashing up onto the mudflat to a high place among the trees where I could look out on the slope that led into the watershed. I lay on my stomach, rain dripping from the overhang on my back and head, and watched the leader of the five men come down the dip in the land that would give him access to cover and a chance to reconnoiter the area.

He paused, evidently confident that I was not in immediate proximity to him. He looked to the left and to the right, scanning the trees, checking to see where his men had stationed themselves. I propped my elbows in the dirt and aimed the .45 at his rib cage with both hands, allowing for the climbing effect of the recoil, and tightened my finger inside the trigger guard. Surprise time, motherfucker.

"Iberia Parish sheriff's detective! Throw away your weapon and place your hands on your head," I said.

He jerked around just as a pool of yellow electricity flared inside a cloud. His expression was like that of a cowled monk in a Reformationist painting caught in an iniquitous act. In that instant I also saw his eyes, and I knew he had entered the brief interior monologue with himself that I call "the moment." Inside the moment, which is usually not longer in duration than two or three seconds, you choose either to give it up or roll the dice. His face looked grainy and full of lumps, as though insects had fed on it. His eyes were lustrous and black, his mouth slightly parted, as though he were oxygenating his blood. Rain slid down his brow and over his eyes, but he never blinked.

"You're having impure thoughts, podna," I said. "They're about to get you wasted. Don't let that happen."

Almost as though he wished to bring a touch of class to his moment on the edge of the abyss, his mouth softened with a lackadaisical grin. He swung the muzzle of a cut-down pistol-grip pump shotgun toward me. I fired twice, my muzzle flash spearing into the dark, the two ejected shell casings tinkling somewhere off to my right. I didn't think the second round had found a target, but the first one did. The hooded man took it under the armpit, and I suspected the hollow-point round had flattened on bone and torn up through the lungs and perhaps exited through the far shoulder. Regardless, his knees buckled, and blood spewed from his mouth, and his jaw jacked loose when his knees struck the ground. When I pulled his shotgun out from under him, I realized he was both a taller and heavier man than I had thought.

I crawled back into the trees, dragging the shotgun with me, and opened my mouth to clear my ears. I couldn't see the other four men, but I knew I had to turn the situation around on them and get out of the defensive position I was in. They were inside the tree line now, on either side of me, and I had a swollen river at my back and an empty field with little cover in front of me. I sat up on the slope and slipped the pump on the shotgun far enough back so I could be sure there was a shell in the chamber. It was a Remington, and if the sportsman's plug was removed, there were probably five shells in the gun, each probably loaded with double-aught buckshot.

One bad guy down and four to go, I thought. The odds weren't the best. But what had been the odds for the man I had just shot and killed? Before he died, he must have believed his day's work was almost at an end and soon he would be enjoying a steak and fried potatoes and a mug of beer, or filling his mouth with a woman's breasts, or snarfing up a few lines in a French Quarter apartment above a lichen-stained courtyard whose flowers told him the season was unending, as was his life and the pleasures it brought him.

I got to my feet and, like our heavy-browed, thick-armed, shoulder-slumped ancestor, headed along the water's edge toward the southern horizon, the .45 stuck down in my belt, my dead enemy's weapon in my hands, my throat tight with a thirst of such intensity it seemed to belong to someone else.

CHAPTER 17

THE TWO MEN to my south had sought cover when they heard me fire. I was sure they could distinguish the difference between the report of a pistol and a shotgun, and by now they had concluded their leader had made a serious mistake in judgment and had taken himself off the board. I hoped the loss of their leader would cause them to cut and run, but I knew better. They were obviously professionals, probably with military or mercenary backgrounds, and if the crop duster I had seen was actually part of their operation, they had radio communication with people who had far more authority and power than the man I had just killed.

Don't try to figure it out, I told myself. Just get through this afternoon. The storm will pass, the sun will break out of the clouds, and these men will go back under their rocks. At least that is what I told myself.

I strained my eyes against the darkness. The undergrowth was shiny with rainwater, the canopy dripping. I could see no movement among the trees. Nor could I hear any sounds that didn't belong in a drenched woods. Which meant that perhaps, with good luck, the two men to my north had gone to ground and had not decided on a plan. I stood up behind a water oak and studied the underbrush and the riverbank and the slash pines and the gum trees and the willows and the direction the wind was blowing and the patterns it created in the leaves and pine branches. I remembered how the wind had been my friend years ago when it swept through the elephant grass in a tropical country and how it redefined the shapes of the trees on a rubber plantation; I remembered it swelling inside the canopy of a rain forest where the birds had gone silent and where the shadows that did not move abruptly came into focus and caused your breath to seize in your chest.

But I saw nothing except the foliage of a riparian environment that for me had become a black-green tiger cage.

I looked to the south again and saw something that instilled in me more fear than even the two men who were probably crouched in the undergrowth. At the mouth of the river, where it widened into a fan and met a saltwater bay, I saw the same double-decker I had seen on Bayou Teche. I saw its twin scrolled stacks, its scrubbed finish, its rows of passenger cabins, its pilothouse, and the water cascading off the paddles of its great steam-powered wheel, all of it caught inside a column of translucence that looked more like ether than light. I knew that what I was watching was not a delusion, and I knew what the paddle wheeler represented and who the crew and passengers were and why all of them were here, beckoning at me, their lips moving without sound, saying, *It's time.*

I ducked back behind the trunk of the tree, my chest quivering, my clothes all at once cold, as though my body were no longer capable of generating enough heat to warm the soaked fabric. I peered around the tree and in the distance saw only the blackness of the sky. The paddle wheeler was not in sight, but I heard a bush shake and raindrops scatter on the ground and I knew my adversaries were still with me. I pressed my spine against the tree trunk, holding the pump shotgun straight up in front of me like a human exclamation mark, a rock in my left hand.

"You two guys try to follow my logic," I said. "Your leader was probably the smartest guy among you, but he got himself smoked because he assumed other people think the same way he did. So where does that leave you? Before it's over, you'll probably cool me out. But I'm going to get at least two of y'all before I go down, or maybe three, or maybe all of you. You wonder why that is? It's because I'm old and I dread the thought of dying in a bed, and I get off splattering the grits of guys like you."

I flung the rock in a high arc so that it fell through the canopy and landed on a solid spot outside the tree line, indicating that perhaps I had bolted from behind the water oak and was coming up hard on their flank, on the high ground, the sawed-off twelve-gauge pump about to spray buckshot all over their position.

If that was their conclusion, they were only half wrong. I ran through the trees like a broken-field quarterback, crashing over the undergrowth, weaving through the tree trunks directly at them. One man rose from a pool of water where he was crouched and began firing with a semiautomatic rifle on a wire stock. But the electricity in the clouds had died, and the stand of trees was almost totally dark; I doubted if he had a clear idea where I was. I heard a round blow bark out of a gum tree, and I felt wood splinters sting the side of my face, but I was already raising the shotgun in front of me and not thinking about anything other than killing the man whose gun had jammed and who was trying to knock a shell casing loose from his rifle bolt with his hand.

He twisted his body away from me when I squeezed the trigger, holding out his palm in a pushing position, his eyes squeezed tightly shut. I saw his fingers fly loose from his hand as though they had been snipped off with shears. I ejected the spent shell and jacked another one into the chamber, then realized that my adrenaline-fed confidence had been an illusion.

The second man had positioned himself behind the root-ball of a downed tree by the water's edge, perhaps even sacrificing his friend so he could get me in his sights. I tried to swing the twelve-gauge toward him and lay down a masking shot before he let off the AR-15 he had raised to his shoulder. But I tripped on a log and tumbled down an embankment into a cluster of palmettos, the shotgun skittering down with me. The man with the AR-15 let off four rounds, but they were all high, clattering away in the trees like the sound of wood blocks falling down a staircase. I picked up the shotgun with both hands and, without aiming, fired at the shooter. But the barrel had become clotted with mud or clay. It exploded in a red-and-yellow balloon, the muzzle swelling into the deformed shape of a split sausage. I dropped the shotgun to the ground and reached into my belt for my .45, except I knew that this time my appointment in Samarra had come round at last.

I heard the sound of a car horn blowing and tires spinning on grass and mud. The shooter continued to hold the stock of his rifle against his shoulder, but he dissolved back into the darkness so quickly I had to blink to make sure my vision hadn't failed me. I got to one knee with the .45 and scanned the trees and the undergrowth but could see no sign of him.

"Dave, are you in there?" I heard Clete shout.

I got up and started running up the embankment

through the trees. I burst through the undergrowth and ran between two thick slash pines that whipped back into my face, then saw Clete behind the wheel of his Caddy, his window down, rain blowing inside, his porkpie hat clamped down on his brow. He looked like a giant albino ape hunched between the seat and the wheel. "What the hell is going on in there?" he said.

I pulled open the passenger door and piled inside. "I killed one guy and blew the hand off another. Four guys, including the wounded one, are still in there. Where's your cell phone?"

"In the glove box. Who are these guys?"

"I don't know. Cleaners, maybe. Vidor Perkins is dead. Get moving."

He started to accelerate, but he was still looking at me. "You capped Perkins?"

"No, they did. They were shooting at me. Come on, Clete. Step on it. We'll try to box them in."

"You mean cleaners like government guys?"

"I didn't say that. Will you get us out of here?"

"They're already boxed. Let's call the locals and pot them as they come out of the bush."

"You don't listen. You never listen. Your head is wrapped with iron plate," I said.

I rolled down my window and opened up on the tree line, hoping to drive back anyone who was trying to set up on us.

"You don't have to be so emotional about it," Clete said. He mashed down on the accelerator, fishtailing two swampy tire tracks past the Acadian cottage.

I looked through the back window at the tree line but couldn't see anyone emerging from it. I had the cell phone in my hand and dialed 911. There was no service. "What have you got on you?" I asked.

"Just my piece."

"We're going to be okay," I said. "They've got the river at their back, and we're between them and their vehicles. We can pin them down until somebody sees us and calls in a 911."

"That van and the white car are theirs?"

"Yeah, Perkins's body is inside the van."

"You're sure you killed somebody down there on the river?"

I looked at him and didn't answer.

"You saw him close up?" he said.

"He took it through the lungs. He went down like a sack of horseshoes. You think I'm making this up?"

Something caught his attention. I looked through the windshield but didn't see anything.

"At nine o'clock. They cut their lights," he said.

To the left, angling off the paved road into the field, the grass flattening under their bumpers, were two black SUVs. They were neither official vehicles nor the vehicles of choice for people in this area, most of whom were poor. The SUVs divided in the field, creating a pincer movement, trying to seal us off from the road. In the dash light, the raindrops on Clete's face looked like beads of water on a pumpkin.

"I don't get this," he said. "We were dealing with a bunch of local shitheads. Now we've got an army coming down on us. What do you want to do?"

He waited. I didn't want to say what I had to say. "Cut your lights."

"They've already seen us. That doesn't solve the problem. Tell me what you want to do."

"They're behind and in front of us. Head south on the road. We'll use the phone at the crossroads and then come back. Do it, Cletus. We're running out of options."

He stared hard at me, sweat and raindrops running out of his hair. "They're gonna skate," he said.

"I'm sorry I got you into this."

"Forget sorry. We're sending a real bad message to these guys, like they can spit in our mouths any time they want."

"We'll nail them later."

"I've got a truck flare under the seat. We can set fire to the van. You said Perkins is in there?"

"It's what they want, Clete. We'll never get out of the field. Nobody will know what happened to us, and these guys will be around to piss on our graves."

He gazed at me for a long time, fighting with conclusions he didn't want to accept, steering with one hand. Then he angled toward the south, exhaling, depressing the accelerator. In the silence I could hear the grass raking under the Caddy's frame. "How'd you know where I was?" I asked.

"I went to that filling station at the crossroads. The clerk in there said he'd talked to you." The Caddy thumped onto the asphalt. Clete floored the accelerator, glancing in the rearview mirror at the same time. "Try the cell again."

"No service."

The flooded fields on either side of the road were flying past us. "We're gonna get these guys, we're gonna get these guys, we're gonna get these guys," he said.

I was used up and too tired to offer any support for his fantasies about revenge. My adrenaline-fed high had gone the way all dry drunks come and go, like a brief revisit to the psychological and moral insanity that had constituted my life when the cathedral I entered every afternoon was an empty New Orleans saloon with a long mahogany bar at the end of which a solitary corked bottle of charcoal-filter whiskey and a shot glass and a longneck Jax waited for me. Inside the amber radiance filtering through the oak trees outside, I was a faithful acolyte and was always respectful of the spirits that lived in the corked bottle and the power and the light I could acquire by simply tilting a small glass to my lips.

For me, unslaked bloodlust was no easier to deal with than unslaked sexual desire or a thirst for whiskey that at one time was so great I would swallow a razor blade to satisfy it. My skin was hot, my palms as stiff and dry as cardboard. I wanted to return to the field with as much ordnance as I could get my hands on and blow our hooded adversaries into a bloody mist. But I knew how things were going to play out. The men who had killed Vidor Perkins and who had tried to kill me had sanction. Perhaps it didn't come from local or state officials, but a group as well organized and trained and financed as this one was not born in a vacuum. The question was whom did they serve.

We pulled into the filling station at the crossroads and called the Jefferson Parish Sheriff's Department. My report on the gun battle up the road and the death of Vidor Perkins obviously seemed surreal and was probably more than the dispatcher could assimilate. I had to keep repeating who and where I was. In the background I could hear a half-dozen dispatchers trying to talk over one another. There were obviously power outages and downed electrical wires in people's yards and automobile accidents all over the parish. A large-scale shots-fired called in by a police officer from another parish who said he'd just killed a man and wanted backup at the scene he had fled probably sounded like the ravings of a lunatic.

Clete was staring at me as I hung up. "So?" he said.

"They'll probably put us in straitjackets," I replied.

Clete and I drove back up the road, wondering how long the response would take. Surprisingly, two cruisers showed up at the field at the same time we did, their spotlights piercing deep into the darkness, sweeping over the Acadian cottage and the rusted tractor and the acres of grass and weeds that stretched all the way back to the line of trees along the riverbank. I could still see swaths of tire tracks in the grass. I could see the coulee that I had raced down and hidden inside. I could even see the two slash pines where I had exited the tree line. But all the vehicles, including my pickup truck, were gone.

"Do you believe this?" Clete said.

"No, I don't," I said.

A plainclothes detective named Huffinton walked with us through the field. The rain had slackened, and the sky was turning pale at the edges. He was a big man whose clothes fit him badly, and he wore a felt hat with a wide wilted brim and a necktie that was twisted in a knot. Halfway across the field, I pointed out the spot where Vidor Perkins had died.

"There's nothing there but dirt," Huffinton said.

"That's the point. Somebody spaded out the grass," I said.

He walked a few feet from me and swept a flashlight over the ground. "This is about where you took cover behind your truck and started firing at the van? Because if it is, I don't see any brass."

"You're not supposed to. If they'd take my truck, they'd take everything else."

He nodded. Then he lit a cigarette. He puffed on

it in the breeze, the smoke damp and smelling of chemicals and blowing back into my face. I knew any serious investigation of the crime scene was over. Huffinton stared at a golden flood of sunlight under the cloud layer in the west. "Let's take a look down by the river," he said.

We walked along the coulee and stood on the spot where I had shot the hooded man. My .45 shell casings were nowhere to be found. The body of the man I had killed was gone. There was no visible trace of blood on the ground. Nor did we find any ejected shells inside the stand of trees that grew along the river embankment. There were boot and shoe marks in the dirt, but none of a defined nature. The only tactile evidence of the gun battle were the gouges in the tree trunks from the AR-15 and a thin spray of blood on a persimmon branch at the spot where I had taken off the man's fingers with the twelve-gauge.

"Come on down to the department and we'll write it up," Huffinton said.

"This isn't our parish. Dave's job is not to 'write it up.' Dave's truck is probably on a semi headed for a compactor," Clete said. "Call the state police."

"Why don't you do it?" Huffinton said.

Clete looked away at a distant spot, hiding the angry light in his eyes. "There was a crop duster flying around. Where's the closest airport?" he said.

"Anywhere there's a flat space. You have someplace else you need to be?" Huffinton said.

"I'll be back tomorrow and take care of the paperwork," I said.

"Yeah, I'd appreciate it," Huffinton said. "No offense meant, but somebody might say you were back on the sauce when this one happened."

"Tell me which it is: Streak is delusional or I'm a liar," Clete said.

"Say again?"

"Forget it," Clete said.

Huffinton walked toward his vehicle, his back to us, his blunt profile pointed into the freshening breeze.

"I hope his wife has congenital clap," Clete said.

"During the firefight, I saw a steamboat down by the mouth of the river."

"You mean a floating casino?"

"That's not what it was. I've seen it before. On Bayou Teche."

"I don't know if I want to hear this."

"I thought that was where I was going. I thought they were waiting for me."

"Who?"

"The people on board."

"Don't talk like that."

"You're the best, Cletus."

"No, *we're* the best. One is no good without the other. The Bobbsey Twins from Homicide have one agenda only. We make the dirtbags want to crawl back in their mothers' wombs. We're gonna hunt down the cleaners or whatever they are and salt their hides and nail them to the barn door."

"You've already said it for both of us. It's only rock and roll."

"That's because I was ninety-proof. You don't have permission to die." He grabbed my shirt. "You hearing me on this?"

"I was just telling you what I saw. Who else am I going to tell?"

I cupped my hand on the back of his neck as we walked to his car. I could feel the hardness in his tendons and the heat and oil in his skin. I could feel his heartbeat and the fury and mire of his blood in his veins, and in his intelligent green eyes I could see the misty shine that my words would not make go away.

MONDAY MORNING I went into Helen Soileau's office and told her everything that had happened in the field and river basin during the storm on the southern end of Jeff Davis Parish. She listened and did not speak, her gaze never leaving my face. When I finished, she continued to stare at me, her lips pressed together, her chest rising and falling.

Unconsciously I cleared my throat. "I'm going back over there in a few minutes," I said.

"Really? That's interesting."

"I'm going to the courthouse and try to find what I can on the seven arpents of land owned by Bernadette Latiolais."

"Can you tell me what Clete was doing with you yesterday?"

"He saved my life."

"What you mean is he *had* to save your life. That's because you went over there without backup or informing me or coordinating with the Jeff Davis Sheriff's Department." Before I could reply, she raised her hand for me to be silent. "You killed one man and wounded another?"

"I did."

"You shot one guy's hand off with the twelve-gauge?"

"His fingers."

"But you're sure you wounded him, and you're sure the guy you hit with your forty-five is dead?"

"I don't know how else I can say it, Helen."

"I don't get Vidor Perkins's relationship to these guys."

"There was a red knot on his collarbone with two puncture marks in it. I think he was tortured with a stun gun. They made him walk to me and shot him by mistake."

Her irritation with me had passed; she was looking at the broadening circumstances of the case. "And you saw a plane you think might have been the control center for these guys?"

"I saw the plane. Its purpose is a matter of speculation."

"We can start checking the hospitals for gunshot admissions, but I doubt the wounded man sought conventional treatment if he's working for the sophisticated operation you describe. You think these guys work for Timothy Abelard?"

"It's a possibility. He was a big defense contractor. He'd have the connections."

"That's not what I asked."

"I don't want to believe it of Mr. Abelard," I said.

"Am I developing a hearing defect?"

"I want to believe Mr. Abelard is an anachronism, a decayed vestige of the old oligarchy. All of them weren't bad. Some of them probably did the best they could with what they had."

"Hermann Göring loved his mother, too," she said. "The guy you shot with your forty-five?"

"What about him?"

"You okay with it today?"

"He dealt the play. I identified myself and told him to throw his weapon away."

"That's the ticket," she said. "But it wouldn't hurt to take a couple of days off, would it?"

I didn't even bother to answer. My eyes were lidless, staring into hers. She smiled to herself.

"Something funny?" I said.

"Why is it in any conversation with you I always know what you're going to say and not say? Why do I even have conversations with you, Pops?"

It was a light moment, reminiscent of the days when she and I were investigative partners and both prone to err on the side of immediate retaliation in dealing with the army of miscreants who like to make life unpleasant for the rest of us. But I knew Helen's cheerful expression was only a temporary respite from the morgue photos that were still in my file cabinet.

I got up from my chair and walked to her window. Helen's potted petunias were overflowing in the vase, and down below I could see the trusty gardeners from the stockade trimming the grass around the grotto that was dedicated to Jesus's mother. I propped my hands on the windowsill.

"Did you want to drink last night?" she asked.

"I thought about it."

"You think you ought to find a meeting today?"

"I have drunk dreams every third night. They're not dreams of desire. They're nightmares."

"I don't understand what you're telling me."

"Wanting to drink is not really wanting to drink. It's like a desire to cup your hand over a candle flame and snuff it out."

She stood next to me and touched my arm. I didn't want to look at her. Two or three women lived inside Helen's skin, and one of them was not only androgynous but had no erotic parameters. "Slow down, bwana. We're going to avenge those girls. I give you my word."

I kept my eyes straight ahead. I felt her fingers on top of my wrist, felt them run along the hairs on the back of my hand and rest on my knuckles. Then her fingers moved away from me, and in the silence I could hear her breathing.

"I think there are two sets of killers in this case, two sets of interests, and two sets of motivation," I said.

She didn't reply until I was forced to turn and look into her face. Her gaze was steady and curious, her head tilted slightly to one side, her mouth red, her cheeks somehow leaner than they were a few minutes earlier. "What do you base that on?" she asked.

I had to concentrate in order to answer. "I think our mistake is that we keep looking for a single motive that will fit only one or two individuals. That's natural in a sex-related homicide. But we keep discovering information that doesn't fit the profile. Now we're dealing with guys who seem to be cleaners. Guys like this don't get involved in sex crimes. What I'm saying is we need to turn the pyramid upside down."

"Too abstract, Pops."

"You said Hermann Göring loved his mother. That's the point."

"What point?"

"He probably did love his mother. That doesn't mean he wasn't a sonofabitch. There's nothing reasonable about human behavior. Did you see *Citizen Kane*?"

"About William Randolph Hearst?"

"On his deathbed, he whispers the word 'Rosebud.' No one can figure out what it means. Rosebud was the name of the sled he played with in the snow when he was a little boy. All his life this man who created a war in order to sell newspapers was driven by memories of his lonely childhood."

"That's what you think we're dealing with?"

"Maybe. But whatever it is, we're looking right at it. We just don't see it."

"I'm going with you to Jeff Davis."

"What for?"

"I don't like the way they treated you," she replied. I started to speak. She raised one finger. "Not a word."

TWO HOURS LATER, in the Jefferson Davis Parish courthouse, I didn't find any documents that were revelatory in themselves. However, I did find a pattern. During the previous three years, within an area of approximately five hundred acres, blocks and strips of land had been sold at nominal prices to seven buyers. Most of the acreage was fallow or partially underwater. It possessed neither great agricultural or mineral value. The buyers were located in Louisiana, Dallas, Oklahoma City, and Jackson, Mississippi. In the middle of the five hundred acres were the seven arpents apparently inherited by Bernadette, all fitting like narrow pieces of a pie along the bank of the river where I had almost been killed. Under old Napoleonic law, inherited land had to be divided evenly among all the children of the deceased. When access to a navigable waterway was involved, the key issue was equal access: Hence the strange pie-slice divisions along a riverbank.

The land around Bernadette's arpents had been sold eighteen months ago. Bernadette's land was still in her name, although I suspected the title had reverted to the grandmother.

I made a list of the seven buyers and underlined the name of the group that had purchased other land that was part of the Latiolais estate: Castaways, Ltd., in New Orleans.

A floating casino operation? It was possible. When it comes to twenty-four-hour casinos that serve free booze to lure the compulsive and the uneducated into their maw, the altruistic oversight provided by people from Vegas and Atlantic City, the state of Louisiana is always ready to rock.

Or maybe somebody had a marina in mind. But people who build marinas don't have young girls killed because they happen to inherit a small amount of land on a mud-choked river in a part of the country known for its poverty and illiteracy.

It had to be a casino.

When Helen and I got back to New Iberia, I dialed the number of Castaways, Ltd. The man who answered sounded young and earnest, with a voice like that of a scrubbed-face Bible-college student tapping on your door. When I told him who I was, he seemed anxious to please.

"I was looking at some properties in Jeff Davis Parish," I said. "I see that your company purchased some acreage down by the river. Can you tell me if y'all are planning to build a marina there?"

"Could be. I remember that deal. We build boat docks and waterfront resorts and such. But you might be talking to the wrong guy."

"How's that?"

"We got all kinds of initiatives going here, particularly since Katrina and Rita. Let me switch you over to Edward. He's more up to speed on that Jeff Davis deal."

"Who is Edward?"

"I'm fixing to put him on right now. Just hang on. Thanks for calling Castaways."

Thirty seconds later, someone else picked up on the line. "This is Edward Falgout for the St. Jude Project. How can I help you?" the voice said.

I leaned forward in my chair, the phone pressed a little tighter against my ear. "The St. Jude Project?" I said.

"Yes, sir, what can I do for you today?"

"I'm trying to clear up some title information regarding a tract in Jeff Davis Parish," I said. "Specifically the Latiolais estate."

"If this is about oil rights, we don't own them. You'll have to check the courthouse for that information."

"My name is Dave Robicheaux. I'm with the Iberia Parish Sheriff's Department. We're investigating a shooting that took place near the old Latiolais property."

"Sorry, I was confused. I thought you were a landman with an oil company. We get a lot of inquiries about oil rights."

"I'm writing up a report, and I was confused about some land boundaries. The Latiolais land belongs to the Castaways Corporation?"

"Yes, sir, to my knowledge. Right now it does."

"I didn't catch that last part."

"It does and it doesn't. The St. Jude Project is a charitable group. I think that piece of land you're talking about is being transferred to us. We get land donations from various corporations. One of those corporations we work real close with is Castaways."

"Yes, I think I've heard of you guys. You all do a lot of good," I said.

"Castaways and the St. Jude try to create what we call 'empowerment zones,'" he said. "I'm not qualified to speak on it, but the short version is that Castaways buys run-down properties and rejuvenates and donates them to the St. Jude, more or less to put local people back to work."

"That sounds like a noble endeavor. I'm glad to learn this. My question concerns seven arpents in the name of Bernadette Latiolais. Know anything about them?"

"No, sir, afraid not."

"Just out of curiosity, does that empowerment zone include a casino?"

"Not likely."

"Say again?"

"These are religious people. They don't believe in legalized gambling. The St. Jude Project is real big on the work ethic, what they call 'workfare, not welfare.'"

"Do you know what they might be building down there? That's one of my favorite duck-hunting spots."

"Maybe nothing. Or maybe something ten years from now."

"What kind of something?"

"I got no idea."

"I appreciate your time."

"Yes, sir, happy to help," he replied.

I set the phone back on its base. The man named Edward Falgout may not have given me the keys to the dark tower, but inadvertently he had dropped the dime on the St. Jude Project, which meant he had put Robert Weingart and Kermit Abelard and, by extension, Timothy Abelard right back in the middle of the investigation.

CHAPTER 18

As it turned out, we didn't need the personnel at Castaways, Ltd., or the St. Jude Project to focus our attention once again on Robert Weingart. He did it for us.

That same afternoon Weingart went to a branch bank located in a residential neighborhood where most of the transactions involved the commonplace deposits and withdrawals of middle-income people. Weingart wanted to close out an account that had over two hundred thousand dollars in it. So far, no problem. Weingart wanted to have the money wired to a bank in British Columbia. The teller consulted with the branch manager, who was a black woman, and said a phone call or two would have to be made and wire and account numbers might have to be confirmed, but the transfer would be made that day.

Then Weingart was told what the exchange rate would be when he deposited American dollars in a Canadian bank. "That's six percent less than the real value of the dollar. Check again," he said.

"I already did," the teller said. She was a Cajun woman in her late sixties, with gray skin and knots of veins in her calves, her bottom as wide as a washtub, probably someone's relative who had been given the job at the bank to help her through her declining years. "I'm sorry, Mr. Weingart. I'm just telling you what the bank in Canada tole me."

"Look, this is a simple matter. Try to concentrate on what I'm saying. Each American dollar I deposit in Canada should translate into a dollar and a quarter Canadian. You look like a reasonable person. If you were in my shoes, would you let someone throw twelve thousand dollars of your money away?"

"No, suh, I wouldn't do that."

"That's good. We're getting somewhere. What's your name?"

"Lavern."

"Okay, Lavern, go back to your manager, Mrs. Sasquatch over there, and tell her to drag her lazy rear end out of the chair and to get on the phone and straighten this out. Can you do that for me, Lavern?"

"I don't like the way you're talking to me, suh."

"Sorry about that. My twelve thousand is insignificant when it comes to helping along a grand program like affirmative action. I apologize. Tell your manager I said fuck me. I apologize to you, too, Lavern. Fuck me twice."

Robert Weingart was just backing out his white Mustang convertible from his parking slot when the deputy who responded to the bank manager's call pulled in to the lot. Weingart was wearing shades and a stylish beige fedora and a scarlet silk shirt with blown sleeves. He cut his engine and smiled pleasantly into the deputy's face. "If this is about me, the ladies inside worked out my problem," he said. "It was a misunderstanding about a change in currency rates. I got a little hotheaded. Sorry about that."

"Don't tell me. Tell them," the deputy said. He was a red-haired man with a florid complexion and a brush mustache and a chest that resembled a beer keg. His nickname was Top because he was a retired marine NCO, although he had been a cook and never a first sergeant. As a department comedian, he was considered second only to our dispatcher, Wally.

"I told both ladies I was out of line, sir," Weingart said. "They seemed satisfied. I don't see the problem."

"You're the author?" Top said.

"I'm *an* author."

"My mother read your book. She wanted me to read it. That's why your remarks were real hurtful to her."

"Miss Lavern is your mother?"

"No, the branch manager, the black lady, is my mother. The one you called Mrs. Sasquatch."

Weingart grinned from behind his glasses and inserted his hand in the top of his shirt and massaged his chest. "You're pretty good."

"Take off your glasses."

"What for?"

"Because it's rude to talk to people with sunglasses on."

"I never heard that one."

"You have now."

"Anything to please."

"That's better. Thank you. I hear you've been down three times."

"More than three if you count juvenile time."

"So who taught you it was okay to come to a town like this and use the word 'fuck' in front of my mother?"

"Nobody did, sir," Weingart replied, ennui creeping into his voice.

"You know you have a twitch in your face?"

"I wasn't aware of it."

"Right under your eye. You don't have a couple of fried circuits, do you? Like a little too much crystal in the system? Because that's what you look like to me. I think that's why you said 'fuck' in front of my mother."

Weingart stared straight ahead, his expression self-effacing, his hands resting on the spokes of his steering wheel.

"When is the last time you UA-ed?" Top asked.

"I'm not on parole. I was commuted out, all sins forgiven."

"I can always spot a guy who has dirty urine. I think that's why you have a twitch in your face."

"I'm getting a crick in my neck. Do you mind if I get out of the car?"

"You're not dropping or snorting or smoking or shooting or any of that stuff?"

"You've got it."

"But if you're not under the influence, what's your excuse for using the word 'fuck' to my mother and Miss Lavern? Bet you didn't know I was a lifer in the Crotch."

"In the *what*?"

"I think guys like you are draft dodgers. You hide out in jails while other people go to war. Look at your face in the mirror. Half of it looks like a glob of Jell-O trembling in a bowl. It's embarrassing to look at."

"There's nothing wrong with my face."

"Are you calling me a liar?"

"Listen—"

"You giving me orders now?"

"No, sir."

"First it was my mother, now it's me. You don't know when to quit, do you?" Top said. "You've got a red ant."

"What?"

Top slapped Weingart hard on the side of his head. "There," he said. "Those things can really sting you."

"Want to roust me? Do it. I've seen it all. I was in Huntsville."

"From what I hear, you saw it on your knees. Or draped over a chair. There you go with that twitch again. Hang on, another red ant."

Top slapped him on the back of the head, this time so hard Weingart's eyes watered. Then he pinched something off Weingart's neck and held it up in front of him. "See, an ant. I told you. I got to get going. Drop by the department and have coffee sometime. But get a doc to check out that twitch. If people didn't know better, they might think you're a yard punk who's scared shitless of authority."

When Weingart drove out of the parking lot, one wheel went over the curb and came down hard in the street, the exhaust pipe and back bumper scraping on the concrete.

THAT EVENING AT twilight, on a back road in St. Martin Parish, Weingart parked his Mustang in front of a crowded nightclub that catered to people who drifted back and forth across the color line. In a more primitive time, some of them had been derogatorily called "redbones." Most of them were probably part white, part Chitimacha Indian, part Cajun, and part black. As a rule, they referred to themselves as Creoles, a term that, in the early nineteenth century, connoted the descendants of the Spanish and French colonists who settled New Orleans and created the plantation society that surrounded it. In general, they were a handsome people; they often had green or blue eyes and reddish or jet-black hair and skin that looked as though it had been blown with brick dust. In St. Martin Parish, this back-roads club was their special place.

Clifton Chenier, the man most emblematic of zydeco music, had been a regular performer there and is buried in an unmarked grave not far from it. In spite of its reputation for underage drinking violations, outrageous amounts of noise, and erotic trysts back in the woods, the club had an innocence about it, perhaps because it was part of the pagan ambience that always lurked on the edges of our French-Catholic culture.

The top was up on Weingart's convertible when he turned in to the lot, so no one paid particular attention to him until he stepped out on the gravel in his pleated white slacks and navy blue terry-cloth shirt and ostrich-skin boots with silver plate on the tips and heels, his clean features lit by the Christmas-tree lights that stayed on the club's windows year-round.

He entered the club, his expression benign, his chin tilted slightly upward. He passed the bar and the propane stove where a big cauldron of robin gumbo was simmering. He passed a green felt table where men were playing bourree in a cone of yellow light given off by a bulb inside a tin shade. He sat at a table by himself not far from the dance floor and the bandstand and ordered a longneck beer and a basket of french fries that had been cooked in chicken fat.

The girl who joined him wore a sundress printed with big flowers and had skin that glowed like a bright penny. Her hair was mahogany-colored and blond-streaked and was tied in back with a purple ribbon that had sequins on it. She was smiling when she pulled out a chair, and anyone watching the scene would have assumed she knew Robert Weingart. But that was not the case. He turned his palms up and jutted his head forward, as though silently saying, *Care to tell me who you are before you flop your ass down at my table?*

"I'm Tee Jolie Melton. My sister cain't be here tonight," she said. "So I came instead."

"I'm not sure I'm cluing in on the message here."

"I know you was suppose to meet her down the road, like you done before. About the audition, right?"

"News to me."

"You was gonna take her for the voice test."

Weingart shook his head, his lips crimped. "Sorry, not me," he said.

She looked away, smiling tolerantly, then brought her eyes back on his. "See, my sister kind of misled you. She's only sixteen. Our mama don't want her going out late at night. But I sing, too. I sing at church and wit' a band in Breaux Bridge and Lafayette sometimes. She tole me you like to come in here for french fries and a drink before you pick her up at the grocery."

He thought hard on it. "You're talking about the girl I gave a ride to when it was raining. She works in that store in St. Martinville across from Possum's. That's your sister, huh? Yeah, I see the resemblance. I think your sister got the wrong idea. I probably said something about her voice and the fact that I know some people in the entertainment business, but she's just a kid."

Tee Jolie gazed into space as though not quite understanding everything she was being told. "I bought your book."

"No kidding?"

"Why you call it *The Green Cage*? Is the cage bamboo or somet'ing?"

"You didn't read it?"

"I got to use the dictionary a lot. You know some words, you."

"In the Texas farm system, you see a lot of green. Oceans of it. Everywhere you look. I have post-graduate degrees in tractor operation and bucking bales."

"You went to school in there?"

He pulled at the flesh under his chin with two fingers. "What are you, three or four years older than your sister?"

"That's about right."

"Actually, you look more mature than that. In the best way. She's not as pretty as you, either."

"I t'ink she is."

"That's because you're a good sister. You want a drink?"

"I don't mind."

"I'm sorry, I forget your sister's name."

"Blue."

"I'm sorry I gave Blue the wrong impression. She seems like a nice kid. I hated to see her standing in the rain like that."

"But you took her out before? She knows everyt'ing about you."

"If I see somebody walking along a road, particularly at night or in the rain, I give them a ride. People are killed every three or four days by hit-and-run drivers around here."

"But you was gonna pick her up tonight, right?"

He put a french fry in his mouth, then pushed the basket toward her. He stared at her for a long time. "You weren't messing with me? You sing professionally?"

"I did an ad on TV in Lafayette. I sang on TV once with Bonsoir Catin, too." Then she blinked as though remembering he had not answered her question.

"You're putting me on," he said.

Her gaze was fixed on the way the orange and purple floodlights on the bandstand lit the haze that floated above the dance floor. She watched the musicians taking the stage. Her mouth was parted slightly, as though she were transfixed by the moment and the promise of the evening and the glitter on the cowboy costumes worn by the zydeco men. She swallowed drily.

Weingart motioned to the waitress. "What are you having?" he said to Tee Jolie.

"Whatever you are."

"Can your bartender mix a Manhattan?" he said to the waitress.

The waitress looked at the bar and back at Weingart. "I can ax."

"Can he handle two Diet Cokes?"

"That's all?" the waitress said.

"Put some lime slices in them. Bring us some of that gumbo, too."

"I don't t'ink we have limes," the waitress said.

"Don't worry about it. The Cokes are fine," he said.

Tee Jolie rested her chin on the heels of her hands. "Blue said you was nice."

"Don't believe everything you hear," he said.

"The gumbo is made from robins. It's illegal to do that. But we eat them anyways."

"A couple of movies got made around here. Nobody asked you to try out for a part?"

She shook her head, smiling coyly. "Why you ax that?"

"Because you're photogenic."

She looked sideways, then back at him. "I don't know what that means."

He pointed at her. "That expression right there. Your face is an artwork. No matter when the camera freezes, the frame tells a story. Robert De Niro and Meryl Streep are like that. Your face has the same quality. It's called photogenic. No one has ever told you that?"

"Not recently."

"Look, this is a nice part of the country. I love the weather and the accents and the food and the music and all that stuff. But maybe you ought to think about expanding your horizons a little bit."

She was smiling at him, more tolerant than flattered, interested perhaps more in the manner of his presentation than its substance. "I'm gonna be a movie star?"

"A writer doesn't have a lot of influence in Hollywood. But I have friends in both the music and film industry who trust my instincts, God only knows why. I also know people who run an acting school, one that gives scholarships. I can make a couple of inquiries. It's like prayer. What's to lose?"

The waitress returned with their gumbo and drinks. "I had him put candied cherries in the Cokes. He was gonna put some old lemons in there. I tole him not to do that," she said.

"Appreciate it," Weingart said, nodding profoundly. He waited with his hands in his lap while the waitress seemed to take forever placing the bowls and glasses and paper napkins and plastic spoons on the table. "We all finished here now?"

"That's sixteen dol'ars," she said.

He counted out twenty-five dollars on her tray, putting the denominations in separate piles so the amount of his tip was obvious to anyone watching.

"T'ank you," the waitress said.

Tee Jolie dipped her plastic spoon into the gumbo and placed it gingerly in her mouth. "You gonna ax me if I want an audition now?"

"I'm not sure that's what you want. I think you're a woman who goes her own way in her own time."

"But you're fixing to leave, aren't you?"

"Why do you think that?"

" 'Cause don't nobody in a club give a big tip till he's fixing to leave. I used to work in a restaurant."

"You're pretty smart. I've got a key to a sound studio in Lafayette. We'll be there in thirty minutes."

"You didn't try to kiss Blue in your li'l car?"

"She told you that?"

"No."

"She didn't say that?"

"I was testing you. She didn't say that at all. She said you was nice."

He wiped his mouth with his paper napkin and pushed his bowl of gumbo away. He seemed to study the zydeco men on the bandstand without actually seeing them. The lead player, a gargantuan black man, had an accordion that rippled like purple ivory. His fingers were as big as sausages, but they danced across the keys and buttons as delicately as starfish. He had gone into Clifton Chenier's signature song, "Hey, Tite F'ee," rocking back and forth, his voice a flood of rust into the microphone. In the background, the rub-board man whipped the thimbles on his fingers up and down on the corrugated sheet of aluminum strapped to his chest.

"I'd like to do something for you, if you'd let me. But it's up to you," Weingart said.

"Do what for me?"

"Give you some exposure. Improve your life. Introduce others to your talent. What do you think we've been talking about, girl?" He paused. "I wrote novels and short stories for years. Nobody would touch them. I was dirt in the eyes of other people. Then I found somebody who believed in me."

"Who?"

"Kermit Abelard." He waited. "You don't know who he is?"

"No."

Weingart smiled. "Wonderful."

"Why?"

"Nothing. Kermit needs a little humility once in a while. You're something else. Want to take a ride?"

She smiled and shrugged. "You giving me a ride in the rain? 'Cause if you are, it's not raining."

"Girl, if you don't have a career waiting for you, I'll swallow a thumbtack. Cross my heart."

She picked up her purse and looked at the bandstand as though saying either good-bye or hello to it. Weingart pressed his palm into the small of her back and walked outside with her under a blanket of stars that perhaps the girl believed had been created especially for her.

IN THE SHADOWS on the edge of the parking lot, a St. Martin Parish deputy sheriff was smoking a cigarette. She was short and slightly overweight and had gold hair, and her lipstick was thick enough to leave smears on the filter tip of her cigarette. The night was warm, and she wore a short-sleeved blue shirt turned up at the cuffs, exposing the plumpness of her upper arms. On nights when a band played at the club, she was one of several deputies who took turns doing security by the front door, primarily as a visual discouragement to parolees who could be violated back to Angola for drinking alcohol or keeping bad company. The job was boring, but the pay wasn't bad, and it was also under the table.

One of the bartenders at the club was an el-

derly black twelve-string guitarist by the name of
Hogman Patin. Both of his forearms were wrapped
with scar tissue like flattened gray worms from
knife beefs in Angola, where he had done time as
a big stripe under the gun almost sixty years ago.
He bore no animus toward whites or the system,
and did not argue with others regarding his view
of the world, namely, that there was no difference between human beings except the presence
or absence of money in their lives. But he had an
animus, and it was one that went deep into his
viscera. Hogman gave short shrift to those who
exploited the innocent and the weak.

He wasn't sure who Robert Weingart was and
in fact could see only the clean lines of his profile
and the shine of the tonic on his hair, but while
Hogman poured the Diet Cokes and filled the
bowls of gumbo Weingart had ordered, he studied Tee Jolie Melton and the glow on her face. It
was the look of a girl who knew she was loved
and beautiful and desired. Her eyes were bright,
as though she was amused by the flattery she was
hearing, as though the words of the well-dressed
white man did not cause flowers to bloom in her
cheeks. Hogman asked the waitress who the white
man was.

"A famous writer," she said.

"He drives that Mustang out front?"

"That's him."

"Ax Tee Jolie if she got a minute."

"She came to his table on her own, Hogman.
He ain't picked her up."

"I know, he's probably researching a book. We
get a lot of them kind in here."

Hogman went to the restroom, then had to move
two cases of beer from the storage room to the cooler.

When he had finished loading the cooler, Tee Jolie and Weingart had left. He wiped his hands on a dish towel and went out on the front porch of the club.

Weingart escorted Tee Jolie to his Mustang and opened the passenger door for her. But instead of getting in, she rested one hand on top of the door and studied his face and the unnatural glaze it had taken on in the glow of the Christmas-tree lights stapled around the club's front windows, as though the tissue in it had been injected with synthetics. "Can my sister come wit' us?"

"I thought we got that situation out of the way."

"I feel a li'l guilty about her not getting to audition, like maybe I'm taking her chance away from her."

"There're all kinds of legal problems when you start dealing with minors. Record companies will do it if the prospect is big enough, but they don't like it. Besides, kids' voices change."

"You telling me the troot'?"

"I mean this with all respect: Why would I lie to you? Because I can't find a girlfriend? I have to go to barrooms on back roads and make up lies like some kind of molester? Is that what I look like?"

"I didn't mean it that way."

"You're a nice girl. You're bright and evidently have talent. But if you don't want to go to Lafayette, no hard feelings. Maybe you're right. It's not meant to be."

"What isn't?"

"One of those breakthrough moments. Doors open, and we go through them or we don't. If a person lets fear dominate his life, he doesn't deserve the talent he's been given. Believe me, if that's the case, with you or me or anybody who has a gift, it will be taken from us and given to somebody else."

"I never t'ought of it like that. Okay."

"Okay what?"

"I want you to hear me sing. Let's go to Lafayette, Robert."

"You called me by my name. That's a breakthrough in itself."

She sat down in the deep black leather of the seat and fastened the safety belt across her chest while he closed the door behind her. Then he turned the ignition, backed in a half circle, and drove slowly across the gravel toward the road.

He got only twenty feet before the female deputy sheriff stepped in front of his headlights, her eyes watering in the glare.

Weingart rolled down his window. "What's the trouble?"

"Cut your engine and step out of the car, please," she said. The deputy leaned over and peered inside at Tee Jolie. "You doin' all right tonight, miss?"

"I'm fine," Tee Jolie replied.

"Did you hear me, sir?"

"Whatever," Weingart said, lifting his hands from the steering wheel. He turned off the ignition and the lights and got out of the car.

"Walk over here with me," the deputy said.

"Can we pull the plug on this?"

"Do you have a hearing impairment?"

Weingart and the deputy went into the shadows by the corner of the club, ignoring the black bartender who stood on the porch. "You leave that girl alone," she said.

"Somebody made you the patroness of mulatto bar girls?"

"This isn't St. Mary Parish. Your free ride is over, buster."

"If I were short and fat, I'd be mad at the world, too."

"I hope you wise off one more time. I really do. Short of that, you get your sorry ass down the road."

"Gladly."

"She stays."

"That should be up to her."

"I can't tell you how happy I am that you've taken this attitude. There were a couple of times I wanted to do this, but I didn't. I'll always regret that."

"Whoa," he said, stepping backward.

Hogman heard the deputy slide her baton from the plastic ring on her belt.

"Tell me how you like this. I've heard it passes in a week or so," she said, thrusting the point of the baton with both hands into a spot just above Weingart's belt.

He let out a groan and slumped against a car fender, barely able to support himself, his mouth open, his face gray.

"One more little poke, in case you didn't get the message," the deputy said. "That wasn't so bad, was it? Happy motoring."

HOGMAN CALLED AT the office in the morning and told me what he and the waitress had seen and heard at the club the previous night.

"What happened to the girl?" I asked.

"She called a cab."

"I'm not sure what you're telling me here, Hogman."

"Dave, this ain't just some trashy po' white shopping for country girls. When a man like that picks up a black girl, it's 'cause he wants to leave his mark on her."

"But is something else bothering you about what you saw and heard?"

"The deputy and this Hollywood guy talked like they knew each other. Like the deputy knew about t'ings he'd done before. When she come inside later, I said, 'A man like that don't stop being what he is 'cause you poke him wit' a club, no. He just do what you done to him to the next girl he gets his hands on.'"

"What'd she say?"

"That he hadn't broke no law. That she run him off and he wouldn't be back again."

"What's this deputy's name?"

"I just call her Miss Emma," he replied. "I don't know her last name."

George Orwell once wrote that people are always better than we think they are. They are more kind, more loving, more brave and decent. They keep their mouths shut in the torture chamber and go down with the decks awash and the guns blazing. I still believe that Orwell was right. But too often there are times when our fellow human beings let us down, and when they do, all of us are the less for it.

After I finished talking to Hogman, I drove to St. Martinville and walked into the sheriff's department and found Emma at a desk in her cubicle, sorting through a pile of paperwork in her in-basket.

"Sometimes I wrap mine in a paper sack and stuff it in the bottom of the trash can," I said. "The irony is, it doesn't seem to make any difference."

A half-smile lingered on her mouth. "You just passing by?"

"I understand you had a run-in with Robert Weingart last night."

I hoped she would make a joke about it or indicate convincingly that she was busy. I hoped she would be mildly irritated. I hoped she would do almost anything except pause and think before she replied. But I saw her eyes go flat and bright without cause, and impossible to read. "Who told you that?" she asked.

"You've met Weingart before?"

"I know who he is."

"That's not what I asked."

"Clete told me once that Weingart might be using roofies on local girls. So I invited him out of St. Martin Parish."

I pulled up a chair and sat down by the side of her desk, not over two feet from her. "Yesterday Weingart wired a huge amount of money to Canada. You think the book business is that good?"

"How would I know?"

"Because maybe you have a history with him."

"I saw him giving a snow job to a young girl who didn't have enough sense to stay out of his car. So I had a heart-to-heart with him. I don't know where you get all this other stuff. Have you been talking to the bartender?"

"You told Weingart he'd gotten a free pass about something. You were talking as though you'd had a chance to put a stop to something but you didn't. You were talking as though you wanted to make up for what a theologian would call a sin of omission."

"Run that church-basement psychobabble on somebody else, Dave."

"Why is it that every person I know who uses that term has something he or she fears discussing?"

"Because most of the people you know are professional victims?"

"Were you talking about the death of Bernadette Latiolais or Fern Michot?"

Emma picked up a thick sheaf of paper from her desktop, work that seemed to be completed, and set it in the in-basket. Her cheeks were flaming. "Why do you do this to me, Dave? I was always your friend."

"I think you planted Clete's gold ballpoint in Herman Stanga's swimming pool. You're not only a dirty cop, Emma, I think you set up a man you slept with, a man who had great affection for you and who still defends you."

There was a cup of cold coffee on her desk. She picked it up and threw it in my face. Other deputies, both plainclothes and in uniform, were getting up from their desks, staring through the front of the cubicle. I took two pieces of Kleenex from the box on Emma's desk and wiped my face with them. "You're a Judas goat. You lead your own kind down the slaughter chute," I said. "Tell me if there is anything lower."

The sheriff placed his hand on my shoulder. "That's enough, Dave," he said.

"Not even close," I replied.

CHAPTER 19

EARLY MORNING IS a bad time for recovering drunks. The wall between the unconscious and the world of sleep is soft and porous, and the gargoyles have a way of slipping into the sunlight and fastening a talon or two into the back of your neck. Perhaps that is why I have always been an early riser, escaping into the blueness of the dawn and its healing properties before the power of memory and the dark energies of my previous life lay claim on my waking day.

But the funk and depression I brought back to town after my encounter with Emma Poche could not be blamed on the unconscious or my history of alcoholism and violence. A time comes in your life when the loudest sound in a room, any room, is the ticking of a clock. And the problem is not the amplified nature of the sound; the problem is that the sound is slowing, each tick a little further away than the one that preceded it. The first time this happened to me, I was in City Park on an autumn day, the smell of chrysanthemums and gas hanging in the trees. The breath went out of my chest and a sweat broke on my forehead. I sat down on a bench, the camellias and the bayou and the ball diamond slipping out of focus. I waited for the moment to pass, my mouth filling with a taste like pennies or blood from a fresh cut. I took off my wristwatch and shook it to make it stop ticking. Then I realized that people were staring at me, their faces disjointed with pity and concern.

"I've got malaria," I said, my hands knotted between my knees, a weak smile on my mouth.

It's not enough to call this a vision of mortality. In that moment, when watches and clocks misbehave and you feel a cold vapor wrap itself around your heart, you unconsciously draw a line at the bottom of a long column of numbers and come up with a sum. Perhaps it's one that fills you with contentment and endows you with a level of courage and an acceptance that you didn't know you possessed.

Or maybe not.

Maybe you wonder if you blew it, if you flipped away your yesterdays like cigarette butts that left a bad aftertaste. Or worst of all, you realize you have to leave the lives of others behind, the one you didn't live and the ones you did not get to know adequately.

Helen Soileau probably had several women living inside her skin, but I had come to know only one or two of them. My daughter had grown from a terrified five-year-old refugee I had pulled from a submerged plane into an aspiring novelist and law student. My wife, Molly, had been a Catholic nun, a missionary in Central America, a labor organizer in southern Louisiana, and the wife of a police officer who had shed the blood of many men. I suspected that neither woman's story was over. I also suspected I would not see the rest of their stories written.

Thoughts of this kind rob you of both faith and resolve. And my situation was further complicated by a phone call that Alafair picked up in the kitchen that afternoon. "Just a moment, please," she said, pressing the mute button on the console. "It's somebody named Emma. She sounds like she's had a few drinks."

I waited, thinking.

"I'll tell her to call back."

"That's all right," I said, taking the receiver from her. I placed it against my ear. I could hear people talking loudly and a jukebox playing in the background. "What's shaking, Emma?"

"Screw you, Dave. One day I'll pay you back for what you did today."

"Is that the entirety of your message?"

"No. No matter what you think of me, I still have a conscience."

"I'm listening."

There was a long silence.

"Emma?"

"They're gonna cap you and anybody who's with you."

"Who is?"

"God, you're dumb," she said, and broke the connection.

My ear felt cold when I set the receiver down in the cradle.

"What is it, Dave?" Alafair asked.

"That was Emma Poche. She's a deputy sheriff in St. Martin Parish. Her boat must have left the dock a little early today."

But I kept staring at Alafair, my words banal and silly, poorly disguising the portent of Emma's call.

"Why are you looking at me like that?" she asked.

"She said I was in danger, as well as anyone who might be with me."

"Danger from whom?"

"She hung up without saying."

"Let's have a talk with her."

"I did that this morning. Maybe this is her way of getting even or appeasing her conscience. She's a drunk, and nothing she says is reliable."

Alafair sat down at the breakfast table and gazed out the back window. Molly was feeding Tripod on top of his hutch, and Snuggs was watching both of them from a fork in the tree overhead. "I have to tell you something, Dave," Alafair said.

"What is it?"

"I heard two deputies in uniform talking in the booth next to me in McDonald's. They were talking about the guys who tried to kill you and Clete in Jeff Davis Parish. One of them said, 'I wonder if Robicheaux is starting to see black helicopters.'"

"Who cares what he said?"

"I care," she said.

"Did you say something to this guy?"

"I told him he'd better keep his mouth off you or he'd be wearing his Big Mac on his head."

I sat down next to her and put my arm around her shoulders. Her back was as stiff and hard as a stump. "Even when you were a little bitty girl, you were heck on wheels, Alf."

When she looked back at me, there were tears in her eyes. "You're better than all these people, Dave. They don't deserve you."

"I'm better than no one."

"This Poche woman is in St. Martinville?"

"Bad idea," I said.

"Where does she live?"

"Stay away from her," I said. "Are you listening, Alf? Come back here."

• • •

IT WAS DARK and rain had started to fall before Alafair found the cypress house on the bayou where Emma Poche lived. Only one light burned in the house, perhaps in a back bedroom. The light fell out into the backyard, where a barbecue pit with an open top smoldered under a live oak, the smoke rising into the leaves in an acrid flume.

The tide was in, and Bayou Teche was high and swollen with mud, the surface chained with rain rings. A speedboat was moored among the flooded elephant ears, a tarp thrown carelessly over the console and the front seat. Alafair could hear music playing inside the cypress house. She could also hear wind chimes tinkling on the gallery and the sound of someone's voice rising and falling above the music. She stepped up on the gallery and started to tap on the door. Then she realized what she was hearing, a soliloquy of need and debasement, a confession of personal inadequacy made by someone who was either drunk or morally insane or without any vestige of self-respect.

"I've done everything you wanted," the voice said. "But you treat me like fingernail parings. I'm supposed to fuck you on demand and never expect a kind word, and act like that's normal. I bought a roast and a cake and fixed your potatoes just the way you like them. I thought we'd eat and go out in public or go to New Orleans and stay at the Monteleone. I don't have a career or a life anymore. All I have is you. Come back to bed. Let me hold you."

Alafair stepped back, unsure what she should do next. Then she took a breath and knocked hard on the door. The inside of the house went silent. "Ms. Poche, it's Alafair Robicheaux. I need to speak to you," she said.

She heard the sound of feet moving across the floor and a door opening in back. She knocked again, this time harder. "Ms. Poche, one way or another, you're going to talk to me," she said.

She walked around to the side of the house. Someone wearing a flop hat and a raincoat was walking rapidly through the trees and down the slope to the bayou. The electricity leaping between the clouds lit the moored speedboat and the banks of flooded elephant ears and the small waves capping among the cypress knees. The person picked up the weighted painter and stepped up on the speedboat's bow in a single motion, then pushed the electric starter on the engine and backed into the current. In seconds, the boat was splitting a trough down the middle of the bayou.

Alafair went back to the gallery. Emma Poche was standing behind the screen door, backlit by a lamp she had turned on in the living room. She wore jeans and a blouse that exposed a bra strap. "What do you want?" she said, her hair in disarray, her breath rife with the odor of cigarettes and alcohol.

"You called my father this afternoon."

"What about it?"

"You said someone was going to kill him and anybody he was with."

"I have no memory of a conversation like that."

In the glow of the lamp, Alafair could see the streaked makeup on Emma Poche's face, the swollen eyes, the smear of lipstick on her teeth. "I answered the phone," Alafair said. "I handed the receiver to my father. I listened while he talked to you. Don't lie to me."

"What did you say?"

"May I come in?"

"No, you can't," Emma replied, reaching for the latch on the screen.

But Alafair jerked open the door and went inside. "If you want to call 911 and report an intruder, you can use my cell." When Emma didn't reply, Alafair said, "Who was the person who just left?"

"I don't have to tell you anything. Who do you think you are? Your father has hallucinations. Everybody knows it. He's one of those dry alcoholics who would be better off drunk."

"My father is the kindest, most decent human being you'll ever meet. I feel sorry for you, Ms. Poche—"

"It's Deputy Poche."

"I advise you to shut your mouth and listen, Deputy Poche. I found out where you live from Clete Purcel. I also found out you were the woman who tried to set him up for the murder of Herman Stanga. That's about as low as it gets. I had a hard time imagining what kind of woman could do that to a man like Clete. I tried to see you in my mind's eye, but I couldn't. Then I stood on your gallery and heard you begging affection from somebody to whom you're obviously a throwaway fuck. If you weren't so pathetic, I'd slap you all over your own house."

"You little bitch, you can't talk to me like that."

"Who are the men who tried to kill Dave?"

"I don't know."

Involuntarily, Alafair raised her hand.

"You listen to me, girl," Emma said. "We can die and become humps out in a field, and two days after we're gone, nobody but our families will remember who we were. Look around you. You see the trailer slums on the bayou and the crack dealers on the street? You think Dave or you or me can change the way things work here? We're little people. You think I'm the only person around here who's a disposable fuck? You like the way you got treated by Kermit Abelard?"

"What do you know about Kermit?"

"Better question, what *don't* I know about him? He used you. But while he was getting in your pants, he was taking it between the cheeks from Robert Weingart."

Alafair used the full flat of her hand to slap Emma Poche across the face. She hit her so hard, spittle rocketed from Emma's mouth.

Emma sat down on the couch, her left cheek glowing from the blow, her eyes out of focus. "You feel sorry for me? I have a high school degree. You're a Stanford law student. Which one of us got used the worst? Which one of us shared her lover with a sleazy con man who date-rapes teenage girls? I could have you locked up and charged, but I'm gonna let you slide. Now get out of my house."

Alafair's gaze dropped to the coffee table. "What are you doing with this book?" she asked.

"Reading it?"

"Who just left here?"

"No one. As far as I'm concerned, you've imagined everything that's happened here tonight."

"You're reading Kermit's novel about the Battle of Shiloh?"

"You keep your hands off my book."

"Did Kermit give you this, Ms. Poche?"

"Why would you think that? Why wouldn't you assume I bought it at a store?"

"Because everything else on your bookshelf is trash."

"You give me that," Emma said, getting to her feet.

Alafair peeled back the book's pages to the frontispiece. The inscription read:

To Carolyn,
    With affection and gratitude to a champion
on the courts and a champion of the heart.
Thanks for your support of my work over the
years.
        Kermit Abelard

Carolyn?

I DID NOT see Alafair until the next morning, when I was fixing breakfast and she came into the kitchen in her bathrobe. I poured her a glass of orange juice and fixed her a cup of coffee and hot milk and set the glass and the coffee cup and saucer in front of her at the table. I didn't ask her where she had gone the previous night or what she had done. I went outside and fed Snuggs and Tripod and came back in. Then she told me everything that had happened at Emma Poche's house in St. Martinville.

"You hit her?" I said.

"She's lucky that's all I did."

"You didn't get a good look at the person going out the back door?"

"No, but I saw the boat. It looked like the one Kermit owns. I can't be sure. When I saw his novel on her table, I thought maybe Kermit had left it. Except the inscription is to a tennis player named Carolyn. Does that mean anything to you?"

"Yeah, it does. Carolyn Blanchet, Layton Blanchet's widow. She played on the tennis team at LSU.

I think she's still the seventh-ranked doubles amateur in the state."

"Layton Blanchet, that guy who was running a Ponzi scheme of some kind? He shot himself at his camp?"

"I think Layton was probably murdered."

"You think Carolyn Blanchet is involved with Emma Poche? That maybe she was the one who went out the back door?"

"It's possible."

"Like maybe they're getting it on?"

"Could be. A lot of things about Emma would start to make sense."

I set a plate of eggs and two strips of bacon in front of Alafair. She had been frowning, but now her expression was clear, her hands resting on top of the table, her long fingers slightly curled, her fingernails as pink as seashells. "I thought maybe—"

"That Kermit was Emma's lover?"

"Yeah, but that wasn't what bothered me. I thought maybe he was involved with something really dark. With killing Herman Stanga or setting up Clete. But it wasn't Kermit who went out Emma's back door, was it?"

"I'm not sure about anything when it comes to the Abelards," I replied. "Their kind have been dictators in our midst for generations and admired for it. They created a culture in which sycophancy became a Christian virtue."

But she was staring out the window, not listening to abstractions, her food growing cold. "No, it wasn't Kermit. I'm sure of it now. My imagination was running overtime. Are you mad at me for going after Emma Poche?"

"I've never been mad at you for any reason, Alafair."

"Never?"

"Not once."

"Drink a cup of coffee with me."

"You want to tell me something else?"

"No," she said. "Look at Tripod. He just climbed up in the tree. He hasn't done that in weeks. Don't you love our home? I don't know any place I would rather wake up in the morning."

I COULDN'T CATCH Helen Soileau until she came out of an administrative meeting with the mayor after eleven A.M. I followed her into her office, but before I could speak, she gave me the results of her attempt to confirm my account about the shoot-out on the river in Jeff Davis Parish.

"Within the time frame we're using, no hospital in the state has reported a gunshot wound that matches your description of the one you think you inflicted on the man by the river," she said. "Nor has there been a report on any dumped bodies that would match those of Vidor Perkins or the guy you think caught a forty-five round through the lungs. No airports anywhere between Lake Charles, Baton Rouge, and New Orleans know anything about a crop duster flying around during the storm, either."

"Crop dusters don't need airports. They land in farm pastures every day. And I don't *think* I shot those guys, Helen. I blew up their shit at almost point-blank range."

"Does bwana want to be clever, or does bwana want to hear what I've found?"

"Sorry."

"The locals found some bloody rags on the side of the road. There was a piece of flesh with part of a fingernail on it inside one of the rags."

"Enough to get a print?"

"No. But enough to run a DNA search through the national database. So far we still don't know who these guys are or where they're from or who they work for. Timothy Abelard probably did business with the Giacano family in New Orleans. You don't think they're part of Didi Gee's old crowd?"

"No, these guys were too sophisticated."

"The Mob isn't up to the challenge? They kidnapped Jimmy Hoffa in broad daylight on a Saturday afternoon in front of a Detroit restaurant, and to this day no one has ever been in custody for it and no one has any idea where his body is. You think the guys who pulled that off were kitchen helpers in an Italian restaurant?"

"These guys were military."

"You know that?"

"Yeah, I do."

"How?"

"They never spoke. They didn't have any visible jewelry. They wore the same hooded raincoats, like a uniform, so their enemy could not distinguish one of them from the other, so their impersonality would make them seem even more dangerous and formidable. 'Black ops' isn't an arbitrary term and has more than one connotation."

She ticked her nails on her desk blotter. "I hope you're wrong. We hardly have the resources to send our local morons to Angola. What'd you come in here to tell me?"

"Emma Poche called me up when she was loaded and told me I was in danger."

"From?"

"I asked her that. She told me how dumb I was."

"What else?"

"Alafair went to Emma's house last night and confronted her."

"To what degree do you mean 'confronted'?"

"She slapped her. She also caught her with a lover. Maybe the lover is Carolyn Blanchet."

I saw a glint catch in Helen's eye like a sliver of flint. Then I remembered that she and Carolyn Blanchet had been at LSU at the same time, that something had happened involving a friend of Helen. Rejection by a sorority because of the friend's sexual orientation? I couldn't remember.

"Run that by me again," Helen said.

"Somebody was in Emma's house when Alafair was at the front door. Emma was delivering a litany of grief about her mistreatment at this person's hands. But whoever it was left through the back without Alafair seeing him or her. Alafair said a copy of Kermit Abelard's last novel was on the coffee table. It was inscribed to someone named Carolyn."

"That doesn't make it Carolyn Blanchet's."

"The inscription indicated this particular Carolyn was a champion tennis player and a longtime supporter of Kermit's work. Carolyn once told me she was a big fan of Kermit's books. I don't think it's coincidence. I think we've been looking in the wrong place."

I had lost her attention. "That slut," she said.

"Pardon?"

"You and I need to take a ride."

"I can handle it, Helen."

"What you can do is get on the phone and tell Ms. Blanchet we're on our way to her house and her prissy twat had better be there when we arrive."

WHEN CLETE PURCEL was a patrolman in New Orleans and, later, a detective-grade plainclothes, he had been feared by the Mob as well as the hapless army of miscreants who dwelled like slugs on the underside of the city. But their fear of Clete had less to do with his potential for violence than the fact that he did not obey rules or recognize traditional protocol. More important, he seemed indifferent to his own fate. He was not simply the elephant in the clock shop. He was the trickster of folk legend, the psychedelic merry prankster, Sancho Panza stumbling out of the pages of Cervantes, willing to create scenes and situations in public that were so outrageous, pimps and porn actors and street dips who robbed church boxes were embarrassed by them. Whenever I hesitated, his admonition was always the same: "You got to take it to them with tongs, big mon. You got to spit in the lion's mouth. Two thirds of these guys never completed toilet training. Come on, this is fun."

Maybe because of his visceral hatred of Robert Weingart, or his conviction that Timothy Abelard trailed the vapors of the crypt from his wheelchair, Clete decided to take a ride down to the Abelard compound on the southern rim of St. Mary Parish. It was a fine day for it, he told himself. The rain had quit; the clouds were soft and white against a blue sky; the oaks along Bayou Teche looked washed and thick with new leaves. What was there to lose? His gold pen had been stolen from him and used to set him up for the killing of Herman Stanga. He still had resisting-arrest charges against him because of his flight from the St. Martin cops the night he busted up Herman Stanga behind the Gate Mouth club. His best friend had almost been clipped in that gig down by the river in Jeff Davis Parish, then had been dissed by the local cops. In the meantime, Clete had watched a pattern that seemed to characterize his experience in law enforcement for over three decades: The puppeteers got blow jobs while their throwaway minions stacked time or got their wicks snuffed.

He put down the top on his Caddy, made a stop at a convenience store for a six-pack of Bud and a grease-stained bag of white boudin still warm from the microwave, and motored on down the road, Jerry Lee Lewis blaring "Me and Bobby McGee" from the stereo.

Outside Franklin, he drove south on the two-lane through a corridor of gum and hackberry trees and slash pines that grew along the edge of flooded sawgrass and expanses of saltwater intrusion where the grass had turned the color of urine. As he neared the Abelard compound, he saw a pickup truck backed into a cleared area that contained a cast-iron Dumpster. The top of the Dumpster was open, and a large black woman wearing rubber boots was standing in the truck bed, hefting a series of plastic garbage bags and flinging them into the Dumpster.

Abelard's nurse, he thought. What was her name? Had Dave said she was Abelard's out-of-wedlock daughter? A white man was sitting in the cab of the truck reading a sports magazine, his door open to catch the breeze.

Clete turned in to the clearing, cut the engine, and set his can of Bud on the floor. "Need a hand with that?" he said.

The black woman paused in her work, studying Clete, trying to place him. "No, suh, we got it," she said. She flung a heavy sack with both hands into the Dumpster.

Clete got out of the Caddy and removed his shades and stuck them in his shirt pocket. His shoes were shined, his golf slacks ironed with sharp creases, his flowery sport shirt still crisp from the box. "It's Miss Jewel, isn't it?" he said.

"Yes, suh. You came out for lunch one day with Mr. Robicheaux."

Clete glanced at the white man behind the wheel. His hair was peroxided and clipped short, the sideburns long and as exact as a ruler's edge, his jaw square. He never lifted his eyes from the magazine. Clete picked up two large vinyl bags and walked them to the Dumpster and tossed them inside.

"I got the rest of them, suh. It's not any trouble," Jewel said.

Clete nodded and put an unlit Lucky Strike in his mouth and gazed across the road at the wood bridge that led to the Abelard compound. A blue heron was rising from the lily pads that grew in the water by the bridge, the edges of its wings rippling in the wind. "Got a match?" he said to the man behind the steering wheel.

"Don't smoke," the man said, not looking up.

"Got a lighter in there?"

"It doesn't work."

Clete nodded again. "Have I seen you some-where?"

This time the man held Clete's gaze. "I couldn't say." He sucked on a mint. His eyes were of a kind that Clete had seen before, sometimes in his dreams, sometimes in memory. They didn't blink; they didn't probe; they contained no curiosity about the external world. They made Clete think of cinders that had been consumed by their own heat.

"You a military man?" Clete asked.

"No."

"But you were in, right?"

"Ruptured disk."

Clete pulled his unlit cigarette from his mouth and held it up like an exclamation point. "I got it. That's why you couldn't help Miss Jewel out."

The man dropped his eyes to the magazine, then seemed to give it up, as though his few minutes of retreat from the distractions of the world had been irreparably damaged. He closed the door and started the engine, his mouth working on the mint while he waited for the black woman to get in.

"You know where I think I've seen you?" Clete said.

"Couldn't even guess."

"I was looking through some binoculars. You were in a field down by a river in Jeff Davis Parish. It was raining. Ring any bells? Some heavy shit went down. Maybe a couple of your friends got their lasagna slung all over the bushes. I never forget a face."

"Sorry, I'm from Florida. I think you're confused."

"It wasn't you? I would swear it was. You guys know how to kick ass. It was impressive."

"Watch your foot."

Clete stepped back as the man cut the wheel and turned in a circle, opening the passenger door for the black woman. Clete pointed his finger at the driver. "Airborne, I bet. That's how you got that ruptured disk. You're doing scut work for the Abelards and Robert Weingart now? That must be like drinking out of a spittoon. I bet you've got some stories to tell."

As the truck crossed the two-lane and turned onto the wood bridge that spanned the moat around the Abelard house, Clete memorized the tag and dialed a number on his cell phone. Then he lost service and had to punch in the number a second time. The call went into voice mail. "Dave, it's Clete. I'm outside the Abelard place. I need you to run a Florida tag. It belongs to a real piece of work, maybe one of the shitbags from the gig on the river. I tried to rattle him but didn't have any luck." He closed his eyes and said the tag number into the cell. "Get back to me, noble mon. Out."

Clete rumbled across the bridge and up the knoll that formed the island on which Timothy Abelard's columned manor stood like an abandoned shell from a movie set. The pickup truck driven by the man from Florida was parked by the carriage house, but no one was in sight. When Clete knocked on the door, he could hear no one inside. "Hello?" he called out. No response.

He walked around the side of the house, past a chicken coop and an ancient brick cistern that was veined with dead vines. In the backyard the black woman was hoeing in a vegetable garden, a sunbonnet tied under her chin, her big arms flexing as she notched weeds out of the rows planted with carrots and radishes. Clete did not speak when he walked up behind her, though he had no doubt she was aware of his presence. He took off his hat and studied the refracted glare of the sun inside the flooded cypress snags between the house and the bay. "Mr. Abelard home?" he said.

The woman kept her eyes on her work, a line of sweat sliding out of her bonnet onto her forehead. "No, suh."

"Where is he?"

"Gone to Lafayette for his dialysis."

"As his nurse, wouldn't you normally go along with him?"

"I got chores to do here."

"Is Kermit or Robert Weingart around?"

"No, suh, they're in New Orleans for the day."

"What's the deal on our peroxided friend from Florida, Miss Jewel?"

Locks of her hair hung outside her bonnet. They were threaded with silver, damp with her work and the humidity that seemed to rise from the composted soil and the dead water surrounding the knoll. Her hoe was rising and falling faster, thudding into the ground, flashing in the sun. "Your name is Mr. Clete, isn't it?"

"Yes," Clete said.

"You need to leave, suh. It's not a good time for you to be here."

"You in trouble, Miss Jewel?"

"No, suh. I been here all my life. I was born in the quarters, back up the road where the old mill use to be. I just do my job. I go my own way. Nothing bad is gonna happen to me."

"Who's the dude from Florida?"

She looked out of the corner of her eye toward the house. "I got to get these radishes hoed out. Then I'm fixing a big salad for Mr. Timothy. People have their problems and their grief, then it passes. Mess with it and it gets all over you."

Clete heard a screen door open and swing back on a spring. The black woman's hands tightened on the hoe handle, her triceps knotting as she scratched and clicked the blade frenetically between the vegetable rows.

"If you have business on the property, you need to call first and make an appointment," the man with the peroxided hair said to Clete.

"Give me a number and I'll get right on that."

"It's unlisted."

"That kind of makes it hard to call."

"Take it up with Mr. Abelard or his grandson. I'm just the hired help."

"You're doing a heck of a job, too."

"Anything else?"

"Can I park out on the road?"

"Do whatever you want, long as it's not on this side of the bridge."

"I didn't get your name."

"I didn't give it. Go start dinner, Jewel. I'll be along in a bit."

"Yes, suh."

The man from Florida watched her walk into the shade of the house and lean her hoe against the back steps and go inside. Then he fixed his gaze on Clete. His face had the youthful tautness of an athlete's, but there were three parallel lines across his brow with tiny nodules of skin in them, like beads on a string, that gave his face a dirty, aged look. "You a PI?"

"Why would you think that?"

"Leave me a business card. I got my job to do, but I try to give a guy a break if I can."

"I think your job is to keep Miss Jewel from talking to outsiders."

"Then you thought wrong."

"I think you already know my name. I think you didn't answer the door because you were busy running my tag."

The man from Florida glanced at his wristwatch. "In five minutes, I'm gonna look out the front window. Leave or stay. But if you stay, you're gonna be on your way to the parish jail."

"No problem," Clete said. "By the way, Miss Jewel doesn't give up family secrets, whatever they might be. So don't be acting like she did after I'm gone. You got my drift on that?"

The man from Florida stepped closer to Clete, into his shadow, his face turned up into Clete's. His right foot was pulled behind his left and set at a slight angle, the instinctive posture of someone who was trained in at least one of the martial arts. An odor like male musk or stale antiperspirant rose from his armpits. "It's no coincidence you got beer on your breath this early in the morning. You're a retread, pal, way beyond your limits. Eat a big dinner and get drunk or get yourself laid. Do something you can handle. But don't mouth off to the wrong people again. Juicer or not, a guy your age ought to know that."

The man walked back to the house, stooping to pick up the hoe from the steps and hang it on a garden-shed hook, as though Clete were not there.

Clete went back out to his Caddy and sat behind the wheel, biting a hangnail. He drained the open can of beer that rested on the floor, but it was flat and hot and tasted sour in his mouth. He stared at the front of the house, the scaling paint on its stone columns, the dormers upstairs that seemed piled with junk, the nests of mud daubers and yellow jackets under the eaves, the loops of cobweb on the fans that hung over the upstairs veranda.

Clete thought of his childhood in the old Irish Channel and the predawn milk deliveries he made with his father in the Garden District. He remembered a splendid antebellum home off St. Charles Avenue and the kindly woman who lived there and asked him to come back on Saturday afternoon for ice cream. When he had shown up, dressed in his best clothes, the backyard was crowded with street urchins and raggedy black children from across Magazine. He returned later with a bag full of rocks and broke out all the glass in her greenhouse. Now, as he stared at the Abelard home, he tried to think of a term that described it and the history it represented: a cheap fraud, a house of cards, a place where Whitey could boss around his darkies and live off somebody else's sweat.

But he knew those weren't the appropriate words. The house meant nothing, and the people in it, such as the Abelards, were, like the rest of us, eventually dust in the wind. The real story was one that people seldom figured out. It was that the Abelards and their kind had taught others to disrespect themselves, and in large numbers they had done exactly that. Clete poured his beer out on the gravel, crunched the can in his palm, and tossed the can in the flower bed.

As he was driving across the wood bridge, his cell phone rang. He checked the caller ID, then placed the phone to his ear. "Talk to me, big mon," he said.

He turned off the bridge and pulled the Caddy to the side of the road and listened. While he listened, he gazed at the blue Dumpster set back in the cleared space across the road, a bib of flattened trash scattered around its perimeter, a thick green stand of brush and persimmon trees behind it. "Andy Swan, huh?" he said. "Okay, I'm going to do some archaeological research while I'm here, and we'll ROA for dinner when I get back to New Iberia. No, everything is copacetic. I'm extremely cool and serene and mellow and thinking only cool thoughts. Do not worry, noble mon. No, there is no problem here in St. Mary Parish that is not totally under control. Out."

He parked in front of the Dumpster, retrieved a pair of bolt cutters and polyethylene gloves from the trunk, and cut the cable that was locked down in a V-shaped configuration on the Dumpster's steel lid.

He began his search by splitting open the piled vinyl bags and shaking out their contents. Among the persimmons, he found a broken tree branch on the ground and used it to rake among the plastic bottles and tin cans and shrimp shells and Perrier and wine bottles and decayed food that the Abelards and their guest Robert Weingart had amassed in a week's time. He was about to give it up when he spied, on the Dumpster's floor, a strip of white plastic that was tongued on one end and notched with a hole on the other, the sides serrated like tiny teeth.

He dropped the plastic strip into a Ziploc bag. Behind him, the pickup truck driven by the man from Florida rattled over the plank bridge and angled across the asphalt and pulled to a stop lengthwise behind Clete's Caddy. The man got out and slammed the door behind him. "I don't believe you," he said.

"I'm about to leave. I'd appreciate you moving your truck," Clete said.

"What you're gonna do is clean up this mess. What you're also gonna do is put anything you found back where you got it."

Clete scratched the back of his neck as though an insect had just bitten him. "No, I don't think that's on the table today."

"Did you come out here to get beat up or drug off in handcuffs? You just like to walk into buzz saws? You get off on pissing in the punch bowl? Which is it?"

"See, I just found what looks to be a ligature. Or maybe it's just a strip of plastic used to hang pipe. What's your opinion, Mr. Swan?"

"I'm supposed to be impressed because you got somebody to run my tag?"

"No, there's nothing interesting about me. But you, that's a different deal. You were a member of the execution team at Raiford back when they were still using the chair. You were one of the guys who shaved their head and put a diaper on them so they wouldn't mess themselves in front of the witnesses. *That's* major-league impressive. Is it true y'all packed cotton and lubricant up their anus before you put on the diaper? That's what I've always heard. Y'all have to train much for that?"

"I usually try to stay objective about my job and not get personalities mixed up in it. But for you, I think I'm gonna make an exception," Andy Swan said.

Clete lifted his arms away from his sides. "No piece, no slapjack, no cuffs, no shank, no weapons of any kind. I'm no threat to you, Mr. Swan."

"I know. You're just a jolly fat man, probably a guy who got kicked off the force somewhere for taking freebies from crack whores or going on a pad for greaseballs. Now you carry a badge anybody can buy in a pawnshop and stick your dick in Bourbon Street skanks and pretend you're still a player. Maybe I didn't get it all exactly right, but I'm close, aren't I?"

"Take your hand out from under the seat and step back from your vehicle," Clete said.

"Or?"

"I've got enough room to get my Caddy out," Clete said. "When I'm gone, you can call the locals or go about your business. No fuss, no muss."

"You asked about stuffing cotton up their ass. I never did that. I shaved their head and put the electrode paste on and strapped the mask on their face. I strapped it so tight they couldn't breathe. I think some of them suffocated before the electricity cooked their insides. I know for sure blood ran out of their nose and mouth and sometimes their eyes. And I hope every one of them suffered. Why? Because they deserved it. What do you think of that?"

Clete didn't answer. Andy Swan straightened up and turned around, the stun gun in his hand buzzing with a blue-white arc. "Let's trim a little of that fat off you," he said.

"Why don't we do this instead?" Clete said. With all his weight, he rammed the branch he had been using as a rake into Andy Swan's face, the dried, sun-hardened tips spearing into the man's eyes and nostrils and mouth and cheeks. Andy Swan crashed against the side of his truck, dropping the stun gun, pressing the heels of his hands into his eye sockets. Clete grabbed him by the back of the collar and spun him around and drove his face against the truck cab. Then he did it again and again, his fingers sunk deep into the back of Swan's neck, Swan's nose bursting against the metal. When Clete stopped, Andy Swan could barely stand.

Walk away, walk away, walk away, a voice kept repeating in Clete's head.

He stepped back, his hands at his sides. The blue Dumpster, the garbage on the ground, the persimmon trees and the Caddy and the pickup truck were all spinning around him now. Andy Swan's face resembled a red-and-white balloon floating in front of him.

"I'm done," Swan said. He tried to cup the blood running from his nose. "I take back what I said. I don't want any more trouble."

"Who killed the girls?"

"I don't know."

"Who tried to kill Dave Robicheaux?"

Andy Swan shook his head and spat a broken tooth into his palm.

"Are you deaf? Do you think I enjoy this? Answer me," Clete said.

"I don't know anything, man. I just do security."

"You dissing me again? You think I'm stupid? You think I get off knocking around gumballs?"

"Suck my dick."

Clete drove his fist into Swan's stomach, doubling him over, dropping him to his knees. Strings of blood and saliva hung from Swan's mouth. His back was shaking. He raised his left hand in the air, signaling Clete not to hit him again. "I got here three days ago from Florida. Check me out. I work for a security service in Morgan City. I'm just an ex-cop. I'm no different from you."

"You ever say that last part again, you're going to have some serious problems."

Clete picked up the stun gun, walked out into the trees, and threw it into a pond. When he returned to the Dumpster area, Andy Swan was still on his knees. Clete lifted him up by one arm.

"What are you doing?" Swan said.

"Nothing. And neither are you. You're going to get a lot of track between you and Louisiana. And you're going to do that now. You're not going back to the Abelard house and give that black woman a lot of grief. You're changing your zip code as we speak."

"If that's what you say."

Clete's gaze lifted into the trees, his eyelids fluttering. "I don't recommend equivocation and a lack of specificity at this time. Are we connecting here?"

"Yeah."

"Say again?"

"Yes, sir."

"Good man. Take this in the right spirit. Those guys you fried at Raiford? You'll see them again."

"They're dead. We electrocuted them."

"That's the point," Clete said. "Turn east at the four-lane. You got a straight shot all the way to Pensacola."

CHAPTER 20

CLETE'S CALL ASKING me to run the tag of the Florida pickup had come in before Helen and I left the department for Carolyn Blanchet's house outside Franklin. It had been no problem to run the tag; nor had it been a problem to call a friend in the state attorney's office in Tallahassee and ask for a background check on Andy Swan. But I did not tell Helen what I had done until we were almost at the Blanchet home. My timing was not only bad, I think it contributed in the worst possible way to the events that were about to follow.

"Not only is Clete conducting his own investigation in St. Mary Parish, but you're helping him, even asking a personal favor from the Florida state attorney's office?" Helen said.

Her knuckles had whitened on the steering wheel. When I didn't reply, she shot me a look, the cruiser slipping over the yellow stripe.

"We're all on the same side, Helen."

"Clete's on his own side, and so are you."

"Not so."

"I'm really pissed off, Dave."

"I gather that."

"Not adequately. Believe me, we'll talk more about it later."

She turned off the four-lane and drove down a service road to the Blanchet property and the lovely green arbor in which Layton's tribute to himself still rose through the oaks like a Tudor castle covered with cake icing. We were not the only people there. Two SUVs and a silver sedan with a United States government plate were coming toward us through the two columns of oaks that lined the driveway, the sedan out in front. Helen stuck her hand out the window and signaled the driver to stop.

"Helen Soileau, Iberia Parish sheriff," she said. "What's going on?"

The driver of the sedan was young and wore a white shirt and tie and had a fresh haircut. "Nothing now," he said. "We just got served. Somebody ought to explain to you people that this isn't 1865."

"Carolyn Blanchet got an injunction against the United States government?" Helen said.

"You got it. We'll be back later. Have fun, Sheriff," the driver said.

I watched the convoy drive onto the service road. "She probably got a local judge to create some temporary obstacles for the IRS or the SEC. But they'll cut through it with a couple of phone calls," I said.

"Anything these guys wanted from her has already gone through a shredding machine. Carolyn Blanchet gets what she wants and makes few mistakes."

I hated to ask the question that had been hanging in the air every time Carolyn Blanchet's name was mentioned. "Helen, how well do you know her?"

"If you haven't heard, Pops, when we're on the job, I'm your boss. You don't question your boss about her personal life. That said, when we're off the job, you still do not question me about my personal life. Understood?"

"No."

"You want to explain that?"

We were still stationary in the driveway, the

sunlight spangling inside the oak canopy overhead. I kept my eyes straight ahead, the side of my face almost wrinkling under Helen's gaze. "I think you know more about Carolyn than you've let on," I said.

When I looked at her, I saw a level of anger in her face that made me wince. "I have a circle of friends in New Orleans you probably haven't met," she said. "Carolyn Blanchet has had relationships with some of them. All of them were the worse for it. She uses people and throws them away like Kleenex. She's also a degenerate. Black leather, masks, chains, boots. Would you like more detail?"

"Why didn't you tell me this?"

"Because she hasn't been an active part of the investigation of a crime committed in Iberia Parish."

"That's pretty disingenuous, if you ask me."

And in that mood, not speaking, we parked the cruiser in front of the house and walked through the side yard to the tennis court, where we could hear someone whocking balls that were being fired over the net by an automatic ball machine.

Carolyn was wearing blue sweatpants and a sports bra and was hitting the balls two-handed, her platinum hair shiny with perspiration, her skin sun-browned with freckles, her baby fat wedging over her waistband as she put all her weight into her swing.

She wiped her face and throat and underarms with a towel and flung it on a chair by a table set with a pitcher of lemonade and glasses. She asked if we wanted to sit down.

"Not really, Ms. Blanchet," Helen said. "We wanted to offer our sympathies at your loss, and to ask you a couple of questions, then we'll be gone."

"How you doin', Dave?" Carolyn said, sitting

down, ignoring Helen's statement, pouring herself a glass.

"Just fine, thanks. You chased off the feds?" I said.

"No, the federal court in New Orleans did. Layton left behind a mess. But it's not my mess. If somebody else wants to clean it up, that's fine, but they can do it somewhere else."

"Ms. Blanchet—" Helen began.

"It's Carolyn, please."

"We're still investigating the death of Herman Stanga," Helen said.

"Who?"

"A black pimp who was shot and killed behind his home in New Iberia. We wondered if you know a St. Martin Parish sheriff's deputy by the name of Emma Poche."

"Offhand, I don't recall hearing the name."

"Offhand?" Helen repeated.

"Yes, that's what I said. 'Offhand.' It's a commonly used term."

"Do you know any female deputies in the St. Martin Sheriff's Department?"

"No. Should I?"

"But you know Kermit Abelard, don't you?" Helen said.

"I've read his books. I've been to one or two of his book signings. What's the issue here?"

"There is no 'issue.' Did he inscribe a book to you?"

I stared at Helen incredulously because I realized the direction she was headed in, one that would expose the source of our information.

"We're trying to clear up a question about Kermit and his relationship to Layton and their mutual interest in biofuels," I interjected.

"What you need to do is answer my question,

Ms. Blanchet," Helen said, her gaze drifting toward me irritably. "Did Kermit Abelard inscribe a book to you?"

"I just told you I attended his book signing. That's what people do at book signings. They get their books signed by the author."

"Then why is your autographed book in Emma Poche's house if you don't know Emma Poche?" Helen said.

I could feel my pulse beating in my wrists. "Carolyn, it's obvious we're looking at a deputy sheriff for reasons that make us uncomfortable," I said. "Someone may have planted evidence at a homicide scene. We had reason to believe you might know this deputy. We didn't come here to offend you."

I paused and then took a chance, hoping to create a distraction from Alafair and possibly force an admission by Carolyn Blanchet. "We have a report you may have met with Emma Poche at a motel outside St. Martinville. Your private life is your private life, but you're telling us things that don't fit with what we know."

Carolyn was shaking her head even before I finished speaking. "I should have known. There's no end to it," she said.

"End to what?" I said.

"My husband was a paranoid. He convinced himself I was having an affair—in part, I think, to assuage his own guilt for screwing women all over the United States and Latin America. Evidently he hired a fat idiot of a private detective to follow me around, and this is what we end up with."

"How could you be at the motel with Emma Poche and not know her?" Helen said.

"I didn't say I was," Carolyn replied.

"I think you did," I said.

She touched her temples. "I must be having an aneurysm."

The sun was over the trees now, and I could feel the heat rising from the concrete. "Emma Poche has a way of showing up in too many places or with too many people that involve either Layton or you," I said. "I don't believe Layton shot himself, Carolyn. I believe he was murdered."

"By whom?" she said.

"Let's look at motivation," I said. "Layton was a big liability. He was sick mentally and emotionally and seemed determined to go down with the *Titanic*. Who loses if the bank is broke? Who loses if the feds find out others were involved in Layton's schemes?"

"I always liked you and treated you well, Dave. You're saying ugly things about me, and I think I know the source. She's standing right next to you. When you walked onto the court, you began talking about a book you found at this female deputy's house. You served a warrant on her house in St. Martin Parish, where you have no jurisdiction?"

"We have various resources," I said.

"You're lying. Both of you are." She knew Alafair had been our source, and she knew that we knew she knew. She stood up and adjusted the sweatband on her hair. She took a long drink from her glass and set it back down on the table, the ice sliding to the bottom. "I thought that bunch of federal nerds I just got rid of were inept," she said. "But you two are establishing new standards."

"I have morgue photos of two dead girls in my file cabinet," I said. "Somehow their deaths are connected to the Abelards and your late husband and some properties in Jefferson Davis Parish. Both girls were abducted, and I believe both suffered terrible deaths. You can be clever from now to Judgment Day, Carolyn, but if you were mixed up in the murder of those girls, I'm going to hang you out to dry, woman or not."

I saw Helen turn and stare at me.

We walked back through the side yard, past the heavy, warm fragrance of the flower beds and the smell of chemical fertilizer and the odor of something dead under the house, neither of us speaking, a sound like wind roaring in my ears. Helen started the cruiser, and we headed down the driveway toward the service road. In the silence, I could hear tiny pieces of gravel clicking in the tire treads.

"I screwed it up. I'm sorry," she said.

I looked out at the shade on the lawn and at a shaft of sunlight shining through the trees on a sundial.

"She figured out Alafair was our source, but that doesn't mean she's going to do anything about it," Helen said. "Trust me, Carolyn doesn't let her emotions get in the way of her agenda."

"Someone who practices sadomasochism? Someone who may have murdered her husband or had someone do it for her? Someone you call a degenerate and a slut who uses and discards people like Kleenex?"

"You don't take prisoners, do you, Streak?"

"No, I don't," I replied.

I didn't speak again until we were back at the department, and then it was only to ask the time because my watch had stopped.

THAT EVENING CLETE and I drove across the drawbridge in the Caddy and sat down in one of the picnic shelters in City Park down by the water in the gloaming of the day, the air dense, the sky purple and pink and marbled with fire-lit clouds in the west. "So you figure Emma is in the sack with Carolyn Blanchet and maybe the two of them planted my gold pen in Stanga's swimming pool?" he said.

"I'd call it a strong possibility," I replied.

"Which would mean they probably capped Stanga, huh? But why?"

"He knew too much. He'd dime them to save his own ass. He was disposable. He tried to extort them or to extort Layton. He should have brushed his teeth more often. Take your choice."

"So I was bopping a switch-hitter who was setting me up to ride the needle for the woman she was banging? I've been taken over the hurdles a few times, but I don't know if I can handle this."

"Don't fault yourself because you believe in people, Clete."

"Right," he said, his eyes looking at nothing. "I went to Morgan City and checked out this guy Andy Swan. He was telling the truth about working for a security service. But he didn't arrive three days ago. He's been around Morgan City at least three weeks. He could have been one of the guys who tried to pop you. You're going to give that ligature I found in the Dumpster to the crime lab?"

"In the morning. But it's out of context, Cletus."

"Who cares? It's evidence we didn't have before." Clete waited for me to speak. When I didn't, his gaze fixed on my face. "You're thinking about Alafair?"

"Of course I am. Helen blew it."

"Look, Dave, Helen is right about one thing. Because the Blanchet woman knows Alafair found out about her affair with Emma doesn't mean she's going to put a hit on her. Sometimes we got to keep things in perspective."

"Their building is burning down and they know

it. That's why Robert Weingart was transferring his money to a bank in Canada. You put scorpions in a box and shake it up, they sting everything in sight."

"All right, let's talk about Weingart a minute. What's his involvement with Carolyn Blanchet? It's biofuels, it's Herman Stanga, it's the Abelards, it's what?"

"It's all of what you just said. I just don't know how it fits together."

"Big mon, we're not going to let anything happen to Alafair. You're not giving her credit, either. Didn't you say she had an IQ of 180 or something?"

"No, her IQ isn't measurable. It's off the scale."

"It's not genetic, either."

"That's supposed to be funny?"

The shadows were deepening inside the trees, and lights were going on in the houses high up on the slopes along the bayou. I heard the cogged wheels under the drawbridge clank together and saw the bridge separate in the center and rise into the air. I could see the running lights on a large boat coming out of the gloom, and I thought I heard a hissing sound like steam escaping a valve cover and water cascading behind the stern. The sunset had created a gold ribbon down the middle of the current. Against the silhouette of the uplifted bridge, I saw the bow and pilothouse of the boat nearing us, and black men working on the deck and a bearded skipper in a blue cap behind the wheel, a cob pipe clenched in his teeth. I rubbed my eyes with the back of my wrists, as though I were fatigued. Clete looked down the bayou, then back at me. "You okay?" he said.

"Sure," I replied.

"Want to try and catch Andy Swan before he leaves town? I mean, since we now know he could have been one of the guys at the shoot-out."

"He wasn't."

"How can you be sure?"

"Because the guys at the river weren't state employees who work on execution teams."

"So what do you want to do?"

"Go after the guy whose age and infirmities have been giving him a free pass too long."

I could see the connection come together in Clete's eyes. "I'm not that keen on the idea," he said.

"It was old men who sent us to war," I said.

COCKROACHES DON'T LIKE sunlight. Despots and demagogues do not make appearances in environments they do not control. Elitists join clubs whose attraction is based not on their membership but on the types of people they are known to exclude. It wasn't hard to find out where Timothy Abelard would probably be on Friday night of that particular week. I read an article in the Lafayette newspaper and called a couple of patriotic organizations and a congressional office and was told, in one instance, "Why, yes, Mr. Abelard wouldn't miss this event for the world." The "event" that seemed of such global importance was a fund-raiser to be held at seven P.M. at Lafayette's Derrick and Preservation Club in the old Oil Center.

Clete and I dressed for the occasion. The waiters at the club were all white-jacketed middle-aged black men who could not be called obsequious but belonged culturally to another generation, one that knew how to be selectively deaf and to pretend that the clientele they served held them in high regard. The linen-covered buffet tables were lit by candles and sparkled with crystal glasses and silver bowls. The food was sumptuous, the quality you would expect at Antoine's or Galatoire's in New Orleans. The guest speaker was a retired army general who had helped subvert the democratically elected government in Chile and replace it with Augusto Pinochet, who turned the country into a giant torture chamber. He was also a practicing Catholic. When four American Catholic missionaries were raped and murdered by El Salvadoran soldiers, he said at a news conference that maybe the victims had "tried to run a roadblock."

The guests at the banquet and fund-raiser were an extraordinary group. Batistianos from Miami were there, as well as friends of Anastasio Somoza. The locals, if they could be called that, were a breed unto themselves. They were porcine and sleek and combed and brushed, and they jingled when they walked. Their accents were of that peculiar southern strain that is not Acadian nor influenced by what is called Tidewater or plantation English or the Scotch-Irish dialectical speech of the southern mountains. It's an accent that seems to reflect a state of mind rather than a region. The vowels somehow get lost in the back of the throat or squeeze themselves through the nasal passages. The term "honky," used by racist blacks, may be more accurate than we like to think. But their innocence is of a kind you cannot get angry at. They are not less brave than others, nor more sinful, nor lacking in the virtues we collectively admire. You just have the feeling when you are in their midst that all of them fear they are about to be found out, unmasked somehow, revealing God only knows what, because I am convinced their psychological makeup is a mystery even unto themselves.

Clete and I arrived early and went out to the

parking lot, wondering if by chance a vehicle from the shoot-out on the river might show up. We wrote down perhaps a dozen license numbers, but we were firing in the well and knew it.

The decals in the windows left little doubt about the environmental and geopolitical convictions of the vehicles' owners. They ranged from the flag wrapped around the beams of a Christian cross to a child urinating on "all Muslims and liberals" and an image of a bird falling from the blast of a shotgun, under which were the words "If it flies, it dies." But these were the visual expressions of people who got up each morning trying to define who they were. The men at the shoot-out were pros who did not attract attention to themselves or serve perverse abstractions created for them by others. The men at the river had no quarrel with either the mercenary nature of their mission or the black flag under which they carried out their deeds. If you have ever met them, you are already aware they share a commonality that never varies: There is no light in their eyes. Search for it as long as you wish; you will not find it. And maybe that is why they are so good at not leaving behind any trace of themselves. Whatever they once were has long since disappeared from their lives.

It was breezy in the parking lot, and the oak trees that stood on the boulevard and in the Oil Center itself made a sweeping sound in the wind, their branches and leaves changing shape and color in the glow of the streetlamps. Clete stared at the southern sky and the flickers of lightning over the Gulf, his eyes like hard green marbles, his face taut. "It's going to blow," he said.

"It's that time of year," I said.

"I got a funny feeling."

"It's just a squall. It won't be real hurricane season till mid-summer."

"That's not what I'm talking about. I saw something in your face when we were talking in City Park, on the bayou there."

"Saw what?" I asked, avoiding his gaze.

"You were looking at something down the bayou. By the drawbridge. You rubbed your eyes like you were tired, but you were hiding something from me. There wasn't anything down the bayou except the bridge. I looked, and there wasn't anything there."

"That's right, there wasn't."

"Then what were you hiding from me?"

"I don't remember that happening, Clete," I said.

He rotated his head as though his collar was too tight, his eyes uplifted at the sky and the electricity playing in the clouds. "I had a dream last night. There was a big clock on my nightstand, one of those windup jobs. The cover on the face was gone. Then some guy came in the room. I tried to see who he was, but all I could see were his eyes looking at me out of a hood. I kept saying to him, 'Who are you?,' but he wouldn't answer. I tried to get my piece off the dresser, but something was holding me down on the bed, like somebody was sitting on my chest. He walked over to the nightstand and picked up the clock and broke off the hands. Then he put the clock back down and walked out of the room. I still never saw who he was."

"It was just a dream," I said, trying to keep my face empty, trying to forget the room I had rented in Natchez with a clock that had no cover and no hands.

"Dave, we need to get rid of this Abelard gig. It stank from the jump. Nobody is interested in those dead girls except us. I say we smoke the guys who tried to hurt us and let somebody else add up the score. If we bend the rules, screw it. The guy who clicks off your switch is always the one you never see coming. I don't want to buy it like that."

"We're going to be okay," I said. "We always come through things, don't we?"

"It's waiting for us. Out there. I can feel it." He waved his hand at the air as though swatting away insects. "It's like a red laser dot crawling all over us."

"You never rattled. Not in the Channel or the Desire. Not even in Nam or El Sal."

"You don't get it. I'm not talking about me. It's you. I can see it in your eyes when you think nobody is looking. You see it coming. Stop jerking me around."

I hooked my arm around his neck. "Let's go back inside and check out these guys," I said. "Maybe give them something to remember."

"What'd you see on the bayou, Dave?"

I didn't reply and squeezed his neck as though we were two boys in a wrestling match. Then we went inside, Clete behind me, his mouth small and downturned at the corners, his behemoth physique about to split the seams of his clothes.

THE DINERS FILLED their plates and sat at big round tables in a banquet room, at the head of which was a podium and a microphone. Clete and I sat on folding chairs against the back wall. No one seemed to take particular notice of us. Clete kept leaning forward, his hands on his knees, studying the room, the diners, the men who drifted out to the bar and returned with a highball or a dessert for a wife or girlfriend. When the general was introduced and walked to the podium, the entire room rose and applauded. He was tall and wore a gray suit with stripes in it, and was erect in his carriage for a man his age. His clean features and the white strands in his hair gave him the genteel appearance of Wordsworth's happy warrior, but there was a visceral Jacksonian edge about him, physical incongruities that suggested a humble background not altogether consistent with his dress and manner. His ears were too large for his head, and there were lumps of cartilage under his jaw. His hands were square and rough-looking, his wrists ridged with bone where they protruded from his white cuffs. His facial skin creased superficially with his smile, exposing his teeth, which looked tiny and sharp-edged in his mouth. But it was the martial light in his eyes that you remembered most. It was like that of a choleric man who kept his wounds green and treasured his anger and drew on it the way one turns up the heat register when necessary.

Clete watched him, biting on a hangnail, spitting it off the end of his tongue. "I saw that dude at Da Nang," he said.

"What did you think of him?"

"I don't remember," he replied. "He was standing under an awning. We were standing in the rain. Yeah, I remember that. The rain falling on all those steel pots while he was talking to us."

The general had a prepared speech in his hands. But before beginning it, he paused and stared into the crowd, his face brightening. "I know when I'm among the right kind of people," he said. "I was walking through the parking lot a few minutes ago, and I saw a bumper sticker I must share with you. It said, 'Earth First! We'll drill the rest of the planets later!'"

The audience roared with laughter.

But Clete was not listening to the general's joke and the audience's appreciation of it. He was peering at a table in the corner where Timothy Abelard was sitting in a wheelchair, his grandson, Kermit, seated on one side of him and his caretaker, Jewel, on the other. Also at the table was a dark-skinned man who had a thin nose and wore a pencil mustache and whose lacquered black hair resembled a cap. The other man at the table had his back to us, and I could not see his face. His hair was boxed on the back of his neck, and his right shoulder seemed to hang lower than his left, as though he were uncomfortable in his chair or experiencing lower-back pain, trying to shift the pressure off his spine.

"I thought you said Kermit Abelard was the liberal in the family," Clete said to me.

"Kermit is a sunshine patriot."

"A what?"

"Read Thomas Paine."

"I don't need to. He treated Alafair dirty. He's a four-flusher and a punk, if you ask me. Who're the greaseball and the other guy at the table?"

"Who knows? The old man was famous on the cockfighting circuit. He used to fly in a DC-3 to Cuba and Nicaragua with his cocks. He was pals with Batista and the Somozas."

"I need a drink. You want anything from the bar?" Clete said.

"Take it easy on the booze."

"I wish I was stone drunk. I wish I was wearing a full-body condom. You think these chairs have been sprayed for crab lice?"

A man sitting in front of us turned around and gave us a look.

"You got a problem?" Clete said.

The man turned his back to us and didn't reply.

Clete leaned forward and punched him with one finger between the shoulder blades. "I asked if I could help you with something."

"No, I'm fine," the man said, looking at Clete from the side of his eye.

"Glad to hear it. Enjoy your evening," Clete said. He went to the bar, scraping his chair loudly. When he returned, carrying a highball glass packed with ice that was dark with bourbon, his gaze was fixed on the Abelard table. "See the guy next to the greaseball, the one with his arm in a sling? There's a cast or a big wad of bandages on his hand. You clipped a guy's fingers off at the gig on the river?"

"That's what it looked like."

"You remember his face at all?"

"I didn't see any of their faces except the guy who got his ticket canceled."

"The guy in the sling is hinky. He saw me looking at him and turned away real quick, like he'd made me."

A different man in front of us turned in his chair, his brow furrowed. "Will you people be quiet?" he said.

"Mind your business," Clete said.

"Sir?"

Clete leaned forward in his chair. "Call me 'you people' again and see what happens."

I put my hand on Clete's arm. He pushed it away and raised his glass and drank from it, his eyes already taking on an alcoholic luster, and I realized he had probably had a shot or two straight up before returning from the bar.

"What?" he said.

"Shut up."

"These guys all smell like Brut. You know what Brut smells like? An armpit. Take a whiff. The barman could make a fortune selling gas masks."

"Lower your voice."

"I'm very collected and cool and simpatico. You need to lighten up." Clete took a deep drink from his glass and filled his jaw with ice and began crunching it between his molars. He tapped the soles of his loafers, creating a staccato like a drumroll on linoleum. Then he said out of the side of his mouth, his eyes lowered, "The guy in the sling just turned around. He knows who we are. He was on the river. We need to get this guy in the box."

In his own mind, Clete was still a cop. His mistakes at NOPD, his flight from the country on a murder beef, the security work he did for the Mob in Vegas and Reno, his history of addiction and vigilantism and involvement with biker girls and junkie strippers and street skells of every stripe all seemed to disappear from his memory, as though the justice of his cause were absolution enough and his misdeeds were simply burnt offerings that should not be held against him.

But he was not alone in his naïveté. I was out of my jurisdiction, my judgment suspect, my behavior perhaps driven more by obsession than by dedication. I was a neocolonial who had walked in the footprints of German-speaking French legionnaires and whose mark was as transient as tracks blowing in a Mesopotamian desert. My life, as Clete's, was a folly in the eyes of others. And here we were, the court jesters of Acadiana, with neither evidence nor personal cachet, about to take on forces that our peers found not only normal but even laudable.

I went into the men's room and used my cell phone to call a detective-grade cop in the Lafayette Police Department by the name of Bertrand Viator. "I'm at the Derrick and Preservation Club," I said.

"There's a guy here who might be a suspect in a homicide in Jeff Davis Parish."

"I'm not up on this," Bertrand said. "What homicide are we talking about?"

"It's kind of complicated. I saw the homicide. Nobody else did."

The line was silent. Then my friend evidently chose not to attempt working through what I had just told him. "What do you need, Streak?"

"Can you get me some backup? I don't have a warrant, and I'm out of my jurisdiction."

"What's the name of the suspect?"

"I don't know."

"But you want to bring him in?"

"I'm not sure. The guy is sitting at a table with Timothy Abelard. I'm going to have a talk with Abelard and a couple of his friends. I'd like to have a degree of legal authority behind me when I do it."

"You're by yourself?"

"Clete Purcel is with me."

There was another pause. "Sorry, I can't help on this, Dave."

"Want to tell me why?" I asked.

"I don't fault Purcel for being his own man. I just don't want to take his fall. You might give that some thought."

When I got back to the banquet room, the general was finishing his speech. The audience rose and applauded, then applauded some more. Through the crowd I saw Timothy Abelard looking at me, his face lit with goodwill, two fingers raised in a wave.

"Where've you been?" I heard Clete say.

"Trying to get us some backup."

"No dice?"

"They've got their own problems," I said.

I felt his eyes examining my face. "They gave you some flak about something?"

"We don't need pencil pushers."

Clete turned his attention back to Timothy Abelard and the man with the bandaged hand. "What do you want to do?"

"Wait till it thins out," I replied.

"Then what?"

I touched a manila envelope that I had rolled into a cone and stuck in my coat pocket. "We give them a look at some unpleasant realities they won't find in a family newspaper," I said.

But the Abelards and their retinue did not wait for the party to end. Without fanfare, Jewel pushed Timothy Abelard in his wheelchair down a corridor toward an exit, and the other people from the table followed, the man with the injured hand glancing back once over his shoulder.

"Let's go," I said.

Clete swallowed the bourbon-stained ice melt in the bottom of his glass, his cheeks blooming. We walked out into the parking lot, no more than thirty feet behind the Abelard party, the oak trees swelling with wind against the glow of the streetlamps. "Excuse me," I called out.

But no one among the Abelard party chose to hear me.

"I'd like to have a word with you, Mr. Timothy," I said. "It's a matter that concerns your grandson and possibly one of your friends here."

He raised his hand, signaling everyone around him to stop. I walked to a spot between the wheelchair and an enormous SUV that he and the others had been preparing to enter. His bronze-tinted hair was blowing on his pate, dry and loose, like a baby's. When he turned his face up at me, I thought of a tiny bird.

"You're a ubiquitous presence, Mr. Robicheaux," he said. "You pop up like a jack-in-the-box. I didn't realize you were an admirer of my friend the general."

"I'm not."

"So our meeting here is more than coincidental? Well, I shouldn't be surprised. As I recall, your father was a persistent man. He could lay them flat out, couldn't he? What is it about my grandson or my friends that has you so concerned?"

I looked at the man whose hand was wrapped in a wad of gauze and tape as big as a boxing glove. His face was as taut as latex, his eyes liquid with resentment, a scar like a piece of white string cupped on the rim of one nostril. The man with the oiled black hair had turned at an angle toward me, his coat open and pushed back loosely, his nose thinner than it should have been, as though it had been destroyed by disease of some kind and reconstructed by an inept plastic surgeon.

"Your man with his arm in the sling, is he missing some fingers?" I asked Abelard.

"Not to my knowledge. He slammed a door on his hand."

"No, I think I shot him. I think I blew his fingers all over a tree. I suspect he's still in considerable pain," I said. Then I laughed. "I also killed one of his friends."

"You must tell us about this sometime. But right now we need to be going. Good night to you," Abelard said.

"No, I'd like for you to glance at a few photos," I said, pulling the manila folder from my coat pocket and opening it in front of him so it caught the light. "That first shot was taken at an exhumation by the Iberia–St. Martin Parish line. Her name was Fern Michot. She was from British Columbia and eighteen years old at the time of her death. Here, this other shot shows her in her Girl Scout uniform when she was sixteen. It gives you a better idea what she looked like. There was a lot of water and decaying garbage in the grave where her killer dumped her.

"This other girl is Bernadette Latiolais. The knife cut across her throat almost decapitated her, which caused her to bleed out and the muscles in her face to collapse, so it's probably pretty hard to recognize her. Does she look familiar to you? Kermit says he knew her, so I'll bet he remembers how beautiful and happy she was before a degenerate and sadist kidnapped and murdered her."

"What Mr. Robicheaux is trying to say is the girl received a scholarship we created at UL, Pa'pere," Kermit said. "I might have met her at an honors ceremony, but I didn't know her. Mr. Robicheaux is still resentful because of my breakup with Alafair."

"Is that true, Mr. Robicheaux? You resent my grandson?" Abelard said.

"No, I don't spend a lot of time thinking about Kermit," I said. "Here, look at these close-up photos of the ligature marks on Fern Michot's wrists and ankles. She may have died from asphyxiation, or she may have been frightened to death. In your opinion, what kind of man or men would do this to a young girl, Mr. Timothy? You have any speculations?"

"Yes, I do. I think you should seek counseling," he replied.

"Did you know these girls, Mr. Abelard? Have you ever seen them?"

"No, I haven't. And I hope that settles the matter for you."

"You think you can act like this to an elderly gentleman? Who are you?" the man with the mustache said to me.

"Stay out of it, buddy," Clete said.

"Where is your identification? Where is your authority to do this?"

"Here's mine," Clete said, opening his badge holder. "Dave Robicheaux is a detective with the Iberia Parish Sheriff's Department. If you want to find yourself in handcuffs and sitting on the curb over there, open your mouth one more time."

"It's all right, Emiliano," Abelard said.

"No, it is not all right," Emiliano said. "Who are these crazy people? This is the United States."

I don't know if it was the booze, or Clete's hypertension, or the angst over the lifetime of damage he had done to his career and himself, but it was obvious that once again we were about to give up the high ground and load the cannon for our enemies. "You just don't listen, do you, greaseball?" Clete said.

"I have a son at West Point. I have another son who graduated from the School of the Americas at Fort Benning. You will not address me that way."

Then I heard the voice of someone I had completely forgotten about. It was soft, almost a whisper, humble and deferential, the voice of someone who had been taught for a lifetime that her interests were secondary to those of other people. "Mr. Timothy?"

"What it is, Jewel?" Abelard answered, looking up at the woman who was both his nurse and his daughter.

"Mr. Timothy?"

"Yes?"

"Mr. Timothy?"

"Will you please say it?"

"Please, suh," she said, her eyes glistening.

"You're not making any sense, woman," Abelard said. "To damnation with all of you. Get us out of here. I'm sick of this."

There was nothing for it. We had taken on the roles of anachronisms making shrill noises on a stage set in front of an empty theater. We all stood motionless in the parking lot, the trees swelling and bending, our shadows trembling on the asphalt because the streetlamps were vibrating in the wind, none of us speaking, the photos of the dead girls clenched in my hand. But before leaving, I wanted to write my signature on someone's forehead, if for no other reason than pride.

"What's your name?" I said to the man with the bandaged hand.

"Gus," he replied.

"Gus what?"

"Fowler."

"You don't hide your feelings very well, Mr. Fowler. You were one of the dudes down at the river. You're also a nickel-and-dime fuckup who probably couldn't burn shit barrels without a diagram. Here's your flash for the day: Your mutilated hand was a first installment. I'll be talking to you down the track." I gave him the thumbs-up sign and winked at him.

Then Clete and I drove away in his Caddy, down old Pinhook Road under a canopy of live oaks that had been planted by slaves, the moon racing through the branches. Clete was steering recklessly with one hand, his big chest rising and falling, his face white around the eyes. "We gave it up too soon," he said. "You had the old man in a corner. Why'd you let up?"

I remained silent, listening to the tires whirring on the asphalt.

"Don't do that," he said.

"Do what?"

"What you're doing. Don't stonewall me, Dave."

"The tent was burning down."

"Because I called the guy a greaseball?"

"The cops in Jeff Davis found skin tissue and bloody rags on the road by the shoot-out. We're going to get a DNA sample from this guy Fowler. If we'd gotten into it with either him or the Hispanic guy, we'd have been in custody ourselves."

"Fowler will be on a plane by midnight."

Maybe Clete was right, but I was too tired to care. All I wanted to do was go home and fall asleep and not think anymore about the Abelards and the faces of the girls whose photos were rolled inside the manila folder in my coat pocket. I understood Clete's disappointment and anger, but I wasn't up to dealing with it. The system shaves the dice on the side of those with money and power, and anyone who believes otherwise deserves anything that happens to him. We weren't going to bring the Abelards down with physical force or intimidation. I was beginning to believe that the photos of the dead girls and all my case notes and faxes and autopsy forms and Internet printouts would eventually find their way into a cold-case file and end up behind a locked door in a storage room, one that nobody entered without a sense of guilt and failure.

I had no idea I would receive a phone call from someone whose importance in the investigation I had treated in a cavalier fashion, maybe because of a racial or cultural bias of my own. In the era in which I was raised, people of color never gave up the secrets of their white employers. Their silence had nothing to do with loyalty, either. It was based on fear.

Early Sunday morning I heard the phone ring and Alafair pick up in the kitchen. "You're where? I'm sorry, I can't hear you very well," she said. "My father is right here. I'm sure he'll be able to help. No, it's not too early. It's good to hear from you. Hang on."

She handed the receiver to me and silently formed the words "Miss Jewel" with her mouth.

CHAPTER 21

THE TREMOLO IN Jewel's voice was of the sub-
dued kind that I always associated with people
whose sleeplessness and worry and uncertainty had
left them on a desolate beach. "I don't want to be
saying these t'ings, Mr. Dave, but when you showed
us those pictures, I got sick inside, and I was hoping
everyt'ing would get set straight then and there, but
it didn't, and that's why I'm calling you."

"Set straight where?" I said.

"There, outside the banquet room in the Oil
Center. Wit' the wind blowing and the shadows
trembling on the concrete and all of us just standing
there when that lie got tole."

"Which lie?"

"I was looking down at those girls' faces in the
photographs when Mr. Timothy said what he said,
and I didn't believe that it was him talking, 'cause
Mr. Timothy has got lots of faults, but lying isn't
one of them. Now his sin has become mine, 'cause
I didn't speak up. I waited for him to do it, but he
didn't."

"I see."

"No, suh, I don't believe you do. I'm a nurse.
I've worked on people who died in an emergency
room with bullet holes in them you could stick
your thumb in, the gunpowder burns still on their
clothes, except the police report says they were shot
while armed and fleeing. I've seen babies brought in
by parents who said the stroller got knocked over

accidentally or the baby pulled down a hot-water pan on itself. Those t'ings keep happening 'cause other people go along wit' the lie. When I looked into the faces of those dead girls, it was like there were words sewn up inside their mouths like dry moths trying to get out, except nobody wanted to listen."

She was on a cell phone, and I could hear the transmission starting to break up. I had the feeling that if she didn't finish her statement to me, she never would. "Miss Jewel, tell me what Mr. Abelard should have said in the parking lot."

"The one named Bernadette was at the house. She came there in the boat with Mr. Robert and Mr. Kermit. They'd been taking a ride out on the bay, and they tied up the boat at the dock and played croquet on the lawn. Mr. Timothy shook her hand. I saw him."

"How long ago was this?"

"Maybe t'ree months back. I'm not sure."

"Maybe he forgot," I said.

"Mr. Timothy never forgets anyt'ing. Not a face, not an injury, not a weakness in someone, not a show of strength. He's the same wit' loyalty. He always say he gives every friend and every enemy whatever they've earned. He's never been afraid. Those dagos from New Orleans, the Giacanos, used to come here and do business. They were scared of Mr. Timothy 'cause he always tole the troot' and always kept his word. If the troot' hurt him, he didn't care. The dagos didn't know how to deal wit' him. He tole you I was his daughter, didn't he?"

"Yes, he did."

"How many white men would do that?"

"But we haven't gotten to the real issue. Why did your father lie, Miss Jewel?"

"I don't know, suh. But I got to own up about somet'ing. The girl named Bernadette called the house. She wanted to talk to Mr. Robert."

"Robert Weingart?"

"Yes, suh. I tole her he wasn't here. I axed could I take a message. She said, 'Tell Robert I saw him wit' his pimp friend and their whores at the Big Stick club in Lafayette. Tell him I saw what he was doing wit' one of them on the dance floor. Tell him I changed my mind about the land deal.'"

As she spoke, I was putting down on a notepad everything she told me. "What land deal, Miss Jewel?"

"I don't know. She said somet'ing about conservation."

"What, exactly?"

"I don't know about those t'ings."

"Just tell me what she said as closely as you can remember."

"She said to tell Mr. Robert she gave his land to the conservatory or somet'ing."

"Where are you now?"

"At my house."

"Where is that?"

"In the quarters."

"Okay, Miss Jewel. Don't discuss this conversation with anyone. Everything you have told me is in confidence. You haven't done anything wrong. You did everything you were supposed to do. At this point, your responsibility is over. You hearing me on this?"

"I should have called you a long time ago. I t'ink it was me that let that poor girl get killed."

"You shouldn't say that about yourself. You're a good person. It took courage for you to make this call."

"No, you're not understanding me. After I gave Mr. Robert the message the girl left, I heard him talking on his cell phone to somebody. He was standing on the lawn, looking out at the trees in the water. I don't know who he was talking to, but he said somet'ing I don't want to t'ink about, somet'ing that makes me wake up in the middle of the night. I tell myself maybe I didn't hear right, that it was my imagination, but I keep seeing him standing against the sunlight flashing off the water, his face shaped just like a snake's head, and I hear him saying, 'I believe we have a candidate for the box.'"

The box?

ON MONDAY MORNING I told Helen everything that had occurred at the fund-raiser in Lafayette. I also told her, almost word for word, everything Jewel had reported to me. When I finished, she propped her elbows on her desk blotter and touched her fingers to both sides of her forehead. "I'm having some trouble tracking all this. You took Clete Purcel with you on an unauthorized trip to Lafayette and got into it with Timothy and Kermit Abelard and their entourage?"

"No, I asked Mr. Abelard some questions, and he lied to me. That's obstruction."

Her eyelids fluttered as though the fluorescent lights in the room were short-circuiting. "All right, I'm not going to get into procedural problems here. The man with the bandage on his hand?"

"Gus Fowler."

"This guy Fowler, you think he was one of the guys you shot on the river?"

"I can't swear to it."

"Did you run him?"

"He has no record of any kind."

"Go to Abelard's place and pick him up."

"Pick him up for what?"

"I don't care. Make up something. When has legality been a problem for you? I'll talk to the sheriff in St. Mary."

"What about Robert Weingart?"

"What about him?"

"Jewel said he told someone Bernadette Latiolais was a candidate for the box."

She looked around the room, still blinking. "*That's* disturbing. I can't make sense of this. There's a land swindle or scam of some kind involved, but there's something perverse and sadistic going on as well. It doesn't fit together." She lifted her gaze, staring straight into my eyes. "Unless?"

"What?"

"I'm not objective. I've already proved that," she said.

"Not objective about what, Helen?"

"Carolyn Blanchet."

"Go on."

"She's a dominatrix. I've been told stories about her sessions in the French Quarter."

In the silence, I could see a flush spreading across her throat.

"You think Carolyn is capable of murder?"

"You tell me. She was a bitch when she came out of the womb. I hate this stuff."

"What stuff?"

"All of it. Everything we do for a living. I'm tired of living in a sewer. I'm tired of seeing innocent people get hurt. Go see if you can find Gus Fowler. I'm going to talk to the state attorney's office and try to get to the bottom of the land deal."

She got up from her desk and looked out the

window at the bayou, her back stiff with anger or revulsion, I couldn't tell which.

"We're still the good guys," I said.

"You know how many unsolved female homicides there are in Louisiana?"

"No."

"That's the point. Nobody does. Not here, not anywhere. It's open season on women and girls in this country. You bring that asshole in. If he falls down and leaves blood on the vehicle, all the better. His DNA becomes a voluntary submission."

"Can you repeat that last part?"

"Call me when you're at the Abelard place," she said. "By the way, the ligature Clete found in the Abelards' Dumpster was clean. Bring me something I can use, Dave. I want to put somebody's head on a pike."

BUT RHETORIC IS cheap stuff when you play by the rules and the other side does business with baseball bats. No one came to the Abelards' door when I knocked. An elderly man whose race was hard to determine was pulling weeds in the flower bed. He said he had seen no one that morning. He also said he had never heard of anyone named Gus Fowler, nor did he remember seeing anyone who fit Fowler's description. I asked where I might find Miss Jewel.

His eyes were blue-green and scaled with cataracts. They glowed in the indistinct way that light glows inside frosted glass. His skin was a yellowish-brown, leached pink and milk-white in places by a dermatologic disease that often afflicts people of color in the South. The tattered straw hat he wore made me think of pictures of convicts taken at the prison colony in French Guiana. "Jewel Laveau?" he said.

I realized I had never known Jewel's last name. It was not an ordinary one, either. Anyone who ever read a history of old New Orleans or visited the St. Louis Cemetery on Basin Street would probably recognize it.

"If she ain't wit' the family, she's most probably at her house in the quarters," the gardener said.

"You know where I could find Robert Weingart?"

He smiled in a kindly fashion. "No, suh."

"You haven't seen him?"

"No, suh, what I mean is, I ain't sure who that is. Even if I knew, I ain't seen nobody."

I understood that no amount of either coercion or bribery would ever cause this man to give up a teaspoon of information about the Abelards or the people who came and went through the front door. "Can you forget I was here?" I said.

"Suh?"

"Don't worry about it," I said.

I drove east on a winding road between the bay and pastureland that had become a flood zone chained with ponds that were home to clouds of gnats and dragonflies and where, for no apparent reason, cranes or egrets or blue herons did not feed or nest. A gray skein of dead vegetation left by storm surges coated the branches of the persimmon and gum trees and slash pines, and on either side of the road, the rain ditches were strewn with trash, much of it in vinyl bags that had split when they were flung from automobiles. Up ahead, among a few slender palm trees stenciled against the sky like those on a Caribbean isle, I saw the tin roofs of the community where Miss Jewel lived.

The term "quarters," in the plural, goes back
to the plantation era, which did not end with the
Civil War but perpetuated itself well into the mid-
twentieth century. Harry Truman may or may not
have been disliked in the South for integrating the
United States Army, but there is no doubt about the
enmity he incurred when he made ten-thousand-
dollar loans available to southern sharecroppers and
farmworkers at 1 percent interest. That one program broke the back of the corporate farm system
and created the Dixiecrat Party and the career of
Senator Strom Thurmond. But a culture does not
transform itself in a few generations. Except for the
automobiles and pickup trucks parked in the dirt
yards, the quarters owned by the Abelard family had
changed little since they were carpentered together
in the 1880s.

They were painted yellow or blue and resembled wood boxcars with tin roofs and tiny galleries
built onto them. They were often called shotgun
houses because theoretically a person could fire
a single-barrel twenty-gauge through the front
door and send a load of birdshot out the back
without bruising a wall. But Jewel's house was
different from the rest, located at the end of a dirt
street still slick from an early-morning shower, its
walls painted a deep purple, the window frames
and gallery posts painted green, the gallery hung
with Mardi Gras beads. On the tin mailbox out
by the rain ditch was the name Laveau in large
black letters. She was sitting on the gallery steps,
wearing heavy Levi's and an unironed men's shirt
she hadn't bothered to tuck in and a bandanna
wrapped tightly around her hair. She was reading a shopper's guide of some kind, the pages
folded back, clutching it with one hand, turning

it to catch the light as though the words contained great significance. I walked up the path and stopped three feet from her, but she never raised her eyes from the shopper's guide.

"Are you related to Marie Laveau, Miss Jewel?" I asked.

"She was my great-great-grandmother."

"You don't practice voodoo, do you?"

"She didn't, either. People used that against her 'cause she was the most powerful woman in New Orleans."

"I need to find the man with the bandaged hand, the one who calls himself Gus Fowler."

"I t'ink he left."

"Do you know where he went?"

She seemed to study the question. "No, he didn't say. He just drove away."

"We're going to find him. We'd like to feel you're on our side."

"I don't have anyt'ing to say about him or any of the t'ings you got on your mind."

"You knew I was coming, didn't you?"

"Your kind don't give up easy."

"No, you were waiting for me. Do you see into the future, Miss Jewel?"

She rolled her shopper's guide into a cone and stuck it under her thigh and gazed at the shimmer on the dirt lane. "I'm not part of it anymore."

"What's 'it'?"

"Anyt'ing outside of my job."

"You told Mr. Abelard of our conversation?"

Her face was as dark and smooth as melted chocolate, her eyes devoid of emotion. The sorrow and contrition she said she had felt about the deaths of Bernadette Latiolais and Fern Michot seemed to have burned away with the morning mist.

"What did your father say when you told him you called me?" I said.

She waited a long time before she spoke. "He axed me to sit down and have dinner wit' him. He stood up from his wheelchair on a cane and held my chair for me. That's the first time I ever sat at the table wit' Mr. Timothy. He tole me it didn't matter what I did, I was still his daughter."

"This may be a surprise, but I'm not interested in Mr. Abelard's spiritual generosity."

"Don't talk about him like that, suh."

"I think he's an evil man and should be treated as such. I think you're making a mistake in trusting him."

"I don't care what you say."

"What's 'the box,' Jewel?"

"I don't know, me."

"You're an intelligent woman. Don't try to hide behind a dialectical disguise."

"You can go now, Mr. Robicheaux."

"Think about the faces of those girls in the photographs. You're a highly trained medical person. You know the pain and despair those girls experienced when they died. They had no one to comfort them, to hold their hand, to tell them they were loved by God and their fellow man. But you called me on your own and stood up for them. Don't undo a brave and noble deed, Miss Jewel. Don't rob yourself of your own virtue."

I saw her lips form a bitter line; she looked like a person making a choice between two evils and deciding upon the one that hurt her the most, as though her self-injury brought with it a degree of forgiveness. "I got to do my wash," she said.

"Those girls are going to haunt you," I said. "In your sleep. In a crowd. At Mass. In a movie theater.

Across the table from you at McDonald's. The dead carry a special kind of passport, and they go anywhere they want."

She stared into the humidity glistening on the road and at the tin roofs of the other houses. The wind swayed the palms overhead and rattled the Mardi Gras beads that hung from the eaves of her gallery. I walked back to the cruiser, wondering at the harshness of my language, wondering if my oath to protect and serve had not finally drained my heart of pity and left only rage and a thirst for vengeance. Then I heard her voice behind me, muted against the wind and the rustling of the beads. I opened and closed my mouth to clear my ears. Her gaze was fixed strangely on my face, her eyes lit with a bizarre luminosity, her teeth white against the darkness of her tongue, her skin sparkling with moisture.

"I didn't hear you. Say that over," I said.

"I'm sorry."

"About what?"

"About saying it. I didn't mean to say it. Don't pay me any mind."

"Say what?"

"Go back home. Pretend you weren't here. Keep yourself and your family away from us."

"Tell me what you said."

"Don't make me."

"You say it, damn you."

"Somebody is fixing to die at your house."

She took a deep breath, as though a large, thick-bodied bird had just taken flight from her chest.

I DROVE BACK down the winding two-lane to the Abelard home, on the odd chance I would catch someone there before I returned to New Iberia. As

I neared the wood bridge that gave access to the Abelards' island, I saw Robert Weingart in a pair of Speedos on the lawn between the boathouse and a blooming mimosa, performing a martial arts exercise of some kind. Like a flamingo pecking at its feathers, he torqued his body in one direction and then the other, his hands moving delicately in the air, his eyes closed, the breeze caressing his face and the glaze of tan and sweat on his skin.

If I ever saw a man for whom his own body was a holy grail, it was Weingart. His armpits were shaved and powdered like a woman's. His black Speedos clung wetly to the buttermilk texture of his buttocks, his phallus outlined like a rhinoceros's horn. His eyelids were lowered as though he was enjoying the sun through the filter of his own skin. He gave no notice of my tires rumbling across the bridge, nor did he look behind him when I parked and got out of the cruiser and stood silently watching him across the top of the roof. I had to admire his concentration and his indifference. Weingart had mastered the ethos of the cynic and, in my opinion, had successfully scrubbed every trace of decency and humanity from his soul. If he had any feelings at all, I suspected they were connected entirely with the satisfaction of his desires, and they had nothing to do with the rest of us.

Was this aging, self-absorbed product of plastic surgery the sole perpetrator behind the death of the two girls? He was the white man's answer to Herman Stanga, the man we love to hate. He was cruel, pernicious, and predatory. He exploited the faith and trust of uneducated people and forever blighted their lives. But he was also pathetic. He'd had his head shoved in a toilet bowl by Clete

Purcel. He'd been humiliated and slapped across the side of the head by one of our deputies at the bank. Later that same day, Emma Poche had brought him to his knees with a baton and then had tormented him on the ground. Weingart reminded me of the high school hood who moves to a small town from a big city and scares the hell out of everybody until someone challenges him and discovers he's a joke.

But what did I know about him specifically, other than his criminal history and his penchant for getting into it with people who didn't do things by the rules?

He was pulling his money out of a local bank and transferring it to a bank in British Columbia. He was planning to either blow Dodge or set up another nefarious scheme or both. Timothy Abelard had shown Alafair a photo of himself and a man who resembled Robert Weingart sitting in a café on Lake Louise in Alberta, although Abelard had denied to Alafair that his companion was Weingart. What were they doing there? Was it land investment? Were the Abelards taking their long and sorry tradition of environmental abuse and human exploitation to one of the most beautiful places in the Western Hemisphere, if not the world?

What was the box? The term conjured up images I didn't want to think about.

I walked onto the lawn and stood no more than fifteen feet behind Weingart. He rotated slowly in a circle, opening his eyes, a smirk breaking at the corner of his mouth. "Yes?" he said.

"I'm looking for a guy by the name of Gus Fowler."

"Let me think. No, can't place him."

"Guy with a big wad of bandages wrapped around his hand. He's probably doped up on painkillers. Has a pal from Taco-Tico Land, a guy who takes offense just because somebody called him a greaseball."

"Sorry."

"I blew Mr. Fowler's fingers off. I thought you might have heard about it. I guess you're not in the loop."

"Apparently not."

"Heading up to Canada? Maybe Trout Lake, someplace like that?"

"No."

"You've been to Trout Lake, though, haven't you?"

"Can't say as I have."

"Is that where you met Fern Michot?"

"The name doesn't make bells clang."

"She was a Canadian girl we dug out of a landfill. She was buried with some broken teacups that Bernadette Latiolais had purchased at a dollar store just before she was abducted. Of course, you remember Bernadette?"

"Many people come to my book signings. Was she one of those?" He never paused in his exercise, his upper body rotating at the hips, his arms gliding through the air as though he were underwater.

"She caught you at the Big Stick club in Lafayette with some of your skanks. Or were they Herman Stanga's skanks?"

His eyes were roving over my face; a tiny laugh rose like a bubble in his throat. I waited for him to speak, but he didn't.

"You don't hang with skanks?" I said.

"Excuse me. I don't mean to smile. But I've never seen a variation in the script."

"Which script would that be, Mr. Weingart?"

"The outraged father figure always knocking other people's sexual behavior. It's classic. Daddy is always worrying about what other people are doing with their genitalia. Except Daddy's little girl can't keep her panties on."

"Want to spell that out?"

"I'm not one to judge. Talk to Kermit about it. He said Alafair was jumping his stick on their first date. He also said she gives good head."

He turned at an angle to me, his hands and fingers moving with the fluidity of snakes, the sun-bleached tips of his hair tousling in the wind, a smell like dried salt wafting off his skin.

I winked at him and said nothing. His eyes dropped to my waist. "What are you doing?" he asked.

"This?"

"Yeah." He had stopped his martial arts routine.

"That's the strap that holds my holster on my belt. I have to unsnap it to take off my holster."

"Yeah, I know that. What are you doing with it?"

"You have to ask?"

"This isn't Tombstone, Arizona, and you're not Wyatt Earp."

"You're right. I don't trust myself," I said. "That's why I didn't like to carry a weapon when I was alone with Herman Stanga. Want to hold it? I brought it back from Saigon. I got it for twenty-five dollars from a prostitute in Bring Cash Alley. The prostitutes there were all VC. They dosed us with clap and sold us our own guns. Go ahead, get the feel of it. It's a little heavy, but I bet you can handle it."

His gaze shifted from me to the house, then to the empty road on the far side of the wood bridge. "You're an old man. That's what all this is about."

"I'm old, but I can lift five hundred pounds

across my shoulders. Did you know there's a twitch in your face?" I stepped closer to him, smiling, touching the holstered grips of the .45 against his breastbone. "Go on. It won't bite. You've been jailing all your life, fading the action inside and outside, taking on all comers. You know how to handle a gun."

"Your problem is with Kermit, not me."

"No, I want you to tell me some more about my daughter. You were just getting started."

"No."

"I really want you to. It will be a big favor to me. Hold on a second." I walked to the cruiser and threw the .45 on the seat. "There. Now say whatever you wish. We're all pals here, aren't we?"

He shook his head, stepping back from me, his hands useless at his sides, his head turning to look at a motorboat out on the bay, a tiny wad of fear sliding down his windpipe.

"I watched your bud Vidor Perkins die," I said. "I think he was hit by a toppling round. His brains exploded out of a big exit wound right above his eye. I watched a couple of guys in rain hoods pick him up like a sack of fertilizer and throw him in a van. Think that might happen to you, Mr. Weingart? I suspect you never met any cleaners inside. Know why that is? Cleaners don't do time. They're protected by the government or corporate people who use third-world countries to wipe their ass. Guys who are disposable do their time. You ready to go back inside for this bunch? How long has it been since you had your knee pads on?"

When you step on a snake, don't expect him to run. Even in death, he'll try to wrap his body around your ankle and sink his fangs in your foot. I had watched Weingart's face shrink in the wind and become hard and tight, like the skin on an apple. But now he glanced upward at the clumps of pale red mimosa blooming against a blue sky, then fixed his gaze on me, his smirk once again crawling across his cheek, his fear in check.

"There's something else Kermit mentioned," he said. "Alafair is your adopted daughter, not your real daughter. Which is probably how you justified your visits into her bedroom when she was thirteen and just getting her menses. According to Kermit, Daddy helped her into her womanhood and kept helping her all the way through high school. Daddy is quite a guy."

I took a stick of gum out of my shirt pocket and peeled the foil off and fed it into my mouth. "Everybody gets to the barn," I said.

"Oh, really? What's the profound implication there, Detective Robicheaux?"

"When I check out, I'm going to make sure you're on board," I said. "Kind of like a Viking funeral, know what I mean? A dead dog at the foot of the corpse. Welcome to the bow-wow club, podjo."

THAT NIGHT I couldn't sleep. The air was like wet cotton, the moon down, the clouds flaring with pools of yellow lightning that gave no sound. Also, I was haunted by the words of Jewel Laveau. Was she prescient or just superstitious and grandiose, melodramatically laying claim to the powers of her ancestor, an iconic voodoo priestess who today is entombed in an oven off Basin Street? Don't let anyone tell you that age purchases you freedom from fear of death. As Clete Purcel once said in describing his experience in a battalion aid station in the Central Highlands, it's a sonofabitch. Men cry out for their mothers; they grip your hands with an intensity that can break bones; their breath covers your face like damp cobwebs and tries to draw you inside them. As George Orwell suggested long ago, if you can choose the manner of your death, let it be in hot blood and not in bed.

I got up at two in the morning and sat in the kitchen in the dark and listened to the wind in the trees and the clink of Tripod's chain attached to a wire I had strung between two live oaks. The windows were open, and I could smell the heavy odor of the bayou and bream spawning under the clusters of lily pads along the bank. I heard an alligator flop in the water and the drawbridge opening upstream, the great cogged wheels clanking together, a boat with a deep draft laboring against the incoming tide.

I saw the night-light go on in our bedroom, then Molly's silhouette emerge from the hallway. She stood behind me and placed one hand on my shoulder, her hip touching my back. She was wearing a pink bathrobe and fluffy slippers, and I could feel a level of heat and solidity in her presence that seemed to exist separately from her body. "Something bothering you, troop?" she said.

"I get wired up sometimes. You know how it is," I replied. I put my arm across the broadness of her rump.

"You were talking in your sleep," she said.

"That kind of talk doesn't mean anything."

"You said, 'I'm not ready.' Then you asked where Alafair was. You called her Alf."

"I shouldn't call her that. It makes her mad."

"Dave, do you have a medical problem you're not telling me about?"

"No, I'm fine. Did Alafair go somewhere to-night?"

"She's asleep. She went to sleep before you did. You don't remember?"

"I had a dream, that's all."

"About what?"

"You and she were on a dock. Tripod was there. I was watching you from across the water. You were saying something to me, but I couldn't hear you."

"Come back to bed."

"I think I'll sit here for a while. I'll be along directly."

"I'll sit with you."

"Molly—"

"Tell me."

"Sometimes we have to adjust and go on."

"What are you saying?"

Nothing is forever.

"The bridge is making all kinds of noise. It must be broken. Speak up," she said.

"I didn't say anything."

She felt my forehead, then my cheek. "Tell me what's bothering you."

"I'm not drunk anymore. That's all that counts. I'm going to check on Alf."

"You can't leave me with this kind of uncertainty. You tell me what it is."

You know, I thought. You know, you know, you know.

Through the oaks I could see the clouds lighting and flashing and disappearing into blackness again. In the illumination through the windows, Molly's face had the hollow-eyed starkness of someone staring down a long corridor in which all the side exits were chain-locked. I looked in on Alafair, then closed the door so she couldn't hear our voices.

"Don't pay attention to me," I said to Molly. "Guys like us always do okay. We're believers. We've never been afraid."

Molly stood on the tops of my feet with her slippers and put her arms around my middle and pressed her head against my chest, as though the beating of my heart were a stay against all the nameless forces churning around us.

TUESDAY MORNING ALAFAIR called me at the office. "I think I got a breakthrough on the seven arpents of land Bernadette Latiolais owned in Jeff Davis Parish," she said.

"What are you doing, Alf?"

"Don't call me that name."

"What are you doing?" I repeated.

"Jewel Laveau told you Bernadette Latiolais was giving her land to a conservation group of some kind. I talked with a lawyer in New Orleans who does work for the Nature Conservancy. He said Bernadette Latiolais was going to have a covenant built into her deed so that the land could never be used for industrial purposes and would remain a wildlife habitat."

"You found this on your own?"

"Yeah, after I made a few calls. Why?"

"We need to put you on the payroll. But I don't want you at risk, Alafair. The Abelards and their minions have no bottom."

"You've got it all wrong, Dave. Here's the rest of it. Lawyers for the estate of Layton Blanchet are trying to get Bernadette's donation to the Nature Conservancy nullified. At the time of her death, she was only seventeen and not of legal age. Layton Blanchet was backing a group that was going to build a giant processing plant that would convert sugarcane into ethanol. If Timothy Abelard was a player, he was a minor one."

"Don't bet on it."

"Dave, I think Carolyn Blanchet is at the center of all this."

"It doesn't matter what you think. You have to stay out of it. For once in your life, will you listen to me?" I shut my eyes at the thought of what I had just said. I wanted to hit myself with the phone receiver.

"I thought you'd want the information," she said.

"I do."

"You have a peculiar way of showing it."

"Where are you?"

"In my car. What difference does it make?"

"There's little that I understand about this investigation. Timothy Abelard is surrounded by people who seem more connected with his past than his present. I'm talking about Caribbean dictators and paramilitary thugs. Mr. Abelard is a neocolonial and happens to live here rather than on the edge of an empire. But I'm convinced he's ruthless and perhaps perverse. Why else would he abide a man like Robert Weingart?"

"It's because of Kermit, Dave. Kermit is weak and dependent and probably can't deal with the fact that he's gay. That doesn't mean he's a bad person."

"Don't buy into that."

"You're unteachable, but I love you anyway."

"Don't hang up."

Too late.

I called her back, but she didn't answer. I waited fifteen minutes and called home and got the message machine. Molly was at her office at a rural development foundation on the bayou, one that helped poor people build homes and start up small businesses.

I dialed her number, then hung up before anyone could answer. Molly had enough worries without my adding to them. I went into Helen's office and told her what Alafair had discovered.

"An ethanol plant? That's what all this is about?" Helen said.

"Part of it, at least."

"The local sugar growers are already trying to build one. This is a separate deal, though?"

"It's just one more instance of the locals getting screwed by somebody who pretends to be their ally," I said.

She clicked her nails on her blotter. "So maybe Carolyn Blanchet saw her husband's fortunes going down the toilet and decided to blow his head off and take over his businesses. Think that's possible?"

"Yeah, this might explain the motivation for the murder of Bernadette Latiolais, but what about Fern Michot?"

"You don't know Carolyn Blanchet."

"She's not only a dominatrix but homicidal as well?"

"Want me to go into some details I've heard?"

"Not really."

"There's a world out there you don't know about, Dave. I think it's one you don't want to hear about."

"I don't want my daughter to get hurt."

"How is Alafair going to get hurt?"

"Because none of the lines in this investigation are simple, and both you and she think otherwise."

"You really know how to win a girl's heart. Okay, you asked for this." Helen opened a desk drawer and threw a folder in front of me. "These were taken by a woman I used to be friends with in the Garden District. The woman in the mask with the whip is Carolyn. The leather fetters and chains are the real thing. How do you like the thigh-high boots?"

"I think that stuff is a joke."

"A joke?"

"It's the masquerade of self-deluded idiots who never grew out of masturbation. I have the feeling everyone in those photographs is a closet Puritan."

"You're too much, bwana."

"No, I'm just a guy worried about his daughter. I'll buy Carolyn Blanchet as a greedy, manipulative shrew capable of staging her husband's suicide. But she's not Eva Perón in Marquis de Sade drag."

"How about Carolyn Blanchet and Emma Poche working together? Ever think of that? Or maybe Carolyn has a yen for young girls and Emma got jealous. I don't have all the answers, Dave, but don't accuse me of being simplistic or naive."

"Timothy Abelard is a pterodactyl. To him, people like Carolyn Blanchet and Emma are insects."

Helen replaced the black-and-white photos in the folder and dropped them in her desk drawer. "You give the Abelards dimensions they don't have. I'm not fooled by them, but I don't obsess about them, either."

This time I made no reply.

"I was about to go down to your office when you came in," she said. "That guy Gus Fowler?"

"What about him?"

"A body washed up on the shore at East Cote Blanche Bay last night. One hand is missing three fingers. The sheriff says they look like they were recently sutured. The deceased has a white scar cupped around one nostril like a piece of twine. Sound like anyone you know?"

IT HAS BEEN my experience that most human stories are circular rather than linear. Regardless of the path we choose, we somehow end up where we commenced—in part, I suspect, because the child who lives in us goes along for the ride.

This story began with a visit to a penal work gang outside Natchez, Mississippi. Its denouement commenced late in the afternoon with a phone call from one of the players who had sweltered in the heat and humidity next to a brush fire that was so hot, a freshly lopped tree branch would burst instantly alight when it touched the flames. The caller was not a man I cared to hear from again.

Jimmy Darl Thigpin's voice was like that of a man speaking through a rusty tin can. "I'm retired now and was in the neighborhood," he said.

"I see," I replied, actually not seeing anything, not wanting to even exchange a greeting with the gunbull who had shot and killed Elmore Latiolais.

"I'm up at a fish camp at Bayou Bijou. Come out and have a drink."

"I've been off the hooch quite a while, Cap."

"Got soda pop or whatever you want."

"What's on your mind?"

"Need to give you a heads-up. I got to get some guilt off my conscience as well."

"Why don't you come into the office?"

"I don't like being around officialdom anymore. The state of Mis'sippi give me a pension wouldn't pay for the toilet paper in the state capitol building. Guess what color half the legislature is? I got a chicken smoking on my grill. It's a twenty-minute ride, Mr. Robicheaux. Do an old man a favor, will you?"

After I got off the phone, I called Clete Purcel and told him of my conversation with Thigpin. "I'd blow it off," he said.

"Why?"

"If he's got anything to say, let him do it on the phone."

"Maybe he's not sure how much he wants to tell me. Maybe he was paid to kill Elmore Latiolais."

"I say don't trust him."

"Check with you later."

"I'll let you in on a secret, Streak. These guys know you've got an invisible Roman collar around your neck. They use it against you."

"Thigpin has chewing tobacco for brains. You give him too much credit."

"You never listen."

"Yeah, I do. I just don't agree with you," I said.

I called Molly and told her I'd be home for supper a little late. Then I drove down a long two-lane road between oak trees into a chain of fresh-water bays that bordered the Atchafalaya Basin. I wasn't worried about Thigpin. He may have been an anachronism, but I had known many like him. Most of them had become as institutionalized in their mind-set and way of life as the convicts they supervised. Some, when drunk or in a moment of moral clarity, admitted they had gone to work in the prison system before they ended up hoeing soybeans and chopping cotton themselves. Some, upon retirement, looked over their shoulders every day of their lives. Years ago, I knew a guard at Angola who had put men on anthills when they fell out on the work detail. He also shot and killed inmates on the Red Hat gang, sometimes for no other reason than pure meanness. The prison administration allowed him to work at the gate until he was almost eighty because there was not a town in Mississippi or Louisiana he could retire to. The day he was finally forced to leave Angola, he paid one week's rent at a roominghouse in New Orleans, shut the windows, stuffed newspaper under the doors, and went to sleep with his head in the oven, the gas jets flowing.

I drove up on the levee, my windows down, to my left a wide bay dotted with cypress trees, to my right a string of fish camps on a green bib that sloped down to another bay, this one reddening with the sunset, the fluted trunks of the tupelo gums flaring at the waterline, moss lifting in their limbs. The road atop the levee bent into an arbor of trees where the shadows were thicker, the water along the shore skimmed with a gray film, the tracings of a cottonmouth zigzagging through the algae that had clustered among the storm trash left over from Rita.

I passed a yellow school bus with no wheels, all of its windows pocked by BB guns or .22 rounds, its sides scaled with vine. Then I saw a clapboard shack in the gloom, banana fronds bending over the tin roof, a bright red Coca-Cola machine sweating under the porte cochere, a deck built on pilings over the water, a small barbecue pit smoking greasily in the breeze.

I parked in the yard. Thigpin came out the back of the house and greeted me with a can of beer in his hand. He wore his tall-crown cowboy hat, the same one he was wearing when I interviewed Elmore Latiolais on the brush gang. Perhaps it was the diminished nature of the sunlight, but one side of Thigpin's face seemed even more shriveled from skin cancer than the last time I had seen him, to the extent that his grin looked like a surgical wound in the corrupted tissue.

When he shook hands, his grip was too strong, biting into mine like that of a man whose energies are not quite under control. "I cain't crack you a cold one?" he said.

"No, thanks."

"You in one of them twelve-step programs?" he said.

"That pretty well sums it up."

He released my hand. "Nobody is looking. I got some Johnnie Walker, too."

"You said you had a heads-up for me."

"Come on in the kitchen. I got to get me a fresh beer. I'll set out some plates for us."

"I need to get on it, Cap."

"Too bad. I was looking forward to dining with you."

His eyebrows and sideburns were freshly clipped, his jaw shaved. I thought I could smell cologne on his skin. He didn't strike me as a man who had spent much time at his fish camp. The only vehicle in the yard was a pristine Dodge Ram, the tires clean and thick-treaded, the dealer's tag still in the back window. There was no boat in the water. I glanced at the barbecue pit. The chicken on it was black except for a pink slash where a drumstick had been torn off. "You coming?" he said over his shoulder.

I followed him inside and let the screen door slam shut behind me. The linoleum floor was cracked and wedged upward in places, spiderwebs feathering in the breeze along the jambs of the open windows. I waited for him to speak. Instead, he began clattering around in a cabinet, pulling out coffee cups and a coffeepot, fiddling with the feed on the propane stove. I stepped into his line of sight. "You said you had a problem of conscience of some kind. You want to tell me what this is about, or should I leave?"

He clanked the coffeepot down on the stove and released it as though the handle were burning his fingers. "I think Elmore Latiolais was aiming to kill me. I had it on good authority. He walked to the truck and reached inside. I told him to put his hands where I could see them and to back the hell off. He didn't do it. So I punched his ticket."

"From what 'good authority' did you get your information?" I asked.

"I got to be friends with a powerful man in Jackson. I invested my money with his bank. A lot of people lost their money in that bank. But I didn't. I took this man hunting and fishing, and he treated me as a friend." He was breathing audibly, the way ignorant and defensive people do when no one has challenged their statement.

"I think you're talking about Layton Blanchet," I said. "I think you were paid to kill Elmore Latiolais because he was bringing down too much heat on a coalition of lowlifes who are responsible for the deaths of two innocent girls. Is that the problem of conscience we're talking about, Cap?"

"If you're saying I was bribed, you're a goddamn liar." He still wore his hat; his profile was as chiseled as an Indian's, his eyes as clear as glass. But even while he denied his guilt, his thoughts seemed elsewhere, as though he had already moved on in the conversation.

"What's the heads-up?" I asked.

"People like us do what we're told. You go along, you get along."

"Until you start killing people for hire."

He was motionless, one hand resting on the corner of the stove, the other on a chopping table that had a single drawer. "The government is attaching the money I got from that failed bank. I worked over forty years for what I have. Now I'm supposed to live on a piss-pot state pension 'cause of what other people done? What would you do in that situation?"

I saw two fingers on his right hand jerk involuntarily, just inches above the metal handle on the drawer. I said, "I think I wouldn't fault myself for a situation I didn't create. I wouldn't try to correct the past by serving the interests of the same people who cheated me out of my life savings."

His jaw flexed, the skin on half his face wrinkling as coarsely as sandpaper. "You reckon hell is hot?"

"Since I don't plan on going there, I haven't speculated on it."

"This ain't my way. But they didn't give me no choice, Mr. Robicheaux."

"You open that drawer, I'm going to smoke your sausage."

"No, sir, you're not. You're a trusting man, which makes you a fool. Sorry to do this to you."

With his left hand, he lifted up a double-barrel chrome-plated .32-caliber Derringer that he had probably slipped from his back pocket. It was aimed at a spot between my chin and breastbone.

"People know where I am. They know I talked with you," I said.

"Don't matter. Twelve hours from now, I'll be fishing off the Yucatán coast. Turn around. Don't make this no harder than it is."

I could feel my mouth going dry, my scalp tightening. When I tried to swallow, my breath caught like a fish bone in my throat. In my mind's eye, I saw a nocturnal landscape and the flicker of artillery on the horizon, and seconds later, I heard the rushing sound of a 105 round that was coming in short.

I forced myself to look at the Derringer, its two chrome-plated barrels set one on top of the other. The muzzles were black, the handles yellow, lost inside Thigpin's grip. My head felt like a balloon about to burst. "You're typical white trash, Thigpin. You're a gutless thrall who's spent his life abusing people who have no power. Go on and do it, you motherfucker. I'll be standing by your deathbed."

"Good-bye, Mr. Robicheaux. When you get down below with the Kennedys and all the other nigger lovers, give them my regards."

My vision went out of focus. I raised my hand to my holster, but I knew my gesture was in vain, that my life was over, that I was going to be executed by a brutal, mindless human being whose pathological cruelty was so natural to him, he did not even recognize its existence. Then, through the distortion in my vision, I saw a man standing thirty feet from the kitchen window, aiming down the barrel of an AR-15, his huge shoulders almost tearing the seams of his Hawaiian shirt. He seemed frozen in time and space, his breath slowing, the squeeze of his trigger pull as slow and deliberate as the tiny serrated wheels of a watch meshing together. The report was dulled by the wind gusting in the trees, but the muzzle flash was as bright and sharp and beautiful as an electric arc. The round popped a hole in the screen and blew through one side of Thigpin's neck and out the other, whipping a jet of blood across the stove's enamel.

I suspect the round destroyed his trachea, because I heard a gasp deep down in his throat as if he were trying to suck air through a ruptured tube. But there was no mistaking the look in his eyes. He knew he was dying and he was determined to take me with him. Blood welled over his bottom lip as he lifted the Derringer toward my chin. That was when Clete Purcel squeezed off again and caught Jimmy Dale Thigpin just above the ear and sent him crashing to the floor. The top of the coffeepot rolled past his head like a coin, devolving into a tinny clatter on the linoleum.

CHAPTER 22

I HAD MY CELL phone open and was about to dial 911 when Clete came through the back door, the AR-15 held at an upper angle, his gaze fastened on Thigpin's body. Until I had seen him through the kitchen window, just before he fired, I'd had no idea he followed me to the camp. "You calling it in?" he said.

I waited. A pool of blood was spreading outward from Thigpin's head. I stepped aside.

"Bag him as a John Doe," Clete said. "Let the guys who sent him wonder what happened to him. Weingart already seems to be coming apart. Let the Abelards or Weingart or Carolyn Blanchet or whoever is behind this think Thigpin is about to rat-fuck them."

I closed my cell phone. "You warned me about Thigpin. I should have listened."

"Think of it this way. What happens when I listen to my own advice?" He laughed without making any sound, his shirt shaking on his chest. "I need a drink." He opened a cabinet and found Thigpin's bottle of Johnnie Walker and poured four inches in a jelly glass. He saw me watching him. "I shouldn't do this in front of you," he said. "But I need a drink. I'm not like you. I don't have your control or discipline. I don't have your faith, either. So I'm going to put the tiger in the tank. I'll be a lush right through the bottom of the ninth. Bombs away."

He drank all four inches of it as though it were

Kool-Aid, gin roses flaring in his cheeks, his eyes brightening, the world coming back into focus, becoming an acceptable place again.

"You saved my life, Clete. You'll always remain the best guy I ever knew," I said.

"That second shot? The one that flushed his grits?"

"What about it?"

"It was supposed to be my first shot. The one through the neck was five inches below where I aimed. I could have gotten you killed, big mon."

"You pulled it off, didn't you? You always pull it off. You've never let me down."

But I was caught in my old vanity—namely, that I could convince Clete Purcel of his own goodness and heroism and the fact that the real angels in our midst always have tarnished wings. He sat down in a straight-back chair and looked wearily out the screen door at the sun setting on the bay. "We can't keep running on luck, Dave," he said.

"We've done pretty well so far, haven't we?"

"You don't understand. It's like General Giáp said. He defeated the French with the shovel, not the gun. We keep playing by the rules while the other guys use a flamethrower."

"What do you recommend?"

"I've got a bad feeling I can't get rid of. Killing a piece of shit like Thigpin doesn't change anything. He was just a tool. Right now people out there are planning our death. Maybe the guys in the rain hoods. We don't know. That's it, *we don't know.*"

I sat down across from him. Thigpin's cell phone was on the table. I picked it up and accessed its call lists. Then I closed it and placed it back on the table.

"What'd you find?" Clete asked.

"Nothing. It's clean."

"That's my point," he said. "We took a sack of shit off the board that nobody could care less about."

HELEN NOT ONLY agreed with Clete's suggestion about tagging Thigpin as a John Doe, DOA, she suppressed all information regarding the shooting and got Koko Hebert, our coroner, to tell an aggressive local reporter, "Yes, the body of a fisherman has been found. We're trying to determine the cause of death as we speak. We'll get back to you on that, *muy pronto*. This story definitely has Pulitzer potential."

The next morning I received a phone call from a plainclothes NOPD detective by the name of Dana Magelli. He was a good cop, as straight as they come, and always a loyal friend. He was also a family man, one who didn't rattle easily but who walked away when he heard a colleague telling a vulgar joke or using gratuitous profanity. This morning it was obvious he was not happy about the task he had been given.

"You remember No Duh Dolowitz?" he said.

Who could forget No Duh, once known as the Merry Prankster of the New Orleans Mob? He put dog shit in the sandwiches at a Teamsters convention. He tried to cut up a safe with an acetylene torch in Metairie and burned down half of a shopping center. He helped Clete Purcel fill up a mobster's customized convertible with concrete; he also helped with the deconstruction of a Magazine Avenue snitch by the name of Tommy Fig. The deconstruction involved the freeze-drying and wrapping of Tommy's parts, which were then hung from the blades of an overhead fan in Tommy's butcher shop. But No Duh went through a life change when he creeped a house on Lake Pontchartrain owned by one of Didi Gee's nephews, who put seven dents in No Duh's head with a ball-peen hammer.

"No Duh is running a pawnshop over in Algiers," Dana said. "Some of the items in it are a little warm. A guy came in there three days ago and sold No Duh a DVD player for twenty bucks. There was a disk in it. Out of curiosity, No Duh put it on the screen in his store. At first he thought he was watching a *Friday the 13th* or *Halloween* film of some kind. Then he realized what it was and called us."

"No Duh called the cops?"

"He's got his parameters. I recognized the two girls in the film, Dave. I'm sure they're the same girls in the photos y'all sent us. I'm going to download and e-mail you the DVD. I've got the feeling you're emotionally involved in this one. I'm sorry to do this."

"What's in it?" I said.

"See for yourself. I don't want to talk about it," he replied.

I went into Helen's office and told her of Dana Magelli's call. "I want Clete to see the video with us," I said.

"What for?"

"This investigation is as much his as it is ours. I'll put it another way: Outside of you and me, he's one of the few people who cares about the fate of those girls."

"Call him," she said.

It took Clete only ten minutes to drive from his office to the department. We went into Helen's office and dropped the blinds on the windows and the door. Then she hit the download button on Magelli's e-mail attachment.

People wonder why cops get on the hooch or

pills or become sex addicts or eventually eat their guns. It would be facile and self-serving to say there is one answer to that question. But even among the most degraded of police officers, unless they are sociopaths themselves, there are moments when we witness a manifestation of human evil for which no one is prepared, one that causes us to wonder if some individuals in our midst are diabolically possessed. That is what we wish to believe, because the alternative conclusion robs us forever of our faith in our fellow man.

Whoever held the video camera did not appear in the frame. The setting looked subterranean. The dirt floor was damp and shiny and green with mold. The walls were built of stones that were smooth and rounded, like bread loaves. They were not the kind of stones you would ordinarily find or see in this area. Chains were inset in the walls, the anchor pins driven deep, encrusted with rust.

There was no sound in the video, only images. The light was bad, the lens sliding back and forth over stone surfaces that seemed netted with moisture, as though they were sweating. Bernadette Latiolais and Fern Michot were clearly recognizable; their mouths were moving silently in the strobe, their eyes shuttering in the brilliance of the light.

"Jesus God," I heard Helen say.

The video was probably not longer than forty seconds. When it was over, Helen got up and opened the blinds and turned off the monitor on her computer. Clete had not moved in his chair. His big hands rested on his knees, his fingers tucked into his palms, like paws on a bear. His mouth was small and tight, his back humped like a whale's, his eyes fixed on the empty monitor.

Helen sat back down behind her desk, pushing

her thoughts out of her eyes. "Who's the guy who brought the DVD player into the pawnshop?" she said.

"No Duh swears he never saw him. He figures the guy for an addict or a low-rent house creep," I said.

"What about the paperwork?" Helen asked.

"Magelli says the name and address on the bill of sale were bogus. There were no helpful prints on the player, either."

"A professional house creep doesn't unload one item," Clete said.

"It doesn't matter. I think No Duh is telling the truth. He reported the disk. He has no reason to lie about the seller," I said.

"This is what we need to do," Helen said. "We check all area reports of burglaries and home invasions from the time of the girls' disappearance to the present. Maybe the thief is local and went to New Orleans to unload the player. Or maybe he's a friend of the person who stole it."

We were talking in a procedural fashion, spending time on issues that were perfunctory in nature, a deliberate distraction from the images that we had watched on Helen's computer screen. But the room felt as though the air had been sucked out of it. The sunlight that fell through the window was brittle and swam with motes of dust. I could hear Clete clenching and rubbing his hands together between his thighs, the calluses on his palms as rough as horn, his face bloodless and poached-looking.

When I went outside into the coolness of the morning, I sat on a stone bench by the city library, in front of the grotto that had been built as a shrine to the mother of Jesus. The wind was blowing through the bamboo and the oak trees and the Spanish moss, and rose petals from a nearby flower bed were scattered across the St. Augustine grass. Clete sat down beside me and lit a cigarette, not speaking, the cigarette tiny inside his hand. The smoke drifted in my face, but I didn't mind.

"When are you going to stop smoking those?" I asked.

"Never. I'm tucking away a pack of Luckies in the casket. With no filters."

"Don't drink today."

"Who said I am?"

"Some days aren't any good for drinking. That's all I'm saying."

"I'm going to get the guys who did this, Dave. They're going out in pieces, too."

"You'll get them. But not like you say."

"Don't bet on it."

"You're not like them. Neither am I. And neither is Helen. You're not capable of being like them."

We sat there for a long time, neither of us saying anything, Clete puffing on his Lucky Strike, flicking his ashes so they didn't hit my clothes, the mother of Jesus looking silently at the bayou.

COMPUTERS WORK WONDERS. By late that afternoon we got a hit on a home invasion in which silverware, the entire contents of a liquor cabinet, a flat-screen television, a frozen ham, a case of beer, an Armani suit, and a DVD player had been reported stolen. The home invasion had taken place in an upscale subdivision on the bayou, just outside the New Iberia city limits. The owner of the house was a local black attorney. His name was Monroe Stanga, the cousin of Herman Stanga.

We found him in his office, a two-story white stucco building down by the courthouse square, a building with faux balconies that had Spanish grillework overlooking the Southern Pacific railway tracks.

"Y'all found the stuff somebody stole from my house? That's what y'all saying?" Monroe asked, his eyes going from me to Helen. It was obvious he did not comprehend why the sheriff was personally involving herself in the investigation of a comparatively minor crime.

"You listed a DVD player as one of the items stolen from your house, correct?" I said.

"Yeah, right, plus all my silverware and my flat-screen and my Armani—"

"We think somebody might have sold your DVD player at a pawnshop in New Orleans," I said. "What was the brand?"

He told me, then waited.

"I think we've found your property," I said.

Monroe was in his thirties but had his head shaved at a barbershop every two days, as an older man might. He had gotten his law degree from Southern University and specialized in liability suits that involved chemical spills along railroad tracks, pipeline ruptures, oil-well blowouts, or any kind of industrial accident that could provide large numbers of claimants. He wore a pleated white shirt with a rolled collar and a lavender tie and a gray vest. His coat hung on the back of his chair, and when he hunched forward on his elbows, his eyes darting back and forth, his arms and shoulders poking like sticks against his shirt, he made me think of a ferret being worked into a corner with a broom.

"So how about my silverware and the other stuff that was stole?" he asked.

"Do you have a receipt for the DVD player, something that would have a serial number on it or help identify it?"

"No, I don't have anything like that."

"That's too bad. Did you file an insurance claim?"

"Yeah, of course."

"You didn't have to provide a bill of sale or an item number of some kind?"

"They stole my Armani suit and all my silverware and my flat-screen. Stealing a DVD player isn't like hauling off Fort Knox. I'm starting to get a li'l lost here."

"Where'd you buy the player?" Helen asked.

"I didn't exactly buy it."

"Then how did you acquire it, Mr. Stanga?" she asked.

"My cousin Herman told me he wanted me to have it. And his flat-screen. So after he died, see, I brought them over to my house. 'Cause of what Herman told me."

"You ever use the player?" I said.

He seemed to search his memory. "I don't think I plugged it in. But I'm not sure. What's on y'all's mind? I want to he'p, but I don't know what we're ruminating about here."

"I want you to come down to the department and watch about forty seconds of video, Mr. Stanga," Helen said. "Then we'll have a chat."

Outside, the Sunset Limited clattered down the railway tracks, the pictures and framed degrees rattling on the office walls.

"Herman have some porn on there or something?" Monroe said.

Helen exhaled, then looked at me. Monroe may have been a venal man, but he could not be called an evil one. Our knowledge about his cousin's activities was probably greater than his own. After he watched the video, he was visibly shocked and frightened and sat with his arms folded tightly across his chest, his round mahogany-colored waxed head bright with pinpoints of perspiration. He wiped his forehead with a folded handkerchief, then rubbed at his nose with the back of his wrist.

"How come there's no sound?" he asked.

"We don't know," I said.

He huffed air out of his nostrils, blinking like a man who couldn't deal with the brightness of the day. "Think y'all gonna find Herman's flat-screen?"

"I doubt it," I said.

"If you do, give it to the Goodwill. I don't want to ever see it again," he said.

THAT EVENING I asked Molly to take a walk with me. The sky was piled with clouds that looked like golden and purple fruit turning red around the edges. From the bridge at Burke Street, we could see the flooded bamboo behind The Shadows and the flowers growing along the bayou and the deep shade on the water under the overhang of the trees.

"I'd like for you and Alafair to leave town for a week or so. Maybe go to Key West," I said.

"When did we start running away from things?" she replied.

"This one is different. I'm not even sure who the players are."

"What others do or don't do isn't a factor. We don't stop being who we are," she said.

The air was cool puffing up from under the bridge, the surface of the water crinkling in the sunset with the incoming tide. "We're dealing with people who have no lines," I said. "Their motivations are only partially known to us. Part of their agenda is financial. The other part of it is fiendish. It's the last part I'm worried about."

Then I told her about the video we had watched in Helen's office. While I spoke, Molly continued to lean on the bridge rail, staring at the sunlight's reflection on the bayou's surface, like hundreds of glinting razors, her face never changing expression.

"Who would do this?" she said.

"That's it. We don't know. Monsters like Gacy and Bundy and Gary Ridgway and this guy Rader in Kansas torture and murder people for years and live undetected in our midst while they do it."

"We're not going anywhere, Dave."

I watched a garfish roll among the water hyacinths along the bank, its dark green armored back sliding as supplely as a snake's beneath the flowers, down into the depths, while tiny bream skittered out of its way.

I ATE LUNCH the next day at Victor's cafeteria on Main. It was hot and bright when I came back out on the street, the air dense, a smell like salt and warm seaweed on the wind, more like hurricane season than the end of spring.

A Lexus pulled to the curb. The driver rolled down the charcoal-tinted window on the passenger side. Carolyn Blanchet leaned forward so I could see her face. "How about a ride?" she said.

"Thanks. I don't have far to go," I said.

"Stop acting like an asshole, Dave."

I stepped off the curb and leaned down on the window jamb. "What do you want, Carolyn?"

"To apologize for the way I acted when you and Helen Soileau came out to the house. I had just gotten finished with those federal auditors and wanted to take it out on somebody."

I nodded and stepped back on the curb.

"*Dave,*" she said, turning my name into two syllables.

"Have a great life," I said.

"You'd better listen to me. Helen Soileau is carrying out a vendetta. Give me two minutes. That's all I'm asking. Then you can do whatever you please."

Don't do it, don't do it, don't do it, a voice said.

But there was no question about Helen's lack of objectivity toward Carolyn Blanchet. Worse, I wasn't entirely sure that Helen hadn't been involved in the same circle of female friends in New Orleans as Carolyn. Carolyn pulled around the corner, into the shade of a two-story building, and waited. I followed and got into the car. "Go ahead," I said.

"I misled you about Emma Poche," she said. "We had a brief relationship. I didn't tell you the truth because I didn't want Emma hurt. Men gave her a bad time at the New Orleans Police Department. She doesn't need the same kind of trouble in St. Martinville."

The Lexus's engine was running, the air-conditioning vents gushing. Carolyn wore sandals and white shorts and a yellow blouse and blue contacts. She sat with her back against the door, her knees slightly spread, a gold cross and thin gold chain lying askew on her chest. Her eyes roamed over my face, her mouth parting, exposing the whiteness of her teeth. "You just going to sit there?" she said.

"Ever read *Mein Kampf*? Hitler explains how you tell an effective lie. You wrap it in a little bit of truth."

"Let me tell you this. A friend of mine felt bad about something she had done and called me up and made a confession. My friend had taken pictures of me at a girls-only Mardi Gras celebration. Helen Soileau wanted the pictures. When Helen Soileau wants something, she gets it. I have a feeling you've seen those pictures."

I tried to keep my face neutral, my eyes empty. I looked down the street at a black kid doing wheelies on a bicycle under the colonnade.

"That's what I thought," Carolyn said. "Think what you want about those pictures—they're innocent. Now let me ask you this. What kind of person would use them to blacken another person's reputation? Also, if these pictures are immoral, how is it that Helen Soileau is friends with the woman who took them?"

"None of this changes the fact that you lied about your relationship with Emma Poche."

"Have you told Molly everything about your various affairs over the years? Let's face it, Dave, from what I heard, you were never very big on keeping it in your pants."

"It's really been good talking with you, Carolyn. I'll keep in mind that you were protecting a working-class girl like Emma from public scandal. Tell me, how does that compute with your and Layton's record of stealing the life savings of thousands of working-class people who trusted y'all?"

"God, you're a sweetheart to the bitter end." She paused. "Remember the New Year's party at the Blue Room in New Orleans about twenty years back?"

"Not exactly," I said.

"I guess you don't. You'd soaked your head in

alcohol for two days." She was smiling. "Who took you home that night?"

I held my eyes on hers, trying to show no expression.

"You were quite a guy back then," she said. "Enough to make a girl straighten up and fly right and give up her eccentric ways. Remember that line from Hemingway about feeling the earth move? Wow, you did it, babe."

I got out of the Lexus. She rolled down the window and looked up at me, laughing openly. "Had you going, didn't I?" she said.

THAT NIGHT BLACK storm clouds swollen with electricity had sealed the sky from the Gulf to central Louisiana. Waves crashed across the two-lane road at the bottom of St. Mary Parish, and a tornado made a brief touchdown and knocked out a power line. During the night, several emergency vehicles passed the Abelard house and noticed nothing unusual about it other than a few broken tree limbs that had blown into the yard. At around four-fifteen A.M., a deputy sheriff thought he saw flashes of light inside the windows, both upstairs and downstairs. He slowed his cruiser by the wood bridge that gave onto the compound, but the house had returned to complete darkness. He concluded that he had seen reflections of lightning on the window glass or that someone had been carrying a candelabrum between the rooms.

At 8:43 A.M. Friday, the phone on my desk rang. The caller was someone I had not expected to hear from again. "Mr. Dave?" she said.

"Jewel?"

"I need he'p."

"What is it?"

"I was late getting to work 'cause trees limbs were down on the road. When I got to the house, my key wouldn't go in the front lock."

"Which house?"

"The big house, Mr. Timothy's. The key wouldn't work. The lock looked like somebody drove a screwdriver in it. I went around back, but the door was bolted from inside. I banged on all the doors, but nobody answered."

"Who's supposed to be there besides Mr. Timothy?"

"The maid and the gardener, but they probably couldn't get t'rew on the road."

"What about Kermit and Weingart?"

"They went off to the casino in New Orleans for a couple of days. I put a ladder up to the window. I could see a shape inside one of the doors, just standing there, not moving."

"That doesn't make sense."

"I'm telling you what I saw. There's a shape in the doorway. It's not moving. I'm scared, Mr. Dave."

"Where are you now?"

"Right outside the house."

"I'm heading over there. Call the sheriff's office in Franklin."

"No, suh."

"Why won't you call the sheriff?"

"This is still St. Mary Parish. It doesn't change. Y'all want to believe it has, but you're just fooling yourself."

"Look, Mr. Timothy doesn't stay at night by himself. Who else was there?"

"Mr. Emiliano, the Spanish man from Nicaragua."

"I'll be there in twenty minutes. But you have to call the St. Mary sheriff. I don't have authority outside Iberia Parish."

"Yes, suh. I'm putting the ladder up by the sun-porch now. I can see to the hallway," she said. "Oh, Lord, that t'ing is still standing there."

"What thing?"

"Hurry up, Mr. Dave," she said. Then I heard her crying just before she dropped the cell phone.

CHAPTER 23

FIFTEEN MINUTES LATER, my flasher rippling, I came up behind a utility truck and an ambulance and a St. Mary Parish sheriff's cruiser on the two-lane that led to the Abelard house. Men in hard hats and overalls were chainsawing a fallen tree and hauling it in segments off the asphalt. The sheriff, Tony Judice, shook hands with me. "Jewel Laveau said she called me after you told her to," he said.

"It was something like that, I guess," I replied, not meeting his eyes.

He caught my embarrassment. "Don't worry about it," he said. "We didn't treat people of color around here very well. I don't know why we're surprised when they act the way they do."

"I couldn't understand everything she was saying," I said, changing the subject. "Did you get anything out of her?"

"She was yelling about her father. I thought her father died years ago," he replied.

When the utility workers had cleared the road, I followed the sheriff's cruiser to the Abelard home. The sun was white on the bay, the wind blowing stiffly out of the south. There was a bright smell in the air, as though the land had been swept clean by the storm. But Jewel Laveau was a quick reminder that there was no joy or sense of renewal to be found at the home of the Abelards. She sat on a folding chair in her white uniform in the shade of the boathouse, her shoulders rounded, her large hands spread like baseball gloves on her knees. Her eyes were rheumy, her nose wet, when she looked up at us. "What took y'all?"

"The road was blocked," the sheriff said. "What's inside the house?"

"Go see for yourself," she replied.

"That's not helping us a lot," he said.

"That's your problem. I won't talk about it. If you talk about evil, it just makes it grow. Maybe I didn't see what I t'ought. Maybe it was just the shadows. I tried to call Mr. Kermit in New Orleans. But he wasn't at the hotel. Neither was Mr. Robert." Then her gaze shifted on me and stayed there, as though the sheriff were no longer present. "You're disappearing."

"Excuse me?" I said.

"It's like you're being erased—your arms, your legs. They're thinning away, turning into air."

"You stay here," the sheriff said to her. "I'll talk to you again before we leave."

"You cain't tell me what to do. I'm not listening to y'all anymore. I spent my life listening to you. There was evil all around us. But where were you? You were hiding in your offices, doing what you were tole, letting the people in the quarters suffer and work for nothing. Now you're out here to clean up. 'Cause that's what y'all been doing all your lives. Cleaning up after the people that kept you scared just like the rest of us."

"You need to keep a civil tongue, Miss Jewel," the sheriff said. There was no mistaking the racial resentment that even among the best of us sometimes oozed its way through the mix in our struggle with ourselves.

I walked with the sheriff back up the driveway. Two deputies had already tried the doors and windows and had found all of them locked. The sheriff examined the key slot in the front doorknob without touching it. The slot looked like someone had wedged a blade screwdriver into it. There were also two deep prize marks between the edge of the door and the jamb, as though someone had tried to force back the tongue on the lock. "Get us in," the sheriff said to his deputy.

We had all put on polyethylene gloves. The deputy used his baton to break a glass pane out of a side panel, then he reached inside and unlocked the door. The power was still off in the house, the windows tightly sealed, the air dense and warm and smelling of moldy wallpaper and curtains and slipcovers that were never free of dust and carpet stretched over dry rot. The light that filtered through the stained glass on the sunporch seemed to burnish the woodwork and antique furniture with a red flush that was garish and unnatural.

"Smell it?" the deputy with the baton said.

"Open some windows," the sheriff replied. He flicked a wall switch on and off, apparently forgetting that the power grid was down. His eyes traveled up the stairs and along the banister and up the wall to the landing on the second story. "I was really hoping we wouldn't be doing this," he said.

The blood evidence told its own story. The smears along the wall were those of a person who was wounded and had probably fallen and struggled to his feet. The linear and horsetail patterns, stippled and attenuated on the edges, as though they had been flung from a brush, were of the kind you associate with the splatter from an exit wound. The sheriff and I started up the stairs, not touching the mahogany banister that was stained in three places by the grip of a bloodied hand.

Down below, one of the deputies said, "Oh, shit."

"How about it on the language?" the sheriff said.

"Better come look at this, sir. Watch where you step," the deputy said.

We went back down the stairs and walked past the entrance to the sunporch and entered a dark hallway that led to the kitchen. A man hung from the doorframe, his slippered feet barely touching the floor, a clothesline wrapped around his throat and threaded through a metal eyelet screwed into the top of the jamb. His eyes were open, his tongue sticking out of his mouth like a small, twisted green banana.

But Timothy Abelard's ordeal had not consisted simply of being hanged like a criminal; he had also been shot, at least twice.

"Who the hell would do this?" the sheriff said.

"About half the parish, if they were honest about it," the deputy said. The sheriff gave him a look. "Sorry," the deputy said.

The sheriff looked up the staircase. "I hate to think what's up there. You ready?" he said to me.

"If it will make this easier for you, I'll show you the photos of the dead girls who I think suffered much worse than Mr. Abelard did."

"I'm not making the connection," the sheriff said, his expression suddenly irritable if not disdainful.

At that moment I didn't care about the sheriff's feelings or the conflicts he had probably never resolved regarding his role as a public servant in a fiefdom. I hadn't liked Timothy Abelard, nor did I like the dictatorial arrogance that I associated with his class. But that did not mean I believed that an elderly, infirm man deserved to die the way he had.

I glanced at the glass case that held the photos of Abelard standing among friends of Batista and members of the Somoza family, people for whom cruelty toward others was as natural as waking in the morning. Was Abelard a monster? Or was he just an extension of the value system that produced him, a blithe spirit who turned a blind eye to the excesses of the third-world dictators we did business with? I started to share my thoughts with the sheriff. But what was the point? He didn't create the world in which he'd grown up and wasn't responsible for the sins of others.

Upstairs we began to see the rest of the intruder's handiwork. An office that I suspected was Kermit's was torn apart. Books were raked off the shelves, a computer pushed off a desk, drawers pulled out, a gun case shoved facedown on the floor and, behind where the case had stood, a wall safe with its door hanging open, the contents gone.

A trail of blood led from the doorway of the office into a small bathroom. Emiliano lay fully clothed in the bathtub on his back, one leg hooked over the tub's edge, the shower curtain tangled in his right hand. His face and chest were peppered with bullet wounds that probably had been inflicted by a low-caliber weapon.

It wasn't hard to find the weapon. It was by the desk, a six-shot .22 piece of junk, the serial number acid-burned, the front sight filed off, the broken grips wrapped with electrician's tape. The sheriff picked it up and flipped out the cylinder. "The shooter took his brass with him," he said.

I looked at the wall safe and at the dead man in the bathtub.

"What are you thinking?" the sheriff said behind me.

"I'm not sure," I said.

"You don't think it's a home invasion gone bad?"

I scratched the back of my neck, not looking at him. "It's hard to read, Sheriff."

"Maybe somebody sweated the safe combination out of them and then decided to finish the job."

"Could be," I said.

"But that's not what you're thinking."

"No, it isn't."

"You're thinking that whoever did this knew the old man and hated his guts and decided to give him a preview of hell before he saw the real thing."

"That's a possibility."

The sheriff dropped the .22 into a Ziploc bag. "Does a gun like this remind you of anything?" he asked.

"You can buy one like it in any slum in America."

"It looks like a throwdown to me. If we start counting up rounds fired, it's more than six. So our shooter reloaded at least once, but he left no brass behind. Who always picks up his brass, Dave?"

"If a cop did this, why would he recover his brass and leave his piece?"

"Maybe he didn't want to have it on his person if he got stopped somewhere. During the storm, emergency vehicles were all over the highways. I've heard that you and Clete Purcel have had a couple of confrontations with the Abelards and their associates."

"You could call it that."

"Is it true Purcel killed a federal informant years ago?"

"Don't take the bait."

"Would you repeat that?"

"Look back at everything we've seen. Start with the front door. Who tries to bust a lock by using a screwdriver on the keyhole? If the door was pried, the jamb would be torn up, not just dented. Why would the intruder pull open the drawers in a writer's desk and knock the computer on the floor and rake books off the shelves? If he knew the combination on the safe, he wouldn't have to look for it. This place is a stage set."

"So if a burglar didn't do this, who did?"

"Somebody who got his education on the yard. Somebody who wanted to shut some people up and make a big score while he was at it. Somebody who'd like to give Clete Purcel as much grief as he can."

"I'll bite," the sheriff said.

Not on my meter, you won't, I thought.

I walked downstairs and out into the sunlight, my ears ringing. He followed me into the yard. "Where you going?" he said.

"To give Miss Jewel a ride home. If I were you, I'd have a talk with Robert Weingart."

"Who?"

Hopeless, I thought.

But that's the way you think when you realize for certain you're an old man and, as such, like Cassandra, destined to be disbelieved.

CLETE'S SECRETARY TOLD me he had gone home for lunch. I found him by his cottage at the motor court on East Main, reading a book in a lawn chair under the oaks, his wire-frame glasses down low on his nose. Next to him was a card table set with a tray of sandwiches and a sweating pitcher of sangria and cracked ice. The sandwiches were cut in triangles and filled with cream cheese and chives. He lowered his book and smiled.

"*Plutarch's Lives*?" I said.

"Yeah, this is great stuff. Did you know Alexander the Great was AC/DC and his sweat smelled like flowers? He also got plastered every night." Clete picked up a glass of sangria and drank from it, his eyes crinkling at the corners.

"Where'd you get the sandwiches?"

"Somebody dropped them off."

"Would you answer the question?"

"Emma Poche was in the neighborhood."

"I think you have brain damage. There's some kind of tumor loose in your head."

"Look, she feels bad. She apologized."

"For what? Killing Herman Stanga?"

"We don't know she did that. This is what she told me: 'I've done some hateful and bad stuff. I did it because some of the good people took a lick off me. It's my fault, but they got their lick, and I figured I should get something for it.'"

"That's the rhetoric of a female recidivist. What's the matter with you?"

"Want a sandwich?"

"Where's your throwdown?"

"In the glove compartment."

"Check."

"I don't have to. I just saw it. Why are you worried about my throwdown?" He lifted his glass of sangria to his mouth.

"I came from the Abelard house. Somebody killed the old man and the guy you called a greaseball. The old man was strung up with his feet barely touching the floor. Whoever did it to him wanted him to go out slow and hard."

Clete lowered his glass without drinking from it. "Somebody left a throwdown?"

"Yeah, they did."

"Well, it's not mine. Who do you make for it?"

"Weingart," I said.

"My vote would be for the Bobster, too. I never met a cell-house bitch yet who wasn't mean to the core. Where is he now?"

"Supposedly New Orleans."

"What about the grandson? Kermit Dick Brain or whatever?"

"In New Orleans, too."

Clete seemed to study my face without seeing me.

"What are you thinking?" I asked.

"We're the target, not the old man and the greaseball." His eyes came back into focus. He continued to stare at me. "Something else happened over there, didn't it?"

"The black woman, Jewel Laveau, told me I was disappearing."

"You're going to be kidnapped?"

"She said I was evaporating."

I heard his breathing quicken, saw a vein swell in his neck. "You stop listening to superstitious people. You stop believing in stuff like that."

"I didn't say I believed her."

"You've got it painted all over you, Dave. It's a death wish."

He put his glass of sangria on the table and pinched his thumb and index finger on his temples as though the sun were burning down through the tree overhead, eating into his skull.

"What is it?" I said.

"If you die on me, I'm going to get really mad," he replied. "You're not going to do that to me. I'm not going to allow it. You understand me? I'll beat the shit out of you."

THE MURDER OF Timothy Abelard and his friend and the heinous nature of the slayings were all over the front pages of state newspapers and provided the lead in every local television broadcast. Because the story had Gothic overtones and involved a wealthy recluse, it was immediately picked up by the national news services. Each account emphasized Abelard's stature in the community, his contribution as a defense industrialist, the loss of his son and daughter-in-law somewhere in the Bermuda Triangle, his convivial personality, and his iconic role as a plantation patriarch who represented a bygone era.

No mention was made of his ties to the Giacano crime family in New Orleans or the Batista regime in Cuba or the Somozas in Nicaragua. The man who died with him, Emiliano Jimenez, was referred to as a "visitor" and "longtime friend" who had been "interested in developing new markets for Louisiana sugar farmers."

Any serious student of popular media will tell you that the real story lies not in what is written but in what is left out. In this instance the omission was not simply one of airbrushing out the details of Abelard's dealings with New Orleans gangsters and third-world despots. The bigger omission was ongoing and systemic: Timothy Abelard's death was the stuff of Elizabethan drama; the murder of the girls in Jefferson Davis Parish didn't merit the ink it would take to fill a ballpoint pen.

Abelard's funeral was held on a Tuesday at a mortuary home, not a church. The lawn was green from the spring rains, the flowers in bloom. Most of the mourners were elderly and dressed in clothes that they probably seldom had occasion to wear except at religious services. Their accents and frame of reference were of an earlier generation, one that believed there was virtue in allowing memory to soften and revise the image of the deceased, that appearance was more important than substance, because ultimately appearance was, in its way, a fulfillment of aspiration.

They remembered Timothy Abelard for his acts of charity, his intercession on behalf of a Negro servant locked in jail, his kindness to a deranged woman who begged food at people's doors, his rehabilitation of a drunkard driven from his ministry by his own congregation. Abelard's eviction of his tenants from their homes when they tried to join a farmworkers' union was forgotten.

From across the street, I watched Robert Weingart and Kermit Abelard and four other pallbearers carry the casket down the steps to a hearse. Kermit's face seemed to glow with the self-induced resilience of a person who is either heavily medicated or teetering on the edge of nervous collapse. In spite of the heat, he wore a heavy navy blue suit and white dress shirt and dark tie with a white boutonniere. After the casket was rolled into the back of the hearse, he seemed at a loss as to what he should do next. His truncated workingman's physique seemed wrapped too tight, the heat in his suit visibly climbing up his neck.

Almost as though he had heard my thoughts, his gaze traveled across the street and met mine. He disengaged from the mourners and walked through the traffic to my truck, barely acknowledging the two vehicles forced to stop in order to let him pass. "I didn't recognize your pickup," he said.

"State Farm bought me a new one. After my old one got shot up and hauled off by some guys I'd like to have a talk with," I said.

"What are you doing here?" he asked.

"Please accept my sympathies," I said.

"Do I have to restate the question?"

"Sometimes a killer shows up at the funeral service of his victim."

"I don't see your friend Mr. Purcel here."

I let my eyes drift off his face, then return again. "I'm not sure how I should take that."

"Take it any way you wish. I resent your presence."

"Sorry to hear you say that."

He placed his hand on the window jamb. "I cared for your daughter. You treated me with repugnance and disrespect every time we met."

"You 'cared' for her?"

"I'm going to the cemetery now. I'm going to ask that you not follow us."

"Maybe you should do a reality check, Kermit. Your father and mother may have been killed because of your grandfather's iniquitous deeds. Number two, you're not going to tell a police officer what he's going and not going to do in a homicide investigation. Do you understand that?"

"You may have gone to college, Mr. Robicheaux, but you wear your lack of breeding like a rented suit," he said.

He walked back onto the lawn of the mortuary home. Robert Weingart cupped his hand on Kermit's shoulder and looked across the street at me, his eyes laughing.

I TALKED AGAIN to the sheriff of St. Mary Parish and told him of my suspicions about Robert Weingart.

"He's got an alibi, Dave. He was at Harrah's hotel in New Orleans or in the casino all night," the sheriff said.

"Say that last part again?"

"He's a gambler. He was either at the tables or in his room. We checked the time-in and time-out at the parking garage. His car never left the premises."

"Who told you he was at the tables?"

"Kermit."

"Kermit was in the casino with him? All night?"

"No, Kermit says he went to bed and Weingart went to the casino. But a blackjack dealer remembers him."

"Weingart could have been at the Abelard house in an hour and a half."

"I don't think he's a likely candidate. I think you're too personally involved in this. Maybe it's time to butt out."

"Drop by the office, and I'll show you a video that will stay with you awhile."

"Video of what?" he said.

I eased the receiver back down in the cradle. I was at a dead end again. The deaths of Timothy Abelard and Emiliano Jimenez had changed nothing. But one pattern of behavior in the players *had* changed. Emma Poche, while drunk, had warned me over the telephone that I and anyone with me was in danger. She had also put Robert Weingart to his knees with a baton when he tried to work his seductive routine on Tee Jolie Melton. And only a few days ago, Emma had brought Clete a tray of sandwiches and attempted to apologize to him, although her confession avoided the admission that not only had she participated in the murder of Herman Stanga, but she had planted Clete's pen at the crime scene.

I looked at my watch. It was 4:56 P.M. When I was on the dirty boogie, what was I always thinking about when the clock inched toward five? It came in frosted mugs and tumblers of ice and bottles that were smoke-colored or dark green or reddish-black or glowing with an amber warmth. A softly lit, air-conditioned bar with tropical sunsets painted on the walls was not an oasis in the desert. It was a Renaissance cathedral, a retreat for wayward souls whose secular communion waited for them in the first glass they could raise to their lips.

It wasn't hard to find Emma. She had changed into street clothes and was drinking in the same lounge where Clete had met her during his surveillance of Carolyn Blanchet, outside St. Martinville. I sat down next to her at the bar and ordered a Dr Pepper in a glass of ice with a lime slice.

"I always thought that stuff tasted like iodine," she said.

"It does," I said. "You give up on meetings altogether?"

"Stop drinking today, gone tomorrow."

"You know why drunks go to meetings?" I asked.

"Let me guess. Because they drink?"

"Because they feel guilty."

"What a breakthrough, Dave." She was drinking Wild Turkey on the rocks, cupping her hand all the way around the tumbler when she drank from it. Her cheeks looked filled with blood, the fuzz on them glowing against the light.

"Do you know why they feel guilty?"

"I'll take another big leap here. Because they went through severe toilet training?"

"No, because they still have their humanity. The greater the pain, the greater the indication that they're basically decent people."

"Put it on a postcard and send it to the penguins,

will you? I mean it, Streak. Let a girl come up for oxygen."

"I have three still photos here. A guy in the department made them from a video that belonged to Herman Stanga. Take a look."

"I don't want to."

"I think you should."

"You don't have to tell me about Herman Stanga."

"This isn't about Herman Stanga. It's about the two girls in the video."

"I'm off the clock. Bring them by the department."

"No, this is between you and me. No histrionics. No throwing coffee in my face. Look at the pictures, Emma."

"No."

I spread the printouts on the bar right by her glass. "I need to know where that place is. Look at it."

"No."

"You stopped Robert Weingart from harming the girl named Tee Jolie. Your conscience is eating your lunch, Emma. You have to help me on this. It's not up for discussion."

Her eyes dropped to the first photo. She drank from her tumbler, the ice rattling against the glass, the whiskey clotting in her throat. "I don't know what that is. I've never seen that before."

"What do you mean by *that*? What is *that*? The terror in their faces? The collars on their throats? The ooze coming out of the wall?"

"Whatever that place is. Whatever is going on there. I don't know what any of that is."

"Yes, you do. You warned me that I was in danger. You were right. A Mississippi gunbull by the name of Jimmy Darl Thigpin tried to clip me. He was hired by somebody you know. The same person or persons who murdered these girls."

She was shaking her head. "You're all wrong. I didn't have anything to do with this."

"Tell me where the girls were held."

"I don't know. I don't know why you're showing me this. I don't know that place. The rocks in the walls look like pineapples. I think that photo is a fake. Why are you doing this to me?"

"Is everything all right here?" the bartender asked.

"Sheriff's detective," I said, reaching for my badge holder.

"What?" he said.

"Get out of here," I said.

Emma was holding her tumbler in both hands now, staring down into the whiskey as though reading words in the ice melt. "You said this gunbull tried to clip you. If that's true, where is he?"

"Put it this way: A guy who's been abusing convicts for forty years doesn't want to go inside. A guy like that cuts any deal he can. At anybody's expense."

"You've got a cooperative witness?"

"What do you think I'm saying to you, Emma? Wake up. You want to do these people's time? Haven't you been hurt enough? They made their money off the backs of the blacks and poor whites. They repair their own lives by destroying the lives of others. How bad do you have to get hurt before you get the message?"

She stared down at the photos. Then she covered them with her forearm, staring rigidly in the mirror. "I did what I was told. I didn't know anything about this. But no matter how it plays out, I'm the one who loses."

"No, these girls lost. You still have your life. You still have choices. These girls didn't have any."

Her eyes looked feverish, her lower lip sagging. "Fuck you, Dave." She finished her drink and raised her glass toward the bartender. "Hit me again. And a beer back."

CHAPTER 24

DEATH COMES IN many forms. But it always comes. And for that reason, "inevitability" may be the worst word in the English language.

These were not thoughts I wanted to brood upon as I sat beside the bayou that evening, the water swollen above the roots of the cypress trees, the sun little more than a cinder among the rain clouds in the west. Spring had come and gone and been replaced by the heavy and languid ennui of the Louisiana summer, a season that, at the end of day, clings to your skin like a sour vapor.

I heard Molly unfold a wood chair and sit beside me. "I fixed some ice cream and pecan pie," she said.

"I'll be there in a minute," I said.

"Don't let this case pull you down, Dave."

"It's not. I don't think it will be solved. I think that's just the way it is."

She didn't argue. Like me, Molly had ceased to contend with the world. It wasn't a matter of acceptance. It was a matter of disengagement. The two were quite different. "Where's Alf?" I said.

"Why do you still call her that?"

"Because that's the way I'll always see her. A father never sees the woman. He always sees the little girl."

Molly looked at her watch. "She left a message on the machine. She got stuck in the traffic coming back from Lafayette."

"How long ago did she leave the message?"

"About twenty minutes."

I folded up our two chairs and walked with Molly up the slope to the back porch. The ground under the trees had fallen into deep shade, the sun golden on the canopy. Tripod and Snuggs were sitting on top of Tripod's hutch, watching us. "Can you guys handle some ice cream?" I asked.

They both seemed to think that was a good idea. I got the ice cream out of the freezer and put a scoop in each of their bowls and placed their bowls on top of the hutch and went inside the kitchen again. I noticed the red light on the message machine was still flashing. I pushed the play button.

"It's me again," Alafair's voice said. "I'm in Broussard. I ran into somebody I need to talk with. I'll be along in a little bit. Just put my dinner in the refrigerator. I'm sorry."

I looked at Molly. "Ran into who?" I said.

She shrugged.

I dialed Alafair's cell phone, but it went instantly to voice mail.

"It could be anyone. Don't jump to conclusions," Molly said.

"When Alf avoids mentioning the name of a person to me, it's because she knows I think that person is toxic."

Molly started to speak but instead drew in her breath and held it and looked at my face, trying to hide the conclusions she herself was already coming to.

ALAFAIR HAD SEEN the black Saab in front of her on the two-lane highway that wound through mossy oaks in the little sugarcane town of Broussard. The highway was called Old Spanish Trail and was usually empty, and for that reason she had swung off the four-lane and driven through Broussard in hopes of avoiding the rush-hour traffic. Up ahead, by the four corners, the Saab had pulled in to a filling station, and the driver had gotten out and was filling his tank. He seemed to be gazing idly back down the road, his face clean-shaven, his jeans and sport shirt freshly pressed, the tragedy that had befallen his grandfather somehow locked temporarily in a box. Then he saw her and smiled in the boyish way she had always associated with him until he had brought Robert Weingart into their lives.

He stuck the nozzle of the gas hose back in the pump and waved her down. She looked at her watch. She could be home in under twenty minutes. Should she pass him by and pretend she had not seen him on the same day he had buried his grandfather? She had not attended the funeral service. Actually, she had hoped she would never see Kermit again. But how do you ignore someone who was once the center of your life, someone who encouraged your art and read your prose line by line and took as much pleasure in its creation and success as you did?

Without making a deliberate choice, she felt her foot come off the accelerator and step on the brake pedal, felt her hands turn the car in to the station, saw Kermit's face looming larger and larger through the windshield. He walked to her window, the summer light trapped in the sky above his head, his dockworker's physique backdropped by blooming myrtle bushes and oaks hung with Spanish moss. She started to speak, but he raised his hand. "You don't have to say anything," he said. "I know you liked and respected my grandfather. He always held you in the same regard."

"I'm sorry I didn't attend the funeral," she replied.

"He'd understand. So do I."

"Are you doing all right?" she said.

"I'm not staying in the house right now. It's still a crime scene. I want to have it cleaned and painted. I want to start things all over. Not just at the house but in my life."

The gas pump behind him was a dull red, solid-looking, part of the evening, part of Americana in some way. But something about it bothered her.

"Can you have a drink with me?" he said.

"I'm late for supper. I was shopping in Lafayette and got caught in the afternoon rush."

"I really need to explain some things," he said.

"Where's—" she began.

"Robert is not here. That's what I need to talk to you about. I need to clear my conscience, Alafair."

There was a bar across the street, one with neon beer signs in the windows and a termite-eaten colonnade and a squat roof that looked like a frowning man. Her gaze returned to the gas pump and the digital indicators that showed the number of gallons. "If I drink anything, I won't eat supper."

"There's a sno'ball stand on the next block. Pull in to the lot. It'll only take five minutes."

"Let me call home," she said.

"Sure," he said. He walked out of earshot, showing deference for her privacy, showing her once again the gentleman he'd been raised to be.

After she had called and left the second message of the afternoon on the machine, she restarted her engine and drove down the block to the corner, where she turned in to a gravel lot behind the sno'ball stand. The board flap on the serving window had been lowered and latched; the stand was closed. Kermit pulled his Saab up next to her car. But something was bothering her, a detail that caught in the eye the way a lash catches under the eyelid. Back at the filling station, she had been talking, or Kermit had, and she hadn't been able to concentrate. What was the detail that didn't fit inside the summer evening, the gold light high in the sky, the dull red solidity of the gas pump, the smell of dust and distant rain?

Kermit got out of the Saab and walked to her window. He carried a brown paper bag in his hand. It was folded neatly across the top, in the way a workingman might fold down the top of his lunch sack before heading out for his job.

"You bought less than two gallons of gas," she said.

"Right," he said.

"Why would you stop just to buy two gallons of gas?"

"I needed to use the restroom, so I thought I should buy something," he replied, his expression bemused.

"Why not just buy some mints? That's what most people would do."

"Actually, that's what I did." His eyes seemed to flatten, as though he were reviewing what he had just said. "When I was inside. I bought some mints."

"Could I have one?" she asked.

"A mint?" He touched his shirt pocket. "They must be on the seat. We need to talk. Slide over."

He opened the driver's door and turned off the engine and pulled the keys from the ignition. In the rearview mirror, she saw a white Mustang come from the side street and angle across the lot and jar to a stop on the opposite side of her vehicle, dust rising off the wheels, drifting in an acrid cloud through her windows. There was no one else on the street. The wind had dropped, and the leaves on the oak trees looked like the brushstrokes in an expressionist painting—glowing unnaturally, smudged, unreal, trying to disguise in the cheapest fashion the painful realities of death.

The driver of the white Mustang wore shades and a yellow felt hat, the kind a hiker might wear on the banks of Lake Louise. He was eating a hamburger with one hand. A second man, someone she didn't recognize, sat in the passenger seat. There were three deep lines in the man's forehead that reminded her of knotted string. The driver got out of his vehicle, glancing over his shoulder and down the sidewalks. When he sat down heavily next to her, she thought she could see the crumpled lines around his jaw and ears where a plastic surgeon's knife had created the mask that had become the face of Robert Weingart.

Kermit Abelard shook a pair of steel handcuffs from the paper bag he had been holding, just as Weingart thrust a hypodermic needle into her thigh. In seconds, she saw the light go out of the sky and the trees dissolve into smoke. Then she heard Weingart whisper close to her cheek, his breath heavy with mustard and onions, "Welcome to hell, Alafair."

AT SUNSET, FROM the front of his cottage at the motor court, Clete Purcel witnessed a change in the weather that was audible, a sucking of air that drew the leaves off the ground and out of the trees and sent them soaring into the sky, flickering like hundreds of yellow and green butterflies above the bayou. Then a curtain of rain marched across the wetlands, dissolving the western horizon into plumes of gray and blue smoke that resembled emissions from an ironworks.

The barometer and temperature dropped precipitously. Clete went inside the cottage and heard lightning pop on the water. A half hour later, through his front window, he saw headlights in the rain, then heard a door slam and feet running, followed by a loud banging on his door. When he opened it, Emma Poche was staring up into his face, an Australian flop hat wilted on her head, the leather cord swinging under her chin like the bail on an inverted bucket, her breath smelling of beer. Over her shoulder, he could see the backseat of her car piled to the windows with her possessions.

"Let me in," she said.

"What for?"

"You have to ask?"

"Yeah, I don't have a clue."

Her eyes searched the room and came back on his. "I set you up."

"On the Stanga deal?"

"I fucked you in your bed, then I fucked you behind your back."

"You put my gold pen in Stanga's pool?"

She shrugged and raised her face to his. "You got a drink?"

"No."

She stepped around him, forcing him to either close the door behind her or push her back outside. "Can I look in your refrigerator? You must have a beer."

"You clipped Stanga?"

"I didn't say that."

"But you did?"

"Is the world the less for it?"

"You clipped him for Carolyn Blanchet?"

"Don't get me started about Carolyn."

"We're not talking about your love affairs,

Emma. The two of you capped her poor dumb bastard of a husband."

"It didn't have anything to do with you. That's the only reason I'm here. I really did a number on you, Clete. It's the worst thing I ever did in my life."

"Now you're blowing town? See you around Crime Stoppers and all that sort of jazz?"

"No, I'm gonna hang around so I can do Carolyn's time in Gonzales. I always wanted to be an ex-cop in a prison population full of bull dykes. You gonna give me a beer?"

"I think there's one behind the mayonnaise."

She opened the icebox and removed a bottle of Bud and twisted off the cap. She put the cap on top of the breakfast table rather than in the trash basket. She lifted the bottle to her mouth and drank, her eyes on his, two curls of hair hanging down on her brow.

"Who killed the girls?" Clete said.

"I don't know. That's the truth. Carolyn was in business with the Abelards and looking out for her own interests. Stanga was in the way, and so was her husband. But I don't know who killed the girls. I think they got a rotten deal."

"A rotten deal?" he repeated.

"That's what I said," she replied, not comprehending his bemusement.

He looked into her face for a long time, to the point that she broke and glanced away. "Why are you staring at me like that?" she asked.

"Because I can never tell when you're lying."

"That's a lousy thing to say. Dave Robicheaux said I wouldn't ever have any peace unless I owned up to you. So I've done that."

"Yeah, you have. You got anything else to say?"

"It's kind of outrageous."

"So tell me."

She lowered her eyes, then looked up into his face again, her flop hat tilted on the back of her head, the leather cord swinging under her chin. "How about a mercy fuck for a girl on her way out of town?"

He put his hands on her shoulders and turned her around and led her to the door. "Get some coffee down the road. Don't tell me where you're going. Never contact me again, not for any reason. You find my name on anything in your possession, destroy it. I hope things work out for you, but I think you did the big flush on yourself a long time ago. Adios, babe."

Her face seemed to recede in the darkness and rain, the disbelief and injury in her expression shaping and reshaping itself in the overhead light. He closed the door and bolted it behind her.

He heard thunder in the south and through his side window saw a sheet of rain sweep across the water and slap the trees against the roof of his cottage. He watched her drive out of the motor court, her car leaking oil smoke, one taillight burned out, and he wondered if he had developed a capacity for cruelty that, in the past, he had only feigned. Then he realized the phone on his nightstand was ringing.

I LOOKED AT my watch. It was 8:10 when Clete picked up. Rain was drumming on our tin roof, so hard I almost had to yell into the telephone to be understood. "Alafair left a message at six-twenty. She said she was in Broussard and was stopping to talk with someone she met. I haven't heard from her since."

"She doesn't answer her cell?" Clete asked.

"She turned it off. I talked to the cops in Broussard. They haven't seen a car that looks like hers. I called the state police. Same thing."

"Why would she turn off her cell?"

"She didn't want to be bothered while she was talking to somebody I probably don't like."

"Not necessarily. It could be a girlfriend or somebody who needs some help. Look, right before you called, Emma Poche was here, pretty soused, wanting to own up to planting my pen in Stanga's swimming pool."

"How's that relate to Alafair?"

"She said she didn't know who killed Bernadette Latiolais and Fern Michot. I believed her. So I let her go."

"So?"

"I thought I should tell you. Maybe I should have sweated her. I let her get her hooks into me. I don't think I have any judgment anymore."

"Why are you telling me this now?" I asked.

"I just thought I should."

"No, you think whoever killed the girls has Alafair."

"Don't put words in my mouth. Turn on the TV. This storm is tearing up Lafayette. Maybe she pulled off the road. Maybe she can't get a signal."

"I think Robert Weingart killed Timothy Abelard and the Nicaraguan. I think he tried to put it on you and, by extension, on me. I think he's probably convinced Kermit Abelard we're responsible for his grandfather's death."

"Who cares? Kermit Abelard is a fop. Stay where you are. I'm coming over."

I couldn't think straight. Before I could say anything else, he had broken the connection. I called the sheriff in St. Mary Parish and hit another dead end. He said he didn't know where either Kermit Abelard or Robert Weingart was, then added, "Frankly, I don't care."

"Say again?"

"Because they're not the problem," he said.

"Who is, sir? My daughter?"

"Don't you be laying off your anger on me, Dave."

"Don't call me by my first name again," I said, and hung up.

But getting angry at a functionary in St. Mary Parish was of no help. I tried to clear my head, to think in a sequential fashion, to revisit mentally all the evidence we'd uncovered in the murder of the two girls. The video of the subterranean room we had found in Herman Stanga's DVD player contained a detail that I couldn't get out of my mind, one that indicated a story larger than itself. But what was it?

The stones in the walls. They had reminded me of bread loaves, smooth and heavy and rounded on the ends, not given to flaking. Emma Poche had looked at the still photos made from the video and had said they resembled pineapples. Why would she say pineapples? Because of the shape? Was her statement one of those linguistic leaps from an image to an idea based on an association in the subconscious? Did something about them call to mind breadfruit, the food that nineteenth-century plantation owners grew and fed to their slaves in the tropics?

Clete came through the back door without knocking. His slicker was dripping water, his face beaded with it. "Let's go to Broussard," he said. "We start talking to everybody we can along Highway Ninety and the old two-lane."

I had already thought about it. The two-lane was a possibility. It was within the town of Broussard itself, with few places where Alafair could pull off to talk to someone. But the city cops had not seen her car, nor had anyone along the two-lane reported a scuffle or an abduction or anything unusual occurring that evening. The four-lane, also known as Highway 90, was far more problematic. It went for miles and was congested with service stations, fast-food restaurants, bars, convenience stores, and motels, plus any number of business properties where she could simply pull in to a parking lot.

Regardless, one way or another, we had to get off the dime. "We'll each take a vehicle and divide it up," I said.

The phone rang. Molly picked it up in the bedroom before I could reach the kitchen counter. "Dave, it's the state police," she said.

My heart was beating hard when I picked up. I didn't know the trooper who had called. He said he was on a farm road not far off the interstate west of Lafayette. "We've got a Honda registered in the name of Alafair Suzanne Robicheaux. It's been involved in an accident," he said. "I saw the ATL on it earlier. Am I talking to the right party?"

"Yeah, this is Dave Robicheaux, with the Iberia Parish Sheriff's Department. I'm Alafair's father. Who's in the vehicle?"

"We're not sure. It's upside down in a coulee. We're waiting on the Jaws of Life. We had to get them from Opelousas. The vehicle is wedged, so we can't flip it over."

I had to close my eyes to control my frustration. "How many people are in there? Are we talking about a man or woman? Can you be specific?"

"I can see one man. I don't know if anybody is in there with him or not. I hope he's the only one. I sure as hell do."

"Explain that."

He paused. "The guy I can see has space to

breathe. Most every other area of the vehicle is crushed tight as tinfoil."

"Give me your twenty again," I said.

After he gave me directions, I pressed down the button on the phone cradle and looked at Molly, the receiver still in my hand. "It's Alafair's car. There's an injured man inside. The trooper can't be sure if anybody else is in the car."

"Oh, Dave," she said.

"Clete and I are headed there now." Before she could speak, I raised my hand. "You have to stay here in case somebody calls. Maybe it was a carjacking, maybe an abduction. Alafair would have fought. She wouldn't have just submitted to some guy who drove off with her."

There were other scenarios that were much less optimistic. But there was no point in reviewing them. "Weingart is behind this, isn't he?" Molly said.

"That's my guess. But I don't know."

I saw Clete look at me and tap on the dial of his watch. I called the department and asked that a cruiser be stationed in front of our house. Then Clete and I headed for Interstate 10, the emergency flasher clamped on the roof of my new Toyota truck, the rain dividing in the headlights, the highway unwinding behind us like a long black snake.

CHAPTER 25

THE STORM WAS still in full progress when we arrived at the accident scene, the sky roiling with blue-black clouds, the lights of farmhouses barely visible inside the rain. The state troopers had ignited emergency flares along the edge of the coulee where, according to a witness, Alafair's Honda had been hit at high speed by a tractor-trailer that had never slowed down. The Honda had rolled over at least three times before it landed on its roof at the bottom of the coulee, the driver's window pinched into a slit. A trooper with a flashlight in one hand and a radio in the other approached us as soon as Clete and I got out of the truck.

"You're Detective Robicheaux?" he asked.

"Yes, sir."

"It's probably going to be another fifteen or twenty minutes before the Jaws are here. I don't know the status of the guy inside. He's generally incoherent and uncooperative," the trooper said. He had a square jaw and tight mouth and eyes that kept looking at everything around him rather than at me.

"Did you get a name?"

"No. I'm trying to get a crane in here. Did you see one on the road?"

"No," I said.

"The attempt to locate didn't give us very much information. What's the deal on your daughter?"

"I think she may have been abducted."

His eyes met mine before he gazed down the road

again, his expression neutral. "We don't quite understand what happened here. The witness says two other cars seemed to be traveling with your daughter's car. But they didn't stop. From what we can gather, the guy driving the semi may be DUI, but the two companion vehicles fleeing the scene don't add up."

"What kind of description do you have on them?"

"The witness says one was white, the other dark-colored. If you want to talk to the guy inside your daughter's car, you'd better do it now."

"He's not going to make it?" I said.

"We're trying to open an irrigation lock and divert the water out of the coulee. I give it about ten more minutes before it'll be over his nose. If we have to chain-pull the car out—" He didn't finish his thought. "Take a look for yourself."

Clete and I worked our way down the side of the coulee, each of us holding a flashlight the troopers had given us. The rain was warm and pattering on the exposed undercarriage of the Honda. Through the opening between the roof and the window jamb, I could see a man's head and shoulders wedged against the steering wheel, the safety strap still in place across his chest. His face was contorted, the water in the coulee flowing thick with mud and dead vegetation through the broken windows, touching the top of his head.

"Dave, that's Andy Swan, the guy who was on the execution team at Raiford," Clete said.

"You're sure?" I said.

"I ought to know. I kicked his ass."

I got on my knees in the water and leaned down to the window. "I'm Detective Dave Robicheaux. My daughter is the owner of this car. Where is she?" I said.

Swan's gaze would not focus. I realized that one of his eyes had been knocked askew inside the socket. "Did you hear me?" I said.

He didn't answer. I shone the light inside the car, the beam spearing into the crevasses between the crushed metal and the seats, and over the buckled doors and the folded glass that looked like green ice blown from a fountain. I could smell gasoline and oil and brake fluid and the dirty burnt odor of rubber that had been scoured off the tires.

"What are you doing inside Alafair's car?" I asked.

Andy Swan made no reply. Clete knelt next to me, one hand propped against the car body. "Remember me?" he said through the window.

Swan's good eye watered in the glare of the flashlight.

"I'm going to line it out for you," Clete said. "I've got no reason to deceive you. One way or another, we're going to get Alafair back. But right now you've got about eight minutes before you do the big gargle. If you do the right thing now, Dave and I promise you we'll pick up this car with our bare hands and get you out of this ditch and into federal custody and on the way to a federal hospital. Your pals screwed you with a RotoRooter, Andy. Are you going to take their weight on a kidnap and maybe a murder beef? This is Louisiana. You thought Raiford was a bitch? You know what it'll be like on death row at Angola for a guy who was on an execution team? Every trusty in the kitchen will spit in your food before it's brought to your cell. In the shower you'll be anybody's bar of soap. Think the hacks will be looking out for you? Most of them wouldn't blow their nose on your shirt."

Swan opened his mouth to speak, and I realized

that something was wrong with his throat or that something was broken inside his chest. His words were clotted, wrapped with phlegm, blood leaking over his lip from a dark gap in his teeth. "Under the hay," he said, almost in a whisper.

"What hay?" I asked.

"Baled hay. Go through the door. It's under the hay."

"What's under the hay?" I said.

"The place they were taking her. By the river."

"What place? Which river?" I said.

"I'm not from here. There's a tractor—" he began.

"Say it."

The coulee was running higher, the current sweeping along the crown of his skull, startling him, his eyes opening wide. "I don't know the name of the place."

"Who took her?" I said.

He twisted his head and looked straight into my face, his ruined eye protruding obliquely from the socket, his good eye almost luminous, as though it were seeing through me, watching a scene or images that no one else saw.

"Talk to me," I said. "Don't let go. Don't let a collection of shits write your epitaph."

Then he did something I had seen in a dying man only two or three times in my life. His face became filled with dread, the jaw going slack, the tissue transforming to a puttylike gray, even though his blood had already drained into his head. The exhalation of his final breath was as rank as sewer gas.

I hit the side of the car with my fist.

"What was he talking about?" Clete said. "A tractor? Baled hay?"

"By a river," I added.

Clete's face was round and hard in the reflection of the flashlight. "What are you thinking?" he asked me.

"The video from Herman Stanga's DVD player," I said. "The stones in the wall. They're not indigenous to Louisiana. They're the kind that were carried as ballast in nineteenth-century sailing ships. The place in the video was a barracoon."

"I didn't get that last part," he said.

"A jail for slaves. A lot of blackbirders were bringing in slaves from the West Indies after the prohibition of 1809. Jim Bowie and Jean Lafitte brought them up the Mermentau River and sold them into the cane fields."

"That shack or whatever full of hay bales where we got into the shoot-out?" Clete said. "There was a rusted-out tractor next to it. You think that's the place where the girls were?"

"Maybe," I said.

Above us on the road, someone was setting up a generator-powered bank of flood lamps. Suddenly, the coulee was lit by an eye-watering white brilliance. The state trooper in charge of the accident scene was silhouetted against the glare, the rain blowing like bits of crystal in the wind. "We got the Jaws," he called down. "You guys find out anything?"

"The guy's name was Andy Swan," Clete hollered up the slope. "He worked with the execution team that fried Bundy. He's probably checking in with him about now."

But Clete's cynical remark served as a poor disguise for our mood and the hopelessness of our situation. Our investigation into the accident by the coulee had eaten up time that Alafair may not have had. While we dithered, she suffered. We got back on Interstate 10 and headed west toward Jeff Davis Parish while I tried to get through to someone in the sheriff's department there. Finally the 911 operator patched me through to a plainclothes detective who was working an extra duty shift that night. His name was Huffinton. At first the name didn't register. Then I remembered him. "What is it this time?" he said.

This time? "You responded to the 'shots fired' at the river?" I said.

"I'm the guy," he replied, sucking on a tooth or a mint. "What do you need?"

He was the same detective who had gotten into it with Clete and who had made a remark about my history with alcohol. "Down by the river, at the same location where I had to pop those guys, there's an old Acadian cottage. It's stacked with bales of hay. There's a tractor not far from it."

"What about it?"

"My daughter has been abducted. I'm not sure where she's being held, but one of the perps in the abduction described a house or cabin just like the one by the river. I'm on I-Ten west of Crowley, but I need you guys to jump on the place right now. You copy on that?"

"No, I don't copy anything. A kidnap victim is being held in a shack full of hay?"

"I think it was a barracoon."

"A *what*?"

"A place where slaves were kept. We have video that came from—"

"Is this a put-on?"

"I'm talking about an underground jail. It may be underneath that old Acadian house. It's the place where Bernadette Latiolais may have been murdered."

There was a pause. "I tell you what. I'll drive out there. I'll look around, just so everybody is happy. Then I'm going to forget our conversation. But I think you need to get some help, Robicheaux."

"Did you hear me? My daughter was abducted."

"Yeah, I heard you. That doesn't change anything. Every time you and your fat friend come here, you leave shit prints all over the place."

"Call me when you get to the river."

"No, I'll call you when I have something to report. In the meantime, don't patch in to my radio again. Out."

I handed my cell phone to Clete as the truck veered toward the shoulder. "Get the state police," I said.

"Take it easy, Dave."

"You didn't hear that idiot."

"Which idiot?"

"Huffinton, that Jeff Davis plainclothes who got in your face. If this goes south for Alafair—" My throat was closing on my words, and I couldn't finish the statement.

Clete was dialing 911 with his thumb, looking at me in the dash glow, his eyes full of pity. "We're going to get her back, big mon. Andy Swan was working for old man Abelard. I suspect Weingart took over control of the old man's affairs, then decided to do some payback on Alafair. But he's a survivor, Dave. He's not going down in flames just to get revenge against you and me."

"What if Weingart isn't pulling the strings?"

The 911 operator picked up before Clete could answer. He handed me the cell phone, and I made the same request to the state police that I had made to the Jefferson Davis Sheriff's Department.

"Repeat that about Weingart. You don't think he's behind this?" Clete said.

"You already said it. He's a sexual predator and a con man and a bully, but he's not a serial killer."

"You think the old man killed the girls?"

"Think again."

Clete bit the skin on the ball of his thumb, his green eyes dulling over; he was obviously wondering if both of us had not been played from the jump. "Sonofabitch," he said. Then he said it again. "Sonofabitch."

THE ROAD WAS empty as we drove into the southern end of Jeff Davis Parish and looked out on the sodden fields and the gum trees bending in the wind along the river. I could see car tracks winding through the grass toward the doorless Acadian cottage that was used to store hay. But there were no vehicles in the field.

I turned off the two-lane and approached the cottage, my headlights bouncing on the rusted tractor and the tips of the grass waving in the wind. The car tracks we had seen earlier went past the cottage and down to the river. I stopped the truck and cut the headlights. Steam was rising from the hood, the engine ticking with heat. I got out and approached the front of the cottage, my flashlight in one hand, my .45 in the other. Clete was to my right, his blue-black .38 pointed in front of him with both hands. He gave me the nod, and we both went in at the same time.

The building was a typical Acadian dwelling of the mid-nineteenth century. At one time, it had probably contained two small bedrooms, a front room, a kitchen, and a sleeping loft for visitors. But all the partitions had been knocked out, and the floor was stacked to the ceiling with hay bales that had long ago become moldy and home to field mice.

Except for one area in the center of the kitchen. Three bales had been piled lopsidedly, and muddy footprints led from them through the back door into the field. Clete stuck his .38 into his shoulder holster and shoved two of the bales tumbling into the wall, then dragged the third one aside, exposing a trapdoor that looked made of oak. At the bottom of the door was a hole the size of a quarter. I inserted my finger in it and lifted.

Underneath it was another door, this one constructed of several iron plates, cross-fitted with iron bands and big rivets that were orange and soft with rust. It was the kind of door you expected to see on a Civil War ironclad, one that could resist almost any assault short of a direct hit by an exploding cannon shell. An iron ring was attached at the bottom. And so was a padlock.

"Alafair?" I called, my voice breaking.

There was no response.

"It's Dave and Clete," I said. "Can you hear me?"

There was still no answer. I ran to the truck and opened the steel toolbox in back and returned with a crowbar. I wedged it inside the padlock and snapped it loose, then dropped the crowbar to the floor and pulled on the ring with both hands. Clete got his fingers under the lip of the door, and the two of us flung it back on its hinges. I shone my flashlight down into the darkness.

"Jesus, I can't believe this," Clete said.

A set of steep wood steps led down into a subterranean room whose walls were made up of the stones we had seen in the video. The walls were sweating with water seepage, coated with lichen at the bottom and inset with chains at the top. But the chains were not ancient ones that had fettered rebellious slaves. They were steel-link, shiny, practical, economical in design. They had probably been purchased at a local hardware store by somebody who looked just like the rest of us.

We went down the steps into the darkness. I touched the stones in the wall with my hand, then wiped it on my shirt. The air was dense and smelled of mold and feces and stagnant water and maybe human sweat. I could hear my own breathing and feel my pulse jumping in my throat. A plain wood table and a chair stood in the middle of the room. On top of the table was an opened toolbox. I did not want to look at the contents. I did not want to do that at all.

Clete bent over and picked up a piece of crumpled paper from the floor. He smelled it. "They were here. I think we just missed them," he said.

"What is that?"

"A hamburger wrapper." He wiped his fingers across it. "Look, the mustard is still fresh."

"They were eating down here?" I said.

"Let's follow the car tracks down to the river. The state troopers ought to be here soon," he said.

"Don't count on it. It's not their bailiwick." I was trying to think and not having much success. The only words that went through my mind were *Where to now?* And I had no answer to my own question. "Maybe they went back into St. Mary Parish," I said.

Then headlight beams flooded into the kitchen area above our heads. I climbed back up the steps and went outside, my .45 hanging from my right hand, the mist damp on my face. I stared into the high beams of an unmarked car driven by the plainclothes detective Huffinton. He got out of his vehicle, hitching up his pants, his shapeless fedora pulled low on his brow, his expression as blank as a dough pan. "Y'all got here, huh?" he said.

"Where've you been?" I asked.

"I was here. I didn't see anything. Then we had an armed robbery and a shooting by the exit on I-Ten. I took the call."

"You looked in the cottage?"

"I didn't say that. I pulled up on the road and put my spot on it. There wasn't anybody around. Then I got the shots fired on the radio."

"Two sets of car tracks go right past the cottage and down to the river. You didn't check them out?"

"I saw maybe one vehicle down there. But that's not unusual. High school kids fuck down there. What's the big deal? You didn't find anything, either, did you?"

I could hear my breath rising in my throat again. "Go through that back door and look down into the room below the floor. That's where I think my daughter was being held. It's a torture chamber. I want you to go down below and put your hand on the stones. I want you to look in that toolbox on the table and tell me what's on the tools."

I felt myself moving toward him as though I had no willpower, as though a dark current were crawling from my brain down through my arm and hand into the grips of my .45. "Don't just stare at me. You get your ass down those stairs."

"Dave," I heard Clete say softly behind me. "Maybe at least Huffinton stopped it."

I didn't move. My fingers were opening and closing on the grips of the .45.

"Time to dee-dee," Clete said. "The Bobbsey Twins from Homicide are keeping it simple tonight, big mon. We're getting Alf back."

"He's not gonna talk to me like that," Huffinton said.

"You shut up," Clete said.

I felt my right hand relax, and I saw Huffinton's face go in and out of focus then suck away from me in the wind, that quick, like an electronic blip disappearing on a screen. Then I was walking with Clete toward the truck, his arm as heavy as an elephant's trunk across my shoulders.

WE HEADED EAST, back toward New Iberia, with no plan or specific destination, the speedometer needle nearing ninety. At Crowley we picked up an Acadia Parish sheriff's escort in the form of two cruisers with their flashers rippling. I called Molly and told her what we had found. "They took Alafair there?" she said.

"I can't be sure, but I think so. Has anybody called?"

"Helen Soileau, that's it. Where are you going now?"

"Maybe back to the Abelards' place. Is the cruiser parked outside?"

"It was ten minutes ago."

"Go look."

"It's there."

"Go look, Molly."

She set down the receiver, then returned to the kitchen and scraped it up from the counter. "He's parked by the curb, smoking a cigarette. Everything is fine here."

"Call me if you hear from anybody. I'll update you as soon as anything develops."

"What did they do to her in that room, Dave?"

"There's no way to know. Maybe nothing. Maybe they didn't have time," I said, forcing myself not to think about the toolbox.

The Acadia escort turned off at the Lafayette Parish line, and a Lafayette Parish deputy picked us up and stayed with us almost all the way to New Iberia.

"What do you want to do, Dave?" Clete asked.

"We go back to St. Mary. I want to find Abelard's daughter. I don't think she told me everything she knew."

"Waste of time, in my view."

"Why?"

"She'll go down with the ship. You already know that."

"Somebody knows where Weingart is. His literary agent, his business connections in Canada, his publisher. He's got a plan, and somebody knows what it is. We need to get ahold of the sheriff in St. Mary and get in the Abelard house."

"What for?"

"Correspondence, Rolodexes, records, how do I know?"

"I don't think we have time for that, Dave."

I looked at him, my heart seizing up, my breath coming short. Maybe Clete was right and I was creating my own illusions about getting back my daughter. This whole case had been characterized by illusion. The St. Jude Project, Robert Weingart as reformed recidivist, Kermit Abelard as egalitarian poet, Timothy Abelard as the tragic oligarch stricken by a divine hand for defying the natural order, Layton Blanchet as the working-class entrepreneur who amassed millions of dollars through his intelligence and his desire to help small investors, a historic Acadian cottage that hid a barracoon. The Abelards had paneled their sunporch with stained-glass images of unicorns and satyrs and monks at prayer and knights in armor that shone like quicksilver, turning the interior of their home into a kaleidoscopic medieval tapestry. Or perhaps, better said, they had created a glass rainbow that awakened memories of goodness and childhood innocence, all of it to hide the ruination they had brought to the Caribbean-like fairyland they had inherited.

If she was not already dead, my daughter was in the hands of men who were among the most cowardly and cruel members of the male species, namely, those who would take out their rage and self-loathing on the body of a child or a woman. I wanted to kill them. I felt a level of bloodthirst I had never experienced.

Clete seemed to read my thoughts. "Dave, just do what your judgment tells you. I don't have any answers. But whatever we do, it's under a black flag."

I didn't reply.

"No quarter, Streak. Say it. We kill every one of these bastards."

"Whatever it takes," I said.

He put an unlit Lucky Strike in his mouth, his porkpie hat slanted down, the scar tissue through his eyebrow as pink as a rose. My cell phone vibrated on the dashboard. I opened it and placed it to my ear. "Dave Robicheaux," I said.

"Molly gave me your number," a woman's voice said. "Where are you?"

"Carolyn?" I said.

"I have to talk to you. We have to put a stop to this."

"To what?"

"To Alafair's abduction."

"You have some information for me?"

"Maybe. I'm not sure. I don't know how helpful it is."

"What are you trying to tell me?"

"I've found out some things about Weingart. I know some of the places he goes. I have to talk to you on a landline or in person. They can pull transmissions out of the air."

"Who's 'they'?"

"The people who tried to kill you. Where are you?"

"Just outside New Iberia."

"I'll meet you at your house."

I thought about it. Carolyn Blanchet was not about to go down to the department. "All right," I said. "But in the meantime, get on a landline and call Helen Soileau."

"Are you serious? I wouldn't allow that bitch to wash my panties." She clicked off.

I hit the speed dial and called home. "Carolyn Blanchet said you gave her my number. Is that true?" I said.

"Yeah, did I do something wrong?" Molly said.

"No, Molly, you've done everything right. Is the cruiser still out front?"

"Yes."

"If Carolyn Blanchet shows up, tell her to wait outside. We're on our way."

I closed the cell phone and replaced it on the dashboard. We crossed the city limits into New Iberia. Yellow pools of electricity spilled through the clouds and spread across the sky and died without making a sound.

"Carolyn Blanchet was talking about a mysterious group of some kind that can pull cell-phone transmissions out of the air," I said.

"Who knows?" Clete said. He removed the cigarette from his mouth and widened his eyes, unable to conceal his fatigue. "Know what I'm going to do?"

"No."

"Watch." He slid the cigarette back in the package, then rolled down the window and sprinkled all the cigarettes in the package into the wind stream. He took off his hat and kept his head outside the window for a long time, looking back into the darkness. Then he rolled up the window, his hair sparkling with raindrops. "Shoot me if I ever buy a pack of smokes again."

"I promise," I replied.

"Carolyn Blanchet would steal the pennies off a dead man's eyes."

"It's the only game in town," I said.

He didn't argue.

BECAUSE OF FLOODING and the collapse of a sewer drain four blocks up from my house, East Main had been barricaded and the street was virtually deserted. It was strange to see Main devoid of people, like it was part of a dream rather than reality, the asphalt as sleek and black as oil under the streetlamps, rainwater coursing through the gutters, a dirty cusp surging over the sidewalks. The lawns of the antebellum and Victorian homes along the street had been windblown with camellia and bougainvillea and hibiscus petals and pieces of bamboo and thousands of leaves from the live-oak trees. The grotto dedicated to the statue of Jesus's mother was lit by a solitary flood lamp next to the library, the stone draped by the shadows of the moss moving in the trees. I felt that I had moved back in time, but not in a good way. I felt like I had as a little boy during the war years, when I experienced what a psychiatrist would call fantasies of world destruction, of things coming apart and ending, of people going away from me forever.

The temperature had dropped, and fog was rolling off the bayou and puffing through the trees onto the street. Up ahead, I could see a cruiser parked close by my house. No other vehicles were parked on the street or in my driveway. I saw a woman come out my front door and approach the sidewalk, holding a newspaper over her head, jiggling her fingers at us the same way I had seen Kermit Abelard jiggle his fingers. At first I didn't recognize her. She was wearing a raincoat and a bandanna over her hair. It was Carolyn Blanchet.

"Go around the block," Clete said.

"What for?"

"I'm not sure. You called Emma a Judas goat. I think that was Emma's teacher right there." He picked up my cell phone from the dash.

"What are you doing?"

"Calling your house," he said.

"Screw that."

"They're desperate, Dave. It's all or nothing for them now."

"It doesn't matter." I turned in to the drive and cut the engine. My front yard was flooded, the house lights burning brightly inside the rain, like the image of a snug sea shanty battered by a coastal storm, a place where a lamp stayed lit and bread baked in an oven.

I opened the truck door and got out. Carolyn Blanchet smiled at me. "Where's Molly?" I asked.

"She's still in the bathroom," Carolyn replied.

Her statement didn't compute, but I didn't pursue it. The cruiser was parked in the shadows of the neighbor's oak trees, backlit by a streetlamp. I could see the deputy's silhouette behind the wheel, his hat cocked at an angle, as though he were dozing. I heard Clete get out of the truck.

"What kept you?" Carolyn said.

"Nothing. We were doing ninety all the way."

She gave me a funny look. "You don't know, do you?"

"Know what?"

"Alafair got away. We tried to reach your cell phone, but the service was down. Molly was calling you from the bathroom. I thought she got through."

I never took my eyes from her face. Her skin glistened with moisture. Her chin was uplifted, her eyes happy, like those of a woman waiting to be kissed. Her mouth was beautiful and alluring, exuding warmth and affection and a promise of exploration, and I suspected it had charmed many men and women out of their heart and soul.

"You're such a crazy guy, Dave. There she is," she said.

I saw Alafair standing motionlessly in the bedroom window, the curtains pulled back on either side of her. If there was any expression on her face, I couldn't see it. Out of the corner of my eye, I saw Clete moving toward the cruiser that was parked back in the shadows. My heart was racing, my throat dry, the rain clicking on my hat. Behind me, I heard Clete rip open the front door of the cruiser.

"Dave, don't do it!" he called out.

I knocked Carolyn Blanchet on her butt getting into the house.

CHAPTER 26

THE BODY OF the deputy assigned to watch our house never moved when Clete opened the cruiser's door. The deputy's eyes were half-lidded, their stare forever fixed on nothing. His head was tilted slightly to one side, almost in a quizzical manner, a thread of blood leaking from his hat down one cheek. His handheld radio was gone, and the wiring had been ripped out from under the dashboard. The interior light had been manually turned off, and Clete couldn't find the switch to get it back on again. The battery in his cell phone was dead, and a car he tried to flag down veered around him and kept going. Clete pulled the body of the deputy from behind the wheel and left it in the street to draw as much attention as possible to the scene. Then he started running through the side yard toward the back of the house, his .38 gripped in his right hand, water and mud exploding from under his shoes.

AS SOON AS I came through the front door, a man I had never seen kicked the door shut behind me and swung a blackjack at my head. I raised my arm and took part of the blow on my shoulder and the rest just behind the ear, enough to bring me to my hands and knees but not enough to knock me unconscious.

Through our bedroom door, I could see Molly in an embryonic position on the floor, her mouth duct-taped and her arms stretched behind her, her wrists duct-taped to her ankles. The room was in disarray, a sewing box and the cosmetics that had been on her dresser broken and stepped on and tracked across the throw rugs. It was obvious she had put up a fight. Robert Weingart was pointing a .25 auto straight down at the side of her face. Alafair stood in the shadows, staring at me, blood patina'd on the tops of her bare feet, her pink dress streaked with mud, her hair matted. "I couldn't warn you. He was going to shoot Molly," she said.

"Don't worry about it, Alf," I said.

"Lie down on your face, sir," the man who had hit me said. "Arms straight out. You know the drill."

"Who are you?" I asked.

He reached down, ignoring my question, pulling my .45 from its holster.

"You were one of the guys at the river?" I said.

"Just a guy doing a job. Don't make it personal, sir," he said.

"What did they do to you, Alafair?" I said.

"They took my shoes and my feet got cut, but that's all that happened," she said.

"You sure have a way of blundering into things, Mr. Robicheaux," a voice said from the kitchen.

I twisted my head around so I could see the figure silhouetted in the hallway. Kermit Abelard stepped into the light. "Waiting on Mr. Purcel, are you?" he said. "I wouldn't. This time your friend went way beyond his limits."

"You think you can create a clusterfuck like this and just walk away from it?" I said.

"Let's wait and see," he replied. His expression was serene, his cheeks splotched with color as though he were blushing, his eyes warm. He seemed to be waiting on something, like a man whose prescience is confirmed with each tick of the clock. "Ah, there it is. That guttural, puffing sound, like a man with strep throat trying to cough? That's Mr. Purcel eating a couple of rounds from a silenced forty-caliber Smith and Wesson. You put him up to killing my grandfather, didn't you? The quixotic knight-errant, waging war on a crippled old man."

"That's really dumb, Kermit," I said. "I hate to tell you this, but your trained yard bitch in there has put the slide on you. He hung your grandfather up like a side of beef. Think about it. Who else would do something like that? Not me, not Clete Purcel, not anybody you know except the guy you sprung from Huntsville and who paid you back by offing your grandfather."

"I have no illusions about Robert. But he respected my grandfather. He didn't kill him. Your fat friend did, and you and your family are going to pay for it."

The man who had hit me began taping my wrists behind me. "Better talk to your employer, bud," I said. "You guys are pros. This is Louisiana. You pop a cop, you're going to the injection table, provided you ever make the jail."

I could hear the man breathing as he worked, his fingers winding the tape around my wrists, notching it into the bones. Then he taped my ankles. "Who are you guys?" I said. "Mercs? You know the score. Use your head."

But he made no reply.

"Hundreds of millions, maybe even billions, are hanging in the balance, Mr. Robicheaux," Kermit said. "Somebody will end up owning that money. It might be the government or the state or plaintiffs in a civil suit or me and Robert and Carolyn. But somebody will own it. And whoever owns and keeps it will have these kinds of men working for them. Are you so naive that you don't believe the most powerful families in this country aren't guilty of the same crimes Robert and I might have committed?"

He began to rake through a litany of collective sins that ranged from the Ludlow massacre to support of the Argentine junta to the abandonment of a girl in a submerged car by a famous United States senator. Paradoxically, he seemed oblivious that his grandfather had been friends with some of the very people he was denigrating.

"You had better get done with this, sir," said the man who had wrapped my wrists.

"See what's going on in back," Kermit said.

"We can take care of this, sir. I think you should go."

Kermit gazed at Alafair through the doorway, his eyes wistful. "Do everybody except her," he said.

"You're taking her with you, sir? I wouldn't advise that."

"No, Robert will be handling Alafair before we leave."

"Wouldn't miss it for the world," Weingart said.

Kermit pulled aside a curtain and looked out front. "By the way, Mr. Robicheaux, one of our team just hooked a wrecker to the cruiser and is hauling it and the driver away. Don't expect the cavalry anytime soon."

I was on my face, my heart beating against the floor, the soiled odor of the carpet climbing into my nostrils. Down the bayou, I thought I heard the drawbridge clank open and rise into the air and the engines of a large vessel laboring upstream against the current.

Kermit squatted so he could look directly into

my face. "I didn't want any of this to happen. You forced the situation, Mr. Robicheaux," he said. "You hate people of my background. You've spent a lifetime resenting others for the fact that you were born poor. Admit it."

"You're wrong about that, Kermit. The Abelards were a great source of humor for everybody around here. Everyone was laughing at you behind your back, you most of all. You didn't get screwed at birth, Kermit. Your mother did when her diaphragm slipped."

Kermit stood erect. "Get it done," he said to the man who liked to call people "sir."

CLETE PURCEL CHARGED along the side of the house behind a row of camellia bushes and clumps of bamboo and untrimmed banana plants. But he didn't stop when he reached the backyard. Instead, he kept running down the slope, deeper into the trees and darkness, until he had a view of both the bayou and the entirety of the house. He could see the back porch and the kitchen and Alafair's bedroom; he could see Tripod's chain extending from the hutch up into the tree where Tripod was hiding; he could see the shapes of three men wearing rain hoods of the kind the men at the shoot-out on the river had worn.

Their backs were turned to Clete. They were looking down the driveway and down the walk space between the camellias on the far side of the house. Then one of them began to wander down toward the bayou, pointing the beam of a penlight ahead of him. Clete drew himself against a live oak, one shoulder pressed tightly against the bark, and waited. The hooded man walked within two feet of him, his small hooked nose in profile against the green and red lights on the draw-bridge. Clete put away his .38 and stepped quickly from behind the oak tree, wrapping his arms under the hooded man's chin, snapping upward, all in one motion. For a second, he thought he heard a cracking sound, like someone easing his foot down on a dry stick. He pulled the hooded man deeper into the trees and dropped him in the leaves, then retrieved the penlight and the silenced semiautomatic the man had been carrying.

Clete moved quickly up the slope, threading his way between the trunks of the trees, his feet sink-ing into the soft pad of pine needles and decayed pecan husks and the leaves from the water oaks that were yellow and black and still lay in sheaves on the ground from the previous winter. The two men who had been looking down the driveway and the walk space on the far side of the house had returned to the center of the backyard and were now gazing down the slope. "You out there, Lou?" one of them said.

Clete stepped behind a big camellia bush strung with Spanish moss. He pointed the penlight toward the neighbor's house and clicked it on and off three times. Then he stuck the pen between his teeth and said, "Got him."

"You got him?"

"Yeah," Clete said, the pen still between his teeth.

"Why didn't you say something?" the other man said. "This whole gig sucks. These people are out of *Gone With the Wind*."

"No, you got it wrong," the other man said. "They're out of *Suddenly, Last Summer*. It's by Ten-nessee Williams. It's about this New Orleans faggot that gets cannibalized on a beach by a bunch of peas-ants. Lou, quit playing with yourself and get up here."

The bridge at Burke Street was opening, the surface of the bayou shuddering with the vibration of the machinery. The bow of a large vessel slid between the pilings, the lighted pilothouse shining in the rain. "What the hell is that?" one of the men said.

"I told you, it's *Gone With the Wind*. This place is a fresh-air nuthouse."

The two men had started walking down the slope almost like tourists, confident in their roles, confident in the night that lay ahead of them, unperturbed by considerations of mortality or the suffering of the people inside the house they had invaded.

Clete Purcel moved out of the trees with remarkable agility for a man his size. He lifted the semiautomatic and its suppressor with both hands, aiming with his arms fully extended. The hooded men did not seem to realize how quickly their situation had reversed. Clete shot the first man through the eye and the second one in the throat. They both fell straight to the ground and made no sound that he could hear inside the rain.

WHILE KERMIT HELD a pistol on me, the man who had duct-taped my wrists went into the kitchen. I heard the dry sound of a metal cap being unscrewed from a metal container, then a sloshing sound, and a moment later I smelled the bright stench of gasoline. Robert Weingart pushed Alafair on the floor next to me, then bound her wrists and ankles. He removed his belt and looped it around her throat but did not tighten it. He checked to see if I was watching him work.

"You guys can't be this stupid," I said. "You think anybody is going to buy it as anything except arson?"

"You're going to die from a gas explosion, Mr.

Robicheaux," Weingart said. "A big yellow fireball that will go poof up through the treetops. When it's done, you'll all be nothing but ashes."

"Listen to me, Kermit," I said. "You can get out of this. You have money and power on your side. You can claim diminished capacity. There are always alternatives. What do you think Weingart is going to do when this is over? He'll bleed you the rest of your life."

Weingart raised his shoe just slightly, then pressed the tip into my ear, twisting the sole back and forth, gradually coming down harder and harder, crushing my face flat into the carpet.

"That's enough, Robert," Kermit said.

"Signing off now, Mr. Robicheaux," Weingart said. He raised his foot and drove it into my forehead just above the eyebrow, bringing the heel into the bone.

"Don't say any more to them, Dave," Alafair said. "They're not worth it. They're both cowards. Kermit told me when he was little and did something bad, his mother would make him put on a dress and sit all day in the front yard. That's why he's so cruel. He's been a frightened, shame-faced little boy all his life."

"You'd better keep your mouth shut, Alafair," Kermit said.

"You're pathetic. That won't change. We'll be dead, and you'll be alive and pathetic and an object of ridicule the rest of your life. Your lover is known in publishing as a piece of shit. That's what you sleep with every night—a piece of shit. I suspect eventually he'll dose you with clap or AIDS, if he hasn't already."

"Are you going to put a stop to this, or do you want me to?" Weingart said to Kermit.

"Let them talk. Maybe you'll be able to pick up some good dialogue," Kermit said.

"I thought that's what you were working on underground, there by the river," Weingart said. "What did you call it? The flowers of evil having their final say. Remember what you said? They always beg."

The front door opened and Carolyn Blanchet came inside, wiping the rain off her head. "I thought you were going to take them somewhere," she said.

CLETE PURCEL GRABBED one of the hooded dead men by the wrists and pulled him away from the house and dropped him behind the toolshed. Then he went back and got the second man and did the same. He went through their pockets, looking for a cell phone. But neither man carried one. Nor did either man carry a wallet or wear jewelry other than a wristwatch. Apart from coins that might have been used for parking meters, the dead men's pockets contained only keys, each of a kind that might have fit the ignition of a car or SUV or boat. Their wristwatches were identical, the bands made of black leather, the titanium cases and faces black also, the numerals fluorescent. One man wore a tattoo of Bugs Bunny eating a carrot; the other man had one of the Tasmanian Devil. The figures were overly round, the coloration bright and festive, the singularity of the cartoon on an otherwise bare piece of skin like a cynical theft from one's childhood.

The neighbor's house was dark, and there was no sound of traffic on the street. The rain was pattering on the tree limbs above Clete's head, the fog spreading thicker on the ground, rising like smoke around the bodies of the men he had killed. Out on the bayou, he thought he heard the sound of a large boat straining upstream, the draft too deep for the channel, the keel scouring huge clouds of mud from the bottom. But when he looked over his shoulder, he could see nothing in the fog except the lights across the water in City Park.

Clete stripped the raincoat off the body of one of the dead men and put it on. It smelled of wet leaves and humus and tobacco and wood smoke, like the smell of a man who had been sitting in a winter deer camp. Clete removed his .38 from his holster and looked down at the face of the man he had killed. The man's eyes were blue and seemed to have no pupils. His mouth was parted slightly, as though he had been interrupted in midspeech. "Hang tight," Clete said. "I'm about to send you some company."

"SEE WHAT'S KEEPING those guys out there," Kermit said.

The man who had been sloshing gasoline through the kitchen and back bedroom set down the can in the hallway. "They're probably bringing up the boat," he said.

"'Probably' isn't a good word in a situation like this," Kermit said.

The man who had knocked me down and taped my wrists walked to the glass in the back door and rubbed it with his forearm. A cartoon of Goofy was tattooed just above the inside of his wrist. He wore a black T-shirt and bleached chinos and half-topped boots. He was one of those men who seemed ageless, wrapped too tight for his own skin, the modulation in his voice disconnected from the visceral energy in his eyes. He had pushed my .45 down into the back of his belt. He was having trouble seeing into the backyard, and he rubbed the glass again. "I think that's Lou," he said.

"Think?" Kermit said. He went into the kitchen. Weingart walked into the hallway also, unable to contain his curiosity or perhaps his fear, glancing back at us briefly.

Alafair's face was inches from mine. "Molly's got the scissors," she whispered.

Through the bedroom doorway, I could see Molly's eyes bulging and the indentation of her lips behind the tape stretched across her mouth. Her upper arms were ridging with tubes of muscle as she tried to work the pair of scissors from the sewing box between the strands of tape wrapped around her wrists. Then I saw her blink unexpectedly, saw her shoulders expand slightly as she severed the tape.

Carolyn Blanchet walked past me and Alafair into the kitchen. "I'm going now," she said to the others.

"No, you're not," Kermit said.

"I did what you asked, and I'm no longer connected with anything that happens here. So I'll say ta-ta now, with just one request: Kermit, please don't call me for a very long time."

"Do you believe this crap?" Weingart said.

I could see the man in the black T-shirt looking out a window, kneading the back of his neck.

"You're not leaving," Kermit said.

"That's what you think, love," Carolyn replied.

"I wouldn't provoke Kermit," Weingart said. "He has a penchant for certain kinds of female situations I don't think you want to enter into."

"Mr. Abelard, I think we need to concentrate on priorities," the man in the black T-shirt said.

"What's the problem?" Kermit asked.

"My friends and I didn't sign on for a catfight, sir."

"Really? Then why don't you take care of your

bloody job and mind your own fucking business?" Kermit said.

The man in the black T-shirt seemed to process Kermit's remark, his shoulders slightly rounded, his chest flat as a prizefighter's, his face uplifted, his incisors exposed with his grin. "I'll be outside taking care of my fucking business, sir," he said. "I think this will be our last assignment, though. The boys and I have been a unit a long time, Senegal to South Africa, Uzbekistan to the Argentine. I can't say this one has been a pleasure."

The man opened the door and walked out on the porch and shoved open the screen, sending it back on its spring. It swung shut behind him with a loud slap. "Is that you, Lou?" he said into the darkness.

CLETE MOVED QUICKLY, closing the space between himself and the man in the black T-shirt, the silenced .40-caliber semiauto extended in front of him. "Walk toward me, hands out by your sides. Do it now," he said. "No, no, don't put your hands on your head. It's not a time to be clever."

Clete began to back up. The man in the black T-shirt wore no hat, and the rain glistened on his face and hair. His gaze swept across the yard. "Where's everyone?" he said.

"Guess. Walk to me, bub. Play it right and you can have another season to run."

"I've heard about you."

"Good. Now do what you're told."

"You were in El Sal. So was I. Except I wasn't fighting for the Communists."

"I was killing Communists before your mother defecated you into the world, asshole. Now move it."

"You know the expression: A guy just has to try."

Clete raised his left hand, patting at the air, his

body hunched forward like that of a man frightened for his own life rather than someone else's. "Don't do it, pal. Think of all the beer you didn't drink, the steaks you didn't eat, the broads you didn't call up. What you're thinking now is the ultimate impure thought. Look at me. No, no, don't do that. Look at me. Put your hand back in front of— Oh shit."

The man in the black T-shirt had his hand on the grips of the .45 stuck down in the back of his belt. He was grinning, his arm twisted behind him, his body contorted when Clete pulled the trigger. He made a whooshing sound, like a man who had stepped on a sharp rock. Then he sat down heavily in the mud, one hand pressed against the wound in his stomach, his head lowered as he stared at the blood on his palm, his hair separating on his scalp in the rain.

Clete picked up the .45 and went through the back door like a wrecking ball.

I DON'T THINK I learned a great deal from life. Certainly I never figured out any of the great mysteries: why the innocent suffer, why wars and pestilence seem to be our lot, why evil men prosper and go unpunished while the poor and downtrodden are oppressed. The lessons I've taken with me are rather simple and possibly aren't worthy of mention. But these are the two I remember most. When I was a young lieutenant in the United States Army and about to experience my first combat, I was very afraid and had no one to whom I could confess my fear. I was sure my ineptitude would cause not only my own death but also the deaths of the men and boys for whom supposedly I was an example. Then a line sergeant told me something I never forgot: "Don't think about it before it starts, and don't think about it when it's over. If you have nightmares, there's always an all-night bar open someplace, if you don't mind the tab."

The larger lesson I took from the sergeant's statement was the implication about the arbitrary and accidental nature of both birth and death. Just as we have no control over our conception and our delivery from the birth canal, the hour of our death is not of our choosing, and neither are the circumstances surrounding it. An admission of powerlessness is not a choice. That's just the way things are.

I can't say these lessons ever brought me peace of mind. But they did allow me to feel that in the time I was on earth, I at least saw part of the truth that governs our lives.

When Clete came through the kitchen door, he had no idea what to expect. Kermit Abelard and Robert Weingart and Carolyn Blanchet were all standing under the kitchen light. Maybe it was the presence of a woman that caused Clete to hesitate, or the fact that Kermit did not have a weapon in his hand. Or perhaps his eyes did not adjust quickly enough to the change from darkness to light. But by the time he had swung the silenced Smith & Wesson toward Weingart, Weingart had raised his .25 semiauto and pointed it directly at Clete's chest. Then, coward that he was, his face was averted when he pulled the trigger, lest Clete get off a shot before he went down.

The report of the .25 was like the pop of a firecracker. The bullet punched a small hole in the strap of Clete's shoulder holster, inches above his heart. He crashed against the breakfast table, dropping the silenced semiautomatic to the floor, the .45 falling loose from his pants. I could see him fighting not to go down, struggling to get his .38 loose from its holster.

Carolyn Blanchet was screaming hysterically. Out of the corner of my eye, I saw Molly cut through the tape on her ankles and tear the tape off her mouth and come toward me. I extended my wrists behind me, then felt the weight of the scissors wedge between my hands, the blades slicing into the tape. In the kitchen, Kermit was shouting at Weingart, "Shoot him! Shoot him! Shoot him!"

Clete straightened up, grasping the back of a chair with one hand, lifting his .38 in front of him. Weingart shot him again, this time high up on the right arm. Clete went down in the chair, doubling over. For a second, there was no sound in the house except the wind blowing a shower of pine needles across the roof. I took the scissors from Molly's hand and freed my ankles. "Get Alf loose and go out the front," I said.

"You have to come with us," she said.

"Clete's going to die," I said.

"We'll get help," she said, her voice starting to break.

"I'll never leave Clete," I said. "My shotgun is in the closet. You guys go on. Please."

"He's right, Molly. Come on," Alafair said, getting to her feet, the tape still hanging from her wrists and ankles.

I ran into the bedroom and pulled my cut-down twelve-gauge from the back of the closet. My hands were shaking as I got down the box of shells from the shelf and thumbed five rounds in the magazine. Then I dipped another handful of shells out of the box, stuffed them in my pocket, and went into the kitchen.

Clete still sat in the chair, his face white with the first stages of shock. The phone on the counter had been torn from the jack, the receiver broken in half. Carolyn Blanchet was huddled in a corner, trembling all over, her makeup running, her mouth contorted. Weingart and Kermit were gone, and so were my .45 and the silenced semiauto.

"Where are they?" I said.

"Bagged ass down the slope, I think. They were talking about a boat," Clete said. "Maybe down toward The Shadows."

His breathing was ragged, the color leaching out of his hands and arms. A single rivulet of blood was running from the hole above his heart. He looked into my face. "I know what you're thinking, big mon," he said. "Go after them. Don't stay here. If they come back through the house, it'll be to clip us both. Remember what I said. It's a black flag. Don't let these guys skate again."

I turned to Carolyn Blanchet. "You get off your ass and take care of him," I said. "You do whatever he says. If I come back and he's not all right, you'll leave here in a body bag."

I went out the back door into the yard. I could see Tripod on the tree limb above his hutch, shaking with fear, his chain dripping from his neck. The rain had slackened, but the fog was thicker and whiter, the trees and camellia bushes glistening with it. Out on the bayou, I could hear a powerboat coming upstream from The Shadows. I suspected it was the one that Kermit and Weingart had planned to use for their escape. But the boat did not stop or pull into the bank. Instead, the driver gave it the gas, and a moment later it shot past the back of my property, whining into the distance.

Kermit and Weingart were on their own.

"Give it up," I said.

The only sound in the yard was the ticking of the rain on the canopy. Weingart had manipulated the system all his life. Why should he either fear or heed it now? The same with Kermit Abelard. He had been born into wealth and privilege and had managed to convince others and probably himself as well that he was an egalitarian rebel. In reality, he had created an inextricable bond with another dysfunctional man, each finding in the other what he lacked, the two of them probably creating a third personality that was subhuman and genuinely monstrous.

I didn't care to dwell on the psychological complexities of evil men. Whether their kind possesses the wingspread of a Lucifer or a moth is a question better left to theologians. Clete needed me. If I could be certain I had established a safe perimeter, I could return to Clete and let my colleagues take care of Kermit Abelard and Robert Weingart. But that was not the way things would work out.

The fog was like steam on my skin. My eyes were stinging and I couldn't trust my vision. Across the bayou, I thought I saw lights burning in City Park. But I realized the luminosity inside the fog came from another source. The vessel was a double-decker, its passenger windows lamplit, its beam big enough to withstand ten-foot seas. I could hear the engines throbbing through the decks and the sound of water cascading off a paddle wheel on the stern.

"Look what you have wrought, Mr. Robicheaux," Kermit's voice said from the darkness. "You're a controller. You poisoned my relationship with your daughter. You tormented my grandfather. Hubris is your bane. You're like most alcoholics. You've superimposed all your character defects onto others and brought down your house."

"If I harmed you in any way, Kermit, I regret not doing a whole lot more of it," I said.

"If you're so brave, Mr. Robicheaux, walk out here and face me man-to-man."

In the darkness I could see little more than the shapes of the trees and the camellia bushes and the air vines and Spanish moss that dripped with rain. I doubted that Kermit Abelard wanted to duel under the oaks. He was a creature of guile, and I suspected he was trying to distract me until Robert Weingart could position himself and get a clear shot at me.

I knelt on one knee in the leaves and pine needles, the cut-down twelve-gauge tilted at a forty-five-degree angle. I heard footsteps to my right. As a parasite and a narcissist, Weingart had made a career out of earning the trust of others, making them dependent upon him, flattering them when need be, then quickly deflating them and injecting feelings of failure and guilt in them, and finally sucking the lifeblood from their veins. As with all his ilk, he didn't do well on a level playing field. When I heard a rotted branch break under his foot, he was still forty feet from me, not close enough for an unskilled shooter to take out a target in the dark.

The wind gusted down the slope when I saw him. He was standing between a camellia bush and the bamboo border between my property and the neighbor's. The bamboo swayed and rattled in the wind; the leaves and flowers on the camellia bush filled with air and motion. Weingart remained frozen, the only unmoving object in his immediate environment.

I snugged the stock of the shotgun against my shoulder and aimed at the silhouette. "I win, you lose. Throw your piece down. Make sure I hear it hit the ground," I said.

But he chose otherwise. That was when I pulled the trigger. My shells were loaded with double-aught buckshot. My guess was he took most of the pattern in the face.

I ejected the empty casing and moved farther down the slope. Weingart was on his back, still alive, strangling on his own blood. I picked up his .25 auto and dropped it in my pocket.

"Robert?" I heard Kermit call. When there was no reply, he said, "Robbie, where are you? Are you hurt?"

I remained motionless by a slash pine and waited. My palms were sweating on the twelve-gauge. I thought I heard a siren coming down Main. The moon moved out from behind a cloud; a solitary band of cold light broke through the canopy and I saw Kermit standing three feet from an enormous live oak, one in whose heart the rusted mooring chains of a slave ship were encased in the wood.

"Last chance, Kermit," I said.

He held both hands straight out by his sides, like a man surrendering himself for crucifixion. He was holding my .45 in his right hand. "Do it. I want you to," he said.

"That's a job for the state of Louisiana. Bend down slowly, your left hand on your head, and place my weapon on the ground."

"Sure," he said. But he made no move.

"You told Alafair this is your crucifixion year. Sorry, Kermit, but you just don't make the cut."

"Really?"

"Yeah, really. You couldn't even get a job as the Good Thief."

I thought I heard the back door of the house slam behind me. But I couldn't look away from Kermit. I saw him spread his feet in a shooter's position and fold his hands in front of him, and I knew my .45 was aimed directly at my face.

The blast from the shotgun knocked him through a camellia bush. I think he cried out, but I can't be sure. My ears were ringing, the air tannic with the smell of burnt gunpowder. My shoulder ached and my face was swollen out of shape from the blows I had taken in the house, the skin electric to the touch. I ejected the empty casing from the shotgun and watched it roll smoking down the embankment. Then I heard feet running behind me as Clete yelled from the back steps, "Dave, look out, she had a piece in her purse!"

I started to turn around, my left hand working the pump on the twelve-gauge, but it was too late. Carolyn Blanchet had slowed to a brisk walk, slow enough to aim with one outstretched arm, her face twisted like a harridan's. "You thought you could talk to me like that? Who do you think you are?" she said.

And she shot me in the back.

Strangely, I felt little pain. The blow was like a smack from a fist between the shoulder blades, just enough to knock the breath out of me, to buckle my knees for a second or two, to make the trees and the bayou lose shape, to make me drop the shotgun and stumble down the slope to the place I knew I was now going.

I could see the paddle wheeler in the fog, a gangway lowered in the shallows. Behind me, Clete was lumbering off balance down the incline, calling my name. Maybe he shot Carolyn Blanchet, but I couldn't be sure. The sounds inside my head were impossible to separate. I saw Molly and Alafair saying good-bye to me, and Tripod and Snuggs walking back up the slope to the house. I saw a black medic from my platoon pressing a cellophane cigarette wrapper on a hole in my lung, saying, *Sucking chest wound, motherfucker. Breathe through your mouth. Chuck got to breathe.* I heard steam engines roaring and hissing so loudly they seemed to be tearing the paddle wheeler apart. I heard the blades of the dust-off coming in over the canopy, the downdraft flattening the elephant grass, the twirling smoke of marker grenades sucking away into the sky. I felt a syrette of morphine go into my thigh and radiate through my body like an erotic kiss. I felt people gathering me up by my arms and legs and lifting me above their heads, but not onto the Huey. They were helping me to my feet, steadying me between them, leading up the gangway onto the deck of the paddle wheeler, a place I did not want to go.

I saw my father, Big Al, in his tin hard hat and my mother, Alafair Mae Guillory, in the pillbox hat she was so proud of, both of them on the bow, smiling, coming toward me. I saw men from my platoon, their rent fatigues laundered, their wounds glowing with a white radiance, and I saw boys in sun-bleached butternut and tattered gray, and I saw Golden Glove boxers from the state finals of 1956 and black musicians from Sharkey Bonano's Dream Room on Bourbon. I saw grifters and martyred Maryknollers and strippers and saints and street people of every kind, and until that moment, I never realized how loving and beautiful human beings could be.

I heard the paddle wheel churn to life on the stern, showering the air with its spray. Then I saw Clete emerge from the fog on the bank, his face white from blood loss, his clothes streaked with water and dotted with mud. He stumbled up the gangway like an irascible drunk wrecking a party, wrapping his arms around me, locking his hands behind my back, pulling me back down toward the bank. His mouth was pressed against the side of my head, and I could hear the hoarseness of his voice an inch from my ear: "You can't go, Streak. The Bobbsey Twins from Homicide are forever."

And that's the way it went in the year 2009, the two of us locked together on a gangplank on the banks of Bayou Teche, in New Iberia, Louisiana, praying for the pinkness of another dawn, like finding safe harbor inside a giant conch shell, the winds of youth and spring echoing eternally.

TURN THE PAGE FOR A LOOK AT

FEAST DAY OF FOOLS

James Lee Burke's
masterful new novel
featuring Hackberry Holland

now available
from Simon & Schuster

SOME PEOPLE SAID Danny Boy Lorca's visions came from the mescal that had fried his brains, or the horse-quirt whippings he took around the ears when he served time on Sugar Land Farm, or the fact he'd been a middleweight clubfighter through a string of dust-blown sinkholes where the locals were given a chance to beat up what was called a tomato can, a fighter who leaked blood every place he was hit, in this case a rumdum Indian who ate his pain and never flinched when his opponents broke their hands on his face.

Danny Boy's black hair was cut in bangs and fitted his head like a helmet. His physique was as square as a door, his clothes always smelling of smoke from the outdoor fires he cooked his food on, his complexion as dark and coarsened by the sun and wind as the skin on a shrunken head. In summer, he wore long-sleeve cotton work shirts buttoned at the throat and wrists to keep the heat out, and in winter a canvas coat and an Australian flop hat tied down on his ears with a scarf. He fought his hangovers in a sweat lodge, bathed in ice water, planted by the moon, cast demons out of his body into sand paintings that he flung at the sky, prayed in a loincloth on a mesa in the midst of electric storms, and sometimes experienced either seizures or trances during which he spoke a language that was neither Apache nor Navaho, although he claimed it was both.

Sometimes he slept in the county jail. Other nights he slept behind the saloon or in the stucco house where he lived on the cusp of a wide, alluvial floodplain bordered on the southern horizon by purple mountains that in the late-afternoon warp of heat seemed to take on the ragged irregularity of sharks' teeth.

The sheriff who allowed Danny Boy to sleep at the jail was an elderly six-foot-five widower by the name of Hackberry Holland, whose bad back and chiseled profile and Stetson hat and thumb-buster .45 revolver and history as a drunk and whoremonger were the sum total of his political cachet, if not his life. To most people in the area, Danny Boy was an object of pity and ridicule and contempt. His solipsistic behavior and his barroom harangues were certainly characteristic of a wet brain, they said. But Sheriff Holland, who had been a prisoner of war for almost three years in a place in North Korea called No Name Valley, wasn't so sure. The sheriff had arrived at an age when he longer speculated on the validity of a madman's visions or, in general, the foibles of human behavior. Instead, Hackberry Holland's greatest fear was his fellow man's propensity to act collectively, in militaristic lockstep, under the banner of God and country. Mobs did not rush across town to do good deeds, and, in Hackberry's view, there was no more odious taint on any social or political endeavor than universal approval. To Hackberry, Danny Boy's alcoholic madness was a respite from a far greater form of delusion.

It was late, on a Wednesday night in April, when Danny Boy walked out into the desert with an empty duffle bag and an army-surplus entrenching tool, the sky as black as soot, the southern horizon pulsing with electricity that resembled gold wires, the softness of the ground crumbling under his cowboy boots, as though he were treading across the baked shell of an enormous riparian environment that had been layered and beveled and smoothed with a sculptor's knife. At the base of a mesa, he folded the entrenching tool into the shape of a hoe and knelt down and began digging in the ground, scraping through the remains of fossilized leaves and fish and birds that others said were millions of years old. In the distance, an igneous flash spread silently through the clouds, flaring in great yellow pools, lighting the desert floor and the cactus and mesquite and the greenery that was trying to bloom along a riverbed that never held water except during the monsoon season. Just before the light died, like figures caught inside the chemical mix of a half-developed photograph, Danny Boy saw six men advancing across the plain toward him, their torsos slung with rifles.

He scraped harder in the dirt, trenching a circle around what appeared to be two tapered soft-nosed rocks protruding from the incline below the mesa. Then his e-tool broke through an armadillo's burrow. He inverted the handle and stuck it down the hole and wedged the earth upwards until the burrow split across the top and he could work his hand deep into the hole, up to the elbow, and feel the shapes of the clustered objects that were as pointed and hard as calcified dugs.

The night air was dense with an undefined feral odor, like cougar scat and a sun-bleached carcass and burnt animal hair and water that had gone stagnant in a sandy drainage traced with the crawl lines of reptiles. The wind blew between the hills in the south and he felt its coolness and the dampness of the rain mist on his face. He saw the leaves on the mesquite ripple like green lace, the mesas and buttes shimmering whitely against the clouds, then disappearing into the darkness again. He smelled the pinyon and juniper and the scent of delicate flowers that bloomed only at night and whose petals dropped off and clung to the rocks at sunrise like translucent pieces of colored rice paper. He stared at the southern horizon but saw no sign of the six men carrying rifles. He wiped his mouth on his sleeve and went back to work, scooping out a big hole around the stone-like objects that were welded together as tightly as concrete.

The first shot was a tiny *pop,* like a wet firecracker exploding. He stared into the fine mist that was swirling through the hills. Then the lightning flared again and he saw the armed men stenciled against the horizon and the silhouettes of two other figures who had broken from cover and were running toward the north, toward Danny Boy, toward a place that should have been safe from the criminality and violence that he believed was threading its way out of Mexico into his life.

He lifted the nest of stony egg-shaped artifacts from the earth and slid them into the duffle bag and pulled the cord tight through the brass eyelets on the top. He headed back toward his house, staying close to the bottom of the mesa, avoiding the tracks he had made earlier, which he knew the armed men would eventually see and follow. Then a bolt of lightning exploded on top of the mesa, lighting the floodplain and the willows along the dry streambed and the arroyos and crevices and caves in the hillsides as brightly as the sun.

He plunged down a ravine, holding the duffle bag and e-tool at his sides for balance. He crouched behind a rock, hunching against it, his face turned toward the ground so it would not reflect light. He heard someone running past him in the darkness, someone whose breath was not only labored but desperate and used-up and driven by fear rather than a need for oxygen.

When he thought that perhaps his ordeal was over, that the pursuers of the fleeing men would give up and go away and allow him to return to his house with the treasure he had dug out of the desert floor, he heard a sound he knew only too well. It was the pleading lament of someone who had no hope, not unlike that of an animal caught in a steel trap or a new inmate, a fish, just off the bus at Sugar Land Pen, going into his first night of lockdown with four or five mainline cons waiting for him in the shower room.

The pursuers had dragged the second fleeing man from behind a tangle of deadwood and tumbleweed that had wedged in a collapsed corral dog-food contractors had once used to pen mustangs. The fugitive was barefoot and blood-streaked and terrified, his shirt hanging in rags on the pencil lines that were his ribs, a manacle on one wrist, a brief length of cable swinging loosely from it.

"*Donde esta?*" a voice said.

"*No se.*"

"What you mean you don't know? *Tu sabes.*"

"*No, hombre. No se nada.*"

"*Para donde se fue?*"

"He didn't tell me where he went."

"*Es la verdad?*"

"*Claro que si.*"

"You don't know if you speak Spanish or English, you've sold out to so many people. You are a very bad policeman."

"*No, senor.*"

"Estas mintiendo, chico. Pobecito."

"Tango familia, senor. Por favor. Soy un obera-dor, como usted. I'm just like you, a worker. I got to take care of my family. Hear me, man. I know people who can make you rich."

For the next fifteen minutes, Danny Boy Lorca tried to shut out the sounds that came from the mouth of the man who wore a manacle and length of severed cable on one wrist. He tried to shrink himself inside his own skin, to squeeze all light and sensation and awareness from his mind, to become a black dot that could drift away on the wind and re-form later as a shadow that would eventually become flesh and blood again. Maybe one day he would even forget the fear that caused him to stop being who he was; maybe he would even meet the man he chose not to help and be forgiven by him and hence become capable of forgiving himself. When all those things happened, he might even forget what his fellow human beings were capable of doing.

When the screams of the tormented man finally softened and died and were swallowed by the wind, Danny Boy raised his head above a rock and gazed down the incline where the tangle of tumbleweed and deadwood partially obscured the handiwork of the armed men. The wind was laced with grit and rain that looked like splinters of glass. When lightning rippled across the sky, Danny Boy saw the armed men in detail.

Five of them could have been pulled at random from any jail across the border. But it was the leader who made a cold vapor wrap itself around Danny Boy's heart. He was taller than the others and stood out for many reasons, as though the incongruity of his appearance only added to the darkness of his personae. His body was not stitched with scars or chained with Gothic-letter and swastika and death's-head tats. Nor was his head shaved into a bullet or his mouth surrounded with a circle of carefully trimmed beard. Nor did he wear lizard-skin boots that were plated on the heels and tips. His running shoes looked fresh out of the box; his navy-blue sweatpants had a red stripe down each leg, similar to a design a nineteenth-century Mexican cavalry officer might wear. His skin was clean, his chest flat, the nipples no bigger than dimes, his shoulders wide, his arms like pipe stems, his pubic hair showing just above the white cord that held up his pants. An inverted M-16 was cross-strapped across his bare back; a canteen hung from a web belt on his side, and also a hatchet and a long thin knife of a kind that was used to dress wild game. He leaned over and speared something with the tip of the knife and lifted it in the air, examining it against the lights flashing in the clouds. He cinched the object with a lanyard and tied it to his belt, letting it drip down his leg.

Then Danny Boy saw the leader freeze, as though he had just smelled an invasive odor on the wind. He turned toward Danny Boy's hiding place and stared up the incline. *"Quien esta en la oscuridad?"* he said.

Danny Boy shrank down onto the ground, the rocks cutting into his knees and the heels of his hands.

"You see something up there?" one of the other men said.

But the leader did not speak, either in Spanish or English.

"It's just the wind. There's nothing out here. The wind plays tricks," the first man said.

"*Ahora para donde vamos?*" another man said.

The leader waited a long time to answer. "*Donde vive la Magdalena?*" he asked.

"Don't fuck with that woman, Krill. Bad luck, man."

But the leader, whose nickname was Krill, did not reply. A moment that could have been a thousand years passed, then Danny Boy heard the six men begin walking back down through the riverbed toward the distant mountains from which they had come, their tracks cracking the clay and braiding together in long serpentine lines. After they were out of sight, Danny Boy stood up and looked down at their bloody handiwork, scattered across the ground, in pieces, glimmering in the rain.

PAM TIBBS WAS Hackberry's chief deputy. Her mahogany-colored hair was both white and sunburned on the tips, and hung on her cheeks in the indifferent way it does on a teenage girl. She wore wide-ass jeans and half-topped boots and a polished gunbelt and a khaki shirt with an American flag sewn on one sleeve. Her moods were mercurial, her rhetoric often confrontational. Her potential for violence seldom registered on her adversaries until things happened that should not have happened. When she was angry, she sucked in her cheeks, accentuating a mole by her mouth, turning her lips into a button. Men often thought she was trying to be cute. They were mistaken.

At noon she was drinking a cup of coffee at her office widow when she saw Danny Boy Lorca stumbling down the street toward the department, his torso bent forward, as though he were waging war against invisible forces, a piece of newspaper matting against his chest before it flapped loose and scudded across the intersection. When Danny Boy tripped on the curb and fell hard on one knee, then fell again when he tried to pick himself up, Pam Tibbs set down her coffee cup and went outside, the wind blowing lines in her hair. She bent down, her breasts hanging heavy against her shirt, and lifted him to his feet and walked him inside.

"I messed myself. I got to get in the shower," he said.

"You know where it is," she said.

"They killed a man."

She didn't seem to hear what he had said. She glanced at the cast-iron spiral of steps that led upstairs to the jail. "Can you make it by yourself?"

"I ain't drunk. I was this morning, but I ain't now. The guy in charge, I remember his name." Danny Boy closed his eyes and opened them again. "I think I do."

"I'll be upstairs in a minute and open the cell."

"I hid all the time they was doing it."

"Say again."

"I hid behind a big rock. Maybe for fifteen minutes. He was screaming all the while."

She nodded, her expression neutral. Danny Boy's eyes were scorched with hangover, his mouth white at the corners with dried mucus, his breath dense and sedimentary, like a load of fruit that had been dumped down a stone well. He waited, although she didn't know for what. Was it absolution? "Don't slip on the steps," she said.

She tapped on Hackberry's door, but opened it without waiting for him to answer. He was on the phone, his eyes drifting to hers. "Thanks for the alert, Ethan. We'll get back to you if we hear anything," he said into the receiver. He hung up and seemed to think about the conversation he'd just had, his gaze not actually seeing her. "What's up?" he said.

"Danny Boy Lorca just came in drunk. He says he saw a man killed."

"Where?"

"I didn't get that far. He's in the shower."

Hackberry scratched at his cheek. Outside, the American flag was snapping on its pole against a gray sky, the fabric washed so thin the light showed through the threads. "That was Ethan Riser at the FBI. They're looking for a federal employee who might have been grabbed by some Mexican drug mules and taken to a prison across the border. An informant said the federal employee might have gotten loose and headed for home."

"I've heard Danny Boy has been digging up dinosaur eggs south of his property."

"I didn't know there were any around here," Hackberry said.

"If they're out there, he'd be the guy to find them."

"How's that?" he said, although he wasn't really listening.

"A guy who believes he can see the navel of the world from his back window? He says all power comes out of this hole in the ground. Down inside the hole is another world. That's where the rain and the corn gods live. Compared to a belief system like that, hunting for dinosaur eggs seems like bland stuff."

"That's interesting."

She waited, as though examining his words. "Try this: He says the killing took fifteen minutes to transpire. He says he heard it all. You think this might be the guy the feds are looking for?"

Hackberry bounced his knuckles lightly up and down on the desk blotter and stood up, straightening his back, trying to hide the pain that crept into his face, his outline massive against the window. "Bring your recorder and a pot of coffee, will you?" he said.

Mama Würstchen

Wein   Käseplatte
(Bananasplit Eislikör

17^{30} Altheemad

17^{00}

16^{30} bei Elke

rot/trocken gen
weltrock